Edward Ellerton

A Fatal Resemblance

A Novel

Edward Ellerton

A Fatal Resemblance
A Novel

ISBN/EAN: 9783337000806

Printed in Europe, USA, Canada, Australia, Japan

Cover: Foto ©Andreas Hilbeck / pixelio.de

More available books at **www.hansebooks.com**

FATAL RESEMBLANCE

A NOVEL

BY

EDWARD ELLERTON

———

NEW YORK
F. P. LENNON
19 ASTOR PLACE
1885

A FATAL RESEMBLANCE.

I.

In a little nook among the Catskill Mountains, where fifty years ago one might least expect to find a residence, comparatively inaccessible as the mountains were then, there stood an old stone farm-house. Recent coats of whitewash had daubed the exterior walls, but in many places the action of the weather had turned the white to a dirty gray and otherwise mottled the primitive-looking building.

A little distance from the house was a very roughly built barn, around which, on this bright summer afternoon of 1835, straggled a couple of cows. Beyond lay a patch of ground sparsely cultivated, owing probably to the sterility of the soil, and a little farther away still were the many-seried trees of an extensive wood. In the background rose lofty mountains, now so covered by a blue misty haze that one could hardly tell where the mountains ended and the sky began.

There was a pleasant, restful look about the scene, and a drowsiness that might lull one to delightful unconsciousness, were it not for the advent of a lively little girl from the farm-house. She came out skipping and singing, and twirling her calico sun-bonnet round her hand instead of putting it on, and looking with her streaming hair, bright face, and step that hardly touched the ground, as if she might be some little mountain

sprite who only showed herself in the sunshine. Skipping and singing, she took her way to the wood. Evidently it was no new nor fearful place to her. The
close ranks of the trees and the heavy shade of the inte-
rior that might have daunted older and bolder hearts, had
no terror for her young confidence.

She penetrated the dark recesses, springing from eminence to eminence, where the ground between some of
the trees rose into hillocks, and she pushed aside—and
sometimes it needed all her tiny strength—the young
branches that, having twined, obstructed her path. Occasionally she stopped to watch the ugly hoptoads that,
scared at her approach, jumped by her, and to look at
some great, long-legged insect making its toilsome journey
up a tree.

"How sorry I am for you," she said in one of those
halts, "for I guess you must have been naughty, and God
turned you from birds and butterflies into these ugly
things. Just like the little girl that Dyke read about to me
the other night, how the fairy turned her into a frog. He
said it wasn't a true story, but it seems like as if it might
be true, for folks that ain't good ought to be turned into
ugly things. Try and be good, now, poor toads and bugs,
and maybe God'll turn you back."

With which salutary advice she resumed her way.
Arriving at one part of the wood where the trees seemed
of larger trunk and higher growth than any of the others,
she paused as if she had reached the end of her journey.

Far above her through the leaves shone a little patch of
bright blue sky, while all about her was that intense solitude so oppressive to some natures. Neither the twitter-
ering of a bird nor the rustling of a leaf broke the silence,
and after she had stood as if waiting for some sound, she
put her little brown hand on the nearest tree, and said to
it affectionately :

"I couldn't come out here this morning because Meg was
sick, and Dyke asked me not to leave her. But I can
stay with you this afternoon, and I've lots to tell you, and

a story besides—the story that Dyke read to me last night about a wicked old Roman king. I'll tell it all to you, only first I must speak to the other trees."

She went about to three or four of the stately maples, patting their trunks affectionately, and telling them she was glad they were so well and had so many bright green leaves, to which it is needless to say the trees listened in silence.

As if impressed by that silence herself, when she returned to the tree she had addressed first, instead of beginning to impart her promised information, she stood looking up to the patch of sky that beamed down upon her blue and clear.

"O trees, if you could only speak!" she said at length, "wouldn't you have a lot to tell—way up there so high, it seems as if God was always talking to you. I wonder if He ever lets you see heaven that Meg tells me about? I'd like to be a squirrel or some of them climbing things, and then I'd live on the top of the highest tree I could find, and so I'd hear, too, what God says to you all."

A breeze was beginning to rustle the leaves. The imaginative child immediately interpreted it to mean a clamor from the trees for her promised news.

"Yes, yes, I'll tell you," she said, as if in haste to allay their impatience.

"Meg got a letter yesterday. Old farmer Brown, coming up from the village, brought it, and I think it made her awful sad, for she and Dyke talked about it, but they didn't let me hear; only Dyke told me this morning that to-morrow we're all going down to Barrytown to see some elegant place where there's a bigger family of trees than all of you are, and lots of flowers. So, to-morrow I won't be here, nor maybe the next day; but I'll promise that I won't like any of the Barrytown trees as well as I do all of you. And now I'll tell you the story that Dyke read."

And she told the story; the story of the old Roman emperor who did nothing more useful than delight the people with magnificent shows, and who met the end of most of the Roman emperors, assassination.   She told it all in her simple way, but with a correctness of detail and incident most creditable to the instruction of Dyke (whoever he was), and that would have delighted the hearts of our modern teachers of history.   Nor did she end with the conclusion of her tale, but delivered a homily (most probably Dyke's) on the deserved end of such useless lives.

Evidently this child of the mountains was neglected neither in morals nor the sciences, and as one looked at her tiny size, and wondered whether she had yet reached the age of seven, and saw her wide, full, open brow and sparkling eyes, one was still more inclined to wonder that such premature intelligence should be united with such a simple and yet such an ardent imagination.

The shadows had begun to lengthen and the patch of sky to grow dark, and warned by these signs that it was time to return, she made haste to kiss the trees as she had promised to do, and flinging back many a childish good-by, she retraced her steps through the wood.

II.

The next morning, so early that the sun had not time to send his beams far down the mountains, and the inmates of the barn-yard looked as if even they had been rather unduly aroused, an awkward-looking, lumbering wagon, drawn by a horse so superior in aspect to the vehicle that it seemed a sort of burlesque to put them together, waited before the door of the little mottled farmhouse.

In a few minutes there came out of the house the little girl whose acquaintance we have already made, and by her side was a florid-faced, good-natured looking woman of middle age.   At the same time there came from the direction of the barn a country-looking youth of eighteen. He was country-looking in the fact that his face had the sunburnt hue of country men, his hands the large and chubby size produced by country work, and his clothes a certain home-spun, rustic look.

A closer observation of his features and his manner, as he assisted his companions to places in the wagon, revealed some things that were not common to coarse country lads. There was a native grace about his movements that could only come from some cultivation of mind, and an ingenuousness and nobility of countenance indicative of a soul that had far higher aspirations than the breed of cows or the price of pigs.

One of his companions we have already described, and save that her hair and much of her face were concealed by a large close bonnet, she looked the same as she did on the preceding day; the other companion, the woman, had nothing to distinguish her from the rest of her class, unless it might be a striking honesty of countenance.

The drive down the picturesque mountain road, frequently by the side of steep and fearful-looking ravines, and at other times by thick growths of vegetation that in the gloaming might be construed into grotesque figures, was one to be enjoyed by even those to whom it was no novelty. And the eyes of the little girl, looking out with witching brightness from her close protruding bonnet, sparkled with delight at every new scene, and her little tongue hardly ceased from asking questions long enough to give Dyke a breathing spell. But he was nothing loth to answer her; indeed, it seemed to be as much pleasure to him to reply as it was to her to inquire, and he often turned round to look lovingly at the eager face.

They passed but few houses, and these at long distances apart, until they had ridden many miles, and left the stony mountain road far behind them; then they came to straggling settlements, which were dignified by the name of villages, and rode through irregular openings that the few residents expected to become streets by-and-by; and sometimes they came upon open-mouthed, curiously-staring rustic people, who looked as wonderingly as if a one-horse country wagon containing three people was a novelty to them. At length, they stopped to eat the bountiful lunch Meg had provided, and to feed the horse from the bag of fodder carried in the back of the wagon, and to water him from a little bubbling stream near, in all of which proceedings the child took as much interest as Dyke did.

The remainder of the drive for an hour or two was along a hot, unshaded road, and Meg's substantial size and dark stuff dress, attracting the heat most uncomfortably, sent that good soul into a teem of perspiration, drawing from her at the same time a volley of such ejaculations as:

"Bless me, but it's hot! It was unconscionable of Mr. Edgar to send for us such a day as this. I'll melt, I know I shall."

Dyke was equally hot, to judge from his moist face, but he made no complaint, and the little girl, though looking hot also, was still too interested in objects about her to mind that slight discomfort.

Meg at length succumbed to sleep, and Dyke halted to adjust her so that the jolting of the wagon would not pitch her about, and possibly throw her out, and then he took the little girl on the seat with himself and drove on. She seemed to have tired of questioning, and from her silence he thought she too was asleep, but as often as he stooped and looked under her bonnet her eyes were wide open.

"What's the matter?" he said at last, a little puzzled by this unusual behavior. "What makes you so quiet?"

"Because I was thinking of that Mr. Edgar we're going to see. How funny that his name is just like mine. Is he anything like that big dark man that came to see Meg ever so long ago?"

"What a memory you have!" answered Dyke. "Why, that's three years ago, when you were the littlest bit of a tot. Yes; it's the same gentleman, but we won't mind about him now until we get to his place. Let us talk about the birds and the squirrels. See! there is a little red fellow now running along that fence."

And the child, immediately interested, forgot her former inquiry; a forgetfulness that Dyke fostered by beginning immediately a story about the chipmunks.

By that time they had reached the place where a lumbering boat was to take them across the river, and as there was barely room for Dyke's horse and vehicle on the rough, narrow deck, necessitating especial care on his part to prevent an accident, Meg was aroused from her nap, in order to be placed with her little charge in safer quarters in another part of the boat. When they arrived at the opposite side, the sun had turned, and a delightful breeze was springing up; moreover, the rest of their way lay through a heavily shaded road, and the child was in ecstasies with the great old trees that loomed up on each side of her.

Dyke had to tell her their names, and how many years he thought they were growing, and whether the branches that were extended, as if to meet other branches, did not do so out of affection, all of which questions Dyke answered very patiently, and to the best of his ability.

Meg, quite refreshed by the cool breeze, adjusted her costume, and expressed her approval of the change in the weather, and by that time they had arrived at the entrance of a private carriage road, at the end of which, half embowered in trees, they caught occasional glimpses of a large stone house.

III.

Dyke was in some uncertainty about the propriety of taking his lumbering vehicle any further, and he was debating with himself whether it would not be better to have his companions alight and walk up to the house, when a respectable, though country-looking man appeared, issuing from a small dwelling just at the entrance to the road.

"You're the people that's coming to see Mr. Edgar, aren't you?" he said, going confidently up to Dyke; being answered in the affirmative, he continued:

"Get right down, and come into my house here; I'm Mr. Edgar's gatekeeper. He told me he was expecting you, and you can make yourself at home with my wife until you rest a bit; then she'll show you up to the house. I'll take care of your horse," as Dyke stopped to pat the animal.

The offer was gladly accepted, and Meg took a great deal of pains in smoothing out the little girl's hair, and brushing down her somewhat rumpled dress, in order to make her, as she herself expressed it, "at her prettiest." "For," she said, turning to Dyke, "there's no knowing what may happen, and it's our duty to bring things around if we can."

But Dyke looked troubled and made no reply. The gatekeeper's wife conducted them to the house, the largest and the handsomest dwelling the little girl had ever seen, and she looked with wonder at the furniture, so different from what she was accustomed to see in her simple mountain home. Dyke also was a little curious and interested, but Meg acted as if such elegance was not at all unfamiliar.

Mr. Edgar came into the parlor to see them, and the child's description of "a big dark man" exactly described him. He was a big, dark man, so tall and straight and lithe that his height seemed even greater than the six feet it must have been; and his complexion, eyes, and hair were swarthy enough to have justified the supposition of Indian blood in his veins. He bowed, and smiled at his visitors, showing the gleam of large, even, and exquisitely white teeth through his moustache, and crossing to the little girl, he said:

"You have grown very much since I saw you last;" then he paused, during which his eyes went sharply all over her little person.

"What is this your name is?" he asked, somewhat abruptly.

"Ned Edgar," said the child confidently.

The gentleman's face lost its pleasant expression, and he turned with a displeased look toward Meg, who hastened to answer with a courtesy:

"She likes to be called Ned, sir, and I didn't think it was any harm to indulge her."

"Perhaps not a while ago, but she is getting too big to be called by a boy's name now. Give me your name properly, my child."

All the little sprite's self-will was aroused. With her impulsive, childish reasoning she could see no right of this dark stranger to interfere with her privileges. Dyke, who had the most right of anybody, never objected to her boy's name, and she certainly was not going to give it up to please this man. So, with all her temper in her eyes, she answered:

"My name is just what I told you, Ned Edgar. Meg says my mother wanted me called Ned, because her brother that she loved so was Ned, and I *won't* be anything else," stamping her tiny foot.

"Ah!" the gentleman said, turning his face away and retreating, while Meg, having recovered from her horrified astonishment both at the child's outspokenness and at her temper, rushed to her, and almost implored her to tell the gentleman that her name was Edna.

"And please don't mind her temper, sir," apologized Meg; "she'll be sorry for it in a minute, and ready to beg your pardon."

"Oh, it makes no difference," said Mr. Edgar coldly, "but I would like to see this young man for a few minutes," turning to Dyke, and then he led the way to another room, beginning abruptly when he had taken a seat, and motioned the lad to another:

"You are the nephew of this woman who is with you, are you not?"

"Yes; her sister's son," was the reply.

"And you are acquainted with all the circumstances of that child's birth and life?"

"I have heard them," was the brief response.

"And how much does the child know about herself?" The swarthy face had something like a blush for a moment, as it bent with involuntary eagerness toward the young man.

"Nothing; save that my aunt and I love her as dearly as though she were truly our flesh and blood."

In proportion as the swarthy face grew flushed and eager, Dyke's open countenance became calm and determined.

"And if this child should be left with you, should indeed always remain unclaimed, what then?"

Dyke rose.

"Should such be the case, I would hail it as a fourfold blessing. My arms are strong enough to work for her, and all that I need to give newer and better strength to them is the assurance that she never will be claimed."

Mr. Edgar also rose, but instead of replying he began to pace the room. Sometimes he covered his face with his hands as he walked, and again he folded his arms and looked before him with the air of one in deep mental distress. He stopped at length.

"It might be best for myself if I could give you such an assurance, but I dare not do it; the feeling here," striking his breast, "will not permit me to do so. I could curse him who has left me in such horrid doubt."

For an instant his face became savage-looking; then, as the expression vanished, he continued:

"I sent for you because I had not the time to go to you, and I wanted to see Edna before I started on a long journey abroad. I am almost convinced that she is not my child, and yet I cannot promise you that my feelings will not change, and that I shall not claim her as my daughter some day. However, until that day comes, until I have proof that she *is* my own, you may continue to have the care of her, and I shall see that you are paid a much larger sum quarterly than you have been here-tofore."

Dyke's voice was a little tremulous:

"No, Mr. Edgar; I cannot accept your offer. The little farm which we have upon the mountain affords sufficient support for us now, and as the care of Ned or Edna," slightly blushing because he had used the masculine diminutive, "is a work of love, no money can pay us. So, if you insist on our acceptance of money, we must insist on resigning the care of the child."

There was no gainsaying his firm determination, and Mr. Edgar, after a searching look at him, said with a half sigh:

"Well, let it be so."

IV.

Fifty years prior to the time at which our story opens, there resided in one of the country districts of England a gentleman by the name of Edgar. Haughty and reserved, almost to moroseness, he seemed to derive little enjoyment from the vast wealth bequeathed to him as the sole remaining scion of a once titled family, further than was afforded by the collection of valuable paintings and statuary. He was always negotiating for the purchase of some celebrated work, and every apartment in the baronial-like mansion contained more than one piece of rare and exquisite workmanship.

How he spared sufficient time from his beloved occupation to woo and marry a lady from a neighboring district puzzled his few friends, and they were hardly surprised at the rumors shortly after circulated that the lady was not happy in her new position. Be that as it may, she died in childbirth, leaving to her haughty lord and master sturdy twin-sons. Something of the father showed itself then, and for a time it seemed as if the springs of parental tenderness had swallowed up the moroseness and taciturnity that had marked his former life; but, as the boys grew up, and were away for long periods at college, the handsome, middle-aged gentleman returned to all his former ways.

The boys, though twins, were as unlike each other in disposition as it was possible for brothers to be. Edward, the elder, though something like his father in pride and reserve of character had withal a frankness and generosity that endeared him to many. Henry, the younger, developed all the qualities of a dare-devil and bravado, without the traits which sometimes go far to redeem such a character. There was also a trickiness in his nature peculiarly repulsive and exasperating to his brother. So they grew to have little in common, and at length to entertain for each other a bitter hatred. When they came home, the country about was speedily full of accounts of Henry's rollicking actions. Now it was a merry party of companions like himself who went tearing over the country at midnight, and who often left disagreeable evidences of their raid. Again, it was some hunt that wantonly trespassed on private grounds and brought exasperated rustic gentlemen to remonstrate with the father of the wild young man. But Mr. Edgar, with all his sternness, could neither subdue nor frighten that headstrong, wayward character, and at length, after repeated acts that had the whole district in arms, he settled a meagre allowance upon his younger son, and thenceforward renounced all relationship with him. The young man was forbidden ever to step across the threshold of his father's home.

He seemed to take the edict quietly enough, betraying neither remorse for his conduct, nor affection for his relatives. But, to a skilled observer, there was a look in his dark eyes and about his handsome mouth which betrayed a secret, yet deep and bitter vindictiveness.

To his brother, who extended his hand, willing and wishing to part friends, he presented a most scowling countenance, and dashing away the proffered hand, he hissed :

"Never; you are not my brother!"

A little while after, Edward Edgar married, entirely to his father's satisfaction; and, as if to bring disgrace on the family name, his brother married at the same time the pretty daughter of a farm hand, but one of whom report spoke in a light and no guiltless manner.

With strange similarity, both wives gave birth at the same time, each to a daughter, and Henry deferred the christening of his child until he should learn the name of his brother's babe.

Then he hastened to have his offspring also baptized Edna.

Thus, there were two Edna Edgars not three miles apart; but, while one had elegant attendance and the most lavish parental love, the other had little better than abject poverty—Henry's allowance being hardly sufficient to support his debauches—and love, deep enough from the young, illiterate mother, but little more than indifference on the part of the dissipated father.

The wealthy Mrs. Edgar died when her babe was a week old; and before another week had elapsed, her child was stolen—stolen from the mansion and from the very arms of its nurse. The latter was found in the morning insensible from the administration of some drug; and when consciousness was restored, she was so stunned by fright as to be able to tell only an incoherent story about the sudden entrance into the nursery, late the preceding night, of a man who looked like a gypsy, and of his violent application of something to her face, while she was nursing her little charge.

Suspicion settled immediately upon the gypsies who had an encampment in the vicinity, and a thorough search was made, but without success. Singularly enough, Edward Edgar never suspected his brother of the deed; and while the whole country about was excited and dismayed, and sympathized with the anguish of the bereaved father, not a syllable connected Henry Edgar's name with the cruel and daring action; not until he himself sent word to his brother that the missing infant was in his house.

Edward Edgar hurried to the poor abode, there to be confronted with two infants so exactly alike that he could not distinguish his own, and to be told by Henry that it was *he* who had stolen the child, and that he knew the babes apart, having put a hidden mark on the one he had stolen ; but that he would see his brother infernally condemned before he would tell him which was his own, or by what means he had been enabled to put upon the child letters—letters that he alone could reproduce. He further said that the letters were the initials of her own name, E. E., but he refused to say upon what part of the infant he had marked them.

Not even the threat of a prosecution for his crime could move him. He was just as ready to go to prison as to go anywhere else, he said defiantly, and Edward Edgar shrank from the shocking publicity that must be entailed by a criminal prosecution of his own and only brother. His brother's wife, compelled to abject subjugation by her husband, was quite as non-committal, and she was so well instructed that the closest observation failed to detect in her a sign that might betray her knowledge ; she hung over both infants alike, and never pressed one to her heart that she did not lavish on the other the same caress.

There seemed to be but one way out of the agonizing dilemma, and that was suggested by faithful Meg Standish —for Mr. Edgar to take both the babes, and as they grew, something might be developed which would enable him to tell his own.

He determined to follow the advice, and Henry consented to yield the two children, provided that he should receive in return a liberal amount of money. Mr. Edgar acceded to the demand, but he stipulated for legal possession of the infants, in order that the future might be secured from any claim of Henry Edgar or his wife.

To that demand, after some deliberation which was due

perchance to the imploring look of the abjectly obedient wife, Henry Edgar also consented, and the necessary legal forms being complied with, the two babes were transferred to Mr. Edgar's grand home.

Both Mr. Edgar and Meg Standish watched closely the parting of the young mother with the children, feeling that at such a time some instinct of maternity must betray itself. But her husband never left her side for an instant, and under his scowling, determined look, she dared not show a motion other than he had commanded. She hugged and cried over both little ones equally, but that was all ; and the very next week her husband left England, taking her with him, but where he went no one knew.

Nurses from the continent were procured for the children, and Meg set all her wits and all her affection to work to discover in which one there might be such evidence of the lovable disposition of her own young mistress as must establish beyond a doubt the identity of Mr. Edward's child. In the course of the year, when the little ones gradually began to develop physical differences by which they could be distinguished, as well as differences in their infantile dispositions, faithful Meg fancied she had quite discovered which was the child of her master, and her warm heart went out to the little one they called " Eddie," while Mr. Edgar, singularly enough, seemed to think that the other babe, who was called Edna, was his. His father also inclined to that fancy, but as, since the death of his daughter-in-law, to whom he was much attached, he seemed to be somewhat imbecile, Meg paid little attention to his preference.

Strange and miserable were the feelings that warred in young Edward Edgar's breast. Almost convinced that Edna was his child, and at the same time fearful that, after the lapse of years, he might find that he had been lavishing his affection on the offspring of a low woman of doubtful reputation, he came at length to permit himself no attachment to either.

When the children were two years old, some property in America was bequeathed to Mr. Edward Edgar. The bequest, however, required his presence on the spot, and as his father was fast sinking, he waited only his death to make the journey, determining to place the children, before he went, under suitable but separate care. He desired to separate them because he would not have his child the companion of the daughter of such a woman as his brother's wife.

"And where will you send them ? " asked Meg, her heart in her mouth lest the child *she* loved should be sent from her care.

"To institutions probably, if I can find any that will take the charge of such young children."

The woman's honest face was aglow. " You may do what you like with Edna, for there's some'at about her that I can na take to, and that tells me she is none o' yourn, Mr. Edward. But Eddie you'll na take from *me*. She has her mother's own turns wi' her, and it's past me comprehension that you don't see them. Let me keep her, Mr. Edward, and I'll take her wi' me to America, to me sister that's been writin' for me this mony a month. She has a farm there, somewhere, and a bit o' money saved besides, and I'm not without me own savings. " So Eddie 'll be taken good care on, and she'll have the love that they wouldn't gie' her in an institootion."

The gentleman yielded, and on the evening of the same day old Mr. Edgar died. His will, made at the time that he discarded his younger son, and never subsequently altered, gave everything to the elder, who, immediately after the interment of his father, placed the Edna that he deemed to be his own child in a sort of nursery in the suburbs of London, and allowed the other to accompany Meg. Then he went to America, to Barrytown, where was situated the property that had been bequeathed him.

There seemed to be something in his new life that pleased and in a measure satisfied him, for he continued to make his home in Barrytown. As if in projecting and supervising improvements on the estate, he was lulled into temporary forgetfulness of his internal horrid struggle—a struggle to master the yearning of his heart for the companionship of his child. He had loved his beautiful young wife with an intensity of which only strong and stern natures are capable, and his soul constantly longed to possess something that was hers. But his fear of making a mistake with regard to the children, and his utter repugnance to loving the child of that brother whom he now fiercely hated, was equally strong. So while one feeling made him fear to be utterly indifferent to Meg's little charge, the other permitted him to do no more than see that there was paid for her care a fair sum quarterly, and to visit her once in her mountain home. She was four years old at the time, and pretty and cunning enough to tempt him to kiss her warmly. But he could not divest himself of the idea that she was his brother's child, and so, much to Meg's secret indignation, he suffered his demeanor to betray nothing more than the passing interest of a stranger.

He asked all sorts of questions about the little mountain farm, ascertaining that Meg and her nephew, with the assistance of a hired man, were alone in its managment, Meg's sister having died; and he seemed particularly interested in Dyke, then a lad of seventeen. The latter, for a country boy, had enjoyed unusual advantages of education, being under the tuition from his childhood of an erratic but well educated man who, making his home with some relatives in the village of Saugerties, turned an honest penny by giving lessons in the "three r's" to the children of his scattered neighbors. In Dyke—whose correct name was Dykard Dutton—he took a lively interest, not only teaching him the three famous rudiments, but ably imparting much instruction in the higher branches. He lent his own choice books to the lad when he was able to read them, and that was how Dyke was enabled to read for Edna's, or as she delighted to be called, "Ned's" mature delectation such tales as had Roman emperors for their heroes.

Perchance the well-informed, much-travelled, and aristocratic gentleman was amazed to find such mental ability under so rustic a guise, and that he could not help admiring the manliness of the lad. Be that as it may, he paid Dyke so much attention in the matter of respectful inquiries about the youth's daily avocations, that Meg was proud and happy, and almost forgave his indifference to her little charge.

After this mountain visit, Mr. Edgar returned to his Barrytown estate, and lived for three years longer in strange seclusion. His neighbors were not many, and a little too far removed from him to give his life and habits the scrutiny they—especially the unmarried female portion would like to have done. They believed him to be a childless widower, and they would have extended to him their heartiest hospitality, but all their advances were received with a hauteur which repelled any future effort.

He heard at regular intervals from those who had charge of the child he was almost convinced was his own, and every letter spoke of her growing beauty and intelligence. She knew her letters and could read a little, but the nursery, being only for very young children, afforded no further educational facilities, and it was necessary to transfer her to some school. Edgar determined to attend to the matter in person, and it was in consequence of this resolution formed in haste, and leaving little time to prepare for his departure, that he wrote to have Ned brought from her mountain home to visit him.

He would see her before going, in order to compare her with the other Edna whom he would also shortly see; hence the cause for the little one's journey to Barrytown.

V.

As Mr. Edgar would leave for New York on the ensuing afternoon, Meg resolved to depart the next morning, so that "Ned" had little time to explore the woods about the estate, and to make the aquaintance of any of the trees, as she longed to do. Her usual fancies were at work, and not a rustle of the leaves that she heard from the open window beside which she stood waiting for Meg to finish her simple toilet, nor a twitter of the birds that reached her in the early, sweet-scented morning air, but told her a story as sweet and simple as her own little guileless heart.

She yearned to be abroad among all the alluring influences, and calling to Meg that she could wait no longer, she darted from the room, down the broad stair, and through the front entrance, which to her delight was wide open. Along the path she skipped, clapping her hands and singing to herself as she was accustomed to do at home, and indeed with every evidence of forgetfulness that she was anywhere but in her mountain woods. Suddenly she came on the path which led to the garden, and attracted by the scent of the flowers that every breeze wafted to her with an overwhelming sense of odorousness, she pursued her way until she came upon great, variegated beds arranged in all sorts of shapes, and nestling at the foot of hills, and in the midst of greenhouses, through whose crystal panes were seen tall foreign exotics.

She had never seen any but wild flowers, and now the beauty and variety of those before her overwhelmed her for a moment. Then, not daring to pick any, she flung herself on her knees beside one of the beds, and took long inhalations of the fragrance.

"You dear things," she said, "how God must love you when He makes you so pretty." It was her first and usual thought; pretty things were God's favorites, and she continued to apostrophize them in her quaint way, until she was startled by a deep voice saying behind her:

"Wouldn't you like to pick some of the flowers?"

It was Mr. Edgar, big and dark as he was yesterday, and very much out of "Ned's" good opinion because of his unwarrantable interference with her name. But Meg had talked to her a long time about the matter, and had seemed to feel so badly because of "Ned's" temper before the gentleman, that the child with her usual impulsiveness had promised to ask his pardon the moment she saw him ; and with much trepidation of heart she had waited for that moment all the evening. But Mr. Edgar did not reappear. Now, hard as it was, it seemed to be her bounden duty to keep her promise to Meg, and, without waiting to let her courage weaken, she rose, shook back her lose-flowing black hair, and said a little tremuolusly :

" Meg said I was naughty to you yesterday, and that I ought to ask your pardon.   Please forgive me."

She held out her little brown hand, and looked up into his face with a charming blending of confidence and candor in her own countenance.

He was touched in spite of himself, and for an instant he fancied there was something in her expression which resembled his lamented wife, but the next moment he imagined that he detected in her features the closest resemblance to those of his hated brother, and he said half coldly: "I forgive you ; and now you had better pick your flowers, and go back to the house : they will want you for breakfast."

He turned away, and the child, delightedly availing herself of the permission, seemed to forget all about him.

Directly after breakfast, the party left for their mountain home, Mr. Edgar shaking hands with Meg and Dyke and Ned, but not offering to kiss the latter — a slight which was most agreeable to the little one, for she had a sort of fear of this big, dark man.

VI.

Two months had passed, and Farmer Brown coming up from the village brought another letter to Meg Standish, and this time the contents caused more exclamations from Meg, and more private conversations with Dyke than the former letter had done.

" What do you think he's driving at ? " she asked of her nephew, when for the third time the two privately discussed the contents of the epistle.

“ He’s driving at one thing,” answered Dyke gloomily, “ though perhaps he’s not aware of it himself.”

“And what’s that?” asked Meg, mopping her good-natured face with her apron, and drawing closer to her nephew in her eagerness to hear.

“ To take the child away from us altogether, for it will come to that in the end. It’s fear that ‘ Ned ’ after all may be his own that is urging him to this step; else why should he decide now to give her equal advantages with the other child? You told me, Aunt Meg, how bitter he was in his determination not to have the children together ; yet here is his letter saying that the other little girl will be with us in a fortnight, and that both are to go to that school in Pennsylvania.”

Meg’s face was mopped again; the intensity of thought that the subject required brought the perspiration from every pore.

“ But isn’t it wonderful,” she said, “ how he trusts you, Dyke ; to think of his telling *you* to take the children to that place, wherever it is; there must be some’at about you that took wi’ him.”

But Dyke was insensible to the compliment ; he was thinking with a sorrowful heart of this sudden and unexpected interference of Mr. Edgar just as he had begun to be happy in the thought that Ned would remain with him and Meg for at least a long time to come.

“ I had such plans for her,” he said at length ; “ I meant to have given her all my knowledge, and then to send her somewhere for accomplishments, but now he will do it all, and in a little while she will be far removed from us.”

“ He’s the best right to her, he’s her father,” put in Meg.

“ Yes; but he doubts it,” answered the young man almost fiercely, “ and he’ll always doubt it, and perhaps let his doubts cloud her life in one way or another. But we gave her the love without stint or hindrance, and we would always give it.”

“ Well, lad, don’t thee take it so hard.” In moments

of deep feeling, Meg resumed the dialect of her childhood which she had lost somewhat in her long residence among the gentry. " It be'ant so hard after all; thee'll take the child to school, and thee'll go to see her, and Mr. Edgar'll let her spend her holidays wi' us."

But though the youth did not again complain, he took small comfort from his aunt's words.

Meg had many housewifely preparations to make for the little stranger, and many replies to give to Ned's questions concerning her, when she was informed that a little girl of her own age and of her own name was coming from England to visit her; both Meg and Dyke, knowing her passionate attachment to them, were afraid to tell her at first that she was to go away to school with the little girl. So Ned had the brightest anticipations of the visit, and counted the days, and went frequently to her beloved trees, and repeated to them all the news.

" Meg says she's a nice little girl, just as old as I am, and it's so funny, with just my name, only they don't call her Ned. Meg says when we were babies that she took care of us, and that we both lived in an awful big, grand house ; bigger and grander than the one down in Barrytown that I told you all about ; and this little girl's papa is that Mr. Edgar that I told you about also, and he's sending her to see me ; but he is not coming with her himself, he's sending her out with people that's coming—people that he knows ; and when she comes, I'll bring her out here, and show her to all of you, dear maples, and pines, and cedars.

<h2 style="text-align:center">VIII.</h2>

Edna arrived on her mountain visit. It was the afternoon of a lovely October day, when the sun's rays fell genially on the side of the mountains, making deep shadows above and below them, and lighting up with exquisite brilliancy the half turned leaves of the adjacent woods. The little stone house had a more picturesque look in this mellow sunlight, and the inmates of the farm-yard seemed to betray some curiosity as a covered, two-seated wagon drawn by a sleek-looking, well-fed team drew up in front of them, and the driver descended to assist the occupants to alight. At the same time Dyke, and Meg, and Ned appeared from the house, and in a little while the three travellers were made heartily welcome. As age has the preference, we shall say a word first of the worthy couple to whose care the little English girl was intrusted.

They were a well-to-do, honest, and not unintelligent man and wife who had been born and reared on Mr. Edgar's English estate; their only child, a son, had emigrated to America some years before, and having married and settled in Albany, had frequently written for his parents to join him. That fact became known to Mr. Edgar, and as his restlessness was urging him to an immediate course of travel in the East, he availed himself of the opportunity to advise the couple to gratify their son's wish in order at the same time to bring the little girl to Meg; and as a handsome sum of money accompanied his counsel, their consent was soon won.

To Meg their arrival was like that of her own relations, for she knew them well, and only regretted that she could not induce them to stay with her a month. They insisted upon leaving the very next morning.

Such was the good-hearted, simple couple in whose trusty charge the little lady was placed, and now we shall give her a due share of attention. Of course, she did not remember Meg, and she hardly returned that good soul's hearty caress, which coldness the latter attributed to natural shyness. Nor was it to be expected that she should remember Ned, or that the latter should remember her, and when Meg in the exuberance of her own loving heart bade them run into each other's arms, she stood perfectly still, while Ned impulsively obeyed the request and kissed the little stranger warmly.

"Let me look at you," said Meg, when they were all in the house, and the plainly but expensively dressed little girl had removed her bonnet and tippet.

She was the same height and build as Ned, with the same color hair, and dark expressive eyes; but the expression of her face differed; it lacked the sunny candor which fascinated one in Ned's countenance, and while the formation of her features gave promise of much greater beauty than her little cousin ever would possess, just now the latter had the advantage. Meg looked earnestly for some resemblance to Mr. Edgar or his brother; there was the same family likeness that her own little charge had, but nothing more.

The couple had a letter from Mr. Edgar for Dyke, and Dyke opened it to find a more complete detail of instructions than the former missive had contained.

The arrangements for entering the little ones at school had been completed so that Dyke would have no trouble further than the journey with them; and then the letter went on to state that Mr. Edgar preferred the children to be kept in ignorance of their relationship, and that he had sent his own little daughter, as he styled Edna—to Meg's secret wrath—to make this mountain visit first instead of placing her directly at school, in order that the children might become acquainted with each other, and so feel less the loneliness of entering an entirely strange home. A fortnight he thought would make them sufficiently acquainted, and their school-life could begin about the first of November. The same supply of clothes which came with his own daughter, would be found in an accompanying trunk for Meg's little charge.

Ned was impatient to show her young visitor all the things in which she was herself so interested, but the dainty little English miss betrayed a provoking want of curiosity; indeed, she seemed to be holding in constant scorn all her surroundings, and when coaxed out to see the milking, gathered her dress about her, and put her hand to her nose.

"I don't like it," and "I'm afraid of them ugly things," pointing to the great, stupid-looking cows, and recoiling from Ned who would have pulled her forward.

And the next morning, when Ned in delighted and eager haste conducted her companion to the wood, and found that she positively refused to go farther, because of her fears to enter such a dark-looking place, she was ready to cry from disappointment.

"I told the trees you were coming," she said, the tears welling in her eyes, "and I'd have shown you where the squirrels have their nuts stored for the winter, and the berries that come out for the little birds' winter food, and ever so much."

"Told the trees I was coming," said the English Edna, who had lost everything but that first astonishing sentence. "Do your trees here speak?"

"No; not like you and me," said Ned impatiently, "but I understand them, and every time the leaves move I think I hear them saying something."

The little English girl burst into a laugh.

"You're so awful funny," she said in answer to her companion's look of indignant surprise. "I suppose it is because you don't know much, living here with that queer old woman, and that funny-looking man."

Ned's temper was aflame in an instant—such daring aspersions cast on her best beloved friends, and especially Dyke who was her hero, were too much for her childish human nature, and without pausing an instant she flew at her cousin, tearing her hair, and scratching and biting her with all her strength.

The attack was so sudden and unexpected that Edna was completely off her guard, and maddened by the pain, as well as blinded by efforts directed at one and the same time toward her hair, eyes, and cheeks, she could only scream lustily, and endeavor to parry the strokes by thrusting out her arms. The two fell at last, and once down Ned's rage seemed to have spent itself; she rose, leaving her companion still prostrate and screaming, and darting into the wood, was soon hidden from sight.

The little English girl picked herself up, and truly she was in sorry plight. Her dishevelled hair hung partly over her face, and was full of the dirt and tiny bits of brush-wood on which she had fallen, while one of her cheeks bore swollen and bloody marks of the little virago's teeth. Her dress was torn and dirty, and her whole person was suggestive of a most desperate encounter.

Screaming all the way, she returned to the house.

"Bless me soul!" exclaimed Meg when she saw her, and Dyke, brought by the screams from the barn, had his fears aroused for Ned.

"Where is Ned?" he asked, in his anxiety for her, losing concern for the child before him.

But Edna was in too violent a paroxysm of grief to answer, and it was not until Meg had soothed her that they could get any coherent statement from her. Then the blame was all upon Ned; the artful child not telling a word of her own provocation.

Dyke, who knew every shade in Ned's disposition, asked:

"Didn't you say something to her that made her fly at you like that? Just think what you said to her."

"I didn't say anything; only I wouldn't go into the woods with her because it was so awful dark," and the sobs continued.

"Where is she now?" asked Dyke.

"She's in the wood," spoken from the depths of Meg's bosom.

Dyke hurried to the wood, while Meg thought within herself, "Lawks me! if this is the way they're getting acquainted, what'll it be by-and-by?"

Dyke sought the wood; he knew Ned's haunts, for he had often been there with her, and interpreted for her her fondly imagined language of the trees. Now he found her curled up at the foot of one, and sobbing as if her heart would break. Her grief came from a twofold source, a keen sense of Dyke's displeasure—her fits of temper so pained him—and remorse for her savage treatment of the little stranger.

"I've been so wicked," she had sobbed out to the trees,

as she had thrown herself down, "and now God won't love me, and you won't love me either."

Dyke took her up in his strong, young arms.

"Tell me, Ned," he said with that grave air which he assumed whenever her temper broke out and which went to her little heart, "tell me about it."

She put her arms around his neck, and rested her tear-stained cheek against his, while she answered:

"Please forgive me, Dyke; I've been awful wicked. I just went at her and scratched her and bit her, but I'm awful sorry, and I'll beg her pardon too, if you'll only forgive me this time, Dyke."

"But tell me about it," he persisted gravely. "What caused you to do it; did she say anything to you?"

Ned was silent; she had been taught by both Meg and Dyke, but particularly Dyke, to tell the truth strictly, and now did she do so, her answer must reflect upon Edna, and also hurt Dyke's feelings. With all her anger against the little visitor, in her natural generosity of heart, she could not bear to say anything that would reflect upon her.

But Dyke persisted, and at length he won the whole story, with an addition of:

"Don't mind it, Dyke; she'll like you by-and-by, and maybe she's real nice too after all. Don't you think so?"

But Dyke reserved his opinion, and instead, talked in his gentle, yet grave and impressive way of the dreadful future the child might be storing for herself in yielding to those passionate bursts of temper. And she listened while the tears streamed down her cheeks, and looked so pretty and so pitiful that the lad could not refrain longer from comforting her.

She walked with him to the house very soberly; but the moment that she caught sight of Edna, whose tears had long since been dried, and who was amusing herself watching Meg's culinary operations, she darted to her, threw her arms around her neck and burst out with:

"I'm so sorry I hurt you; I know I was awful wicked, but please forgive me, and I'll try to love you very much,"

The humble and penitent speech was received with an indifference that gave but little indication of much generosity of heart.

VIII.

We pass over the days which intervened before the departure of the children for school. The tears and sadness of "Ned," when she found that she was to be separated from those she loved so well, not to mention her friends, the trees, to whom, with touching simplicity, she poured out the complaints of her heart. Nothing but Dyke's promise to bring her home for every holiday that he would be permitted to do so, could make her consent to go, and at the last, when Edna, with an impatience that betrayed itself by pouting lips and a childish scowl, was hurrying to her seat in the wagon which was to take them to Saugerties, thence by boat to the other side of the river, where they would meet one of the primitive conveyances of the time, Ned was hanging about Meg's neck as if she could never, never tear herself away.

And during the journey her only comfort seemed to be in nestling by Dyke's side, holding his hand, and listening with swimming eyes to the interesting descriptions the young man gave of the places they passed, while Edna paid constant attention to her own little person; not even Dyke's animated accounts could win her from her interest in herself; the ribbon fastening her tippet, the gloves fitting so smoothly her shapely little hands, the folds of her dark dress, all were subjected over and over again to fond and prolonged attentions, and her fine eyes were often raised with a very conscious look of her own beauty and importance.

The journey was completed at length, and the first sight of the large gray, plain-looking building conveyed to little Ned a feeling of utter desolation; but for Dyke's sake, who had told her if she grieved it would break his heart, she struggled hard to be very brave and calm. Upon Edna the effect was quite different. She felt instinctively that she was about to meet people more like the well-dressed ladies she had been accustomed to see in England, and that her innate love of elegance and luxury would not be offended by such vulgar surroundings as she had during her mountain visit; besides, she rather longed to be away from Dyke. Child as she was, she had been ashamed of his country look, and had mentally contrasted him with the elegant gentleman who had introduced himself to her as her papa, just before she left England. So that it was with a very sprightly step she ascended the steps of the wide portico, and followed into the parlor the smiling matron who came out to meet them.

Poor litle Ned followed, clinging to Dyke's hand, and shutting her teeth very hard together, to suppress her grief.

The pleasant-looking matron was most tender in her attentions, assuring Dyke, whom, to Edna's surprise, she treated with marked respect, that frequent letters had passed between herself and Mr. Edgar relative to the children, and that the latter should have all the care and comforts of their own home.

"But we are in some dilemma about their names," she continued; "both being Edna Edgar, how shall we distinguish them?"

"This one," said Dyke, putting his arm reassuringly about his own little charge, "we call Ned at home."

The lady shook her head, smiling still. "That would hardly do here, being a boy's name. I suppose we shall have to call one Miss Edgar, and the other Miss Edna."

"Let me be Miss Edgar," put in Edna, who, with the stateliness of twenty-five, was sitting in one of the stiff-backed chairs, and gazing curiously about her. Her cousin, in too much grief to care even about the threatened loss of her pet name, was nestling against Dyke and holding her head down, so that he would not see the quivering of her lips and the filling of her eyes.

The matron, not a little surprised at the rather bold

and unexpected request of the little girl, turned and looked at her somewhat reprovingly ; but Miss Edgar was neither dismayed nor abashed.   The lady turned back to Dyke. " Perhaps this little girl will tell us which she prefers."

But poor Ned had no will, nor voice to speak, and when Mrs. Mowbray, touched by the dejected attitude of the child, would have drawn her to her, and spoken tender words, Ned could restrain herself no longer.   With a great sob she threw herself upon Dyke's breast, and cried as if her little heart would break.   Even the matron's eyes were moist, while down poor Dyke's cheeks streamed tears of which in his manliness he was ashamed, but which he could not restrain; but Edna stared indifferently, now and then arranging some portion of her dress.

The painful leave-taking was over at length, and Dyke went away laden with loving messages to Meg, and equally loving ones to the trees, all of which the young man promised to deliver, but he was heavy-hearted enough himself, and had it not been for the fact that Ned, as she was still to him, though the matron, had decided to call her Miss Edna, could write a very little, thanks to his efforts, and that he was cheered by the prospect of hearing frequently from her, he would have been as inconsolable as she was.

IX.

As the school days went on, Miss Edgar talked constantly to her companions of her elegant English papa and all that she expected to have when she became a young lady ; and she paid as much attention to her little toilet every day as though she were already grown up, and she strove to imitate the manners of those of her teachers who, in her childish judgment, had more claim than the others to gracefulness or elegance.

Miss Edna sometimes spoke, but oftener thought, with a full heart of her simple mountain home and its two fond occupants, and her toilet, or the toilet and manners of those about her, gave her little concern. Her whole anxiety was to please Dyke. He had asked her to be very obedient, and very faithful to her studies, and she followed his requests to the letter, telling him in the little notes she was permitted to write every month how hard the lessons were sometimes, but that thinking of him made them grow easier.

And how Dyke kissed the crooked and cramped writing, especially the signature, " Your own little Ned," of each tiny note, before he put it carefully away. It was well that he could not foresee how one day he would read over those notes when anguish should have broken her spirit and his own.

As the months rolled by, and the character of the children developed, Ned's homesickness somewhat disappearing in constant occupation and her own unwearied diligence, it was evident that Miss Edna, as propriety demands that we also must call her for the present, was becoming a universal favorite. Her heartiness in play in recreation time, her unselfishness, and her readiness to assist, endeared her to the young hearts about her; then her quaint, sweet fancies about the whole vegetable world interested and charmed them. They loved to listen to her, and to draw her out on topics so unfamiliar to their unimaginative minds. Twice she had succumbed to her fiery temper; once, when an atrocious lie had been told by one of the larger girls on a little one, and Miss Edna, knowing the circumstances, flung them unflinchingly in the larger girl's face, and provoked a storm that was only quelled by the interference of one of the teachers. The other occasion was, when her cousin learned by accident that the father of one of her classmates pursued an avocation not in accord with her own elevated notions of a gentleman's business. She flung some scornful remark at the child, and Edna, who was present, with her usual impulsiveness turned upon the haughty speaker:

" She's as good as you are, and you're a mean, hateful

thing to speak so. Nobody knows what your own father is."

"He's a *gentleman*," said Miss Edgar, drawing herself up to her little stately height, and emphasizing the word gentleman in a most decisive way.

"Nobody *knows* that," persisted Edna, hot with the temper which was so easily aroused, "it's only yourself who keeps telling us so, and it 'd be a good deal nicer if you didn't brag so much about him, anyway."

Miss Edgar gave a scornful toss to her head, and answered, with a provoking mimicry of her cousin's tones : "*You* haven't any papa to talk about, unless that ugly-looking greenhorn, Dyke."

Edna could endure no more ; and in the battle that ensued, and in which as usual the little mountain girl was much the stronger, the smaller children, who happened to be the only ones present, fled affrightedly to tell the tale, and to summon help.

Edna was punished for her dreadful conduct ; but, as usual, her remorse for having yielded again to that which gave Dyke such pain was her most acute tormentor, and for hours after she was dissolved in tears and ready to make any amends that would allay her troubled conscience. In her penitence, she forgot the provocation she had received, and she went of her own accord to ask her cousin's pardon, which act of humility made Miss Edgar quite triumphant, and she bestowed her forgiveness with all the haughty grace of a conqueror.

Miss Edgar herself had received a reprimand, for the little listeners had repeated what she said; but, owing to a most cunning, sycophantic way of eluding disagreeable consequences, which, child as she was, she possessed to a remarkable degree, her reproof had been slight, and while poor Edna, driven by her remorse to send an account of it to Dyke, was writing in her little cramped hand a detail that had not a word of blame for her cousin, and only censure for herself, and a pitiful plea for pardon from Dyke, Miss Edgar was carrying herself with haughtier airs than ever, and giving *her* version of the matter to her companions.

When Dyke read that little pitiful note, he shut his teeth hard together, and through them said to himself: "It was that little devil that provoked her to it. I know it was, though Ned doesn't say so in her letter."

Both children learned rapidly, little Miss Edgar, however, requiring less study to master a lesson than did Edna, and she also evinced more talent for music, astonishing Mrs. Mowbray one day by soliciting lessons upon the harp in addition to the piano. " You need not be afraid," she said, lifting her eyes very fearlessly to the pleasant face above her. "My papa will be perfectly willing. I heard him say before I came away from England that I was to learn everything I had a taste for." Mrs. Mowbray was silent from astonishment; the confidence and self-possession of this chit of a girl not yet quite eight years old almost dismayed her, and it was with a shade in her countenance she answered at last :

"I shall write to your papa and tell him of your desire."

" But may I not begin the lessons now ? " persisted the child, her confident air increasing.

"Not until we hear from Mr. Edgar," was the decisive answer.

Could Mrs. Mowbray have known the real motive of the child's request, she would have been painfully concerned. Little Miss Edgar desired lessons upon the harp, not for her love of the instrument, but because it possessed advantages for exhibiting a beautiful arm. She had overheard a conversation between some of the larger girls which enlightened her upon the subject, and having long since learned from some simple, but indiscreet tongue of the beauty of her arms, her childish vanity was immediately fired. She waited impatiently for her father's letter, and when it came, she was summoned to Mrs. Mowbray's room to hear its contents. But that good sensible woman did not, as the little lady thought with secret indignation she had a right to do, read the letter verbatim. She simply quoted from it the parts which concerned the child, and which were to the effect that she might take any lessons she chose, providing always such lessons received the approval of Mrs. Mowbray. Then she quoted another part which said that, as Mr. Edgar intended to prolong his stay abroad, his daughter could spend her long summer vacation either at the school, or in the mountain home of her little companion, the other Edna Edgar. The matron was careful not to read for the little eager ears the part which requested that Miss Edna should receive instructions precisely similar to that imparted to Mr. Edgar's daughter, for the gentleman, for purposes of his own, had from the first sent instructions to the effect that the children were not to know that it was to him Miss Edna was indebted for her education. Mrs. Mowbray also had been made acquainted confidentially with the relationship existing between the children, but she had managed so adroitly that every one else in the institute, including even the teachers, believed them to be only friends, to whom strange accident had given the same name and a singular resemblance.

Miss Edgar's pleasure at hearing she might take lessons on the harp was a good deal marred by her disappointment at learning that her papa was not coming home. She had confidently expected to spend the vacation with him in Barrytown, of which place Edna, with great good nature, had frequently told her, and her delight at the prospect of such a visit making her unwontedly generous, she had said that Edna should spend some of the time with her. But Edna, with becoming spirit, had replied that she loved her own home too well to spend from it even a day of her holidays. Now, however, all little Miss Edgar's hopes were dashed, and she pouted and was sullen with both teachers and companions, and her next letter to her father was a wild plea for him to return, which plea Mr. Edgar answered very fondly, but at the same time he stated that he would not come to America for several years.

X.

Miss Edgar preferred to spend her vacation in the institute, rather than be obliged to travel with rustic-looking Dyke, and her choice was very much to Dyke's satisfaction; for, after so long an absence, the young man wanted Ned all to himself. Ned was also well pleased, for she felt that Edna would have been a sort of discordant spirit in the little home, and not alone have prevented her own enjoyment of the scenes she loved so well, but interfere, perhaps materially, with even Meg's pleasure and comfort. And how the child enjoyed her return home! She could hardly refrain from kissing even the cows, especially the brindle that, at the touch of the little hands, turned with what seemed to be a look of affection in her great stupid eyes. Then her friends, the trees; with what ecstatic delight she embraced each, and talked to them all; telling about her school life, and how she had never forgotten them.

Somehow, that holiday was different from, and more delightful than any succeeding one; for other years bringing more knowledge and experience, destroyed gradually all the sweet quaint fancies that made her life now like some happy dream. And how her delighted enjoyment of everything rejoiced Dyke's honest heart, and made him quick to plan diversions that were at once a surprise and a novelty. Even Meg's heavy step grew lighter, and her hands quicker at their daily work since the whole house was brightened by that sweet, winsome presence. Then the mountain rides the three took behind sleek well-fed Sam, who knew the road so well he needed hardly any guidance, and during which Dyke repeated he mountain legends that had such a charm for Ned. Often in the moonlight, when Meg dozed in the wagon, and Ned with a red cloak about her sat looking like a mountain sprite herself, and Dyke being largely read in mountain lore, repeated story after story, the child had little difficulty in fancying many a fairy among the bushes; even the bushes themselves, to her eyes, looked in the moonlight as if they might be green wood nymphs. She had no fear of any of the mountain genii, for, owing to Dyke's able, though simple instruction, she was quite confident that nothing could hurt her so long as she herself remained strictly truthful and good. How the memory of these times was to come to her one day, when, sick with the hollowness of the hearts about her, and faint with the burden of a cruel wrong, she was to long for even one hour of those happy, guileless, childish times.

XI.

Year after year glided away, unmarked by anything more important than Ned's annual visit to her mountain home, in which visit her cousin always refused to join her. Miss Edgar, now a tall and graceful girl, entertained for Dyke and his plain little home the dislike of her childish days. She grew at length to refuse to see the young man when he came to the institute, alleging, in answer to Ned's indignant reproaches for such unkindness, that Dyke was not *her* relative, nor friend, and that she could not be expected to keep up an acquaintance with such a vulgar-looking, ill-dressed person. It was well the mountain girl had gained at last some control of herself, or Miss Edgar would have experienced, as she did twice before, a most unpleasant contact with her cousin's hands. As it was, Ned contented herself with flinging a sharp and passionate reproach at the haughty speaker, and she descended to Dyke with an agitated face and manner. She had only left him to bring her cousin, and when she returned alone, he understood at once the cause of her agitation. "Edna *wouldn't* come," he said, smiling a little, "is not that it?" But Ned, true to her old childish regard for people's feelings, and Dyke's in particular, could not bear to repeat what Edna had so unkindly said. "I know it all," said Dyke, smiling still. "Miss Edgar is ashamed to know me. I do not look sufficiently like city people to suit her. But 'a man's a man for a' that,' eh, Ned?" with a smile becoming broader as he saw the youthful face beginning to tremble, "and *you* like me despite my clothes, do you not?" For answer, she flung her arms about his neck, and hid her face on his shoulder until her tears were dried.

Ten years: it has been a long, and yet a short period, those ten years that have passed since we first became acquainted with Ned; and how does she compare now with the simple child whom we then knew? She has the same candid, winsome expression of countenance, which, with her beautiful eyes and hair, and tall graceful figure, make her a very attractive-looking girl. Then she has manners that are charming from their very simplicity, and the same loving, forgiving, generous heart of her childhood. She has her temper still; that temper which has cost her so many tears and heartburnings, but which no efforts, and she has made desperate ones, have been able to hold entirely in command; it is true, it no longer takes the vulgar form of a personal encounter, but it blazes out in word and look. She has learned well, having taken so naturally to the languages that she is a better linguist than musician, and better than all, she has a solid foundation of study on which to raise any future super-structure.

Her cousin has developed into an exquisitely beautiful girl, but with the vanity of her childish days deepened and intensified, only now, with the cunning of her sex, it is well concealed; and while she has succeeded in acquiring a charm of manner bewitching to superficial observers, she has also a certain insinuating tact by which she wins easily people who are susceptible to blandishment. She has developed a marvellous skill in music, and a voice whose glorious notes made the professor say, on one occasion, she would have little difficulty in becoming a *prima donna;* that praise the young lady received with apparent modesty, but her heart swelled with secret pride, and her blush and exultant smile when she was alone told how love of admiration had cankered the very core of her heart.

The cousins are hardly better friends than they have been in childhood, for Ned, with her innate love of honesty, and a penetration that comes from her own simple, upright character, is enabled to read somewhat Edna's characteristics, and she shrinks from her accordingly. Still, of late years there have been none of the open ruptures that have marked their early acquaintance; and to casual observers they appear to be on very fair terms of friendship.

This is to be the last year of their school life, and just as both shall have reached that "brightest era of a woman's life," eighteen, they are to graduate with all the honors of the institute. Mr. Edgar has written to his daughter that he is coming home at last—coming home in time to be present at her graduation; and that he will be accompanied by an elderly lady, a widow, who has been a friend of his father's, and who will act as a sort of *chaperone* to his daughter in society; that he has disposed of his English estate, and will henceforth make his home in Barrytown.

Miss Edgar can hardly contain herself for joy, and her delight makes her good-natured enough to rush to Ned with the news. "And you must come and see me, Ned." Latterly she also has evinced a preference for the masculine diminutive, and she has adopted it until her cousin is "Ned" to every one save the teachers. "And you must stay with me a long time. Papa will quite approve of it, I know." But Ned shakes her head even while she smilingly murmurs her thanks. Nothing can tempt her from her own little home among the mountains.

Dyke and Meg are also to be present at the graduation; Ned has written to them so urgently that Meg, though so much older and stouter grown as to make travel in her case almost a hardship, feels herself constrained to gratify her darling's wish, and a dressmaker is engaged to come up from Saugerties to make Meg a new, and for her, quite a resplendent gown. Dyke also treats himself to a new suit for the occasion, but it is not much more city-like than the rest of his clothes. Somehow, Dyke, unlike other young men, does not give much thought to his appearance. He does not go courting as others do, perhaps owing to the isolated position of his home and, perchance, also owing to a love which has dwelt in his heart for over fourteen years. Then his mind is so full of the bits of knowledge with which he is constantly storing it, and more than all, of an invention of which he has been full since his boyhood, that he has little room for other things. The invention is something to economize farm labor and, should it be successful, must bring a goodly profit to the inventor. Recently he has formed the acquaintance of a skilled man of business in Saugerties, and with his help in obtaining a patent and introducing his invention through the country, he expects in time to be quite successful. And how does he look on this morning that he is ready to start with Meg for Pennsylvania? The ten, well-nigh eleven years which have passed since we saw him first sit well upon him. His rugged country life has given a fine bloom to his complexion, and his form has the magnificent development that delights an anatomist. He looks every inch the strong, firm, honest fellow that he is.

XII.

That memorable graduation day! memorable to both our heroines, because it was their first introduction to an audience composed of more than their own school associates, and the occasion to one, of her meeting with a father whom she knew only by letter, and a childish memory that every year somewhat obliterated; and to the other, of gratifying, by the honors she received, the two fond hearts which were so bound in her welfare.

The rules of the institute forbidding elaborate dress, the graduates appeared in simple white, adorned alone by natural flowers.

Miss Edgar's heart was beating to suffocation, as from her elevated position she looked over the audience and selected almost at once a distinguished-looking gentleman, with an equally distinguished-looking elderly lady beside him, and felt that *he* was her father. She longed for the moment when her name would be called to sing a pathetic solo, and to give an exhibition of her skill on the harp. She felt no dread of the embarrassment that might be caused by a first appearance before so many, for, being well assured of her ability, and knowing from the numerous admiring looks already directed at her that her appearance was all she could desire, she imagined that she should be perfectly self-possessed. Ned, seated beside her cousin, with equally beating heart, was looking for Meg and Dyke, reassured when she saw them, and smiling in answer to their looks of fond affection. Her part in the exercises was rather limited, being one instrumental performance and the valedictory.

Miss Edgar was announced to give the solo. She rose, and for the moment had a strange calmness that enabled her to walk with exceeding grace to a position directly in front of the audience. Then she unfolded her music and strove to begin. But a sort of stage fright had overtaken her, owing to the mass of upturned faces; it seemed to her as if every countenance had changed into eyes that were burning through her. Her tongue clove to the roof of her mouth, her knees trembled, and the blush of shame and consternation dyed her face, ears, and neck. But the old professor at the piano understood it all, and he played bar after bar of an inspiriting melody, until his favorite pupil lost her fright, and her natural vanity came to her aid. She sang then as perhaps even her enraptured teacher had never heard her sing before. Her glorious voice rose, filling every part of the large and lofty school hall, and it swelled into magnificent cadences that entranced her hearers. The applause burst forth simultaneously, and was loud and long, people rising in their seats the better to view the beautiful singer, and the distinguished-looking gentleman turned to his companion and said eagerly: "That is my daughter." Her performance on the harp called forth another enthusiastic burst of applause, and again and again the distinguished-looking gentleman bent to his companion and whispered some laudatory comment. He was eager for the close of the exercises when he should press to his heart this peerlessly gifted and beautiful creature.

Miss Edna Edgar was summoned to the piano. She had the same graceful figure and fawnlike step of her cousin, and as she moved to her place, people seemed to evince as great a desire to behold her as they had manifested to see her cousin. From her name and marked resemblance to the preceding performer, though lacking the remarkably brilliant beauty of Miss Edgar, the strangers present supposed they were sisters, and her creditable, though not very able performance, was listened to with flattering attention. To Dyke and Meg no fingers ever touched piano so sweetly, and their honest faces flushed with pleasure, and their hearts beat high at the applause bestowed on their darling.

Mr. Edgar turned to his companion, saying: "That is my brother's daughter, of whom I have told you; she does not yet know that I am her uncle." The expressive face of the stately old lady had a shade upon it for a moment, and she looked more earnestly at the young performer before she answered: "Her resemblance to your daughter, and consequently to you, Mr. Edgar, is very marked. Still, she seems neither so lovely, nor so gifted as your child. Do you intend to tell her to-day of your relationship to her?"

The dark handsome face grew darker for a moment; "I did not intend to do so. What do you advise?" "That you tell her, Mr. Edgar. She is your own flesh and blood, and not to be visited for the sin or indiscretion of her parents." "You are right," he whispered, "but I *cannot* tell her yet."

The valedictory was announced, and as the sweet, dis-

tinct, but at first slightly tremulous tones floated out,
Dyke and Meg squeezed hands under Meg's shawl, and
as the speaker gained confidence, and won a closer and
more enraptured attention by her perfect elocution
and natural manner, Meg cried outright for joy, and her
nephew's eyes for an instant shone with a suspicious
moisture.   When at length all was over, and the pupils
were permitted to receive their friends, Miss Edgar flew
to her father's embrace; but, even in that moment of
honest emotion on his part, when she felt his tear upon
her cheek, vanity and triumph that he was so handsome
and distinguished-looking, so superior to everybody else's
father there, were the feelings uppermost in her breast.

Ned, forgetful of everything but that she was with
Meg and Dyke, was embracing each, and crying and
laughing in turn.

Mr. Edgar was introducing his companion to his
daughter, and the elderly lady, bearing that impressive
something about her which marks the grand dame of
the old school, acknowledged the introduction with a
manner that made her sixty years as charming as sixteen.
She had a sweet face, and so clear a complexion that
one, in looking at her, forgot the wrinkles that marked
her features.

"And now," continued Mr. Edgar, to his daughter,
"bring us to your friends," looking in the direction
of the group of which Ned was the centre.

"Is not that young man Dykard Dutton? He is
very much older and manlier grown; and I suppose
that is Meg Standish with him. What an old woman she
has become."

The young lady obeyed, and she was obliged to affect
a cordiality in her greeting of the mountain friends
whom she had ignored so long, when she saw how
truly warm were her father's salutations.

And the elderly lady, introduced as Mrs. Stafford, shook
hands with Meg in her plain country dress, and placed her
delicate white jewelled hand in the great brown hard

palm of Dyke with as sunny a smile and as much graciousness of manner as if both were her equals in the social scale. To Ned she gave a look which seemed to express her secret confidence that they would be intimate friends some day.

Dyke was interested in watching Mr. Edgar. The decade of years seemed to have made such changes in that gentleman's appearance. His abundant black hair and thick mustache were much streaked with gray, and his handsome forehead was indented with lines that told of harassing care or thought. But the young man's observations were terminated by the object of them insisting on the whole party accompanying himself and his daughter to Barrytown, and there making at least a brief stay before going to their mountain home. Meg was quite willing to do so, for it would recall the old happy times when Mr. Edgar was her master, but Dyke politely demurred. Perhaps he feared that the grandeur of the place would make Ned discontented with her own humble abode, and perhaps also he was selfish enough to fear that Mr. Edgar's generosity would go to the extent of inviting Ned to make a permanent stay with his daughter. Under the influence of such feelings he could not give his consent immediately; but he gave it at length, though his heart was filled with a strange gloomy foreboding.

XIII.

The beauty and luxury of that Barrytown home ravished the young heiress with a delight that reached its culmination when she found that the thoughtful kindness of her father had provided even a trained pony for her use. She and her cousin had been taught to ride at school, and happiness as usual making her exceedingly good-natured, she insisted that Ned should have the first canter on the graceful and gentle little animal. There was a groom in attendance, but Dyke being within sight,

Ned took the responsibility of inviting him to attend her, and Miss Edgar, in her exceeding great joy, forgot to make secret fun of him as she might at another time have done.

So the pair went out to the road, Dyke keeping a little behind, both to admire the graceful rider and to war with his own unhappy thoughts. Something that he had never realized before came to him now. He passed his hand over his forehead and said between his teeth:

"Fool, blind mad fool that I have been, not to have been prepared for this." But Ned was turning in her saddle to see why he loitered, and calling to him with all the simplicity of her early years, reminding him when their horses were again together, of the quaint fancies of her childhood about the trees and plants, and demanding in her playful eager way answers to every one of her remarks.

He averted his face whenever her eyes sought his own, and he replied to her with what firmness he could assume; but every tone of her voice pierced his heart, and every touch of her fingers, as sometimes in her eager conversation, when they were ambling slowly along, she flung her hand upon his arm, was like a cruel blow, for he felt that soon tone and touch must be lost to him forever. That night he sought Mr. Edgar for a private interview.

If the gentleman was surprised, he did not betray the feeling, and he invited the young man to a seat with exceeding graciousness. But Dyke replied:

"Thank you, Mr. Edgar; but my business will be communicated better standing. It is about Edna—" he had almost said Ned—"I have come to know if you have any plans for her future."

The gentleman did not answer for a moment; instead, he looked very earnestly at the young man as if he would read his thoughts, and when he did speak, there was a strange uncertainty about his manner.

"I really have no plans further than to continue

to keep her in ignorance of her relationship to me, and to remunerate you from time to time for your care of her."

"Then you desire that she shall make her home with my aunt and me, as she did before she left us to go to school?"

"Yes; unless you object."

Dyke flushed hotly. "I *must* object, Mr. Edgar, for *her* sake. You have educated her beyond such a life, and it would be unjust, not to say cruel, to bury one of her attainments and gifts in a home so plain and lowly as ours is. Had you eleven years ago resigned all claim upon, and all interest in her, we would have reared her according to our means, and she might not then be so unfitted to be one of us. Now she is a lady, and far, far above us. Also, Mr. Edgar, she is your flesh and blood, and entitled from that fact to much consideration on your part; let the generosity which has impelled you to educate her provide for her now."

How the heart of the speaker rose up and well-nigh choked him as he uttered the last words; but Dyke's was a brave nature, and rather than turn aside from a purpose once surely chosen, he could have borne to pluck out his own heart.

Mr. Edgar was somewhat annoyed; it was the second time in the course of a week that the fact of Ned's being his own flesh and blood was thrust into his face, and much though he might recognize that fact secretly, he disliked any open allusion to it. Besides, he had not now the slightest doubt that the beautiful girl whom he called his daughter was really such, and in proportion as his heart went rapturously out to her, so did his indifference to his brother's child increase. Every time that his eyes rested upon her he fancied that he detected new and marked resemblances to his brother, his hatred of whom neither time nor distance seemed to soften. Having educated Ned, and having offered to remunerate any future care of her, he felt that he had done all that could be required, and no thought of her now disturbed him, until Dyke brought her so unpleasantly before him.

He made a turn of the room before he answered; then, with his hands behind him, and his head thrown slightly forward, he said:

"Marry her, Dyke; I shall dower her well, and then both her future and your own will be assured."

Scorn flashed from the young man's eyes, and his voice was tremulous with sudden anger. "Your niece"—with a fine emphasis on the latter word—"Mr. Edgar, is not a chattel to be disposed of in such a manner. She has a heart to be consulted, and were I her equal by birth and education, as I am greatly her inferior, still would such a marriage be impossible, because she regards me only as a brother."

Mr. Edgar was silent, but his head was erect now, and his eyes looking through Dyke's face. Secretly, he was admiring this blunt, fearless fellow, for he half suspected that the young man loved, and loved dearly, the fair subject of their discussion. "What would you have me do?" he said at length.

Dyke answered slowly; every word was a knell to his own affection. "Since you have given her equal advantages of education with your own daughter, give her the same advantages of a home. They can be like sisters and, after all, they will be the most proper companions for each other."

The gentleman made another turn of the room; he could think best when walking, and he was mentally discussing this proposition with all its advantages and disadvantages.

Did he give his brother's child a home, her companionship might render unnecessary for a longer time the company which, for his daughter's sake, he intended to invite to the house—might secure to him for a year or two that country solitude which now, being enlivened by his daughter, would be doubly delightful—and might indeed procure for him a longer term of his child's society;

for when company, and especially of the opposite sex, came to the house, it was natural to suppose that Miss Edgar's marriage might speedily follow.

Thus it seemed well to agree to Dyke's proposition, and Mr. Edgar did so briefly, and then seemed to consider the interview ended, and the young man went out—out to walk in the dark silent grounds. He needed solitude to compose himself, and something in the darkness seemed to help him also, as if it brought nearer that great, invisible Presence which strengthens for sacrifice, and supports in trial. Then he sought Meg, and broke the news of the change in Ned's prospects to her. At first, delight that her darling would be indeed a lady, having all the grandeur to which she was truly entitled, over-powered every other emotion; then came a feeling of wild grief, as she realized how Ned's good fortune must sever the old relations between them; and lastly her anxieties all turned to Dyke.

"What'll *you* do?" she said through her tears. "It was for her you wanted everything, and now she'll no come wi' us any more."

"Never mind me, Aunt Meg; I'm a man, with a man's strength, and I'll work the same as if it was for her. Indeed, I shall be comforted by the thought that she is well provided for. Some day she will marry one of her own kind, and I shall be proud and happy to see *her* happiness." His voice quivered in spite of himself, and his aunt detected it.

"Ay, lad; thee'lt be proud and happy when thy hair is gray, and thy form is stooped, and thy old aunt is gone, and thee'st ne'er a hearth of thy own to sit by, through loving and waiting, with never the heart to ask and——"

He stopped her with a kiss.

"You wouldn't have me ask, Aunt Meg, when the very asking might make her consent, for fear of ingrati-tude; consent, even though she couldn't give me her heart's love."

"That's true, lad; it might be so." And then her

thoughts reverted to all that Dyke had told her of his
interview; he had prudently reserved Mr. Edgar's pro
posal to him to marry his niece, saying:

"And didn't Mr. Edgar say some'at about your own
matters? And didn't you tell him anything about your
invention?"

Dyke smiled.

"He was too full of the other subject; and besides,
what need to tell him? If the invention succeeds, as it
seems likely to do now, he may hear about it, and then,
you fond, foolish old aunt, there will be enough to gratify your pride."

Again kissing her, he left her.

XIV.

The next morning, after another interview with Meg,
Dyke sought Ned.

"I want to see you alone," he said, for Miss Edgar was
in a part of the room writing an order for something
that was to be brought from Rhinebeck.

The unusually grave, and even somewhat troubled
expression of his face alarmed Ned, and without even
waiting to tell her cousin that she was going into the
grounds, she took his arm and hurried forth.

Neither spoke until they had reached a very secluded
part; then Dyke, motioning his companion to a seat on
the mossy eminence, threw himself down beside her.

It was a harder task than he had thought, this breaking
to Ned of the change in her fortune, and she sat so
quietly waiting for him to begin. She asked no question,
but her great, lustrous, guileless eyes looked at him very
earnestly. He could have looked at her forever, she
formed so sweet a picture with her wealth of raven hair
coiled simply at the back of her head, and her rich, dark
complexion. But he had to begin.

"Would you like to live here always, Ned?"

"No; is that what you had to say to me?" her lips parting into a half smile.

He resumed: "Mr. Edgar proposes that you make your home here with his daughter; you will be treated as if you were her sister."

The smile faded from her lips.

"Mr. Edgar is very kind, but I prefer my home with Meg and you."

Dyke said again: "But Meg and I think it best for you, Ned, to accept Mr. Edgar's offer."

"What! not to live with Meg and you any more—not to consider that dear old place way up among the mountains my home for the future?"

She could say no more for the great lump which came suddenly into her throat, and in another moment she had burst into tears and was crying with all the abandon of her childish days. How Dyke's own heart beat, and how something in his own throat rose up; but he set his teeth firmly together, and fastened his hands into the earth beside him, that he might not, in spite of himself, clasp this beloved one to his heart and whisper that she might make his home always hers if she would.

His nature, strong and ardent as it was, was too noble for such a course. He was not her equal, and if he were, he would refrain from asking her heart's affection until he had given her time and opportunity to test it. So he answered, when he had recovered his wonted calm:

"Remember, Ned, that you are a woman now, and must submit to the dictates of your judgment rather than those of your heart. A residence here will be better for you in many ways. Mr. Patten, who has busied himself about my invention for some months past, has everything in readiness for us to travel together about it now, and Meg being long anxious to see some cousins of hers in Albany, I shall leave her with them while I am away; so, you see, the little mountain home is no place for you. What in the world"—brightening a little—"would you do there ? No piano, no society, no books such as you have been accustomed to ? ”

“ Why did you give me such an education ? ” she asked through her tears. “ Better you had saved the money spent on me, and brought me up simply in that little mountain home. I should have been just as happy, I am sure.”

“ Did I ever tell you that *I* had paid for your education ? ” asked Dyke.

“ No ; but I supposed, of course, you had ; am I not right in supposing so ? ”

He was silent, not knowing what to reply. How he regretted not having obtained Mr. Edgar’s permission to reveal to her the truth about the matter. His silence, however, was giving to her the revelation he fain would have made.

“ I see it all now,” she said, springing to her feet. Mr. Edgar has paid for my education.”

Dyke also arose.

“ He did not want you to know that, Ned, and you must tell him how it has come about, for I do not expect to have an opportunity of speaking to him privately again.”

“ But why should he do so much for me ? ” she persisted.

“ Because he is wealthy, and he knew your family in England.”

She continued : “ It is singular how every one belonging to me died, and that there was only Meg and you to take care of me.”

“ We gave you such care as we could,” said Dyke, anxious to get her thoughts away from her family, lest she should divine other things about herself, as well as she had divined who had paid for her education ; “ and I don’t think in the matter of the affection you gave us it made much difference whether we were your own, or not.”

“ Indeed, no ; ” was the earnest reply. “ You were my brother always, and always shall be my brother.”

With a sharp pang he felt the truth of her words; as a brother, and as a brother alone, would she ever love him. But he went on bravely enough: "You see now, Ned, that, owing so much to Mr. Edgar, you can hardly refuse him when he wishes you to live here for companionship for his daughter."

"Perhaps he just educated me for that," speaking a little sarcastically, and drawing herself up.

"No, no; you are mistaken. I am sure he did not entertain such a thought."

"Well, let Mr. Edgar alone for a few minutes, and tell me about yourself. Are you poor, Dyke?"

He looked at her in surprise, and before answering, demanded to know why she asked.

"Only because, as your sister, I have a right to know all your circumstances, and to know also whether Mr. Edgar, in his great generosity to me, has done anything for you?"

Dyke smiled.

"My circumstances at present do not need any aid from Mr. Edgar; and if this invention succeeds, I shall be a rich man." For one whirling moment a great hope filled his heart; if he became a rich and noted man, and Ned should remain unmarried, perhaps her hand might one day be his. It was a hope so sweet and bright that it gave a more cheerful tone to his voice as he continued: "All my aunt's savings and my own are sunk in this invention, and if it should turn out a failure we would be pretty poor; but there is no fear of that, everything is so promising now."

"And how long before your hopes can be fulfilled?" Her face was flushed and eager.

"A year, perhaps two; for people, especially country people, are so slow to accept improvements."

"Well, for the present then, I shall accept Mr. Edgar's offer of a home."

Her lips quivered and her eyes were full, but she did not let Dyke see.

XV.

Life at Weewald Place, as Miss Edgar christened her father's spacious home (having taken the name from one of the novels she had managed to read surreptitiously at school) was enchanting enough, could Ned divest herself of a certain uncomfortable feeling of dependence. Everywhere she turned there was a haunting reminder of her obligations to Mr. Edgar; a feeling that was intensified by his own cold, stately courtesy toward her; for, while he was careful to see that she received equal attention with his daughter, he could not vail his own feelings sufficiently to treat her with more than the utmost politeness. Her face recalled, or he imagined it did, the lineaments of his hated brother, and he often forbore, even when talking to her, to allow his eyes to meet hers. So, while his countenance kindled with pleasure at the approach of his daughter, it often fell at the coming of his niece; and while his voice frequently assumed an exquisite tenderness in addressing Edna, it was more frequently cold, almost to repulsion, when speaking to Ned. And Ned felt the difference; felt it many times with a sickened heart as she contrasted it with the warm affection of Meg and Dyke.

Mr. Edgar's coldness weighed upon her the more that she constantly remembered how much she owed to him in the matter of her education. In accordance with Dyke's wish, she had taken an early opportunity of explaining to the gentleman how she had learned, or rather of herself had divined her indebtedness, and she had attempted to express her gratitude. But Mr. Edgar sternly desired her to stop, and his manner, even more than his words, had made her feel that she was never to refer to the subject again.

Regarding other things she had nothing of which to complain. The servants were as deferential as if she also were Mr. Edgar's daughter, though they were not slow in ascertaining and repeating among themselves that she was only a dependent, and really belonged to a poor home up among the mountains, and Mrs. Stafford took a kindly interest in her.

Miss Edgar herself, delighted with the novelty and beauty of a home that exceeded even her expectations, and in rapture with a father who seemed disposed to gratify all her wishes, was exceptionally companionable.

It added to her pleasures to have Ned share them, and she often astonished our heroine by a sudden embrace, and an exclamation expressive of her delight that they were together.

The cousins took long daily rides—a gentle, graceful pony having been provided for Ned—and, to her, those hours in the saddle were the happiest ones of the day. There was a sense of independence and freedom on the horse's back that proximity to Mr. Edgar's presence prevented her from feeling in the house, and she was very thankful that the gentleman never offered to accompany them.

It was well she did not divine that she herself was the obstacle to his attendance. He would not endure oftener than was absolutely necessary the company of his brother's child.

One afternoon, somewhat tired from a longer canter than usual, and very thirsty, the riders drew up with longing eyes before a spring bubbling by the side of the road. The groom, in obedience to the imperative order of Miss Edgar, who wanted at all times to be certain that the man could never overhear her conversation, was a long way behind. There was no house in sight, and Ned decided to dismount and help herself to a drink in the manner she used to do when a child; but, ere she could spring from her stirrup, there was a rustling among the foliage on the other side of the road, and in a moment there appeared a tall, graceful young man carrying what might be a portfolio of sketches. He was evidently no rustic, for his dress was of stylish city mode, and it was worn with a certain negligé quite becoming. He seemed to understand the desire of the ladies, and with a bow as graceful as it was courteous, he said in a deep, low, musical voice :

" Do not, ladies, be at the trouble of dismounting; allow me to bring you a drink in our rustic way."

He laid his portfolio down, and darted into the wood which skirted one side of the road. When he returned he bore with him leaves skilfully formed into cups. Filling one with the sparkling spring water, he presented it to Miss Edgar. She quaffed, and returned the leafy vessel; her eyes meeting his, and her face suffused with a hot blush. She had never seen such eyes, nor such a face; to her girlish fancy, all unformed in the matter of manly beauty, both were perfect, and the unbounded but respectful admiration his look expressed set her heart to beating rapidly.

Ned also quaffed from the second leafy cup he presented to her, but further than to thank him briefly she scarcely looked at the bearer, and she was somewhat surprised to find her cousin asking of the groom, who had overtaken them and whom she had beckoned to her side when they were out of sight of the stranger, if he knew the latter.

" Yes, Miss; he is Jim Mackay's son. Jim Mackay, the gardener, that lives a little below there," indicating with his whip a point south of the direction they were taking. " He's never been much good to his father, having ways different from us country-folks, and taking to books, and painting and such things. An uncle of his took him away to Europe a few years ago, and now he's just come back, and his father says he's as bad as ever about books, and making pictures of everything."

Miss Edgar made no reply, and the groom fell back to his usual respectful distance.

The next day they took the same route, Ned forgetti ig the occurrence of the previous day until handsome young Mackay started before them ; there was no excuse to stop, Miss Edgar being afraid to feign thirst as she would like to do, lest her feint should be discovered by her cousin, and so there was only an exchange of bows. But the heiress could devise other means of meeting one who had made such an impression on her susceptible heart; and all that she had heard about him but enhanced her strange predilection. "His ways so different from those of country-folks, his taste for books and painting," what were they all but indications of a refined and cultured mind? It would be like some of the stories she had so surreptitiously read, for her to help him secretly—to lend him books, to impart to him some of her own instruction, and at length to make him feel how much he owed to her; it would be delightful, and quite justifiable, since her father so unaccountably deferred asking company to the house. Also, by making this young man her protegé there would be afforded an opportunity to satisfy partially her craving for admiration, for she felt that the handsome face that had looked up to her while she drank was then and there caught in the toils of her beauty. She had some misgiving about the propriety of this quixotic plan of hers, and of the stern disapproval of her father should he hear of it; but her misgiving was of short duration. She craved excitement, and since Weewald Place furnished none, she would embrace this opportunity of making it for herself.

Thus Dick Mackay found himself the recipient of an order for some sketches of the scenery about Barrytown, and he was further delighted by the present of a valuable book on the art of sketching. The note that accompanied the present besought the utmost secrecy, and contained at the same time a most flattering offer to assist the young man in any way that was in the writer's power.

Dick had one confidant—a sister a year younger than he was; a fragile, delicate girl, but one so gentle and winning in disposition that she gained love as easily as she breathed. She sympathized with Dick; she entered into all his tastes, she admired him, and she wellnigh worshipped him; all of which feelings the handsome, dreamy, poetical young fellow returned. To her then

Dick showed the note, and told everything, even to the revelation of his own sudden but deep attachment for Miss Edgar, and he laughed at the castles in the air which his sister built. She could see neither the impossibility nor the improbability of a future marriage of her brother to the heiress. In her eyes, Dick was handsome and clever enough for a princess, and good enough to win even Mr. Edgar's warm regard could that gentleman but know him; at which sweet praises Dick laughed again, but he did not contradict her. Stranger things *had* happened, and love that stops at no barrier might even overthrow Mr. Edgar's opposition.

XVI.

The canker of discontent entered more and more into Ned's heart, being enhanced by the change which had come into her cousin's manner; for Edna, fast in the toils of an attachment she dared not reveal, and for the secrecy of which she was always anxiously planning, had grown unaccountably estranged from Ned. She seldom rode or walked with her, and often seemed disposed to avoid all conversation, and the sensitive, spirited girl was too proud to seek any explanation, or to make any complaint. She never dreamed of the secret acquaintance progressing under her very eyes, nor that it was fear of her own truthful, straightforward character which made Miss Edgar assume so chilling a demeanor.

She heard rarely from Dyke, as his frequent journeys and ceaseless business pertaining to his invention left him little time; he did not add that by this infrequent writing to her he was schooling himself; schooling himself to be prepared to yield her entirely, when occasion should demand it; and Meg, since Dyke was not likely to be home until spring, had decided to spend the winter in Albany.

It was now November, and as Ned counted the months until summer, before which season she could not expect to make the briefest visit to her mountain home, her heart sank.

"I cannot endure it," she said, pressing her forehead against the window of her own room by which she was standing; that room, in whose comfort and elegance she found less charm than in tracing in imagination against the sky the outlines of her own loved mountains. Then she thought, as she had often thought lately, about Dyke's means, and whether she might not earn her own livelihood; and a livelihood that might even enable her to make frequent remittances to Meg. She was sure she could be happy doing something like that, and then her summer visit would be truly delightful.

She went to her desk, and wrote to Mrs. Mowbray, the womanly and kind-hearted principal of the Pennsylvania institute.

It was a characteristic letter, honest and open as her own nature, and so clearly stated that to the good lady who received it, it was a complete mirror of the writer's feelings.

She waited for the answer with feverish impatience. It came promptly, and she read:

"My Dear Miss Edna Edgar:—It was, as you surmised, with a good deal of astonishment that I read your letter. I think I understand the feelings you describe so clearly, and knowing your nature as I do, I must admit that I sympathize with them. Whether, however, it will be best for you to choose a self-supporting life while Mr. Edgar's home so generously shelters you I cannot say. I would advise you to place the matter before him.

"Singularly enough, at the very moment of receiving your letter, I was handed another from a very wealthy, but exceedingly eccentric friend of mine. She is a widow, and living now on the Hudson, not many miles from your present home. She desires a companion, a young lady who will be willing to accommodate herself to whims and vagaries; her duties will be exceedingly light (but I add from myself that I fear they will be very trying) and her remuneration will be quite liberal.

"If, my dear Miss Edna, you are disposed to try this position, and that you gain Mr. Edgar's consent and approval, the place is open to you."

Ned went with the letter to Mr. Edgar; she met him in the broad entrance hall, and at the same moment a servant crossed, carrying a rare and exquisite southern exotic. The gentleman, attracted by the beauty and rarity of the flower, stopped the bearer.

"Mr. Dick Mackay sent it, sir; it is the first of the kind that has blossomed in one of the new sort of greenhouses his father's had put up, and Mr. Dick cut this flower off to send to Miss Ned Edgar."

Mr. Edgar frowned, and looked with something like angry wonder at the young girl who was now standing beside him; but he said no more, only motioned to the servant to deliver the gift.

Ned, being full of her errand to Mr. Edgar, took it mechanically, and she gave hardly a thought to the strangeness of Dick Mackay—whom she rarely saw, and then never to bestow upon him the slightest recognition—making any such gift to her, and she turned immediately to Mr. Edgar to ask him for a private interview.

That gentleman was secretly very much displeased; was the bad blood of his brother already showing itself in his child, that she could, in defiance of all propriety and all obligations to him, form such an acquaintance with a gardener's son as emboldened the latter to the presumption he had just witnessed; a presumption that amounted to familiarity, judging by the fact that the plant was sent to Miss "Ned" Edgar; in the house, owing to his daughter's preference for the name, she was called Miss Ned Edgar. Such being the case, Ned was no companion for *his* child, and he led the way to the library with his wonted courtesy, but with a very grave and stern face. At the door he paused to say with an ill-concealed sarcasm:

"Allow me to ring for your flower to be taken care

of; it may wilt before you can give it your attention," with a slightly marked emphasis on the word your.

But unsuspecting Ned noticed neither his sarcasm nor his emphasis; she noticed nothing save his sternness, which chilled and frightened her, and when the servant appeared she gave up the flower mechanically, heard like one who heard not, Mr. Edgar's directions for its care, and sank into the seat he drew forward for her like one cruelly oppressed.

" You wished to see me," he said coldly, when he had waited an unusual length of time for her to begin.

She was roused at last; the old hot spirit flamed within her, and while her cheeks flushed and her eyes sparkled with secret indignation that she had borne this servitude so long, she handed him the letter.

"This will tell you my object in desiring this interview."

Her very voice was trembling from suppressed indignation.

He read the letter, and evidently more than once—it was so long before he looked up.

Did she wish to leave Weewald Place so as to facilitate, perhaps, her marriage with Dick Mackay? Such was the thought that flashed through his mind and which kept his eyes fastened to the letter, even after he had perused it. Had she, even in her bold-facedness, come to tell him that she had made this low match for herself, as her father before her had done for himself?

He looked up and waited for her to speak.

She arose.

" I thank you, Mr. Edgar, for the charity "—there was a trembling emphasis on the last word—"which has educated me and given me a home; I thank you particularly for the education which I now feel will enable me to gain my own support."

She was obliged to pause; for pride, anger, regret that she was indebted for anything to this proud, stern man were overmastering her.

He also arose.

Her spirited face and manner disgusted him; he fancied that she lacked all gratitude, indeed, all heart, and that she was incapable of the very candor which he considered his due.

"You are old enough, Miss Edgar, to decide for yourself in this matter. To a young lady who has undertaken such a step as this letter indicates, without consulting me, neither my approval nor my consent are necessary."

She was stunned; in her natural simplicity and impulsiveness, she had never thought of acquainting Mr. Edgar with her intention to write to Mrs. Mowbray; as he was not her relative, and that she was merely a dependent, it did not seem to be any part of her duty.

She answered, as soon as she recovered her voice:

"I was not aware that in writing to Mrs. Mowbray before I acquainted you I was wanting in any regard for you. If such has been the case, I am very sorry."

It was her old fashion of asking pardon for a fault in almost the same breath with her temper; but Mr. Edgar was not to be appeased. He looked upon her now as somewhat of an actress, and he was really anxious to have her influence removed from the house.

He answered with an unmistakable decision: "I wish to say no more upon the subject, and whenever you decide to leave your present home, I shall see that you are provided for your journey."

He held the door open for her to pass out, bowing as she did so. Then he sent for his daughter.

Miss Edgar obeyed the summons in some trepidation, having learned that Ned had just come from a private conversation with her father, and not knowing but that conversation might have had some reference to herself. Still, she felt assured that Ned *knew* nothing, and she congratulated herself on the forethought with which she had instructed her lover always to call her Ned Edgar. She had carefully forborne to tell him at the same time that she was usurping the name of her companion, for

every hireling in Weewald Place termed our heroine by
the masculine diminutive; and though Mr. Edgar never
used it, he at no time, after discovering his daughter's
preference for it, disclaimed against it.

Knowing all this, Edna smiled as she saw the plant
borne to her cousin's room.

"My dear," said Mr. Edgar, leading his daughter
fondly to a seat, "I want you to answer very frankly
some questions I am about to ask."

Her heart beat wildly; had he, despite her efforts at
secrecy, heard anything about herself and Dick?

"Do you know anything of Miss Edna's acquaintance
with Mr. Mackay's son? Has she made you her confidant?"

She breathed freer.

"No, papa," opening her beautiful eyes very wide.

"She must have permitted him to make her acquaintance, for he has been bold enough to send her a handsome floral gift to-day. She has also acquainted me with
her intention of engaging as companion to a lady in
C——. Has she said nothing of all this to you?"

Miss Edgar breathed very freely; she could truthfully
answer, "no, papa," to his last question; but she was
careful not to add that it was her own coldness which
repelled every confidence on the part of her cousin.

"Well, my dear, it is evident that Miss Edna is not a
companion for you; I am very glad that she has not
given you her confidence; there might have been con-
tamination in it. She is enamored, I fancy, of this gardener's son, and perhaps wants to leave us in order to
marry him. She probably feared my displeasure too
much to tell me; but as she is not my daughter, her
marriage with this low fellow can neither hurt nor annoy
me. You, my love, will never disgrace your father by
an unequal marriage."

He stooped and kissed her.

Ned was too proud to yield to tears; but the quivering

of her lip, the heaving of her breast, and the moisture which came into her eyes despite herself, when she was alone, told how much she suffered.

She wrote at once to Mrs. Mowbray, assuring her of Mr. Edgar's consent, and urging her to complete all arrangements with the lady in C——, that she might enter at once upon her new position. She did not write to Dyke, fearing to give the honest fellow increased anxiety, and feeling that she could write to him with better heart when she should have become accustomed to her new home.

Such arrangements as Mrs. Mowbray could make were speedily completed, and Mrs. Doloran, the wealthy and eccentric widow of C——, wrote to Miss Edna Edgar that she was quite ready to receive her.

Her departure was marked by nothing save the motherly solicitude of Mrs. Stafford; that lady would be assured that Ned was amply provided for her journey, and when the girl protested at so much preparation, she insisted that she must obey Mr. Edgar's orders, at which Ned bit her lip and was silent.

XVII.

Mrs. Doloran's eccentricities took most extravagant turns, not alone in the matter of dress, which made her secretly a constant subject of ridicule, but in the friendships she formed and in the disposition of her vast wealth. Her ample house was always open to every one whom she chose to honor with her acquaintance, and were it not for the prudent care exercised over her by a nephew to whom she was very much attached, she might often be the prey of those who were most benefited by her lavish kindness. She insisted on having about her for weeks at a time any one who pleased her fancy, or contributed to her amusement by the gift of story-telling, no matter how brief might have been her acquaintance with the person, or how contrary to the rules of propriety might be her favor to him, and in this way she often tried sorely her elegant, reserved nephew. Nothing but his affection for this strange woman—his dead mother's only sister—and his firm conviction that, left to herself, she would become the speedy prey of dishonest persons, retained him with her. He had an ample fortune in his own right so that he had no need of his aunt's wealth, though gossiping tongues attributed all his devoted attentions to the fact that he expected to become her heir.

Ned's arrival was too late for her introduction to Mrs. Doloran or even to Mrs. Doloran's nephew, Mr. Carnew, and after refreshments had been provided for her, she was shown to her room. The apartment was pretty and home-like enough to invite to rest one even less wearied, but she was too full of sad emotions to slumber. Again and again she enacted her parting with Mr. Edgar; he had given her his hand, and told her to apply to him when she should be in any need, but the manner of his speech had seemed to freeze her very soul, and it renewed her determination to endure the most abject want in prefer-ence to any future aid from him. Miss Edgar, in the moment of parting, had resumed the affectionate manner with which she had treated Ned when they first came to Weewald Place. Her affection was resumed, not because it had returned (it could scarcely return, for, correctly speaking, her nature was incapable of feeling any affection save for those who ministered to her own selfish wants), and not because she experienced any sudden pity for her orphan companion going forth to earn her living, but be-cause she was delighted at Ned's departure; and, as usual, anything that made her happy made her good-natured. She knew not what spy-like qualities her cousin possessed, nor what unhappy discovery she might make, if she con-tinued to live beneath the same roof; so, under the influence of joy that there was removed at least one person who she felt would denounce her secret attach-ment did she know it, she had thrown her arms about Ned's neck, and kissed her warmly enough. And sensitive, loving, forgiving Ned, touched by even that late mark of affection, had thawed under it, and forgiven and forgotten all the coldness that had gone before it.

"Write to me," Miss Edgar had whispered, with her cheek, to all appearance, pressed fondly enough against that of her cousin, "write to me frequently;" and Ned had promised to do so, as well as she was able for the gulp in her throat.

These were the memories which banished sleep, and which made it, when it did come, so brief that she awoke with the dawn. She dressed herself, and waited for the November day to be fully ushered in; and when the sunlight broke upon everything with a radiance that seemed to belong to an earlier season, she threw a shawl about her and descended.

Early as the hour was for a gay country house, where breakfast was served late, some one had evidently gone out before her, for the door of the main entrance was wide open. The air was somewhat chilly, but bracing, and under its invigorating influence, as she pulled her shawl about her and hurried on with elastic step, she felt her spirits rise. She had that sweet, ardent youth which requires so little to elate or depress it, and as she passed through walks, the beauty of which in summer time must have equalled those of Weewald Place, and looked about her at the vegetation that, not yet bare, was even bright with the colors which indicated its decay, she felt her griefs grow lighter and lighter. Independence was before her, and it only needed a patient, enduring will on her part to achieve it.

Suddenly she came to a hedge of evergreen higher than herself; looking through the interstices, which in some places were large enough to admit of the passage of a hand, she saw a broad and well-kept gravelled walk. Wondering whether it led directly to the house, and how she could get upon it from her present position, she was further attracted by the sound of approaching footsteps on the gravel.

In a moment there came into sight a very tall, stout woman, followed at a respectful distance by a tall, thin, awkward-looking man carrying a cup and saucer. The woman was dressed in a flowing robe of the brightest yellow silk, that trailed on the walk behind her like some gay plumage, a shawl of light green of the same material thrown scarf wise over her shoulders, and a red lace veil depending from her hair. Her hands were bare, but beautifully white and covered with sparkling rings, and her countenance, when she came into full view of the astonished and amused Ned, was that of a very handsome woman about fifty years of age. Her form was straight to stiffness, and she made it more painfully so, by holding her shoulders rigidly back and keeping her head at the highest possible elevation. She took such long heavy steps, that her gait was more like a manly stride, and it taxed her awkward-looking attendant to maintain the precise distance which she evidently required, for she turned once, and said sharply:

"You're too far, Donald; too far by two paces." Donald exerted himself to make up the two paces, and the lady, satisfied, resumed her walk; but she had only taken a stride or two, when she stopped again, and demanded Donald to bring to her the cup he held.

He obeyed, but with the air of one most dissatisfied with his work, and she, having sipped from the cup extended it for him to take. Instead of doing so, he dashed it from her hand, breaking the vessel, and sending abroad a very appetizing odor of coffee.

"I'll noo be your lap-dog any longer, wi' your 'Donald keep two paces farther, and Donald keep two paces nearer, and Donald hand me me coffee, and Donald carry the cup agen.' It's fine wark Donald Macgilivray's come to when he's after a leddy's beck and call like a cur that's afeered o' a beatin. You'll just get some other dog to do your biddin'."

He was standing as erect as was the astonished lady to whom he delivered this unexpected tirade, with his arms folded, and his stubble-indented Scotch face set in sullen wrath.

The lady burst into a loud laugh, and at that moment an elderly and somewhat strange-looking gentleman appeared upon the scene. He was strange-looking, both because of his deeply bronzed and parchment-like face and his odd dress, pantaloons like a sailor's and a short cloak slung over one shoulder. With an air of protecting freedom he advanced to the lady's side.

"I heard Donald's voice, and I heard you laugh," he said in such deep, clear and pleasant tones, that they seemed out of harmony with his appearance. "What is the matter?"

"The matter?" Why that fool of a Scotchman objects to being my dog any longer. He'd rather be an ill-treated slave than a well-fed cur." And she laughed again; a laugh so loud, so hearty, and so prolonged, that it set peeping Ned to laughing also.

But the Scotchman was not disposed to take any mirthful view of the occurrence; he stood looking as angry and dogged as ever.

The lady turned her mirthful face to him, and said, as soon as she recovered her voice:

"I don't much blame you, Donald, and tell Cawson when you get to the house to find a place for you somewhere, at whatever work you choose to do."

The Scotchman's face changed instantly: he had expected to be summarily discharged, and instead he was promoted.

"O me leddy," he said, looking as if he was ready to fall on his knees at her feet, "you are too good, and——"

She waived him away, and taking the arm of the elderly gentleman was turning to pursue her course, when she caught sight of Ned through the interstices of the hedge. Ned had been so interested and amused, that she did not once think of changing her position.

"What have we here?" said the lady, dropping in her astonishment the arm on which she leaned.

"What are you?" she continued, as Ned, violently blushing, started back; and too impatient to wait for an answer, she continued to her companion:

"Take one of your flying leaps, Mascar, and let me know all about it."

The gentleman obeyed, retreating to the opposite side of the road, and there collecting such force and energy for his spring that it brought him flying over the top of the hedge and placed him almost at the feet of the astounded girl. She was frightened enough to scream, and only restrained herself by a great effort.

"Do not be alarmed," he said in that strangely pleasant voice. "My flight to you has only been for a very harmless purpose. Since you are on these grounds you must be acquainted with some one in Mrs. Doloran's house. It is she who has commissioned me to get your name."

"I am the person whom Mrs. Doloran expects to receive as a companion; my name is Edna Edgar," was the trembling reply.

"Edgar," said the gentleman with a sudden and strange excitement in his manner. "Did you say *Edgar?*"

"Yes;" she answered; but there was no further opportunity for him to question, for Mrs. Doloran was screaming from the other side of the hedge:

"Bring it over here, Mascar; I want to know all about it."

He laughed as heartily as Mrs. Doloran herself had laughed a short time before, and said with a merry twinkle of his sharp, black eyes at Ned:

"*It* is a young lady who doesn't know how to leap over hedges; *it* will go back to the end of this path and meet us where the path converges to the road," indicating with his hand as he spoke the direction Ned was to take, and then he prepared himself for another flying leap back to his impatient companion.

Ned pursued the course indicated, her mind very much divided between anxiety lest she should not please this exceedingly eccentric lady, amusement at the oddities she had already witnessed, and astonishment at the surprise which the mention of her name had occasioned in the strange gentleman. Lost in the maze of her thoughts she reached the end of the walk before she was aware of it, and saw approaching her the strange couple.

"Miss Edgar, the young lady who has come to be your companion, Mrs. Doloran," said the gentleman, gracefully relinquishing the arm that leaned upon his, and bowing low to both ladies.

"Umph!" said Mrs. Doloran, holding her head at a greater elevation, while she inspected this new addition to her household.

"And what's your Christian name?" when she had finished her survey.

"Edna!"

"Faugh! it's like most women's names, good for neither sense nor sound.

"I used to be called Ned," ventured our heroine, anxious at any hazard to win the favor of this woman, without which she might be returned to Weewald Place.

"Ned, eh! well that was sensible; nothing like masculinity in some shape for raising a woman to dignity; eh, Mascar?"

Mascar assented by a bow to the speaker, but a look at Ned expressive of his secret mirth.

The lady continued:

"Women are such emotional creatures, running after their fancies one moment and running away from them the next, adoring the men in one breath, and vilifying them in the second, that they have become the fools of the world; but you are young yet and may be educated to better things. How old are you?"

"Almost nineteen."

"Umph! not so young as you look—have you any followers? Are you in love?"

The young lady blushed violently as she answered in

the negative, and the gentleman's face was contorted with suppressed mirth.

They were within sight of the broad porch of the house, and Ned in her embarrassment, turning unconsciously to look in that direction, saw a gentleman descend the steps and come toward them. Mrs. Doloran, following the course of Miss Edgar's eyes, also observed him, and said eagerly:

"There's Alan!"

She seemed to have forgotten Ned in the watch she maintained on the approaching person; indeed, she appeared to be secretly admiring the easy grace and manly swing of his gait; as he came nearer, even Ned was struck with the clear, eagle-like look in his dark eyes, and the firm, yet kind expression about his mouth, the upper lip of which was covered by a thick, black moustache.

Waiving all forms, Mrs. Doloran grasped Ned's arm and pulled her forward with a jerk, holding her as if in a vise, while she said:

"This is Ned Edgar, Alan, the companion you made me engage. She isn't nineteen yet, and pretty enough to have you noticing her, and she making a fool of herself by falling in love with a man who wouldn't marry her if he could. She says——"

At which point of her unnecessary speech, an angry flash from Alan's eyes stopped her; it was evident, that, if to no one else, at least in some things she succumbed to the will of this young, slender, but firm-faced individual.

He said quietly, but in a voice that was deep, and like his face, firm:

"Now that you have so summarily introduced the young lady, be good enough to introduce me."

Mrs. Doloran broke into one of her hearty laughs; so hearty, so prolonged, and so funny that it was irresistible; Mascar joined in it, while the gentleman, called Alan, bit his lip in a fruitless endeavor to maintain his own gravity, and Ned laughed also in spite of herself.

Mrs. Doloran only stopped when the tears came into her eyes, and then, placing her arms akimbo—a fashion which she severely deprecated in every other female, but leniently tolerated in herself—she said :

" Alan's my nephew—Alan Carnew—he is a good fellow enough when his will is not opposed, and a pretty bad one when anybody attempts to drive him. He likes women when they're women, because he hasn't sense enough to see that women were only made after all the brains had been given to men, and he won't know what the world is till he gets a wife that will fool him to the top of his bent. Now, I'm going into breakfast and to see what Cawson's done for that poor fool, Donald; I'm going in with Mascar, here," taking that gentleman's arm, " and you, Ned, can follow with Alan. Use your opportunity, for you won't have many of them, as I don't intend to allow you and him to be much together."

" A wholesome introduction, upon my faith," exclaimed the gentleman, called Mascar, laughing as he received the arm extended to him, and turned to accompany its owner; but young Carnew was flushed with anger; he did not answer, however, and after a moment, during which it might be he held some wrathful struggle with himself, he turned to Ned, saying, with a smile that seemed to change his whole countenance and make him very handsome :

" Obedience, in this instance, seems to be the only course for us. So we shall follow my eccentric aunt."

She smiled in reply, and he continued as they walked :

" I have read Mrs. Mowbray's correspondence to my aunt concerning you, so that I know whence you come, but she did not say what relation you were to this Mr. Edgar of Barrytown."

" I am no relation," was the answer.

" That is a little singular, since you bear his name and he has taken such an interest in you; but fate sometimes provides for us strange coincidences "—he sighed faintly, as if he was oppressed by the memory of some gloomy coincidence in his own life—" and," he continued, " it is rather unusual for a young lady like you to give up voluntarily a home such as Mr. Edgar provided in order to eat the bread of strangers."

" But it will be earned bread," she could not refrain from answering.

" Why ? Have you found it so hard to eat bread that is bestowed ? " And then, as if he was anxious to leave the topic he himself had introduced, he did not wait for her answer, but continued :

" Your duties here will be light, but they will be most trying ; my aunt's whims sometimes change every hour, and I fear she will make you the puppet of them ; however, when her yoke presses too hard, you can return to your recent home."

They were now on the porch itself, and he was ready to pass her gracefully into the house, little dreaming how his last words had evoked within her a stern determination to submit to the most extravagant of Mrs. Doloran's whims rather than return to Weewald Place.   ·   -

XVIII.

Ned's duties, as Mrs. Doloran's companion, *were* exceedingly trying ; but there was so much amusement in the lady's various oddities that often our heroine's tears, on the point of secretly flowing, were checked by the remembrance of the laughable whim which had given rise to the awkward or unpleasant duty.

Mrs. Doloran's house, which she insisted upon calling Rahandabed, after the hero of some wild East Indian story told to her by the gentleman she had called Mascar, was constantly full of guests, among which, in spite of her frequently avowed contempt for the sex, it was fairly represented. The guests were mostly New York people, Mrs. Doloran's residence having been there until the death of her husband left her free to follow the caprices which were the bane of her unfortunate consort's life, and that made him hardly sorry when his demise came, since it was his only chance of release from so odd and exacting a companion. Their union had been childless, and that perhaps was an extenuating cause for her frequent sudden and amusing infatuation for chance acquaintances. Alan Carnew, an orphan at an early age, when not at college or travelling, made his home with the Dolorans, taking his aunt abroad on the death of her husband, and fondly hoping that on their return some change would be effected in her eccentric ways. He was doomed to disappointment: foreign scenes but imbued her with a deeper love for the grotesque in dress and the singular in forming friendships. She returned with her trunk full of the bright hues of nearly every foreign loom, and accompanied by a gentleman whose acquaintance she had insisted on making.

Her strange fancy was caught first by his odd and striking dress, as he stood in an outer room of one of the Italian palaces that Alan had brought her to see, and next by his conversation with a companion; it was in English, and was a spirited account of some exciting adventure in India. Had not Alan restrained her, she would have gone up to him and asked him to repeat his narrative; as it was, she gave her nephew no rest until he learned that the stranger was an unmarried English gentleman, who had resided for some years in India, which country he had left to return to England in order to receive a fortune bequeathed to him, and that he was now about to make a tour of the world for pleasure.

"Then we shall have no difficulty in inducing him to come to America with us," said the impetuous lady.

"Aunt Doloran, are you crazy?" replied her astonished and indignant nephew.

"No, my exemplary Alan, but very much in love with a project of my own which could never be complete without this delightful Indian gentleman. I intend, when I return, to transfer my residence from New York to some pretty spot along the Hudson, and summer and winter my friends shall have a carnival. This gentleman, with his exquisitely horrid stories of all that he has seen and heard in the Indian jungles will be just the thing. Maybe he'll consent to become my steward, or head man in some way."

Alan, horrified, could only gaze at her. But, as every woman does, she carried her way, and the Indian gentleman, though he was not asked to become her steward, did actually accompany herself and her nephew to America. The latter, in spite of all his protests and entreaties to his aunt to have some regard for propriety, was obliged to manage the introduction; and Mr. Mascar Ordotte (his very name being such an odd one was in his favor with Mrs. Doloran) was in no wise loth to attach himself to the train of a woman who, from the moment of his acquaintance with her, afforded him infinite amusement. He accepted very readily her invitation to accompany her to New York, and once there, required little persuasion to prolong his visit until they should be settled in their country home.

To Alan, this new acquaintance was most undesirable, even though occasionally there was a fascination about Ordotte's manner and conversation that he found hard to resist, but as his aunt was neither to be moved by entreaties, nor by threats to deprive her of his own companionship, and as he feared that his departure might give rein to some unpleasant gossip from those who were unacquainted with the guilelessness of her motives, and as he hoped for a termination of Ordotte's visit, he tolerated all, and treated the visitor with a rather cold, but marked politeness.

Nor did the grave, handsome, and scholarly nephew mingle as much as might be expected from his youth, being hardly twenty-six, with his aunt's guests; he joined their pastimes occasionally, but it was a well-known fact that he preferred his solitary rides across the country, and his books, to all their sports, and many a feminine heart grew sick with disappointment that no charm of beauty seemed potent enough to win the heart of this handsome heir of "Rahandabed."

Ned, of course, was thrown much with the company, being in constant attendance upon Mrs. Doloran; but she was so shy and reserved that she attracted little attention save when some absurd request made to her by the widow drew every eye upon her.

She was a month in her new home, and during that time she had heard once from Dyke, his letter being sent to her from Weewald Place. She had answered, informing him of the change she had made; but she had done it in such a manner that, unless of his own intuition, he could never divine the unhappy feelings which had prompted her. And she had also written to Miss Edgar, according to her promise, a brief, but friendly note, and received in reply from that young lady quite a gushing epistle, detailing how Mr. Edgar had decided to throw open his house to company that winter, and previous to doing so, intended to take his daughter for a brief visit to New York.

December's chilly blasts had set in, and the evenings found the gay company in the spacious winter parlor—to which blazing grate fires at opposite ends of the room, and crimson moiré curtains, imparted an air of delightful comfort—deep in the amusement of charades, or tableaux, or laughable puzzles that taxed alike mental and mirthful faculties. Mrs. Doloran was the queen of the assemblies, and with her grotesque and startling dress, to which her unusual height imparted greater oddity, she presented a most novel sight. Her jewels she wore upon all occasions, varying them only as to kind, and insisted upon adorning her hair with either lace or silken drapery. Her dress, ample enough in the skirt to have clothed two ordinary women, trailed far behind her, and was always of some hue of the rainbow.

Poor Ned was obliged to be constantly in the shadow of this great, ill-dressed woman, and she never knew what moment would call forth such requests as:

"Sing me a lullaby, Ned; I want to forget that I am a woman, and go back to my cradle days;" or, "tell me about that delightful story you were reading yesterday, where the namby-pamby heroine fell into a pond and was mistaken for a fish by the fishermen, and for a goose by her fool of a lover."

And Ned was obliged to obey, while her face burned with blushes, and her voice was painfully tremulous, for Mrs. Doloran's whims were as likely to want gratification in the presence of the whole assembled company as when she was alone with her young companion. One evening, the lady's fancy settled upon Ordotte, rather than upon Ned. Calling him from the group with whom he had been deciding on the manner in which some game should be played, she said in the loud tones she always used:

"Give the company that story, Mascar, that you said Ned's face here put you in mind of."

The allusion to Ned's face brought every eye upon the young girl, even the piercing look of Alan Carnew, who happened to make one of the party that evening, and she dropped her eyes beneath the battery of glances, and blushed until she thought she must suffocate under the sudden rush of blood.

Young Carnew pitied her; her modesty charmed him, while the quiet, uncomplaining way with which she attempted to do the absurd things so often required of her appealed to his heart, and frequently made him strongly inclined to interfere in her behalf; feeling, however, how futile would be his efforts in such a cause, and interested in watching the struggle that he saw it cost her to discharge such repugnant duties, he remained aloof, never seeming to take further notice of her than courtesy required.

Neither had Ordotte noticed her particularly since the morning on which he had showed such surprise at the mention of her name. Now, however, when he was thus loudly and impetuously appealed to, he left the group to which he had been talking, and, approaching Ned, said, with the air of one who was stirred to mention deeper things than might be prudent:

"Miss Edgar's face reminded me of a mystery—an Indian mystery—that is all."

"All?" vociferated Mrs. Doloran, "why, we want the mystery, the whole mystery; how delightful that it occurred in India. Who knows but that Ned here, with her Indian hair and eyes, will be the solving of it."

A strange look passed over Ordotte's face, a look at once sad and fierce, and catching it for the instant that her eyes lifted, Ned involuntarily shuddered.

"The mystery," answered Ordette, "has the same elements as other mysteries—a woman's face, a wayward life, and a burning wrong. Nothing more, I assure you."

He dropped his hands, and turned smiling to Mrs. Doloran.

She would have the details.

"Weave your elements into a narrative," she demanded, "don't leave us to imagine that Ned is really the woman of the mystery."

In her eagerness she had risen from her seat, and stood with one hand on the back of Ned's chair.

Ordotte shrugged his shoulders and laughed; one of the laughs that were so good an imitation of Mrs. Doloran's own as to set most of the company laughing, despite their extreme curiosity aroused by the gentleman's words.

"My mystery," he resumed, when his mirth had subsided, "must remain such even to me, the time has hardly come for its revelation; but if, by the singular fact of Miss Edgar's face reminding me of it, there can be won for that young lady the regard which her amiable qualities deserve, then shall my mystery have its just revelation."

To one person, and one person alone, did his words convey a double meaning, and that person was Alan Carnew.

Watching the tawny face of the speaker, he imagined that he had read in its expression, not alone what the words had conveyed to the company, that the amiable qualities of the young lady deserved different treatment from Mrs. Doloran, but also that Ordotte had a knowledge of something pertaining to Ned.

Mrs. Doloran, however, was too dull of comprehension to assume any part of the remarks to herself, and eager only to gratify her desire of hearing an account of the mystery, she persisted:

"This is frightful of you, Mascar, to plunge us all into such doubt. I insist that you tell us at least what you know."

At this moment a servant entered with some message, which he delivered in a low voice to Mr. Carnew, who immediately arose and crossed to Ned.

"There is a gentleman to see you; he is in a great hurry, and begs if it be possible that you will see him immediately."

Mrs. Doloran also heard the message delivered by Alan, and with her wonted impetuous drift of attention from one subject to another, immediately said:

"A gentleman to see you, Ned? I thought you had no followers, no lovers, no males of any kind in your wake."

Ned had arisen, and between embarrassment at the situation in which she found herself, and shame at the loud and coarse remarks of Mrs. Doloran, she presented a pitiable but most interesting picture. Carnew's manhood came to her rescue.

"Allow me to escort you from the parlor, Miss Edgar," he said, presenting at the same time his arm with an exquisite grace. She gladly took it, and under cover of his courtesy made her exit.

XIX.

The gentleman who wanted to see Ned was Dyke—Dyke, travel-worn and with a strangly haggard look in his honest countenance. Ned almost flew into his arms, but he avoided much of her embrace, without exactly seeming to do so. Since he loved her so passionately he must guard every avenue by which that love might escape and show itself unbidden to her unsuspecting eyes; so, did he suffer the warm caress which in her sisterly love for him she would have given, he must have snatched her to his breast and told how day and night she had been the star that guided him. And the time had not come for that, for he had not yet made his fortune, nor had she had the opportunity of giving her heart to a worthier lover.

He held her at arm's length on the pretence of noting the changes in her, and she laughed and cried in a breath with joy, and could hardly keep still in her desire to do something for him, and to ask him so many questions in the same moment.

"I did not expect to see you until summer," she said; "how did you get here, and at such a time of the night? But you must stay to night; Mr. Carnew told me that any friend of mine should be treated with the hospitality extended to the guests."

Dyke shook his head:

"I cannot Ned, for I must travel all night in order to catch up with Mr. Patten; I turned out of my way to see you, because I could not rest after your last letter—I could not understand why you had left Weewald Place."

"Was not I plain enough?" she said laughingly, and then she cunningly endeavored to throw him off the scent of her true motive in going away, but he was not to be turned from the clew he had shrewdly divined on reading her letter.

"You were very unhappy at Weewald Place," he said, looking at her with that peculiarly searching expression which as a child she could never withstand; and it had something of its old power over her now, for she dropped her eyes and blushed. "Tell me, Ned," he said, "tell me frankly."

But, after all what was there to tell? A coldness on the part of Mr. Edgar which she in her sensitiveness might have exaggerated, and an estrangement on the part of

Edna that she considered atoned for by that young lady's last outburst of affection.

Dyke, however, knowing so well Ned's loving, generous nature, comprehended as much from her meagre and hesitating statements as though he had really been a witness of Mr. Edgar's manner, and he treasured all up in his own heart.

"Now tell me about your life here," he said; and she told him, reserving only the humiliations which her duties sometimes entailed upon her; and the account sounded satisfactory enough, with her light tasks that, as she enumerated them, hardly seemed to deserve the name, and the company with which she said the house was filled, and the pastimes that occupied many hours of each day. Dyke said he was glad she had so much variety, and he strove to make himself believe that he *was* glad that she was so happily situated, even though she might be already on a course which would bear her far from him.

The last moment of the time he had allotted for his stay arrived, and no persuasions of Ned could induce him to prolong it, even though she repeatedly urged Mr. Carnew's invitation.

"Who is this Mr. Carnew," he said at last smilingly, "that you lay such stress upon *his* invitation?"

"Oh, I didn't think to tell you; he is Mrs. Doloran's nephew, and in some sense master of the house."

At this instant there was a knock at the door, and a message from the servant to say that refreshments awaited the stranger, and a room was at his disposal, all by Mr. Carnew's order.

"There, did I not tell you?" laughed Ned, delighted that Dyke should have such attention; but the young fellow would not wait, and half ready to cry that Mr. Alan's kindness should be so slighted, she accompanied him to one of the side doors that led to the grounds. There he had to wait a moment while she brought a servant with a lantern, and in doing so she encountered Mr. Carnew.

"Alick, the man, tells me that your friend refuses to accept our hospitality; do you think it needs my personal invitation?"

He spoke so kindly that it banished her embarrassment at meeting him, and she answered:

"I think not; he is in a great hurry."

"Nevertheless, I shall take it upon myself to try," he said, and so he accompanied her back to Dyke.

She performed the introduction, and Mr. Carnew acknowledged it as gracefully and graciously as if the great, country-looking fellow was his equal in the social scale, while Dyke could hardly refrain from staring so intently at the handsome man before him as to lay himself open to the charge of rudeness. Carnew was so eminently handsome, with that clear, penetrating honest look in his eyes which never failed to win Dyke's admiration.

But he could not be persuaded to stay, and Alan, with a kindly expressed regret and adieu, turned away and left the two together.

"When shall I see you again?" asked Ned, clinging to the great, hard brown hand, that was of itself loth to withdraw.

"Not until summer, I fear; there is so much to be done in the way of travel yet, that I shall not have an hour for myself until then."

She had already asked him all about his invention, and while he had answered truthfully, he had still managed to conceal from her that his prospects were hardly as bright as they had been. Now, whether for the moment that he was off his guard, or that his gloomy anxiety had overmastered him, there was a despondency in his tones that startled her.

She looked up, the lamplight from the hall on the verge of which they were standing, showing fully her anxious countenance, and bringing him back instantly to his wonted guard. He forestalled the question that he felt she was about to ask, by saying, with his accustomed cheerfulness :

"You must ascribe my heavy-hearted speaking, just then, Ned, to my fatigue, having journeyed a long distance to-day, and to my anxiety to meet Patten. In June next, Meg will be home, and then I shall come for you to spend your summer with us, like you used to do when you were *little* Ned."

He stooped suddenly and kissed her and was gone, following the flash of the lantern which at that moment appeared round the angle of the house.

She went back to Mrs. Doloran, and found herself an object of most undesirable attention on the part of that lady, who would know all about Ned's "follower," as she termed Ned's visitor; but here again Alan Carnew came to her rescue, and so diverted his aunt's questions by amusing interruptions of his own, that the attention of the company was withdrawn from Ned, and after a little, amused herself by the wit of her nephew, Mrs. Doloran forgot the blushing, embarrassed object of her searching and pointed observations.

XX.

Mr. Edgar was preparing for his trip to New York with his daughter, when a servant announced that Dykard Dutton wished to see him.

The gentleman's brow clouded slightly ; he imagined that he knew the object of Dyke's visit; it had reference to his niece, and he was not a little annoyed that he was perhaps about to be reproached for what his own conscience more than once had twinged him—suffering Ned to leave his house so unprotected—and while the scowl deepened upon his brow, he ordered the young man to be admitted to his presence.

Dyke's manliness was never abashed, no matter into what haughty presence he might be ushered, or amid what splendid surroundings he might find himself, nor what might be the nature of his errand. His singular honesty of purpose raised him above the awkwardness and embarrassment of coarse and conceited minds, and gave to his bearing a grave simplicity which won and retained involuntary respect. And Mr. Edgar felt this when Dyke was ushered into his presence, perhaps more than he had done on any previous occasion, for his brow cleared, and he accorded to Dyke the gracious salutation he might have given to an equal.

The honest fellow stated his errand at once. Had Mr. Edgar renounced all interest in his niece?

"She has withdrawn herself from my interest," was the quiet reply.

Dyke grew hot. "Would you suffer the merest friend, especially if that friend was a young girl who had accepted the hospitality of your house, to leave it in such a friendless condition; would not your *manhood* have prompted you to accompany her to her destination, and ascertain for yourself that her new home was her proper place? Would not your sense of common charity have impelled you to impress upon any unprotected orphan thrown into your charge, that you were her friend, and not one of whom she was to be afraid, and by whom she was to be repelled? The orphan you have suffered to go forth in such a manner has a tie upon you which you will not be able always to conceal and repudiate, and it may be a part of the justice of Heaven to show you one day that you have made a bitter mistake."

Edgar himself was now stirred to wrath; words like these burned into his soul, and his eyes flashed with the foreboding look of a temper which once loosed knows little bounds.

"You are insolent, young man; I shall brook no such language."

"Hear me out," said Dyke with a firmness which Mr. Edgar felt impelled to obey.

"Since *you* were satisfied to let her go, why not have written to me of her desire; I, at least, would attend her, as I have attended her before, and ascertain the suitableness of the life she had decided to accept. Instead, you sent me no word, and I only learned from her letter that she had gone forth to earn her living. Better you had surrendered all claim to her long ago, and permitted Meg and me to educate her for a simple, useful station. Now she is a lady, and yet she is compelled to be a hireling."

"Cease your insults," thundered Edgar, so maddened by reproaches, the truth of which he could not deny, that he was unable to hear more.

But Dyke was undaunted. Drawing himself to his full height, and looking unflinchingly into the flashing eyes before him, he resumed:

"I have come to-day to get your final answer: Will you resign forever all claim of, and interest in Ned?" The name came so readily to his lips he would not change it for another.

"And if I do, what then?" replied Edgar.

"Then I shall not be so hopeless of her hand one day; unprovided for by you, she will be somewhat nearer to my own station in life, and when I have won the competency that will insure for her a happy home, and if her hand be not given to a worthier suitor, I shall lay my heart at her feet. Did your interest continue to provide for her, my hope could never be realized; the difference in our social scale would close my lips."

In spite of Mr. Edgar's indignation at what he considered the unabashed impertinence of this young man, he could not but secretly admire him, and also secretly pity him; remembering the incident of the flower sent by Dick Mackay, and Ned's own, as he considered it, want of candor, he felt that her affections, if not already bestowed upon Dick, would in all probability be given to some one like him, handsome but worthless, in preference to the honest country fellow before him. He wondered to himself if it would not be truer kindness to tell this trusting man all that he had observed so unfavorably in his niece; but when he attempted to do so he failed—he had not sufficient heart to crush Dyke's hopes, and he said instead :

"I renounce from this moment all interest in my brother's daughter. You are at perfect liberty to do for her whatever your regard may prompt. When I meet her I shall salute her with the courtesy of an acquaintance; further than that she is and she shall be nothing to me."

He bowed and turned away, and Dyke went out with a strange sense of oppression and gloom.

XXI.

The cloud that had suddenly overcast Dyke's prospects regarding his invention, instead of brightening, became darker, until it burst upon him one morning in the reception of a letter from a person that he did not know, and which, owing to his own frequent change of abode, was some time after date in reaching him.

The letter told him that Mr. Patten, whom he had so trusted and depended upon, had but used that trust and dependence for his own gain and the aggrandizement of an influential company to whom he had imparted all the secrets of Dyke's invention; that a patent had been obtained in their name for what Dyke's long years of patient thought and work had achieved, and that Dyke's very efforts, which he had been so painfully and determinedly making during the past four months, had actually gone to help the success of the company.

"I write you all this," the letter went on to say, "because I know this scoundrel Patten and hate him thoroughly, and I have also heard something of *your* hard-working, honest life. It has been proposed even to dupe you still further by keeping you in ignorance of Patten's treachery, and have you continue to canvass the country. All this I overheard yesterday; for your sake I am sorry that the revelation came to me so late. I do not know that you can gain any redress, as might and money are hard to be overcome, and this company has enough of both to save themselves and to protect even this wretch Patten."

That was all, save the utterly strange signature, and Dyke read it over and over like one trying to make out a foreign language. Recently, he had himself doubted Patten, the man's actions and statements being strange and unsatisfactory ; but his doubts, wanting proof, had taken no tangible form, and he had sought to dismiss them.

Now they all came before him and gave vivid color to this written accusation ; still, he would not believe it ; the consequences to him, should it be true, were too dreadful. He put the letter into his pocket and ordered a conveyance. By hard driving, he could reach the station, whence he knew Patten was to board the train for New York. It was only the night before he had received a message from him to that effect, and there was nothing in its plausible tenor to indicate an iota of the treachery he had already perpetrated.

His horse was in a foam of perspiration, though it was a sharp bracing winter day, and Dyke himself was little better from his hot thoughts as he drove into sight of the rude depot, where a few straggling passengers awaited the coming of the down train. Springing from his wagon, and throwing his rein to a lounger, he bounded on the platform of the depot, for already the whistle of the approaching train sounded, and the few passengers were stirring themselves in preparation. Among them was a little, nervous, wiry man ; he threw uneasy glances on all sides of him, and fairly started when, flushed and perspiration-covered Dyke strode up to him.

"You can't go aboard this train, Mr. Patten," said the young man, "nor aboard any train until you settle accounts with me."

"But I must, Mr. Dutton," pretending not to see in this summary check anything more than an ordinary detention of business. "Our interests demand my presence as soon as possible in New York."

"*Your* interests may," said Dyke, with a fine, sarcastic emphasis. but *my* interests demand your presence here."

The train puffed into sight, and Mr. Patten stooped for his valise beside him ; but Dyke grasped his shoulder.

"Patten," said he, "you are dealing with a desperate man, and if it goes to the length of brute force, by God I shall use it."

It was the first time an oath had ever passed Dyke's lips, but the sense of his bitter wrongs had transformed him.

And Patten cowered beneath the angry eyes above him, and trembled under the strong grasp upon his shoulder, and made no further effort to board the train, seeing which, Dyke said, with a quietness that was so stern it was almost as terrible as his anger :

"Come with me."

They entered a house which made pretensions of being a hotel, and, amid the bustle occasioned by the departure of the train, they were comparatively unnoticed. Both knew the place, for both had sojourned there, and no one questioned or opposed when Dyke led the way to a private apartment in the rear of the bar. There, closing the door, and standing with his back against it, he took from his pocket the accusing letter, and extended it to his companion.

"Read, Patten," he said, and give me one word for answer, yes or no."

Patten, in mortal fear, knowing his puny strength beside this great athletic fellow, read as he was requested to do ; then he was silent, overwhelmed that his treachery had been so speedily and so accurately discovered.

"Speak," commanded Dyke, reading in the man's very silence a confirmation of his worst fears.

Patten recovered himself ; it was necessary to tell some story to be saved from the summary vengeance which threatened in Dyke's eyes, and he said, trying to assume a confidence and courage he was far from feeling.

"This is not the first time, Mr. Dutton, a man has been vilified by a malicious enemy. The patent this company has obtained, though for an invention similar to your own, will not entrench upon yours when you get it."

"When I get it," repeated Dyke sarcastically. "And," he continued, "how is it you have never said a word about any invention similar to mine being in the market? Was it because you were in the interest of this company from the first, and that you had made your plan to deceive me?"

"No, no, Mr. Dutton; believe me, I made no plan to deceive you. I——"

But Dyke cut him short.

"I want no quibbling, Patten; I want the truth, and I shall have it if I have to force it out of you."

He strode to the now trembling wretch.

"For God's sake, Mr. Dutton, you would do no violence; remember that I am unarmed, and much smaller and weaker than you are."

"Yes," muttered Dyke, "unarmed, but armed with the wrong and ruin you have brought upon me. Answer me, Patten; have you sold the interest you pledged to me, to this company? Are you *their* hireling?"

He caught Patten by the throat as he spoke, and his eyes had the glare of frenzy.

"Spare me," whined the cowering man, now in mortal fear for his life. "Spare me, Mr. Dutton, and I will tell you all."

Dyke relaxed his grip, and listened with what quietness he could assume to the account of a duplicity which not alone had stolen from him the work of a score of years, but cruelly impoverished him and destroyed by one fell blow every bright hope of his future. He had assisted the broken and hesitating statement by questions that the deceiver, through fear, was forced to answer, and he knew now the full extent to which he had been duped; and as he looked at the whining, cowering wretch before him, and realized the bitter blight wrought by his treachery, it seemed as if a demon rose within him, and impelled him to crush this author of his ruin. Twice he clinched his hands and lifted them as if about to strike, but each time that restraint which he had all his life exercised over himself came to his aid, and he suffered his hands to drop.

"Go," he said at length, when he had mastered his passion sufficiently to speak; "go and complete your infernal treachery. I spare you only because you are too contemptible to suffer at my hands."

He opened the door, and Patten, glad of the opportunity to escape, darted forth.

Dyke paced the room to quiet himself and to think; but all his thoughts resolved themselves into the same stern facts—the loss of the combined savings of Meg and himself, the ruin of all his future prospects, and the hopelessness of any redress. Still, something must be done, if nothing more, something to keep Meg from knowing the extent of the blow, and with no very clear thought as to what he should do after he reached New York, further than to consult a lawyer, he went out to ascertain the time of the next train down.

In New York, the lawyer to whom Dyke applied was one of the first in his profession, and he became singularly interested in the young man's deplorable story; but it was a hopeless case, and he said so frankly. Not all his skill could avail to take it into court, and if it could, nothing but Dyke's simple word of mouth was to be adduced as evidence against Patten; Dyke had not even a voucher of any kind for the secrets regarding his invention which he had imparted; nor a paper to show that Patten was pledged to his interests. It was simply a case of cruelly misplaced confidence, and, as such, there was no help for the poor ruined victim.

The young man did not answer when the lawyer delivered his opinion; he sat looking straight at the finely cut intelligent face before him, with an expression that, inured as the lawyer was to harrowing looks on the faces of his clients, moved him to the soul. It corroborated so painfully all of the sad facts he had heard. That Dyke's was no common nature he well judged, and prompted by his sympathy, and by the fancy which he had taken to the young man, he said:

"Since your circumstances have suffered such a reverse by this wretched business, will you accept a position in a large business house here? The remuneration may be somewhat small at first, but it will increase with the development of your business qualities."

Dyke hailed the proposition. It would give him work for mind and body, and provide for him that subsistence for which he scarcely knew where to turn now; it might also, after months of close economy, restore to his aunt a portion of the savings he had so miserably lost. He could possibly let the little farm among the mountains, induce Meg to make a longer stay with her relatives, and not yet undeceive her with regard to his expected success. So he accepted the offer, and in a week, having completed his few arrangements, he was installed as one of the junior clerks in a large wholesale commission house, and his letters to Meg and Ned, without being in the least untruthful, were so carefully worded that neither dreamed of the bitter and blighting change which had come over his prospects.

XXII.

The winter and spring passed, and Ned—who in every trying hour, and sometimes she had many of them, comforted herself by thinking of the summer when she should go home, as she fondly regarded the little mountain farm—had begun to count the days that must elapse until June arrived, the time she had set for her departure. Her remuneration was, as Mrs. Mowbray had said it would be, quite liberal, and even more than that, for Mrs. Doloran had frequent impulses of generosity, in which she made the young girl handsome presents. Ned happened to suit her whimsical disposition, and even to win by her gentle, reserved demeanor a little of her affection, though these facts did not restrain any of her absurd requirements. And Ned had been as saving as the veriest miser; not a cent went for any purpose save the one, that of hoarding in order to be able to pour into Meg's lap all of her little earnings. Not that she thought Meg needed it, but it would be an outlet for that affectionate gratitude which impelled her to make some return for all the love and care that had been bestowed upon herself.

Dyke wrote as infrequently as ever, and his carefully worded letters gave her no intimation of what he was doing. She supposed that his long sojourn in New York was in the interest of his invention, and that when she saw him in the summer time, he would give her all the particulars he omitted to write now.

So, as the summer came on apace, and Rahandabed assumed all its summer glory, inviting the guests, of which the house was wellnigh full, to constant out-door pastimes, Ned seemed to grow as gay-hearted as any of them. Her eyes frequently sparkled with pleasure, for she was constantly thinking of her summer visit. How she pictured every object in the surroundings of her mountain home: the mountains themselves, the lofty objects of her childish fear and wonder; the wood, to the trees of which she had given in her childhood a human individuality; the little farm, with its patches of late ripening vegetables, its rude barn, and its two stupid, patient cows; the house itself with its few low, roughly ceilinged rooms, and lastly, warm-hearted, loving Meg and Dyke. She saw them all, and thinking of them so much by day, she dreamed frequently of them by night. In her last letter to Dyke, a letter written in the early part of May, she wrote very joyfully of her expected visit, reminding him that there were scarcely four weeks until the arrival of the time appointed for him to come for her. It had been part of Dyke's plan to obtain a vacation of a few weeks, during which he would take both Ned and Meg home, and enjoy with them a brief season of repose and happiness, continuing, however, to conceal from them his misfortune. But, on the very day that Ned's letter came, he was informed of his promotion to a department of the business which would require his closest personal supervision; the increase in his salary was not large, but the promotion itself was a compliment to the young man's business tact and integrity; and his friend, the lawyer, whose interest in the young fellow continued, strongly counselled him not to refuse. It seemed to be much the better course despite the disappointment it would entail upon Ned and himself, and after a night's deliberation he accepted it.

Then he decided to write frankly to Ned; he could not keep her in ignorance longer without telling untruths, and Dyke's whole soul shrank from such a course.

So he broke his news to her very gently, very tenderly, but very honestly, without, however, letting her know the poverty of his financial circumstances, and he concluded with:

"The blow was very hard at first, Ned, but, thank God, I am recovering and able to hope that good will come out of even all this wrong; if a man keeps his heart right, it makes little difference after all what befalls him, for life is so short, and God is overhead to protect and support us.

"I am so sorry for your disappointment and for my own, for, like you, I had been counting the days which must pass until we were once more together in our little home; but my own brave sister" (what control he was obliged to exercise, not to pen a warmer term), "you will bear this as you have borne other things, and perhaps in the course of another year our wish may be gratified."

"Jake" (by Jake was meant the hired man who had helped Dyke in the care of the farm) "has married, and he and his wife are living in our little home, and will take care of it for us.

"My heart fails me to tell Aunt Meg what I have told you, and she is so easily satisfied so long as she thinks I am doing well, that I fancy it will be the better course to say simply that I am needed in New York, and cannot spare the time to see her for some months. She is quite happy in Albany, being the recipient of an affection from her nephews there, as fond and lavish as she herself bestows; indeed, they have more than once written to me that they, having as natural a claim upon her as I have, would like to keep her with them always."

With a tender, brotherly remembrance, the letter ended.

Ned, full of delight and expectation, had flown to her own room to read it; now she felt as if her heart would burst with agony. So rudely shattered all her summer hopes; but it was not that thought which gave her the keenest pain; it was the thought of Dyke's bitter blow. She remembered so well what he had said to her that morning nearly a year ago in Weewald Place, that if he failed, how poor he and Meg would be; he *had* failed, and consequently he must now be poor; poor, and perhaps even struggling in his poverty to remunerate for Meg's support, despite all that he said about the affection of her other nephews. She flew to her trunk and brought forth her hoarded savings; they amounted to a little over two hundred dollars. How delighted she was to have such a sum, even though she did not know whether it would be of much assistance to Dyke. But he should have it immediately, and she gathered up the shining pieces and put them into her purse. Then she wondered how she would get them to him; she was ignorant of the forms of sending money, and could only think of giving it in charge of some of the servants who occasionally went to the city. But she shrank from that plan, not being certain of the honesty of the person to whom she might intrust it, and feeling some repugnance to acquainting a servant with her business.

She also shrank from asking Mrs. Dolaran, fearing that lady would in turn ask her all sorts of unpleasant questions. At last she thought of Mr. Carnew; he would know and direct her, and though she hesitated a little to approach him, because of the gravity and reserve which always marked his manners, she felt assured he would treat her graciously, and not being a woman, he would be unlikely to concern himself more than was necessary with her business.

So, to Mr. Carnew she applied, finding him in the library, and astonishing him not a little by her errand, which she stated in a very straightforward and modest manner.

"I can give you a check payable to the order of your friend," he replied, "and you can inclose it in a letter."

"Thank you; that will do," and she pulled out her little purse.

He drew up the check on a city bank, payable to Dykard Dutton, thinking within himself as he wrote that Dutton—whom he remembered the instant he heard the name, as the country-looking fellow to whom Ned had introduced him—was Ned's lover, and that he was worthless and unmanly enough to take this poor girl's earnings, for Ned had told him nothing of the circumstances that might render sufficiently laudable Dyke's acceptance of her gift. And he pitied Ned, and at the same time had a sort of contempt for her; contempt that she had so little character as to love this worthless fellow; but he suffered none of his feelings to appear, and he handed her the check with charming courtesy.

"Thank you," she said again in her simple, modest manner, raising her clear, frank eyes for a moment to his, and taking her way gracefully out.

He watched her, admiring her in spite of himself, and feeling for an instant something like a secret pang that she had a lover. But the next moment he laughed at his odd fancy, and turning to his books again, forgot her for the time.

XXIII.

Ned's affectionate letter, with the check inclosed, safely reached Dyke, and when he saw that evidence of her loving generosity, and read the tender little message which came straight from her heart, he was well nigh unmanned. Again and again he pressed the written characters that had something of their old childish cramp still, to his lips before putting them away with the bulky parcel of her other letters.

Then he replied, returning the check, with the assurance that his salary was sufficient for all present wants, and that he had been touched to the heart by her loving thoughtfulness.

Ned was sorely disappointed; she felt so certain that Dyke needed it, if not for himself, for Meg, and with the letter and check in her hand, she was trying to think how she could get the money to Meg; to send it by check to that good simple soul would it make it necessary for some of the Albany nephews to know about it, and Ned wanted her gift to be secret. She could think of but one plan: to go to Albany herself; it was only to step on the train, and to be whirled in a few hours to her destination; surely, nothing extraordinary nor venturesome in that, save the fact that she would travel alone; but she had travelled alone from Barrytown, and now she was even more of a woman than at that time. She knew Meg's address, Dyke having incidentally mentioned it in one of his letters, and she felt that her native intelligence would guide her safely. Then, how delighted Meg would be to see her! Her own spirits rose at the thought, and she went with fleet steps to return to Mr. Carnew his check, and to get back her money.

"So your friend refused to take your gift," he said, slightly smiling, but thinking that her lover was a better man than he had deemed him to be, and again he was conscious of a moment's secret pang that she had a lover; but, as before, he was only grave and courteous.

Her chief anxiety was acquainting Mrs. Doloran with her intended absence of a week, and her heart sank a little as she imagined that lady refusing to let her go; but Ned determined to make her journey at all hazards, and, should her determination cost her her present position, she was sanguine enough of another, even though it might be only that of nursery governess.

Mrs. Doloran, however, was exceptionally reasonable, and even kind, on hearing Ned's request. They were alone when the girl told her, the latter being careful to choose the time, and the widow, in her impulse of generosity, said Ned might take a month, and insisted on presenting her then and there with a sum of money which was more than sufficient to defray all the current expenses of her absence. And Ned went to bed that night thankful and happy.

But the next morning, when the whole company was assembled on the lawn after breakfast, and Mrs. Doloran attacked by a sudden indisposition which, not sufficient to confine her to her room, was yet enough to make her unusually whimsical and fretful, began to revert to her promise of a month's absence made to Ned the night before, she regretted extremely having given any such pledge. Who would take Ned's place while the latter was gone; who would be the shy, sensitive, obliging, and uncomplaining butt that this poor, tried lady's companion had been during all those months? No; she could not have it, and impelled both by her peevishness, and by the hope of badgering Ned out of her intended journey, she said suddenly, when there was a momentary lull in the noisy conversation:

" You did not tell me last night, Ned, that there was any real necessity for this journey of yours to Albany. What is it that is taking you there? "

Everybody in the company looked up, and looked directly at poor Ned; even Alan Carnew sat with a book before him; he was the more interested, as this was the first intimation he had of Ned's intended journey, and not knowing whether she meant to take her final leave of Rahandabed, he waited anxiously for further development.

She was sitting slightly in the rear of Mrs. Doloran, whose ample person partly shaded her, and she answered only loud enough to be heard by that lady:

"I am going to visit an old and very dear friend."

Captious Mrs. Doloran was not at all satisfied with the reply.

"Going to visit an old and dear friend," she repeated, in her loud unfeminine voice, "that is all very well to say; it sounds very sweet, and very true, too: *he* is an old and dear friend—a very *dear friend,* no doubt. I dare say he is the same that called on you here, a little while after you came; now be frank, Ned, and tell us all about it; you are going to be married, are you not, and you are going to do it in a very sly, quiet manner, coming back to us as if nothing at all had happened; or, perhaps, you are already married——"

Would nothing stop this woman's tongue? Ned was bursting with indignation; surely no remuneration could pay for such insults as these; but Mrs. Doloran was mounted on one of her favorite hobbies, and she was going to ride it until she was tired.

"I do not doubt in the least but that you *are* married; you are so quiet, and so shy, and so just like what a married woman would be, and——"

But Ned could endure no more; her whole fiery temper was aflame. She rose from her seat forgetful of everything but that she was the butt of most heartless insults.

Her large, lustrous eyes sparkling with anger, her cheeks of the richest crimson, and the firm indignant poise of her graceful form as she stood excited universal, though secret, admiration. Alan Carnew's eyes were piercing her through, as she said:

"It may belong to wealth to insult the poor, Mrs.

Doloran, but it is a base womanhood which insults the defenseless of her sex."

Her voice trembled painfully while she spoke, but the firm poise of her person had not once yielded, and when she had finished she walked away with the mien of a queen.

"By Jove!" said Mascar Ordotte, seated on the other side of Mrs. Doloran, "I never felt so much like applauding anybody in my life; that girl has the right kind of spirit."

A remark which Alan Carnew echoed in his secret heart.

Mrs. Doloran, with her wonted sudden change of temper, had gone instantaneously from her peevish and wanton attack upon Ned, to fear and dismay lest Ned should leave her altogether.

"Go after her, Mascar," she pleaded, "tell her I am sorry for all that I said, that she can have two months to visit her friends in Albany; and here, take her these as peace offerings——"

Hurriedly divesting herself of a diamond ring, her necklace of brilliants, a lace handkerchief, whose purchase price must have been at the very least a couple of hundred dollars, and she would have poured into Ordotte's hands more of her personal adornments but that he stopped her, saying, laughingly:

"No doubt the young lady will come to terms without requiring so many gifts."

He was nothing loth to go upon the errand, for he had his own secret reason for wishing Ned not to take her final departure from Rahandabed. Did she do so, it might entail upon him some trouble to keep constantly informed of her whereabouts.

Ned's temper, according to its old fashion, was quickly succeeded by penitence, and calling to mind the many favors she had received from Mrs. Doloran, and remembering also that the lady, owing to her whimsical mind, was hardly responsible for what she said, and that she, on accepting the position, had been warned of the trying nature of its duties, she was full of censure for herself. So Ordotte came upon her crying heartily, and looking almost as lovely in her tears as she had done in her temper.

He delivered his errand in a very pleasant, kindly way, and she was touched anew by these proofs of Mrs. Doloran's generosity.

" Take them back," she said, "and tell her that it is I who crave forgiveness for having forgotten my place so far as to make that hasty, angry speech.   Tell her I am very, very sorry."

And the pretty mouth quivered again, and the eyes filled once more, and Ordotte hurried back with his message, in order to be out of sight of so much beauty in such touching distress.

In the exuberance of her delight, Mrs. Doloran would go herself to Ned, and in a little while, during which the company were on the pinnacle of amused expectation, she returned, with one of her ample arms about Ned's waist, and her face expressive of the utmost satisfaction.

So, Ned's journey to Albany was amicably settled and the next day, promising to return in a week, but being assured she might remain two months, she was driven to the station by Donald Macgilivray.

XXIV.

The Albany relatives of Meg Standish consisted of a single and a married nephew—children of her only deceased brother—who lived and worked together They were carpenters and in sufficiently comfortable circumstances to enable them to keep their own shop adjoining their own very cosey little dwelling, so that Ned, when arrived at her journey's end, tired, dusty, and hungry, having been too timid to seek refreshment anywhere, found herself ascending the stoop of a very neat and substantial-looking house.   It was evening and too dark to distinguish well the face of the woman who admitted her, but the voice that responded to her inquiry for Meg was cordial and pleasant.

"Yes, Miss, she lives here; come in and I'll tell her."

Ned went into a little room opening from the hall, and in which a lighted lamp emitted rays enough to show the neat and tasteful appearance of the apartment; in a few minutes she recognized Meg's well-known step.

The fond old creature could hardly credit the evidence of her eyes; was it really Ned in the flesh that stood before her, and not some cruel deception of her own imagination? But Ned's voice calling to her, and Ned's arms open to enclasp her, assured her; she embraced her darling, while tears of joy streamed down her wrinkled cheeks.

What an evening that was! Meg was so proud and happy to show the young lady to her relatives, to mark their admiration of her beauty, and their wonder and pleasure at her unaffected manners. She won them all, from the brawny, cordial nephews themselves and the good-hearted wife, to the little toddling, two-year-old child, who took to nestling on the young lady's lap, with the same confidence that she showed to her mother and Meg.

And to Ned, the affectionate hospitality of these people was delightful; it was so honest, so simple, so different from the regard shown to her in Rahandabed. Her own loving nature expanded under it, and she ate and drank of the simple but inviting repast prepared for her, and laughed and talked with perfect abandon.

Meg's relatives knew Ned's whole story, both from Meg's own frequent recitals, and from Dyke's letters, which, owing to his aunt's inability to read writing, they were obliged to read for her; and it was no slight subject of indignant wonder to them that Mr. Edgar should persist in concealing his relationship from his niece, as she was, if indeed she was not his daughter; but as it was his desire to do so, and Meg would not displease him, her relatives were equally careful to drop no word that might reveal her identity to their young visitor.

The next day, when Meg and she were alone, the men being at work, and the good woman of the house engaged in extra culinary operations for the benefit of her young guest, the latter took out her purse and poured its contents into Meg's lap.

"All for you, Meg," she said, her eyes sparkling with delight; they have been so good to me in Rahandabed that I have been enabled to save it."

But Meg could not speak; she was so touched by this proof of affectionate gratitude that a lump rose in her throat, and a film came over her eyes; she could only throw her arms around Ned's neck and kiss her. And when she recovered herself, she put the money back into the little purse, and said through her tears:

"It's a proud and happy day for me to have you remember me so, but I can na take it, my darling; I have na need of it, being well provided for by the boys here, God bless them. They seem glad enough to have me with them, and were well pleased when Dyke's last letter came, saying that he couldn't go back to the mountain home yet, and that I'd have to stay here another while."

All Ned's persuasions could not induce her to accept the gift. She constantly replied:

"I have na need of it."

Then Ned begged Meg to keep the money in trust for her, but even at that the old woman demurred; at length to satisfy the young girl, who seemed so pained by all these refusals, she consented to keep half of it in that manner.

"Keep the other half yourself," she said, "for there's nae telling now that we're off from each other, Dyke and you and me, and you among strangers, what may chance that you'd need a bit of your savings."

And Ned was obliged to yield.

The good people provided for their young visitor such entertainment as was afforded by drives to places of

interest in and about the city, and they were extremely
sorry that her stay must be so limited; but she had said
she would not remain longer than a week, and she felt it
to be her duty to keep her word, even though she had
Mrs. Doloran's permission to stay two months.

Fate decreed, however, that Ned should be unable to
fulfil her promise, for, before the close of the week, she
was confined to her bed with some sort of a fever. The
physician, who was hurriedly summoned, could not tell at
first whether it was the contagious illness raging in
another part of the city, but for safety's sake he advised
the family to send their patient to the hospital. They
were indignant at the proposition, and he, seeing that, and
being touched by their unselfish regard for one who, by
some chance, he learned was no relative, induced them to
appropriate a part of the house for her especial use, and
to be content to have one person alone in attendance upon
her. Of course that person was Meg, and never was
patient nursed more tenderly, nor even skilfully; for the
old woman in her youthful days had acquired a quantity
of valuable knowledge regarding the sick, added to which
she had strong common sense, and affection now made her
quick and certain in the use of both.

One of her nephews suggested sending word to Dyke,
lest the young lady should die, and he, thinking so much
of her, would hardly forgive them for such neglect, but
Meg shook her head, replying:

"There'r na need of it; we'll bring her through with
the help of the Lord, and what 'd be the use of worrying
that poor fellow, and bringing him from his business all
the way up here. Na, na; her disease is a slow one, but
she'll come round all right in a few weeks."

The disease was a slow one, consuming five weeks before the poor, weary, wasted patient could even sit up in
the bed.

Then one of her first questions was, had any word been
sent to Mrs. Doloran.

"Na, dear; we didn't know rightly the directions to

send to, and you were too sick to tell us; but what's the differ? When you're well enough to go back, if she wants you she'll take you and welcome, and if she don't there's plenty of other places for the like of you; so don't be troubling yourself, but take your rest."

And truth to tell, Ned was glad to follow the advice; she was so weak and tired that it was an exertion for her even to think of Rahandabed.

How kind everybody was to her in the little household, and not one would hear of remuneration in any form; she used to lie awake sometimes in the night, wondering whether God gave all the heart and feeling to the people in humble circumstances; her experience of the rich had been so different from all this tender treatment. Eight weeks from the day of her arrival in Albany, she was ready to leave the historic city; she would have gone a week before, but every voice was raised in protest, and she felt obliged to yield to their combined and earnest entreaties.

She had not written to Rahandabed, being content to trust to what Meg had said about other places being obtainable; and so long as Mrs. Doloran had given her two months, it might be as well to explain matters in person as by letter.

She looked pale and emaciated, and her strength seemed very fragile, but she insisted that she was stronger than she appeared to be, and she allayed their fears by promising to write immediately, and in case Mrs. Doloran decided not to re-engage her, to return to them without delay.

Meg and one of her nephews accompanied her to the train, where the young man purchased her ticket and saw that she was comfortably seated. She looked so ill, owing to her pallor and emaciation, that, as she raised her veil to bid him good-by, many a pitying eye was directed to her, and he himself felt like purchasing another ticket and accompanying her all the way, but, when he intimated his desire, she protested so energetically that he was obliged to forego it.

And so she was whirled away with Meg's fond face looking up to her from the side of the track, where the old woman would insist upon standing, so as to get a last view of her darling.

Could Ned have foreseen the circumstances under which she would next meet that fond old countenance, she would rather have journeyed to the most distant part of the earth, than go to Rahandabed.

XXV.

Not expecting to find at the C—— station any of the Rahandabed carriages, Ned was about to engage one of the public conveyances in waiting, when some one behind her said, with a strong Scotch accent:

"Eh! Miss Edgar. This way." It was Donald Macgilivray, with his Scotch face all aglow from delighted surprise.

"They'll be glad eneuch at the house to see you," he continued, "for Mrs. Doloran's gang daft wi' thinking you never meant to come back, and Mr. Ordotte's gang up to Albany looking for you; but he had noo directions to find you. So I was thinking it 'd be nae easy wark for him to get you. He's thought to be coming back on this train, and that's why I'm here to fetch him, but to my mind it'll be as good if I fetch you."

All this time he was leading the way to a handsome open carriage, and as Ned took her seat, feeling considerably relieved that she would not be sent away from Rahandabed, the man seemed struck with her changed appearance. She had thrown her veil back, so that her white, wasted face was fully seen.

"You've noo been sick?" he said, with an honest concern in his tones.

She replied with a brief affirmative, as she leaned back with a sense of delightful rest among the cushions.

Donald attended to his horses, waited another moment to be sure that Ordotte had not arrived and was not loitering somewhere, and then drove off, turning speedily into the shaded fragrant roadway which led to Rahandabed. But he could not keep from communicating scraps of news to the young lady. Every few minutes he turned to tell her something of the doings at the house during her absence, and at length he imparted that which immediately aroused her indifferent attention.

"There's anither young lassie at the house wi' a name like your ain, an' a face the same as if you war twa beans on ane stalk. The company war all talking about it. She came wi' friends of Mrs. Doloran, an' they say she's verra weel to do in the matter o' the siller. Her father lives in Barrytown, but he's in England now."

Ned was surprised; that it was Edna she did not doubt, but it seemed so strange that *she* should come to Rahandabed. She was not displeased, however, for since their last parting she entertained only kindly feelings for her cousin, and she was also gratified to find that she would not be compelled to meet Mr. Edgar; with all her generosity, she could not divest herself of a certain fear and dislike of that gentleman.

Donald, instead of driving all the way up the main carriage-road, turned into another that led to a side entrance of the house.

"I war thinking you'd nae want to meet wi' Mrs. Doloran and the rest o' them, till you'd have a bite and a bit o' rest. They'd be fashin' ye wi' questions, an' ye noo weel able to answer them. So I drove ye here, instead of the front, that ye wouldn't meet wi' any of them. Ye can bide aweel in one of the rooms; an' I'll get some of the lassies to bring you a bite."

Ned was grateful for this thoughtful kindness. She felt so weak, and tired, and ill able to meet Mrs. Doloran just yet, and with a "thank you," the sincerity of which went to honest Donald's heart, she accepted his offer.

Macgilivray had hardly exaggerated when he said

Mrs. Doloran had gone "daft" over Ned's protracted absence. Her captiousness, which had delighted in making poor Ned its victim, having now no especial butt, vented itself sometimes in most disagreeable freaks, often causing her to break into disgraceful fits of temper, during which any servant who had occasion to go to her presence, and who was luckless enough to manifest any awkwardness in the discharge of duty, was likely to have the most convenient object hurled at his or her head. Immediately after, however, the delinquent was sure to be presented with some valuable gift as a token of forgiveness; so the domestics scarcely objected to this vulgar mode of chastisement, since they knew that it meant in every instance an accession to their purse. The guests, however, were a little tired of ebullitions of temper, which were as likely to occur in the middle of a most enjoyable repast as at any other time, and though Mrs. Doloran's wealth and lavish hospitality covered all her sins, still, with a selfish desire for their own comfort, they devoutly wished for Ned's return, that the eccentric widow might go back to the old tenor of her ways.

So, when Ned quietly walked into the summer parlor, where Mrs. Doloran, in most peevish mood, sat with some of her guests, there was a general brightening of countenances and a chorus of glad exclamations. The widow, in her delight, rose so suddenly as to throw down her chair, and to throw it with such force that it fell against a tall, slight, heavy-faced young man who had been standing just behind her; the blow sent him to display his full length on the tapestried floor. Mrs. Doloran, however, did not pause to look behind her, nor was she deterred by the burst of "oh's" and "dear me's" which followed the young gentleman's ludicrous fall, accompanied by audible attempts, in the shape of sudden coughs, to suppress laughter.

She took her wonted strides to Ned, and having folded that young lady in a very undesirable embrace, brought her forward to the company, most of the members of which by this time had gained a semblance of composure, even to the fallen young man, who had picked himself up and retreated blushingly to a curtained embrasure.

Ned looked like the ghost of her former self, and now that Mrs. Doloran had time to notice that fact, she began at once:

"Have you been to the spirit land, Ned, or have those friends of yours done what Ordotte tells us they do in Ireland, sometimes—kept yourself and sent us your wraith?"

"I have been quite ill," was the gentle response.

But Mrs. Doloran was full of another subject, about which she was more anxious to inquire than to ask the particulars of Ned's illness, and with her wonted sudden transition to a different topic, she resumed:

"We have a young lady here of your name, Edna Edgar, and with the strangest resemblance to you, only that you are not as brilliant nor dashing. She told us how you were schoolmates, and that it was by accident you came to have the same name and such a marked resemblance, for you were no relation. Now *you* tell us all about it, Ned."

"I can only tell you what you have already heard," was the reply, the speaker thinking at the same time how fortunate had been Donald's thoughtfulness in her regard, for Mrs. Doloran evidently did not dream of asking her "companion" if she needed refreshment or rest; possibly she thought it unnecessary, as it was almost time for the late dinner.

Disappointed in Ned's answer, she said, with some asperity:

"It is very improbable, such a statement as that; nature doesn't give such striking resemblances to people without a cause. Has it never struck you that you might be related to these Edgars in some way? How did they get to know you in the first place? Here, sit down, and tell us all about it," struck, perhaps, by the increasing pallor of Ned's countenance. The girl was glad to sink into a chair, and she answered as gently as she could, feeling, however, a little of her old indignation at such impertinent probing into her family history.

"Mr. Edgar knew my parents in England, being perhaps drawn the more to them because of the similarity of the name; when they died, he was prompted, both by his pity for my orphan condition and by the singular resemblance I bore to his own child, then also an infant, to take the interest in me which afterwards culminated in his sending me to school with his own daughter, and giving me a home previous to my coming here. Such are the facts, Mrs. Doloran, told to me by those whose veracity I know too well to doubt." The last words were spoken with a decision intended to silence Mrs. Doloran on any further questioning; but, if the self-willed widow could not pursue her inquiries, she could at least give vent to her thoughts on the subject.

"It's a remarkable case of coincidences," she continued, "and the most wonderful thing about it is the way you two girls just accept what has been told you. That Miss Edgar, who came while you were away, doesn't see anything strange in the coincidences any more than you do."

"Why should she?" broke in Ned with some impatience, "it is not the first case of curious resemblance between people who are no relation—even history records such things."

"Ugh!" said Mrs. Doloran, shrugging her shoulders with an affection of disgust, "you are too practical; if you had a bit of romance in your soul you would make a clear case out of this. But I wish Miss Edgar would come; I want to compare her with you—not that the resemblance will be such a marked one, now you're so white, and sick-looking—and I wish Mascar was here, not that he's much good in this case, for he professes to believe implicitly just what you and Miss Edgar say about yourselves. There she is now—" happening to glance in the direction of the open window, just beyond which appeared

Miss Edgar, on horseback, attended by Mr. Carnew, also mounted.

The whole company rushed to the veranda to see the dismounting, and Mrs. Doloran, pulling Ned along with her, followed in their wake.

How beautiful Edna looked; how magnificently she sat her horse, and with what charming grace she just touched the palm of Alan's hand, extended for her dainty foot, as she dismounted. He must have whispered some compliment, for her face and neck were dyed for an instant, and the confident way in which she took his arm to ascend to the veranda gave evidence that his attention pleased her.

Ned, as she saw it all, experienced a sudden and most unaccountable pang, whether of jealousy or envy of her cousin, or sudden love for handsome Alan Carnew, she could not tell, but she was most distressed that it should be so, and she was very angry with herself for her weakness.

Up the steps came Edna, looking like some beautiful picture—as, with one hand, she held her whip and the train of her riding habit—and so full of bewitching animation, that it was little wonder Alan Carnew bent to her in the tender way he did. She caught sight of Ned's pale face over Mrs. Doloran's shoulder, and dropping Carnew's arm, she rushed to her with the prettiest grace imaginable.

"I am—" the sweetest of kisses on one cheek—"so glad,"—another sweet kiss on the other cheek—"to see you,"—a third sweet kiss on Ned's mouth—"you naughty dear; never to tell me in your last letter that you were going away for a while, and I took the trouble to write to you that I was coming here on a visit, which letter, of course, owing to your absence, you did not get. And when I got here, no one could tell me further of your journey, than it was to see some one in some part of Albany. O you darling! I have so much to tell you."

All of which gushing effusion looked very pretty, and very condescending to the company, for they remembered that Ned was only a hireling after all, beholden to Mr. Edgar's bounty for her education, and as a consequence of these things, to be regarded in the social scale very much below the heiress, Miss Edgar.

Upon Ned herself, this lavish outburst, although it was a little too lavish to accord with her shy, sensitive nature, had the effect of opening her heart all the more to Edna. That Edna was sincere she did not for a moment doubt, and Ned's generous soul always warmly responded to affection.

They looked very pretty together, being the same height and having the same graceful pliant figures, had Ned's form not lost its wonted curves by her recent illness. Mrs. Doloran was observing them very critically even to the secret amusement of the company, applying her eye-glasses which she wore on a chain, but never before had been known to use.

"When Ned gets back her color and her flesh," she said, looking over her glasses instead of through them, "there will not be much difference between them. I wish Mascar was here, to tell me what he would think now."

Alan Carnew, having waited until the first gush of Miss Edna's salutation was over, advanced to give his own greeting to Ned.

"Have you been ill?" he asked, struck as everybody else had been by her appearance, and putting into his tones so deep a concern, and into his magnificent eyes, as he looked down into her own, such an earnest solicitude, that she was thrilled through and through. Tones and look were in her dreams all that night.

Just as the summons to dinner sounded, Ordotte drove up to the house in one of the public conveyances, Macgilivray having taken it upon himself to imagine that, as Ordotte did not arrive from Albany when expected, it was most improbable that he should come from any other place, at least on that day, to give him (Donald) the trouble of harnessing up and taking the carriage again to the station. And Mrs. Doloran, who sometimes happened to see just what would be most desirable to pass without her observation, saw Ordotte driving up in the public and inelegant vehicle. Not even her delight at seeing him could make her impervious to the fact that he had arrived in such a manner, when her orders had been for Macgilivray to meet every train up or down, Ordotte having written that he might go to New York from Albany, but that in any case he would return that afternoon or the next. Nor could the gentleman's own assurance, that it made not the least difference, pacify her. She would rebuke the offender without delay; and while Ordotte went to his room to dress for dinner, she dispatched a summons to Macgilivray to come at once to the dining-room.

"You're in for it, Donald," said the servant who brought the message; "I heard her talking to Mr. Ordotte about your not taking the carriage for him."

Donald gave a dry laugh.

"Weel, weel! I was a match for me leddy before, when she wanted the coffee carried behind her, leek a gale in the wake of a ship—" putting forth a most inappropriate simile—"an' maybe I'll noo be found wantin' this time."

And quite unabashed he took his way to the resplendent dining-room. The company were all seated, and the waiters were serving the first course when Donald entered. As the entrance to this summer dining-room—so situated that the windows on two sides of it looked out on a spacious veranda—was broadly open, he did not think it necessary to use any preliminary courtesy before entering, but took up immediately a position near the door, facing Mrs. Doloran who sat in state at the head of the table.

"Your favor, me leddy, and what would you leek to say to Donald?"

Mrs. Doloran suspended her gastronomic operations, and so did everybody else, for the appearance of the Scotchman in his stable dress, and the odor of the stable from his clothes, was exceedingly disagreeable to sensitive eyes and nostrils. Handkerchiefs were taken out quickly and applied. Alan Carnew flushed hotly, and looked disgusted enough to leave the table, but Miss Edgar, who sat next to him, with admirable tact sought to draw his attention from the threatened scene.

The lady of the house, however, was no respecter of persons, and since Donald was in her employment, it was her right to rebuke him when and where she would, regardless of the visionary or olfactory organs of her guests.

"You disobeyed my orders," she said in her most severe tones, and shaking at Donald with every word the head dress of gay-colored feathers that surmounted some lace drapery of equally gay colored hue. "I told you to meet with the carriage to-day the train from Albany and the train from New York, in order to drive Mr. Ordotte to Rahandabed."

"Right, me leddy; them war the orders you gev Donald. Always wi' your leddyship's favor, ye said I war to meet the Albany train. I done so, an' fetched up Miss Edgar; an' wi' your leddyship's favor still, I war iver so weel minded to bide by your leddyship's instructions as to take out the beasties agen, but it war noo in me power."

With every word, Donald had advanced to Mrs. Doloran, the stable odor from his clothes causing a closer application of the scented handkerchiefs by those he passed, and—as the shrewd Scotchman intended it should do—now pouring full into Mrs. Doloran s face.

But the lady could endure that—she scorned even to apply *her* handkerchief, and she looked with a little contempt about the table on those who were making such conspicuous use of their gossamers.

"What do you mean?" she said, very severely still, and with a toss of her head that set her feathers into a ludicrous quiver.

"Why, you see, me leddy, old Mollie got a sudden

colic, and her mate, brown Jim, war threatened wi' the spavin, an——"

"There were other horses on the place," interrupted Mrs. Doloran, angrily. "Rahandabed does not depend on the two you mention."

"Right, me leddy," answered the Scotchman, with the stolid earnestness of one before a court of justice, "that war so, but the other likely team war out wi' Mr. Breakbelly." The name was Brekbellew, but from the first, Donald had humorously twisted it into Breakbelly, and as the owner of the luckless name was present at the table, and was the same whom Mrs. Doloran's chair had prostrated that afternoon, handkerchiefs had to be taken from noses and crammed into mouths to prevent a most impolite explosion of mirth. Even the unfortunate gentleman had a sort of ghastly smile upon his lips.

Mrs. Doloran could endure strongly unpleasant odors, but it was one of her whimsical hobbies to tolerate no language that bordered on the vulgar. She rose from her chair, and while her feathers kept time in most tragic vibration to every indignant word, she waived Donald away, and said:

"Go, vulgar man; go back to your own proper place."

"Ay," said Donald, turning right about, "an' why did ye summon me from me ain proper place?"

And he walked as soberly out as if he was not keenly conscious that he had given to the company, when they should be out of sight and hearing of Mrs. Doloran, an occasion for as hearty a laugh as ever had emanated from any (especially the masculine portion) of her guests.

XXVI.

Ordotte met Miss Ned Edgar—in search of whom to Albany, being sent by Mrs. Doloran, he had been nothing loth to go—with an expression of ludicrously affected surprise. He even assumed a ridiculous attitude, and said, with an imitation of absurd rant :

"My dear young lady! where *have* you been? I scoured nearly all the haunts of civilization in Albany without obtaining news of you, and as a last and desperate resource I thought of securing the services of a balloon that I might hover over chimney tops in order to spy you by some quiet hearthstone. But, as it was summer, my aërial flight would have been in vain—you would hardly have been found by a hearthstone."

At which nonsensical speech Ned laughed, as did everybody else, but she did not feel called upon to tell the precise locality of her sojourn in Albany, and so she was silent.

Ordotte resumed :

"Having failed so ignominiously to find you, I could not return immediately to Rahandabed. I visited New York first, to restore my courage."

From the manner in which he lowered his voice, there might seem to be some strange significance in his words, but if there was, it passed unnoticed.

Life now at Rahandabed was exceedingly pleasant, even for Ned, Mrs. Doloran's exactions being rendered lighter by Edna's good-natured response to them, as if she would save the "companion," and by Carnew's frequent kindly interference, to spare Ned the mortifications which had marked her earlier stay in the house.

Whatever might be Edna's motive in being thus amiable, she carried that quality to such a degree that Ned's warmest affection was won for her, and she hailed the private *tête à-têtes* which the two occasionally had, with an intense delight. Miss Edgar, with remarkable shrewdness, was careful to say nothing in those seeming confidences that could wound Ned's nice sense of truthfulness, nor shock any of her rigid ideas of propriety. The communications were very innocent, detailing only such facts as that, when her papa took her and Mrs. Stafford to New York the previous winter, she made so many pleasant acquaintances, and enjoyed the city life so much, that he, to please her, deferred his plan of opening the Barrytown house to company, and permitted her to remain in the metropolis, of course remaining with her and escorting her everywhere.

"Then," the sweet, confiding tones continued, "I induced papa to let me have Annie Mackay for my maid. You remember Annie, Ned; she was Dick's only sister, that handsome Dick whom papa could not bear, and who has gone away to be a painter or a writer or to embrace some of the lazy professions, as papa calls them ; well, she came to me, and she was so gentle and so sweet that I quite loved her.

" Then papa got news from England—sudden news— about a brother of his that he had thought dead; it excited him very much.   He decided to start in the next steamer for England, and wanted me to accompany him. Think of it ; such a fatiguing voyage on so short a notice— it was out of the question.   So he went without me. Immediately after, I received an invitation to visit some of my newly made friends who lived on Staten Island, and as Mrs. Stafford, whom papa insisted on retaining with us everywhere, was somewhat indisposed, I induced her to remain with her maid in the hotel, while I went to visit for a few weeks my Staten Island friends.   Annie Mackay, my maid, accompanied me ; that was in the beginning of last June, and she became so ill that I was obliged to limit my stay to a month.   We rejoined Mrs. Stafford, and she, kind soul, was so concerned about the poor girl that at my suggestion she accompanied her home, and permitted me to accept the invitation of some friends to Rahandabed.   So I only arrived here a few days before your own return from Albany.   Papa has written that he will be home in a couple of months. Mrs. Doloran made me write in reply that he must come here, as she will not suffer me to leave her for some time, and I confess, Ned, that I enjoy it here very much."

Ned fancied that she knew why Edna enjoyed it very

much; Alan Carnew's rather marked attentions to her
were no doubt the source of the enjoyment, and her own
heart suffered again one of its little pangs that made her
almost despise herself.

Of such tenor were Miss Edgar's artless communications, and as Ned listened to her, and looked at the bewitching play of features that were well-nigh perfect in
their beauty, she did not wonder that Carnew seemed to
be caught in the toils. Then Edna was evidently no flirt,
for, though every gentleman in the house looked and
acted as if he would have given his dearest possession for
a smile from her lips, or a favor from her hand, and poor
Brekbellew was like a faithful cur in his attentions, she
treated all with the same eminently proper lady-like
courtesy, but nothing more. On occasions even when
remarks were made intended to evoke laughter at Brekbellew's ludicrous devotedness, she, instead of taking part
in the mirth, dropped in her graceful way some very
pretty pitying expression that won, as she felt it would
do, Alan Carnew's approving and admiring look.

With that tact and shrewdness that had showed themselves in her very earliest years, she had read Carnew's
character, and all her amiability to Ned, and all her
avoidance of flirtation, and all her reluctance to make
sport of poor, sheepish, but wealthy Brekbellew, arose
from the fact that she knew such a course of acting would
please Alan Carnew. With her overweening, though
well-concealed vanity, she yearned to have at her feet this
handsome scholarly gentleman, even though a secret tie
that she dared not acknowledge, and could not repudiate,
must prevent upon her part any reciprocation of his
tender feelings.

There was one person in the house from whom she unaccountably shrank—Mascar Ordotte. Whether it was that
his shrivelled, tawny face, rendered so by his long sojourn
under a fierce Indian sun, repelled her, or the way that he
had of looking through her with his little keen black eyes,
as if he doubted every word she said, or was inwardly

sneering at her gracious manner, made her feel very uncomfortable, certain it was that she avoided him whenever she could.

And our poor Ned! how was she disciplining this unbidden and unwished for regard on her part for Alan Carnew? A regard now so strong that she thrilled at the sound of his voice and flushed beneath the glance of his eye; but she was certain that he loved Edna, and knowing that, it became her duty to restrain herself by all the stern measures in her power. So she resolved to avoid meeting his eyes, and when he spoke, and was not addressing her, to fix her attention determinedly upon something else; a resolution that was not so difficult regarding her looking at him, but which *was* extremely difficult in the part that referred to his speech. His voice so deep and firm, and so harmoniously changing its tones to suit his topics, thrilled her through and through, and, as it were, despite every effort chained her attention to it.

After a little, Carnew observed how Ned's eyes steadily refused to meet his own; and amused and interested, as well as wondering what could be the cause, he as steadily endeavored to make them turn upon him. But they flashed over him, below him, beside him, everywhere save directly at him, and while Edna's eyes at every opportunity were looking into his with most bewitching earnestness, Ned's were either cast modestly down or fixed at some point beyond him. He became *piqued* at last, not understanding sufficient of the feminine heart to know that this extraordinary manner was really a delicate compliment to his power, and he refrained from noticing her save when it became absolutely necessary.

Ned felt the change most keenly, but she had too much womanhood to yield to her feelings. She went bravely about her duties, thinking that Alan would marry Edna as soon as Mr. Edgar returned, and then her attachment, which cost her so much pain now, having its object removed—for certainly Mr. Carnew and his bride would not continue to live at Rahandabed—would speedily die.

Such was the future pictured by our heroine for Alan Carnew, while he at the same time held a struggle with himself to maintain toward her the cold demeanor he had assumed. Her very reserve but increased his regard, and he found himself frequently wondering whether that Mr. Dutton was really her lover; and yet every time he so wondered he called himself a fool for thinking in the least about anything pertaining to her.

November had come again, and Rahandabed, with its color-changing and falling leaves, its great trees swaying with half-bare branches in the sighing winds, and its few last and fast-fading blossoms had a melancholy beauty particularly pleasing to Ned. She delighted in taking long, solitary walks, whenever Mrs. Doloran chose to spare her, sometimes extending her excursions to romantic spots beyond Rahandabed. One of these was an old, deserted, and half-ruined mill, beneath which a clear stream still wended its way, and within which some lover of the picturesque had placed a rustic seat. A bridge, partly new from recent repairs, led to the mill from one side, though to a climber the mill was easily accessible from the opposite side. The country boys sometimes climbed from that side in through the old, ruined windows, and played their games on the mouldy floor. The rustic seat in the mill was a favorite haunt of Ned's, the whole place was so deserted every time she had gone there that she felt quite sure of the seclusion she desired; then its romantic and half-weird surroundings charmed her, and, added to the pleasant sound of the water going gently over the dam, afforded her keen delight.

On this November afternoon, she took her way to the spot, regretting the lateness of the hour, for darkness set in so speedily on these short autumn days. However, she would have a few minutes to spend in her favorite haunt, and she hurried on, drawing a gratified breath when at length she was esconced in her nook, looking out from the old mill-walls at the weird scene before her, and listening to the monotonous plashing of the miniature waterfall.

Her thoughts went back to her childhood and to her talks to the trees, and though the darkness began to creep apace, she still lingered, lost in her retrospection. Suddenly she heard the sound of indistinct voices from the side of the mill accessible only to climbers, and she started up in some affright. But there was no other sound, only those indistinct tones floating up, as if the speakers stood directly under one of the ruined windows.

Impelled by that curiosity which is sometimes experienced by the least curious of us, Ned, instead of immediately departing, as she had arisen to do, waited. One of the voices was suddenly raised, and it was pitched in such a key that every word was borne to Ned.

"No love is deep that will not make every sacrifice; have I not given you proofs enough in all the risks I have run? What would you have? An open acknowledgment? It would be my ruin, and the moment that you oblige me to make such, I, rather than endure the anger and obloquy that must follow, shall die by my own hand."

To Ned's horror she recognized Edna's voice, and, without waiting to hear further, she rushed from the mill, intending to confront her cousin and let her know what she had heard, and how she had heard it. She did not stop to question the identity of the party, whether male or female, to whom Edna was addressing such strange and shocking words; she only felt that the speech must be due to some imprudence, and that it was her duty to tell that she had heard it. But the noise of her footsteps on the floor of the mill and across the bridge which she was obliged to pass in order to get round to the other side, where were the strange parties, alarmed the latter, and they took to flight, for which they had ample time, Ned requiring two or three minutes to cross the bridge and go up the road far enough to effect a passage to the other side of the mill. When she arrived on the spot, it was deserted, and as it was quite dark, with not even a glimmer from a star, it was fruitless to seek to discover what direction the mysterious parties had taken. But Ned called her cousin's name aloud, thinking she must be hiding somewhere near, and that she would be assured by the sound of her voice. There was no response; and growing a little timid herself in the now almost perfectly black solitude, she hurriedly retraced her steps, and pursued her way to Rahandabed. What was her astonishment to see in one of the brilliantly lighted parlors that she passed, Miss Edgar, sitting calm and composed, with not the slightest evidence of having been so recently out of the house; her hair was not even ruffled, as the wind had ruffled Ned's, and she was talking to Brekbellew, who hung over her chair, with that sweet graciousness that was no more than she bestowed upon every one, but that kept him, poor sheep that he was, in a constant fever of love.

Ned could not understand it; in the first place, unless by extraordinary rapidity, Edna would scarcely have had time to return to the house, and then the quickness of her return must surely preclude such absolute composure as she had witnessed. Could it be that she was mistaken; that the voice she would have sworn was Edna's, was only made such by her imagination? She knew not what to think, and lost in a maze of doubt, she watched her cousin all the evening; but Edna was the same beautiful, brilliant girl, with not the slightest evidence about her of any secret imprudence.

And she seemed to be especially courted that night, as if her charms had grown more attractive, even Carnew leading her again and again to the piano, where her magnificent voice rang out with exquisite force and sweetness.

Mrs. Doloraïn said, in one of the pauses between the music:

"That creature seems to have all the gifts under the sun. It is no wonder the men are half-mad about her. I declare she has turned *my* head; and there's Alan, who's been holding his heart against every sortie for the last six

years, ready now to yield everything to her. The lad 's
gone, as anybody can see by looking at him."

Ned forgot herself and looked at him, and judging by
the expression of his face as he bent to Edna to whisper
the name of the song he wanted next, Mrs. Doloran was
quite right.

That eccentric lady continued:

"Matters can be settled very speedily as Mr. Edgar has
written to say that he is coming home much sooner than
he expected to do; that we may expect him about three
weeks from to-day; his letter came this afternoon, and
Edna wanted to show it to you, Ned," turning to her
companion, "but you were out on one of your walks."

Here was another incident to confound her conviction
that it was Edna's voice she had heard near the mill;
surely, if her cousin were in the house looking for her in
order to show her father's letter, she could not be at the
same time in the spot where Ned was so sure she had
heard her speak.

XXVII.

Mrs. Doloran was seized with a whim to give Mr. Edgar
a gorgeous reception on his arrival, and though his
daughter, whose cultivated taste shrank from the vulgar
display that passed for elegance and brilliancy with the
eccentric lady, remonstrated with her, and assured her
that her father was a man of very quiet, simple tastes,
Mrs. Doloran would have her way. As Mr. Edgar had
named the very day of his expected arrival in New York,
and had said that he would proceed immediately to Rahandabed, it was not difficult to calculate almost the
precise hour of his coming. Thus preparations were
begun that turned the spacious winter drawing-room into
a sort of *outré* apartment from the quantity and quality
and striking color of the velvet hangings with which the

walls were dressed, to the total exclusion of the costly pictures that had previously adorned them. Whence she derived her odd and execrable taste no one could conceive, and while everybody laughed secretly, no one save Alan and Edna were bold enough to remonstrate, or to condemn. But she was not to be restrained by either remonstrance or condemnation, and every day found her superintending something more and more grotesque. Her absurdity reached its height when she ordered a handsome dais at the extreme end of the drawing-room.

"What for?" asked Alan in angry amazement.

"To receive my guest, sir," was the haughtily given answer.

"Do you propose to put him and yourself on exhibition, then?" spoken with an angry scorn that awed for a second even his indomitable aunt; but it was only for a second: her will was too strong to be put down by anything short of death, or perhaps poverty.

"I propose to do just as I like, sir, with my guest, and with everything else that is mine. Is not that the proper womanly spirit, Mr. Brekbellew?" turning to that poor, timid gentleman who, whenever he could not be by Edna's side, was the constant attendant of Mrs. Doloran.

And Brekbellew answered with becoming meekness:

"Yes, ma'am: an eminently proper spirit;" at which Carnew, too angry to speak further, turned on his heel and left the pair.

Of course, Ordlotte was constantly appealed to, as the preparations progressed, and actuated by the exceeding amusement the whole affair afforded him, he frequently gave such a suggestion as turned into newer and stranger extravagance Mrs. Doloran's own preconceived whim.

The eccentric lady was quite in her element; her days rose upon work in which she delighted, and which was an effectual bar to those fitful moods of temper that made her a burden to herself, and an annoyance to those about her. Even the servants basked in her good humor, not being in their wonted constant fear of a sudden and violent contact with the article most convenient to Mrs. Doloran's hand, and Macgilivray said in his dry way :

"It's the fine speerit me leddy's in just now ; but bide aweel, and see how the auld hornie 'll make her her ain self again."

Ordotte was bidden to have ready his most exciting Indian stories, the lady saying :

"I have no doubt a gentleman of Mr. Edgar's wide travels and cultivated tastes will enjoy the terrible and the mysterious in nature, as you depict it, Mascar, in your dreadful tales."

"I have no doubt of his enjoyment of *my* Indian stories," Mascar repeated, with an emphasis on the word my, and a singular intonation of the other words, all of which, however, owing to Mrs. Doloran's preoccupation with her own excited thoughts, were lost upon her.

The preparations extended even to arrangements for illuminating the grounds, and as the season was exceptionally fine, Mrs. Doloran's anticipations were very bright.

Carnew could hardly restrain his anger and disgust.

"Your father," he said to Edna the afternoon before the expected arrival, when they were taking a stroll together through the grounds, " will think we are all fools here."

"No," she said in her most bewitching way, " my father will understand the case almost immediately, and while he may be much amused with your good aunt, he will draw the line between her and those who in sheer kindness pander to her whims ; all that he does not understand I shall make clear to him."

"Thank you," he said, his face slightly flushing.

Her heart was beating with painful rapidity ; what was this concern that he expressed about her father's opinion but a sign of his regard for herself, and, if so, might she not hope that one day this regard would be all that hers was now for him ? Nay ; might she not even now be assured that his affections were her own ? True, no word had been spoken, but all the little signs by which a susceptible woman judges of the regard she may have inspired, were time and again betrayed. And how in her heart she cursed and loathed the secret folly that must prevent her acceptance of his hand should he offer it.

In the midst of her burning thoughts she glanced at him, but he was not looking at her; indeed, he seemed to be in some far distant reflection. Secretly piqued, she put her hand on his arm.

"Do you know that, glad as I shall be to see my father, I am also a little sorry at his coming."

"Why?" spoken without looking at her.

"Because he will be anxious to return to Weewald Place, and I shall have to accompany him."

Carnew looked at her then; a look which frightened her a little by its intense piercing earnestness, and she hastened to add:

"This place with its endless varieties and its gay company is in such contrast to my lonely life at home. Do you wonder that I dislike to leave it?"

She had such a wonderfully child-like, confiding way of putting the question, and she raised such trusting, innocent eyes to his, that he was won, as he had been many a time before, by the spell of her beauty and her artless manner. She saw her advantage, and she pursued it.

"And I have learned so many life-long lessons here."

"What are they?"—he was suddenly interested.

"One, that true goodness of character triumphs over every ill. I have reference now to your aunt's companion, and my dearest friend, Ned Edgar. Knowing, as I am aware you do, that she could have had a home always with us, have you never wondered that she should leave it to become a sort of servant?"

"Yes, at first I did wonder a little, but I am not wont to concern myself about other people's business."

"Her leaving it was a surprise to me, the more so that she never by a word hinted at the cause; and it was only when my father himself asked me if I knew anything about her secret acquaintance with the son of a gardener on our place, a Dick Mackay, and expressed his disapprobation of her conduct, that I began to think his manner to her might have driven her from us. As she was so reticent, I have never had courage to mention the matter to her, but, studying her as I have done since I have been here, and being brought into daily contact with her unselfish goodness, I believe that which my father said of her to be false. Some one must have misled him, and I only fear that his manner to her when he meets her here will be as cold as it was during the last days of her stay in Weewald Place."

She sighed most feelingly, and looked down at the pretty white hand resting upon his arm.

"Tell me another of the lessons you have learned," he said, too much charmed with his companion just then to speculate upon what she had so unnecessarily told of her cousin.

"The other lesson," she spoke with some hesitation, as if not certain of the propriety of her communication, "is that a woman's heart undisciplined is the scourge of many."

"You have reference to my aunt," he said dryly, "but give me your third lesson, if you have learned so many."

"The third," putting both her hands upon his arm, "is that he who judges, but reserves his opinion, who loves, but yields not to his attachment, is wiser in his generation than the fools who make honest speech of all they know, and gushing revelation of all they feel."

She had spoken wildly and more frankly than she had intended to do, impelled by a certain recklessness arising from the fact that her own ardent wish could never be fulfilled.

And Carnew blushed as hotly as any girl might have done. Had she penetrated his secret attachment to Ned? That attachment to which he struggled so hard not to yield and which, having heard what he did about the gardener's son, even though the story were not true, must now speedily die. Such was the thought that animated him, and made his voice a little tremulous as he asked:

"Who taught you the last lesson?"

The answer came in a whisper:

"You."

No more was said until they reached the lawn where the whole gay company was assembled to watch the completion of the preparations for illumination. They stood, also, ostensibly to watch, but there was on the part of each a desire to compose hot and unpleasant thoughts. Ned stood near them, pleasantly interested, and Carnew, when he could do so unobserved, studied her face. It attracted him despite himself, though he linked with it the unfavorable story which Edna had told him, and he thought that Ned's own marked reserve toward him since her return from Albany might be even an evidence of the truth of that story; if her troth was plighted to this gardener's son, she might deem it her duty to be thus excessively modest, and was such the case, her modesty was certainly to be commended. But strange thoughts flashed through his mind: what if her visit to Albany during all those weeks had anything to do with this Mackay? And did Dykard Dutton, whom Carnew had long since regarded as Ned's suitor, know all about it, and was he hurt by it? But at this stage of his uncontrolled thoughts, the young man became suddenly ashamed of himself, and he turned resolutely away to give all his attention to some arrangement of colored lights that Mrs. Doloran was insisting was quite wrong. A little commotion in the vicinity of Ned drew his attention to her again; the commotion was made by a man in a laborer's dress approaching her with a note which he said was for Miss Ned Edgar. She took it in dumb surprise, but in an instant her keenest fears were aroused for Dyke; possibly it was some bad tidings from him, and she asked tremblingly, as she looked at the superscription.

"Miss Ned Edgar," written in an entirely strange hand :

"Who gave you this ?"

"A gentleman out on the road; and there's to be no answer," was the reply; and the man, with the best bow he knew how to make, took a hurried departure.

It was well that Mrs. Doloran was too much engaged to notice her "companion," or she probably would have insisted on knowing the contents of the note; as it was, everybody in Ned's vicinity was watching the young girl, and though she did not look at any of them, by a peculiar intuition she felt their critical observation, and she blushed hotly as she opened the note, and in perfect amazement read:

"Within an hour the last and greatest sacrifice I can make shall be completed. Can any love demand more ?"

That was all; neither date nor signature, and the penmanship was so utterly unfamiliar. She looked up, and in her bewilderment directly across at Carnew and his companion, Edna. Carnew was watching her so intently that his eyes to her heated imagination seemed to be flaming through her, and Edna, slightly leaning forward in her eagerness to watch her cousin, was pale as death.

In an instant Ned's brain was whirling with excited thought; the words that she had heard at the mill, "No love is deep that will not make every sacrifice," and which she was so sure had been uttered by Edna's voice, came back to her and startled her with their similarity to the expressions in the note. Then Edna's present appearance, her unusual pallor, the evident anxiety with which she watched her cousin, all told that she had some, and perhaps imprudent, secret; but again, the superscription made her hesitate. "Miss Ned Edgar—" surely it was meant for her, for never by any possible chance was her cousin addressed as Ned. To end her suspense, she would go immediately to Edna, give her the note, and ask for an interview. But, at that instant everybody's attention was attracted by the sudden and rapid advent of a carriage into the grounds, and the sudden scream of:

"My father!" from Edna, who had recognized its solitary occupant, as for an instant he put forth his head from the carriage window.

Immediate excitement ensued, rendered ridiculous in no small measure by Mrs. Doloran's indignant outburst of:

"The man's come too soon; here are the lights not half completed, the dais in the parlor isn't finished, nor the velvet drapery, nor the antlers hung in his room, and I don't believe Mascar has his stories ready, and I am not in costume, and—why didn't he wait?"

Appealing to everybody about her, but looking longest at her nephew, who was secretly delighted at this early arrival; it would probably spare him much mortification.

Edna, with an apparent forgetfulness of self which seemed very charming, had broken from the company and dashed after the carriage, in order to meet her father when he alighted, on seeing which Mrs. Doloran commissioned Alan to do the honors of receiving the guest, until evening, when she would present herself in state.

."And we can have the illumination to-night," she said, taking Ordotte's arm, and going on a tour of survey.

The company scattered; some to accompany Alan to the house, others to take their accustomed strolls through the grounds, and Ned, in uncertainty as to what she had better do, stood twirling the note between her fingers. Carnew said as he passed her:

"Come with us to the house, Miss Edgar; my aunt will not need you for some time, and I am sure you are anxious to meet your old friend, Mr. Edgar."

There was the faintest touch of sarcasm in the last words, but faint as it was, Ned caught it, and wondering why he had used it, she forgot her usual prudence and looked him full in the face. He returned her look carelessly and passed on. She followed, and was in time to see Edna hanging on her father's arm, with all the delight of an eager and happy-hearted child. There was no pallor no anxiety about her now. She was brilliant and joyous, and proceeded to make the introductions with inimitable grace.

"And Ned, papa," she said, putting her cousin forward the moment she saw her; "here is Ned, our own Ned."

How Ned's heart throbbed with gratitude for this affectionate recognition.

But Mr. Edgar only bowed in his stateliest manner, and suffered his fingers to close coldly over hers for an instant, while he asked for her health with the same conventional courtesy that he might have extended to any acquaintance. She answered as coldly, and blushing hotly, withdrew to another part of the room, while Carnew, watching the scene with intense interest, recurred again mentally to all that Edna had told him.

Father and daughter; they were a pretty sight together; she so beautiful and so affectionate, and he so handsome, although strangely careworn, and so exquisitely tender to her. The tears rose in Ned's eyes as she watched them, and feeling that she would suffocate if she remained, she hurried out of doors for one of the solitary strolls that generally composed her. Taking a secluded part of the grounds, she wandered on, so absorbed in her thoughts as to be quite unconscious of the scenes she passed, until she came suddenly upon a little group of men whom she recognized as farm hands of Rahandabed. They were grouped about something which they seemed to be examining with great earnestness, and as they started on hearing her footsteps, and turned with something like dismay to look at her, a man who had been inside the little circle rose from a crouching position, and seeing her, came forward. It was Macgilivray, with a more solemn expression than even his grave Scotch face usually wore.

"Take yoursel' awa', Miss Edgar; its noo sicht for your

eyes; a puir daft lad that's killed himsel' is doon there; he's shot through the heart; wi' a paper pinned to his breast that says it's for love he done it—a dour love that makes a man do the leck o' that."

" Who is he?" asked Ned, white and trembling.

" There's nae telling yet; we don't leck to touch him till the authorities gets here. I'll gang to the house wi' word now."

And he left Ned, who also retraced her way to the house.

XXVIII.

The excitement was intense among the servants, and extended even to the guests when it became known that a young man had shot himself on the grounds of Rahandabed. " The authorities," as Macgilivray had termed the country coroner, was not long in coming to the spot, and after such an official investigation as he best knew how to make, the suicide was borne to one of the barns on the estate, and there laid out with a sort of rude and shrinking kindness. No one knew him, and nothing was found upon his person to reveal his identity. Not even a portemonnaie was found in his pocket; nothing but a little scrap of paper pinned to his breast, on which was written in a bold, manly hand:

" For love I have done it."

The pity of the female servants was excited by his handsome appearance. Not even the throes of death had disturbed his regular features, and save for the ghastliness of his face, one might well think him sleeping.

With that morbid curiosity that sometimes actuates alike high and low born, the guests went out to see him. Indeed, everybody went except Ned, Mrs. Doloran, Mr. Edgar, and Edna.

Mrs. Doloran, in strange contradiction to herself, refused to share any of the morbid curiosity, replying in angry astonishment, when asked to accompany some of the guests to view the suicide,

"What! ask *me* to look at the dead fool? The only pity is he didn't blow out his brains instead of his heart, that we might see how little he had, and what poor stuff they were. For love, indeed, he shot himself. He'd better said, for lack of honest sense."

And she went on the instant to select the toilet in which she intended to receive her new guest. With ludicrous whimsicalness, she was determined on not appearing in his presence until she should meet him in state that evening, on that account intending even to dine in seclusion.

Mr. Edgar refused to see the suicide, because he had no interest in the matter, and Ned did not go for the reason that such a death had an appalling horror for her; but it was none of these things that deterred Edna.

It was the horrible fear that she should recognize the dead man, and her heart beat with sickening speed, and her face paled and flushed in a breath at every observation upon the event made by the company. And yet, with the feeling that restrained her, there was at the same time an almost irresistible desire to see him, but to see him alone, to look upon the dead face when no curious eye would be upon herself, and involuntarily she glanced about the room, as if she feared she was even then the object of suspicious scrutiny.

But, there were no eyes fixed very earnestly upon her save those of Ned, who was longing for an opportunity to speak about the mysterious note she had received. Strangely enough, though its words seemed printed before her everywhere she turned, she did not dream of connecting them with the suicide.

To stricken, guilty Edna, Ned's anxious look conveyed a verification of all her fears. She, too, thought constantly about the note, feeling assured that it was for herself, and perhaps contained a warning of the dreadful thing that had happened. What should she do? Where could she flee for help?

In whom could she confide? Was it necessary for her

safety to tell her wretched secret to Ned? Ned, whose rectitude was so strong that she would die rather than betray any confidence, or violate her slightest promise? She looked at her father, beside whom she was seated, and to whom Carnew was showing some rare prints, and she shuddered as she pictured the anger and scorn with which he would greet the knowledge of his daughter's foolish conduct; and then she looked at Carnew, and a vise seemed about her heart as she imagined *his* contempt. What if Ned should be impelled to speak to him about the note she had received, and the suspicions that, in connection with the suicide, it must have engendered in her mind? Her face became ghastly at the thought, and, feeling that she must do something to prevent such a revelation, she excused herself to the two gentlemen, and crossed to Ned.

"You are going to dine with Mrs. Doloran, in her private parlor, are you not?" she said in a half-whisper, though Ned being seated in an embrasure, there was no one to overhear.

"Yes," was the reply.

"Then meet me as soon as you can leave her, will you?" spoken quite in a whisper now; "I shall be in my own room."

"Yes," said Ned; "for I also have something to say to you, and——"

She was about to add what she thought of the note she had received, and indeed to give it to Edna, but at that moment Brekbellew came up to them and claimed Miss Edgar's attention.

Mrs. Doloran was so unusually and vexatiously captious at the meal which she and her companion ate together in that lady's private parlor, that it seemed as if poor Ned was to be deprived of all opportunity to have her promised interview with Edna; but few mouthfuls passed her own lips. She was too full of anxiety and of a nameless, nervous dread to be able to eat. But the voluble, whimsical lady did not notice that. Ned was a figure-head, so to speak, at which she could direct all her remarks, and she was in no humor to care whether they were replied to or not, but she was in a humor to talk, and babble, babble she went, to the agony of the young girl who saw hour after hour pass away without bringing Mrs. Doloran any nearer to the end of her garrulity, or to the close of her meal, having, in the interest of her tongue, suspended eating so frequently and so long. And did the poor companion venture to request a brief leave of absence, it would have brought upon her such an avalanche of impertinent questions that it were better to refrain altogether from seeing Edna that evening. But, at last a message came to the effect that the company were impatiently waiting the presence of Mrs. Doloran. That recalled the eccentric lady, and made it necessary that she should conclude hastily her meal and deliver herself into the hands of her maid; so Ned was free for a little while. She hurried to Miss Edgar's room. Edna opened the door to her; her face as white as the white, fleecy dress she wore, and she was trembling in such a manner that the very hand she extended to Ned shook like that of an old, palsied woman.

"I thought you would never come," she whispered, "and I am so wretched."

To Ned's astonishment she was crying—crying as if her very soul would melt.

Her cousin could not speak. She was too much astounded to find a word of comfort, or even inquiry; but her tender heart ached in sympathy with this strange, unknown grief; nay, every instinct of her true womanly nature was aroused, and all went forth in pity and love to Edna, as if she had been an own sister. She forgot even her previous suspicions, her half-distrust, her doubt, and she wound her arms about the sobbing girl and pressed her closely to her.

Edna roused herself.

"I have so much to tell you. But may I trust you? Will you think of me as a sister and guard my troubles in your own breast? Will you swear, Ned, never to betray my secrets if I tell them to you? Will you swear solemnly?"

She disengaged herself from the tender clasp, and drew back as if to study Ned's face.

Ned was startled. An oath was to her something dreadful; and this oath, once made, would bind her so sacredly—she who regarded a mere promise with a martyr's sense of duty—that, no matter to what it committed her, it would still be inviolable. Then also her previous suspicion, and distrust, and fear of Edna came suddenly back, and all her emotions showed themselves in the troubled working of her countenance.

"You shrink, you hesitate," said Edna, "and I shall not force you. I have no right to burden you with my sorrows, and I shall not. But you were the only one in the wide world I could turn to, and I felt that you loved me."

The last words touched anew the sympathetic listener; still, true to that prudence with which she was unusually gifted, she said gently:

"Your father surely is your truest friend. You will not refuse to confide in him?"

"I cannot," spoken in a strangely rigid way.

"Then, will it do if I promise to keep your secret just so long or so far as it is consistent with duty to keep it?"

"No; I must have your oath to keep it unconditionally. Otherwise, there is but one course for me to pursue—one dreadful course at which even you, when you hear it, with your gentle charity, will pity more than blame. Could you take the oath I ask, you would be able to advise and to console me. You have suspicions; you had them before even I asked for this interview. You think I have been guilty of imprudence, perhaps of wrong. You are in some measure right. In any case, since you refuse what I ask, I shall be soon beyond the reach of all earthly consequences."

She turned away and threw herself sobbing into a chair,

leaving Ned aghast at the implied terrible threat in the last words. "Beyond the reach of all earthly consequences" could mean nothing else than self-destruction, and, too guileless to dream for a moment that it was only a part of her cousin's shrewd and clever acting in order to work upon Ned's too easily enlisted sympathies, she had but one thought, that it was now her duty, even to the taking of the oath, to prevent this last dreadful crime.

"Only tell me," she said, kneeling beside her cousin, "that *my* keeping of this secret will not do a wrong to anybody, will not bind my conscience in a dreadful remorse, and I shall take the oath."

Edna turned to her, even slipping from her chair, until she too was on her knees, and with her arms about Ned, until their faces almost touched.

"There is no wrong done now," with an almost inaudible emphasis in the last word, "to anybody but me."

"Then I swear," said Ned, "never to reveal what you shall tell me."

"Solemnly swear?" said Edna.

"Solemnly swear," repeated Ned, and Edna's heart beat with exultation, for Ned had taken the oath, and had taken it upon her knees.

She arose, and Ned rose also.

There were no more tears now, no further passionate abandon to grief. She could be something of her own old self again, and tell her secret how she would, for it would be as safe in Ned's breast as if it were buried in the grave. Still, she affected to shiver, as she said: "I am a married woman, Ned.

"I was married by a clergyman not very far from Weewald Place, but so secretly that no one in my father's house dreamed of such a thing——" She paused through sheer fright at Ned's appearance; the girl was ghastly, and she seemed to have difficulty in breathing.

"What is it, Ned? why are you so affected? Surely it is no more than others have done before me—and I loved him."

Ned had regained her breath, and she answered sternly :

"How could you marry without the knowledge of your father? How could you be so false to your duty as to receive any suitor without acquainting him?"

Edna sank to her knees and sobbed :

"Do not upbraid me; I was imprudent, erring if you will, but at least pity me now; I am sorely punished, for I feel that the suicide whom they have found on the grounds, is my husband."

Her listener started back in terror and dismay at the announcement.

"*Your husband!*" she repeated.

"Yes,' said Edna starting suddenly to her feet, "and I have felt that the note which was given to you this afternoon was meant for me, and was only given to you in mistake."

The note; she had forgotten it for the moment in the feelings excited by Edna's strange revelation; now, she pulled it from her pocket, and put it into her cousin's hand.

Twice, three times she read it; then she put it to her lips and moaned :

"My God! it is he; that is his farewell to me."

In her excitement Ned forgot to inquire just then why the note was addressed to her, but she was thinking of the mysterious words which she heard at the mill. She repeated them now, and asked if Edna had uttered them.

"Yes," was the reply, "and I heard you call my name, but fear lent wings to my feet. He concealed himself in the vicinity, but I fled to Rahandabed, and had just time to be in the house and assume a most composed attitude when you arrived, and were no doubt surprised at my unruffled presence there. But come with me now, Ned, and let me convince myself whether my dreadful fear be true. In company with you, I can summon courage to look at him; alone I could not. Nobody will miss us"—as Ned shrank from the proposition, and Edna attributed the shrinking to the unseemliness of leaving the house unescorted at such an hour—"for my father thinks I am confined to my room with some sudden, slight indisposition, and Mrs. Doloran will hardly want you for an hour yet. Come! do not refuse me I am beside myself as it is, and to bear this dreadful suspense longer will kill me.'

She put her hands to her head in a wild way that frightened Ned and made her consent, in spite of her aversion to look upon the suicide.

Flinging a long dark wrap to her cousin, Edna folded another about herself, and putting into her pocket a piece of wax candle and some matches, the two went forth, and descended by a back staircase to the grounds.

Edna had taken care to inform herself just where he was laid, and as the night was a bright, clear one, they had little difficulty in finding the path to the out-houses. No one seemed to be about, for which Miss Edgar was thankful, though if they had been met by any of the servants, the only persons likely to be on that part of the grounds, she was prepared to say quite frankly that they were only gratifying their curiosity to see the suicide.

There were so many out-houses that the difficulty was to find *the* one, and with a nerve that to Ned was most appalling, Miss Edgar lifted the latch of door after door, of milk-house, and wash-house, and barn, and lighting her candle went forward undismayed. Her search was unavailing, until they came to one temporary structure, the door of which was broadly open. A gust of wind seeming to bear the very breath of the charnel house assailed them, and blew out the candle the moment it was lighted. Nothing daunted, she lit it again and went forward, Ned slightly in the rear. The corpse was there, on some rudely improvised trestles, and covered face and all by a sheet. Without a moment's hesitation, Edna, holding the candle aloft in one hand, drew down the sheet with the other. Impelled by a feeling strangely apart from herself, and yet seeming to centre within it every emotion of her soul, Ned too leaned forward as the sheet was drawn, and beheld the still white features of handsome Dick Mackay.

She could not speak. She could hardly breathe, and in her agonized surprise she turned to her cousin, but at that same moment Edna flung the candle down, and in the darkness that succeeded, the candle going suddenly out from the force of the fall, her sobs could be heard as if she had dropped on her knees beside the dead man.

Ned found her voice and groping, clutched Edna's shoulder, seemingly from its low position on a line with the suicide's pallet.

"Come back," she whispered, "I am getting ill."

The girl arose, and the light from without showing in through the open doorway being sufficient to guide them, she did not again light the candle, but retraced her way hurriedly and silently, not a word being spoken until her room was reached. Then Ned, who had somewhat recovered herself, and was influenced in turn by feelings of pity, disgust, indignation, and sorrow, said with some severity:

"How could you marry *him*, and marry him without acquainting your father?"

"Ask me why women have been foolish before my time?" answered Edna impatiently; "why they fall in love with handsome faces, and give their hearts before they know what it is to have a heart? O Ned! if I could undo that one mad act, and restore *him* to life, I would gladly die myself." Her grief was real this time, for a transient remorse had seized her; remorse for the dreadful crime of which she knew but too well she had been the cause.

"His family," gasped Ned, "his poor old father, his young sister of whom you have spoken to me so often— ah! I understand now the strange interest you seemed in your conversations to take in them all. But none of his people know that you are his wife, do they?"

"His sister knows."

"And will she keep the matter secret now, when her

brother has committed suicide—will she not rather in her grief be likely to tell everything about him ? ”

“ I don’t know ; that is what I fear ”—and Edn a’s tears burst out afresh ; “ but I have one hope--no one has recognized him ; he may be buried unidentified.”

“ *Edna !* ”

The appalling tone in which her name was uttered compelled the weeping girl to look up ; but she cowered from the stern-looking face that met her.

“ Would you add further crime to what you have already done, by not, if no other means can be found, yourself telling that you have recognized in this suicide the son of poor old Mackay ? Would you leave this aged father to wait in an agonized suspense for tidings of his missing boy ? The most dreadful certainty is better than an uncertain waiting. O Edna ! do not let this first wretched act of yours crush every kindly impulse of your womanhood.”

“ But what will become of *me ?* ” moaned Edna. “ His sister may, as you say, tell all when she knows of this dreadful occurrence, and what then shall *I* do ? ”

“ Bear the consequences ; they will hardly be so dreadful since the unfortunate man is dead, and you are a widow instead of a wife. Your father, in consideration of that, will condone your act, I think.”

“ You don’t know my father ; he is unforgiving—he is even vindictive—and he would never, never consider me his child again.”

“ Then accept it, if he does not,” said Ned warmly ; “ will it be anything to what you have brought that poor wretch who lies dead by his own hand ; to the grief you have brought upon his family ? You were daring and defiant enough to marry him : be equally daring to confront the consequences.”

“ I cannot, oh, I cannnot,” she moaned.

“ Then *I* sha’ll reveal the identity of the dead man ; the oath you exacted does not bind me in that respect. I can say at least, that *I* have seen and recognized him.”

"And will you say that I was with you when you recognized him?" asked Edna, her voice so tremulous that she could hardly enunciate the words.

"If circumstances require the truth, I shall; but your conscience is making a frightful coward of you. Why should it be more remarkable for you to have looked at the suicide, than that the other guests of the house should have done so?"

Edna roused herself:

"You are right; my fears are making a coward of me. I shall tell my father that I have seen and recognized Dick"—pronouncing the last word with a gulp—"and —" a knock at the door interrupted her. It was a message from Mr. Edgar to know how his daughter was, and the messenger at the same time stated that Mrs. Doloran was searching the house for Ned.

"I shall go to Mrs. Doloran immediately," said the young lady, rising to depart.

"And I," said Edna to the messenger, "shall join the company in the parlor in a few moments. Tell my father so."

XXIX.

What refined, fastidious, quiet-looking Mr. Edgar thought of the great, ill-dressed, loud, and forward woman to whom he was presented by Carnew, it required his most stern self-control to prevent from showing, at least in his face. She gave herself the most absurd airs and with her immense size, and her dress of gay-colored satin that shimmered in the light like a great surface of metallic sheen, and her head dress of plumes that added to her height, and made her seem like a female warrior, she was a most novel and ludicrous sight. Those of the company who were not within the range of her vision were convulsed with laughter, and those who were, had to resort to many manœuvres to hide their mirth.

Carnew was crimson from anger and shame, but with his imperturbable self-command, he permitted no more evidence of his feelings to appear than the flush itself gave, and he fulfilled his part of the presentation of his aunt with a quiet, gentlemanly grace which charmed Mr. Edgar. That done, he turned away; but Mrs. Doloran, whose whim it was to keep him just then, caught his arm.

"Now do, Alan, let your gallantry come to my rescue awhile. You know that Mr. Edgar, having travelled so much, will expect to be entertained by a varied conversa tion. And what variety can a *woman's* poor mind devise? You know, Mr. Edgar——" with a languishing raising of her eyes, and an affected setting back of her head that was most mirth-provoking.

"I am one of those who know the true value of the sex: the little insipid nothings that fill the female mind; the vagaries, the emotions that upset the female heart. Therefore I am anxious to retain about you something that savors of brains." With a look at her nephew meant to be conciliatory, but that only roused his indignation to white heat.

Mr. Edgar bowed; the only thing he could do under the circumstances, as in the character of such an honored guest he could neither reply as he would to that unwomanly speech, nor, in deference to the nephew whom he very much admired, betray by a look his utter disgust of the speaker.

But, Alan, who was bound by no such regard, and who was now so angry that even his wonted command had deserted him, said a little hotly: "It is better for me to go, Aunt Doloran, than stay to witness your inoculation of Mr. Edgar with ideas so disparaging to yourself as a woman." He bowed low to his aunt, and before she could recover from her astonishment and indignation at his boldness in administering such a public reproof, he had bowed also to Edgar, broken from her grasp, and was hurrying away.

"There's a fool for you," in her anger bursting out into her customary inelegant speech; "he can't take the truth, and never could; but here is one—" catching sight of Ordotte, who had just entered the parlor and was approaching her, "who holds my views of things."

Ordotte had been presented to the guest earlier in the evening, and he now came forward with that ease of manner which to thoroughly cultured Edgar savored a little too much of ill-bred familiarity, and began at once with clever tact to soothe Mrs. Doloran's irritation and to draw out the guest. In her new-found interest the lady forgot her previous uncomfortable feelings, and talked volubly and nonsensically enough to corroborate her previous assertion of the impotency of the female mind.

"But your stories, Mascar; your Indian stories," she said suddenly, in the very middle of one of her pointless tales, remembering that that part of the programme arranged for Mr. Edgar's entertainment had not been yet carried out.

Ordotte laughed—a laugh that showed in full his white even teeth, whiter looking by contrast with the tawny hue of his face—and snapped his eyes at the new guest in a way that rendered the latter a little uncomfortable.

"My Indian stories," he said, when he had ceased laughing, "will have, I have no doubt, a very singular and fascinating interest for Mr. Edgar. Which shall I tell, Mrs. Doloran? The one where I lay in a jungle all night with the dead tiger on my breast, or——?"

"No; don't tell any of them yet;" said Mr. Doloran, rising. Wait until I get Ned here; I enjoy your stories better when I have her face to watch, ever since you said her face recalled one of them to you."

But the messenger dispatched for Ned reported that the young lady was neither in her own room, nor in any of Mrs. Doloran's apartments.

"Then search the house for her," said the lady, impatiently; and so messengers were sent in different directions. Mr. Edgar, taking advantage of the slight lull that had occurred in the conversation, begged to be excused, while he also sent a message to his daughter.

Ned entered the parlor, pale and tremulous from her recent emotions, and pitiably indisposed to make one of the party awaiting her. But she nerved herself to it, and bowing, dropped into the chair beside Mrs. Doloran.

It was well that that lady was so anxiously interested in the anticipated Indian story, or Ned would have been assailed by most sharp and impertinent questions. As it was, she hardly noticed her after having motioned her to the chair beside her own.

Ordotte begun :

"Klipp Kargarton, the hero of my tale, was one of the strangest fellows I ever met. He had all the qualities to win hearts, but they seemed to have been so smothered by some blight that it was only at times one knew that he was not the heartless, sullen, and taciturn man he seemed to be. When I met him for the first time in Singapore, he was doing business there for some firm, but shortly after, at my suggestion, he gave up his position and accompanied me to Calcutta, where I had already invested some capital in an English house. I obtained for him a position in the same house, and we became such warm friends that he occasionally gave me scraps of confidence which wonderfully enhanced my interest in him. He was an excellent sportsman, and one of the memories that I shall never forget, is of his face when he, with some others, were out for a day's hunting in the jungles. At such times he seemed to be like another being, and his courage in pursuing and attacking the fierce beasts was a source of envy to more than one of us.

"On one occasion he and I, owing to his ardor in the hunt, an ardor which I unconsciously caught, became separated from the rest of the party, and we found ourselves actually on the lair of a tiger with her cubs. The tiger we dispatched after some trouble and a scratch or two upon ourselves, but the two cubs, strange to say,

Klipp would bring home alive with him. No argument of mine would dissuade him from his project, nor make him see that he would get just as much for the skins, which we could take off as we had already taken the mother's, and at the same time be spared the trouble of of carrying the live beasts. He would have his way, and I was forced to carry one of the cubs, while he took the other. Our great fear was to meet the father of the animals, unless, perhaps, he had been met and dispatched already by some of our party. Our stock of ammunition was very low, so we courted no more game, but made our way to civilized haunts as quickly as possible.

"Then Klipp stated his object in bringing the cubs alive. Only a day or two before, a female tiger captured for some zoölogical show that was to leave for England in a few months, had given birth to cubs which had died. The grief of the beast, they said, was excessive, and Klipp, with his great, kindly heart, thought of her when he saw the cubs in the jungle.

"And the bereaved tigress actually welcomed the little strangers, and fondled them as if they were indeed her own departed ones. At which Klipp, to my surprise, looked disgusted.

" ' Her nature is as little to be relied upon as if it were human,' he said to me; and when I laughed, he said again :

" ' They say parental instinct is so strong that in the face of any deception a father would recognize his child'; but it is not so.' "

Up to this point of the story, no one save Mrs. Doloran had manifested anything but a polite interest; now, however, Mr. Edgar was sitting erect, his face as pale as the snowy bosom of his shirt, and his eyes flaming through Ordotte. But he, pretending not to notice the sudden and strangely awakened interest, proceeded :

"As I said before, Klipp was a very strange man; indeed, some thought that his mind was not altogether sound, but those people did not know the singular events in his life. He went every day to see that tiger and her adopted children, and every day he returned more and more disappointed and disgusted with her increased fondness for them.

"One day, in his deep disgust, he said to me:

"'We are all brutes, and a man may be pardoned when he does a great wrong because of his brutish nature. I expected to see in that animal something that would shame us men; an instinct that would make her turn away from these strange cubs, and not receive them as men do who have other children palmed upon them for their own.'"

The perspiration was standing on Mr. Edgar's brow, and the fingers of the hand that rested on his knee worked convulsively.

Mrs. Doloran, who was angry that Ordotte had not told *her* that Indian story, could contain herself no longer:

"Why did you keep that tale from me, Mascar?" she said with indignant reproach.

He answered with a laughable assumption of penitence and humility:

"My dear madam, it was hardly of a kind to interest you; but Mr. Edgar," with a profound bow to that gentleman, "has, no doubt, encountered so many strange phases of character that I thought it would not be uninteresting to add one of my experiences to his own."

The lady was somewhat mollified: "Well, Mascar, I shall forgive you. And now finish the tale."

"The tale is finished," with another bow, and a quick, sharp look at Edgar.

"But Klipp, and the cubs, and the dear old tiger, what became of them all?" asked Mrs. Doloran, her voice raised in trembling eagerness.

"The dear old tigress and her cubs were taken to England; and Kipp, I left him in Calcutta."

"Couldn't you ask him to come here? O Mascar, it would be delightful! Just write and invite him here."

And her gushing eagerness set the plumes on her head to quivering in a most ludicrous manner.

"I can't do that very well," answered Ordotte, stealing again a sly, sharp look at Edgar, "owing to Klipp having left Calcutta without leaving any trace of his destination; so letters from my Indian friends informed me over a year ago. But if you wish, Mrs. Doloran, I could write to the managers of the zoölogical show in London, inviting the tigress and her cubs here, providing the interesting beast is still alive. They might consent to let them come."

The last part of his speech being spoken with the same imperturable gravity and earnestness that the former had been, rendered it irresistibly comic, and Ned, who had paid but little attention to the story, laughed in spite of herself; but Mrs. Doloran arose, and said with offended dignity:

"No, sir, you will do nothing of the kind; I shall not have Rahandabed turned into a jungle."

Mascar dropped on one knee in front of her, and clasping his hands, said with an excellent assumption of the tragic-comic air that it convulsed with laughter most of those who witnessed it:

"Pardon, a thousand pardons, madam; I but thought to minister to that inherent love of nature which in you is so beautifully developed. On my bended knee I assure you that I shall not write for the illustrious tigress."

It was of little moment to Mrs. Doloran that such speeches and attitudes made her supremely ridiculous: they gave her prominence in her own eyes, and that gratified her vanity; then the homage of Ordotte, assumed and ludicrous though it was, pandered to her innate vulgar love of display; she might be laughed at, but, at the same time, if she could attract attention, it made little difference to her. She had the one comfort of vulgar minds—the thought of her wealth, which in the eyes of many covered all her oddities.

And so she said, with what she considered a graceful

bending of her person to the suppliant, and a pretty tapping of his cheek with her fan:

"When you sue for forgiveness in such a manner, I cannot refuse you."

Mr. Edgar looked and acted like one in a dream, and in an unpleasant dream. His face still retained its snowy pallor, and as if that bleached hue had driven out the lines upon his forehead and about his mouth, they appeared more numerous and prominent than they had done since his arrival. His eyes were fixed upon Ordotte, nor did they seem to have the power of withdrawing themselves until his daughter, escorted by Brekbellew, came up to him. She arrived in the very middle of Ordotte's ludicrous plea for pardon, and with difficulty preserved her composure; the poor sheep by her side so lived in her presence that he scarcely saw the laughable incident before him.

How beautiful she looked; not a trace of any secret grief, or recent emotion about her; certainly nothing to indicate that she felt even half as much as Ned felt the terrible thing that had happened.

Vigor and joy seemed to return to Mr. Edgar with the advent of his daughter; it was as if her presence dissipated some ugly unreality; and he rose, thanked Brekbellew for his attention, and immediately transferred her to his own arm.

"Edna and I will have a little saunter together," he said, bowing to Mrs. Doloran, "and later," turning his eyes to Ordotte, "I shall be happy to have some conversation with this gentleman."

"Ah! his Indian stories have interested you, then," said Mrs. Doloran enthusiastically.

"Yes; a little," replied Edgar with some hesitation, as if afraid to commit himself.

And he turned rather hastily away with his daughter.

Ned watched them. She wondered if her cousin would tell her father then of her ghastly discovery, or if she would wait until the morning. They turned away in the direction of the conservatory and, at the same time, Mrs. Doloran called Ned to accompany her and Mascar; they were going to attend to some detail of the illumination that was to take place at midnight.

XXX.

The opportunity of speaking to Ordotte that Mr. Edgar desired, arrived just before the guests went out to view the illumination. Edna having been claimed by Carnew for the songs which she sang so well, and to which it was his delight to listen, had gone with him to the music-room, and Mrs. Doloran having disappeared to change her toilet for one as gorgeous perhaps, but a little more suitable for the grounds, Mascar was for the moment free. He had not forgotten Edgar's wish to converse with him, and seeing that gentleman apparently holding a sort of dreary conversation with Brekbellew, he went up to him.

Edgar changed color; he was aware that he did so, and he fancied that Ordotte's eyes twinkled mischievously at the sight. He chafed secretly that it should be so, without well knowing why, in the first place, he had any need to give such an exhibition of his feeling, and, in the second place, why he should care particularly for what Ordotte thought. But that gentleman said in his easy, familiar way:

"Thinking that Mr. Brekbellew would like to go to the music-room, I came to offer you my company."

Brekbellew was intensely grateful; his heart and his eyes had followed Edna when she went away leaning upon Carnew's arm, and though, through politeness, he had offered to remain with her father, he had found it difficult to concentrate sufficient attention on what Mr. Edgar was saying to be able to reply intelligently. To be delivered then from such a situation, and to be free to go after his heart's idol, and to imagine also that Ordotte had come to his rescue purely for his (Brekbellew's) benefit, was something to make his breast swell with gratitude, and his poor little insipid face kindled as he looked his thanks to his deliverer, and murmuring to Mr. Edgar a polite excuse for availing himself of the opportunity offered, he hurried away.

Edgar and Ordotte looked at each other after his departure; a look on the part of the one that told of hidden fear and agony; on the other, of contempt and triumph. But each look was so brief, the faces returning immediately to their wonted expression, that a spectator might imagine all to be only the outcome of his own heated fancy.

Edgar was the first to speak:

"Your Indian tale had a deeper and more subtle point than you cared to have appear on its surface."

Ordotte shrugged his shoulders.

"Every tale, every common incident of life, may have its deep and subtle point if our consciences are pricked."

"What do you mean?"

There was suppressed passion in Edgar's low tones.

"Nothing, save as you interpret it. As I told you in the preface of my story, I have had much experience with the different phases of human nature. Men have been, and are my study, and when I speak, it is out of the fulness of a heart that often, unawares, has touched the keynote of another's secret trouble. Whether I have done so in your case, I leave you to judge."

Edgar stared at him. Who was this man who seemed to know his secret trouble? For, despite his love for Edna, and his absolute conviction that she was his daughter, at times a strange haunting doubt mingled with it all. Fight the doubt he did, and crush it; but it rose again, and with it rose more than once Ned's face in mute reproach. What, if she after all were his child, and that all those years he had been holding to his heart the daughter of a woman of loose and low character?

Ordotte's tale had roused anew these horrid doubts, and they raged until they were dissipated by Edna's presence, which he had hailed as a drowning mariner might hail a plank. Now, however, they were back in greater fury. He stooped toward Ordotte, and said in a broken whisper that was somewhat painful:

"If you have guessed that I have a secret trouble, you have guessed well. Whether your intuitive knowledge leads you to think it is a crime also, I know not. I only ask, I adjure you to tell me if you are in possession of any secret that will help me."

Ordotte rose. Perhaps he felt it was time to end the conversation; it was coming so near a dangerous border. Edgar rose also.

"No, Mr. Edgar; you are wrong in thinking that I am in possession of any secret of yours, or that it is in my power to help you. I have learned to read faces a little, and your face has given me my knowledge of your character."

"An unfavorable knowledge, eh?"

Spoken with almost a child's eagerness, and of which speech he was heartily ashamed the moment he had uttered it.

But Ordotte answered with a gravity that was almost sorrowful:

"I fancy that you have been blinded in many instances by pride and self-will. But pardon me, Mr. Edgar, for my great freedom of speech. As you have found out by this time, I am an odd fellow. Here is Mrs. Doloran"— spoken with such a change of voice that it seemed like another person—"bearing down upon us, and armed with all the accoutrements of war, to judge from the glistening things about her."

The glistening things, as Ordotte termed them, consisted of a silver banded cloak that was already about the lady's ample person, and a veil of silver tissue thrown over her nodding plumes. In her wake followed Ned, looking more ready to weep than to laugh, and wishing with a sick heart that the night's festivities were over.

Supper was to be served immediately after the illumination, and as the guests passed into the grounds there could be heard the clatter of the servants' work in the dining-hall. Somehow, Ned connected the sounds with the falling of clods upon a coffin, and when the handsome and many-colored lights broke upon her view, showing a scene so weirdly and picturesquely beautiful that the guests became enthusiastic in their admiration, she saw everywhere the still white face under the sheet in the out-house.

After supper, Mrs. Doloran would put into execution her pet scheme of exhibiting herself and her guest on the dais. She had the colors arranged purposely to throw into startling effect her own already startling costume, and now since Mr. Edgar was so handsome and so distinguished-looking, he would certainly add to her appearance there. Seated in that elevated position, she would be what she wanted to be at all times, the cynosure of every eye, and even, as in her vain, secret, unstable heart she wanted to do, enhance Ordotte's admiration for her. It did not occur to her what her guest might think of such a proceeding; as her guest, he would be obliged to acquiesce politely in what she wished, and her absurd vanity cloaked everything else. But Alan was watching her. He had watched her secretly all night, throwing many a covert, but angry glance at the dais, which he felt was destined to bring him new shame. So, when his aunt was designedly leading Mr. Edgar to that part of the room, Carnew whispered his fears to Edna, whom he had been escorting since supper.

"Let us forestall her," said Edna mischievously; "it will hardly be as ridiculous for us to mount there, as for your aunt in her absurd costume, and my father, who certainly will not like it. And we can keep the places so long that she may lose the desire to do likewise."

He hailed the suggestion, and together they hurried, easily getting in advance of Mrs. Doloran, who did not dream of their desire, until to her amazement she saw Miss Edgar in the very place designed for herself, and beside her, her provoking nephew.

Anger made her dumb for the moment; then her wrath burst out regardless even of the presence of her escort:

"How dared they? Those seats were intended for us. But I shall order them down immediately."

"Do nothing of the kind!" It was Ordotte's voice just behind her. He had seen and divined the purport of Carnew's manœuvre, and he had hastened to Mrs. Doloran to prevent, if he could, the outbreak which he feared would follow.

He continued:

"The lady and gentleman who are in the places fill them very acceptably, and Mr. Edgar, did you invite him to such a position, might plead his inability, or his reluctance to be raised to so great an elevation."

She was hardly mollified, but Ordotte rattled on, and Edgar, were he not so heart-sore and disgusted, might have found it in him to laugh at the ludicrous positions in which this woman delighted to place herself.

Edna and Carnew did fill the places very acceptably and most becomingly. The bright colors of the dais harmonized well with her simple white costume, and the dark beauty of her blushing face was never seen to better advantage. Looked at there, as she sat in most graceful attitude with her head modestly drooping, she was an exquisite creature, and Edgar's heart beat once more with all a father's swelling triumph and admiration. She was *his* child. No doubt could move him from that conviction. Perhaps her beauty assumed even a deeper hue from contrast with the young, erect, and handsome man by her side, and many a female heart in the little assembly sickened from pangs of its own jealousy and envy. When, to throw a little playfulness into the impromptu scene, and make the guests think it was a premeditated pantomime, he, with a talent which no one suspected was in him, feigned to be the wooing lover of a sly, coy, and bashful maiden, Edna took the cue, and the little pantomime went well and gracefully on, to the guests' intense surprise and delight. Even Mrs. Doloran was won at last, and she applauded and laughed louder than anybody else.

But Ned was silent and shivering. The pantomime was but a succession of pangs to her, for, now that Edna was free to marry, would not all this dumb show of love on Carnew's part become a reality? What fortune seemed to surround the girl—a happy home, a tender father, and now the removal of the very consequences of her own imprudent, if not erring act, that would have impeded her marriage with a rare good man, as Ned regarded Alan; while she, who had no real home, no father, and who loved Carnew with all the strength of her large, loving heart, must stifle her affection and behold him the husband of another—and such another. In her bitterness she almost wished that Annie Mackay would reveal her brother's marriage. Then she was frightened at herself for having such a desire, involuntary and brief as it was. Still, if Edna did but show even in her countenance a little trace of feeling for what they had both endured in the early part of the evening, Ned imagined that she would not feel quite so bitter. But the longer Ned looked ed at her, the brighter grew the lovely face, and it was only too evident that no shadow of the dead man rested upon her.

The festivities closed, and much to the satisfaction of Carnew, without the further exhibition of any ridiculous whim by Mrs. Doloran. He seemed to feel that it was due to Edna's timely thought. Accordingly, he was very grateful, and he said his good-night to her with a tenderness that set her cheeks glowing and her heart beating violently. She had hardly recovered from her emotion, when her father, who had found it impossible, without a rudeness of which he was not capable, to leave Mrs. Doloran until that moment, came up to her to give her his escort to her room. But at his own sumptuous apartment, which was just above one of the parlors, he stopped suddenly, and opening the door drew her in with him. She wondered somewhat, and was a little bit dismayed, for her guilty conscience sent up its fears at once. Still, his manner was that of inimitable tenderness; and when, having closed the door behind them, he drew her forward until the softened light from a large shaded lamp fell full upon her face, and folding his arms about her, said with a voice so tremulous and strange it hardly seemed to be her father:

"O my daughter!" Her own feelings gave way, and she cried upon his bosom. He felt her tears and thought they were the evidence of her affection for him, of her sympathy with his own emotions, at once so intense and so inexplicable. He did not dream that her tears were those of relief; relief from the horrid fears his strange manner to her had engendered, for she knew not what might have become known to him. Now, however, that she was assured her secrets were still safe, his paternal love still undiminished, she grew confident and demonstrative in her return of his affection. She wound her arms about his neck, she drew his face down to her own, and she held him as if she would never let him go.

"My own, *own* child!" he murmured, with a peculiar and lingering emphasis on the word own; and he continued to repeat the phrase as if there was a balm in it for his doubting and agonized heart.

Never had Edna known him to be so demonstratively tender, and encouraged by that fact she was more than once on the point of telling him of young Mackay's suicide. Something whispered that it would be easier to make the revelation now, than to defer it until the morning. Yet an inexplicable fear restrained her, until he said, noticing that she continued to weep:

"Why do you cry, still, my child? Surely you are not unhappy."

"Ah, papa, not unhappy myself, but unhappy for others."

Again he folded her up to him.

"My darling! You have your mother's tender heart.

Did only a servant have a sorrow which she heard, she made it her own.   For whom, my child, do you weep?"

She lifted her streaming face.

"They have discovered that the suicide who was found on the grounds, papa, is Mr. Mackay's son, Dick."

"What!" and with his exclamation he started from her in wonder and dismay; he asked rapidly, and it seemed to her—fear-stricken as she had again become—sternly:

"Who recognized him!"

Her cowardly heart, lest she should be asked for explanations which she would be unable to make, would not let her say as truth demanded: "I did," and though a moment before she had not intended to tell a lie, now she said without faltering:

"Ned came to my room to ask me to accompany her to see him."

"Did she know that the suicide was young Mackay?"

How stern was his voice; Edna cowered from it, and cowered from him as he looked at her.

"I don't know.   She only came to me to go with her, and we both saw that it was he."

"And her manner while she looked at him," the stern voice resumed, "was it such as to make you think there had been any great affection between them?"

"I don't know.   After looking a moment she said she was getting ill, and we returned."

Edgar said again, but more as if he were talking to himself:

"My surmises have been correct; there must have been some bond of affection between them, or else why should he come here to die? She, perhaps, actuated by a late prudence, has refused to reciprocate his affection, and he may have been driven by his despair to this deed.   In any case, I feel that his death lies at her door."

"Oh, my darling!" suddenly approaching her and again folding her to him: "that I have subjected you for any time to the influence of this woman!"

"O papa! do not be too hard upon her; women sometimes cannot help being weak, and she may not have been guilty of what you think."

Her own fears that she had gone too far in criminating Ned, and that the meshes she had woven about another might extend far enough to entangle herself, made her earnest and touching in her plea for her cousin. But her father answered:

"It is your gentle charity which urges all this; you are too guileless to suspect the wrong-doing of others. And has she proclaimed the discovery she has made, or does she mean to let the poor wretch fill an unknown grave?"

"O papa!" with a passionate burst of tears, "she asked me if I would tell you that we had recognized him."

"*Asked you to tell me?*" he repeated; "she would not dare to tell me herself, feeling, no doubt, that I should penetrate whatever mask she might assume."

In his indignation he forgot that his own coldness to Ned must have imposed a most effectual barrier to any voluntary communication on her part.

He was silent then, recalling the sad, pale, anxious face which his niece wore all the evening, a face in such unfavorable contrast to the bright, happy-looking one of his daughter. That was another and a strong link in the chain of corroborative evidence against the unfortunate girl; the bad blood of her low mother was showing in her, and once more the doubts raised by Ordotte's tale were allayed. He was more convinced than ever that Edna was *his* child.

Edna continued to weep, more from her secret fears than any other cause, and when she saw that her father was still absorbed in his stern reverie, she said with a sob:

"Forgive her, papa!"

He roused himself. To her dying day she never forgot the expression of his countenance. Her novel-reading had given her a vague idea of stern and vindictive-looking faces, but this one, with its compressed mouth, its rigid lines, its corrugated brow, and more than all, its flaming, piercing eyes, was much more terrible than anything she had ever imagined. After that first wild look at it, she felt that she must scream with terror if she saw it again, and she covered her own countenance with her hands.

"Forgive her! Was it you, Edna, my own daughter, who had done a thing like this, my heart and my home should be closed to you at once and forever. Provide for you I might at a distance, but never should I consent to see again a woman who could so degrade her family by stooping to such an affection; a daughter who could so disgrace her father by receiving for a moment clandestine attentions, and from a suitor so much beneath her. Ned is to me now, and shall be henceforth an utter stranger."

"But, papa," said Edna, taking her hands from her face, and keeping her eyes down, "you will not tell these suspicions of yours to any one—you will not let Mr. Mackay know——"

"No," he interrupted, "for the satisfaction of your poor, little, tender, foolish heart, I shall promise you that nothing of this shall pass my lips to any one. It would do little good now, since the poor wretch is beyond all earthly help, and it might only add to the grief of his poor old father to feel that, at the bottom of it, was a woman who had been one of my household. Let Ned keep her guilty secret, if it be through her, as I now firmly believe it to be, that this man has come to his death. I shall not reveal it."

That assurance made her tears cease to flow, and well knowing there was no danger of any private conversation between Ned and her father, in which perhaps her falsehoods might be detected, she looked up and became something of herself again.

"I had decided to leave here to-morrow, Edna, " Mr. Edgar said. "and now all that you have told me makes me more eager to go. I shall give orders for the transportation of poor Mackay's body to his home. His father is a worthy old man, and deserved a better son than that scapegrace."

"To-morrow?" repeated Edna.

"Yes; you can be ready, can you not? I am most anxious to remove you from many influences here—that ill-bred, coarse Mrs. Doloran, and Ned. With Carnew I am charmed. It seems one of the strange freaks of nature that he should be so nearly related to that vulgar woman."

"Oh, yes, papa; I can be ready, and I shall be glad to go."

And that assertion was truthful; she was glad to get away from meeting Ned. Knowing how she had calumniated her, she was not yet so hardened in guilt as not to feel a little qualm of conscience for her fiendish work. Her great hope was that their departure might be so hurried as to leave no time for a private interview with her cousin. For Carnew there was no regret at leaving him; since her father admired him so much, she knew he would be invited to Weewald Place, and she doubted not his immediate acceptance of the invitation.

XXXI.

The events of the succeeding day, with that strange fate which is often more propitious to the evil-doer than to the good, were quite in accordance with Edna's secret wishes. Her father, unable to sleep after she left him; waited only the first glimmer of the dawn to go and look at the suicide. And he remained so long by the side of the dead man, impelled to his unseemly vigil by a strange fascination, that he was found there by some of the servants. Later, when it was by his order the body was prepared for removal to Barrytown, everybody believed that it was he, who, in taking an early stroll about the grounds, had recognized the dead man. Nor did

Edgar drop a word to contradict the belief. For Mrs. Doloran, when she heard that her guest was bent upon his departure, and that, immediately after the late breakfast, her anger knew no bounds.

Nice return for her hospitality to take himself away just as she thought she should enjoy him. She hated him now, and hoped she would never meet him again. And when Alan came to say that Mr. Edgar was waiting to bid her adieu, she refused to see him, nor would she permit Ned, who was really ill enough looking to be in her bed, to leave her for a moment, lest *she* perhaps should say a courteous farewell.

And so Alan had to apologize with what grace he might, for his aunt's lack of courtesy.

He was, however, assured by Mr. Edgar's manner, and by that gentleman's earnest invitation to himself to visit Weewald Place, that Mrs. Doloran's eccentricities were quite understood.

" But Ned, papa," said Edna, with a charming warmth " I cannot go without bidding her adieu."

Mr. Edgar, in the indignation that the very mention of Ned's name aroused, forgot for the moment the presence of Alan, and answered sternly :

" It is my wish that you should not see her." After which his daughter said no more, but dropped her eyes very becomingly, and appeared to be somewhat sorrowful. Carnew was disturbed and pained. Linking what Miss Edgar had told him only the day before of Ned's secret acquaintance with young Mackay, and Mr. Edgar's coldness to her because of that acquaintance, with the facts that, in the suicide, Edgar had himself discovered this identical Mackay, and was now so eager to leave Rahandabed, and so stern in his order to his daughter not to see Ned, he could come to but one conclusion— that the story of the previous day, which his informant wanted so charitably not to believe, must be quite true, of which truth, perhaps, Edgar had even some secret proofs, but that, in his magnanimity, he would not openly condemn the imprudent, if not erring girl. Then her own pale and sick-looking countenance that he saw when he went to speak to his aunt in the latter's apartment, seemed to be a proof of the unpleasant things against her. Well might she look pale and sick if, as he now believed, young Mackay's suicide lay at her door. And not until that moment did he realize how much he himself loved Ned. But he knew it now, knew it by the agony of his own thoughts, and though he performed all the parting ceremonies with perfect courtesy, it was with somewhat of a pre-occupied air, but little flattering to Edna.

Piqued and saddened by it, she said, as he assisted her to a place in the carriage: "May I be assured that you will accept my father's invitation to Weewald Place?"

She lingered purposely, as she spoke, with her hand upon his arm, and her eyes looking fixedly into his own, so as to throw all the witchery of her exquisite beauty about him. But the effect was lost, for he saw only one face—the face that he must learn to forget. He bowed, however, and murmured that she might be quite assured of his acceptance of her father's invitation.

Poor, old honest Mackay! It seemed a strange turn of Heaven to give him this reward for his long life of struggle and rectitude. Perhaps, had the news been broken to him by another than Mr. Edgar, he might not have exercised such stern control of his feelings; but as it was, even in his intense grief—for he loved his boy, scapegrace though he deemed him to be—he was impressed and, after the manner of poor human nature, a little flattered by Edgar's unusual condescension. He bowed his head when told the news, and for a few minutes let his tears have their way down his furrowed cheeks. Mr. Edgar had thought it better to tell at once all that was known of the circumstances attending young Mackay's suicide, but he did it very gently, impelled to that course by the same feeling which had caused him, in the first place, to assume the charge of the body—a feeling that because, through kin of his, trouble had come to these poor people, it was in a measure his duty to show them some kindness.

"And a paper pinned to his breast, you say, Mr. Edgar?" the poor old father repeated, when the gentleman had told the ghastly story.

"Yes; saying for love he had done it. Do you know anything of his private affairs, Mackay; anything that might have driven him to such a deed?"

"Nothing; but how should I know? He was away from home so much. In the last eighteen months he has scarcely been here a week. His sister, Annie, may know. They took to each other warmer than most brothers and sisters; only she's away now with her aunt in Rochester, and so delicate that I'm afeared this news will be the death of her too, and——" He stopped suddenly, for the thought of the loss of both his children caused a great lump to rise in his throat, and he turned away, unable to say more.

Edgar was really touched. He placed his hand on the old man's arm and said with a strange tremulousness in his own tones:

"Do not let her know anything about it yet, and when she returns she may be strong enough to receive the information. How long is she to remain with her aunt?"

Mackay, having by an effort recovered his voice, answered:

"As long as she likes; I wasn't particular, so long as it was doing her good."

"Very well, then, let her stay, and send her no word of this."

To which proposition the old man assented.

And Edna, when told all that by her father, felt intensely relieved. Annie Mackay away from home, and not likely to hear about her brother's shocking death for some time, lifted a weight of fear from her own heart. She knew not whether the pledged and faithful secrecy of the young girl in the past, would or could be maintained in the face of such a tragedy, and though she hoped much from her own influence over Annie, and from the latter's affection for herself, still it seemed to be a lucky stroke of fate to have her absent just now. She wrote to Ned how Annie Mackay was away, and too ill to be made acquainted with what had happened, but she did not say a word to indicate her own feelings. Indeed, the letter was as bright and chatty as the effusion of a gushing and guileless school-girl. In vain Ned tried to gather from it some little trace of remorse or penitence, or at least of that deeper feeling which is at all times the accompaniment of a truly Christian heart. There was nothing of the kind, and the very sympathy expressed for old Mackay had a cold, unfeeling ring about it that made Ned turn away from the letter with bitter disappointment.

Young Mackay was laid to rest in the little country cemetery, on a bleak afternoon, when the dreary aspect of nature seemed in mournful keeping with the bereaved old father. Quite a concourse of the country people witnessed the interment, for the Mackays were well known, and old Mackay much liked and respected.

Edgar did not attend the funeral, but he assumed all the expense, and to make further amends, he offered the old man the better and more lucrative situation of head gardener in Weewald Place, which offer was gratefully, if not gladly, accepted.

Edna was gay and melancholy by turns; for, hardened as she had become, she could not keep down the still white face that rose so often to reproach her. Her father, because of his deep affection, singularly watchful of her, noticed her fitful moods and attributed them to the lonely contrast that Weewald Place was to Rahandabed. Mrs. Stafford, though kind, and gentle, and cultured, was hardly sufficient society for a girl of Edna's lively temperament, and he himself was perhaps too old and too much inclined to melancholy reticence to prove an agreeable companion. Such were the arguments he pleaded to himself in extenuation of her varying disposition, even though his secret heart sent up a little protest against it all. He could not help feeling that, having been absent from her father so long, she might surely enjoy having him to herself for a little, and show that enjoyment by appearing happy in his presence, instead of manifesting, as she frequently did, a listless, almost dejected air, and an absent, half-sad look.

One day that he had contemplated her thus for some time, he said suddenly:

"What do you think of my asking Mr. Carnew to visit us immediately? I thought to wait a month or so before renewing my invitation to him, but there is really no reason to wait so long."

"O papa," she answered, "it would be so delightful," and the sudden color that glowed in her cheeks, and the immediate straightening of her form, with the pleasure showing in her whole changed countenance, attested the truth of her words.

Edgar felt he had made a new discovery: that his daughter loved Carnew, and that her manner, which he had been attributing to other causes, was due solely to the fact that her heart was in another's keeping. Wondering if the affection was mutual, and if so, whether Carnew had openly professed it to Edna, he asked:

"Has Mr. Carnew paid you very marked attention during your stay at his home?"

"No, papa," opening her beautiful eyes with that look of innocent wonder which she knew how to assume with such excellent effect, "nothing beyond that which he would pay to any lady guest. I was the latest arrival to Rahandabed, and being unaccompanied by any male escort as the other ladies were, I supposed he deemed it his duty to attend me when I rode, and to pay me some attention at our evening parties."

Her father was somewhat relieved; charming and devoted as he thought her to be, he still feared that she might have been receiving marked attentions without first asking his consent, and in that case there would have been a strange parallel between her and Ned.

But at the same time he felt also a little throb of pain that this child whom he loved so intensely could so soon and so readily give her affections to another; could be willing to leave his home to brighten that of a stranger. Still he took himself to task for the feeling. Why should he expect to keep her more than other fathers kept their children, and why should he want the very brightest of her years bound to him, an old man now as he imagined himself to be, though hardly in his fiftieth year, when the law of simplest reason demanded that she should move in a different and more useful sphere? Then, even in the event of her marriage, she need not be separated from him. Her husband might be induced to make Weewald Place his home, and in that case Edgar would not only have the society of his daughter, but that of a son. That view cheered him a little, and he resolved to watch Carnew closely when he came, and should he prove, on a longer acquaintance, to be as deserving of regard as he already seemed to be, he would not only not object to his attentions to Edna, but even try to forward them. Having thus resolved, he went immediately to write a note of invitation to Carnew, which note he intended to dispatch by hand, so that the bearer might bring to him immediately Carnew's answer.

Edna was still blushing with pleasure. Her father's desire to invite Carnew, the absence of any censure or remonstrance on his part when he interrogated her about the gentleman's attentions to herself, indicated that he would not object to the young man as a suitor, and Edna determined to wind about him when he came every coil of her many charms. She did not dream for a moment that it was shy, reserved, calumniated Ned, who, without knowing it herself, had won the heart of handsome Alan Carnew.

XXXII.

Mr. Edgar's departure caused Mrs. Doloran to have one of her most tantalizing moods. Her vanity had been sorely wounded by it, for, had that gentleman been at all impressed by her blandishments, he certainly would not have departed so soon. And, as was usual, everybody about her paid the penalty of her miserable failing; but the keenest brunt of it fell upon Ned. She made the most absurd demands of the poor girl, often by so doing exposing her to the ridicule of many of the guests, and she querulously censured her in public and in private, until Ned, in desperation, was seriously determining the question of leaving the lady's service. She could at least go to Albany to Meg's relatives, to whom she punctually wrote, and she had sufficient money saved to defray her expenses until another situation could be found. But she must write to Dyke first; she could not take such a step without consulting him. And accordingly she wrote, detailing pretty fully the many ills to which she was subjected in her present home, but withal saying that, as it was now the beginning of winter, and perhaps rather an awkward time to think of securing a position in any family, if he thought it better, she would endure her present abode until the spring.

Dyke read that letter with eyes that very nearly swam with tears of pleasure; it, as it were, gave him an assurance that her heart was still her own, and might (ah! how his own heart beat at the thought) one day be his. He had given so much satisfaction to his employers that already it was contemplated to promote him to a position beyond his most sanguine hopes; the fact had been hinted to him that very day, and he had ample reason to expect that by the spring he would be in a position to offer Ned at least a comfortable and an assured home. As his wife, his large loving heart could shelter her from every ill such as she now endured. So, in the fulness of his delight, he wrote that he could not for one moment expect

her to remain in a place where her daily annoyances were
so great, and that he quite approved of her proposal to go
to Albany. In April, he was positive he would be able
to secure a position for her, and in the mean time her stay
with Meg and Meg's relatives might afford her perhaps a
little rest and recreation. If she would tell him the pre
cise time of her departure, he would endeavor to get a
couple of days' leave of absence in order to escort her.
Not a word had he said of his real intention, and yet he
flattered himself that she would see through it all, and
understand that the position he would be able to secure
for her would be that of his wife. Ned, however, was
obtuse in that respect. She divined nothing of the kind
from the simply-worded letter; and while her heart beat
with renewed affection for the honest, large-hearted fellow, it was the affection of a sister, nothing more. She
soliloquized about the contents of the missive:

"Since he is so certain of securing a position for me in
the spring, why should I not endure Mrs. Doloran until
then? After all, if I go to these good people in Albany,
they may insist upon doing as they did before, charging
nothing for my expenses, and then I should feel not a
little unhappy. No, I have changed my mind, I shall
endure Rahandabed until April."

And she wrote to that effect to Dyke; and he, blinded
by his own love, took her resolution to remain at Rahandabed as a proof that she understood the true meaning
of his letter, but that, with her natural and beautiful
modesty, she had refrained from a single question which
must draw him out upon the subject. Nor would he be
any more explicit until the actual moment arrived when
he could pour out at her feet that affection which had
begun when he first saw her as a baby, and which had
increased since with every year of his own life.

Carnew dispatched an immediate acceptance of his
invitation to Weewald Place. Indeed, he was rather
glad of the change it would afford. He was tired of the
frivolity about him, disgusted with his aunt, whom his

manhood would not permit to abandon to the sharp practices and the unkind gossip of many about her, and he was bitterly disappointed in, and heart-sick at the thought of Ned. Having by accident seen in the mail-bag her recent letters to Dykard Dutton, all sorts of unpleasant reflections arose in his mind. Was it for the sake of Dutton she had discarded Mackay and driven the latter to suicide? Had she been frank enough to tell Dutton anything about the wretched affair? And then he tried to hate Ned, to stigmatize her to himself as a secret flirt, a schemer for a husband; but one look at the sweet, pale, sad face, disarmed him and sent him back to other thoughts with a sigh in his heart, and a great wild longing that she was what he once thought her to be.

He departed for Weewald Place very quietly, no one knowing of his departure until he had actually gone, and then a brief note to Mrs. Doloran borne by Macgilivray, who had driven the young master, as the Scotchman always termed Alan in speaking of him, to the station, informed that lady of her nephew's intended absence for a few weeks, but the place of his destination was not mentioned. Why Alan had acted with such secrecy he perhaps could hardly have explained to himself, save that, as his aunt so avowedly disliked Mr. Edgar, it would but add fresh fuel to her anger did she know he had gone to visit that gentleman, and in that case her temper would be more disagreeable than ever to those about her during his absence. But his present course was hardly better. Upon reading the note, she turned in a perfect fury to Ned:

"What do you think of that? Alan leaving home without consulting me, and then daring to write that he has gone, and never to name the place that he has gone to?" But she did not wait for Ned's reply. She burst out at astonished Macgilivray. "When did he give this note to you?"

The Scotchman did not lose his prudence. Divining from the information that Mrs. Doloran had already imparted that there was some motive for secrecy on the part of the young master, he determined to be very careful not to reveal the precise time of Alan's departure, nor the train he had taken.

"Me leddy, he put that note into me han' just as the carriage stoppit doon at the station, an' just before he steppit into the car. But if you want mair precise information, it war just as I war a thinking aboot tightening the girths of black Bess the off horse, an' war aboot to get doon to luik at the left fore shoe of Jim the near horse, an——"

"Stop," commanded Mrs. Doloran, more infuriated than ever, "I didn't ask you for such stuff as that. What train did Mr. Carnew take?"

The Scotchman's face assumed a most bewildered expression, and he looked from Mrs. Doloran to Ned in such an amusingly helpless way, that at another time the girl would have been provoked to laughter.

"Speak, man!" thundered the irate woman.

"Well, you see, me leddy, a train war going up and a train war coming doon, and what between the note that he gart me gie you, and Jim's left fore shoe——"

"You're an utter fool," interrupted Mrs. Doloran; "can't you tell whether he went up or down; did you see him get on the car?"

Macgilivray was averse to downright lying, but he could easily reconcile his conscience to a little equivocation or prevarication, and in this case the latter seemed especially commendable:

"Yes, me leddy; I seen him steppit aboord the car, but then it might be the car gang doon, and then agen, it might be the car gang up, for, as I said before——"

But again he was interrupted.

"Since you are such an unmitigated idiot about the trains, tell me about the time that he boarded the car."

This time, to insure success in the part he was playing, Macgilivray assumed rather a knowing look.

"I think I can tell you that, me leddy, if ye'll noo hurry me, but bide aweel while I get it straucht."

Mrs. Doloran seemed to be trying to possess her soul in patience, and the crafty Scotchman, with the forefinger of his right hand pressed to the side of his nose as if to help his recollection, resumed :

"It war verra near twa hours, an' twenty-one minutes after lunch, when I got the order to be ready to drive the young master doon to the station, an' when we started it war verra near three o'clock."

"Oh, then he must have taken the train up," interrupted Mrs. Doloran.

"Bide a weel, me leddy; we had a stappage on the road; Black Bess's shoe hurtit her, and we had to stop round to Payne's the blacksmith to have it fixed; the young master said there war time eneuch. That took twenty-seven minutes and a half, and there war muckle mair time in getting to the station, for he gart me not to drive fast. Sae I dinna haud in my mind the exact hour you want, me leddy, but if it war noo much past four o'clock, then it war verra near to five o'clock."

Mrs. Doloran's temper was at white heat by this time, and she almost drove the Scotchman from the room.

He went, congratulating himself that his departure had not been summarily hastened by the advent of a missile at his head ; probably he had been saved from the unpleasant contact only because there was nothing very convenient to her hand.

But Ned had to bear the woman's tirades, and to listen to passionate speeches, flung with demoniacal injustice at Carnew, until her head ached as well as her heart.

At length, Mrs. Doloran seemed to have found an anchor for her restless thoughts. In her denunciations of Alan's conduct, she had named first one place, and then another as his likely destination, but only to discard the idea as soon as she had given it expression; now, however, she seemed to conclude that it was after Edna he had gone, and immediately she said so, adding :

"Why did I not think of that before ? The girl bewitched him, and of course he cannot live without her.

Depend upon it, Ned, he's gone to Weewald Place, and he'll come back, I suppose, with his bride."

Had she been a grain less selfishly absorbed than she was, she must have noticed the change which her words caused in the face of her companion. Pale before, it was ghastly now, and the dark heavy lines under the big black eyes seemed to grow darker and larger.

But Mrs. Doloran continued:

"I wouldn't object to his marrying her; I don't object to *her*, I only object to her father. I shall write to him immediately, and tell him just what I think of his sneaking away from Rahandabed like this."

XXXIII.

Was Carnew not the firm, grave, thoughtful character that he was, he must have been so won by the exceedingly pleasant cordiality with which he was received by the Edgars, as to have fallen easily into the trap rather set for him by both father and daughter.

But, though he basked in the kindness, earnest and simple as it was on Edgar's part, and was often fascinated to a degree by the charm of Edna's beauty and accomplishments, there was something about her which kept him from the slightest desire to make her his wife. Perhaps it was that in her violent desire to hasten matters she forgot herself sometimes and betrayed a faint and undefinable lack of modesty that, above all other virtues, Carnew prized in woman; and perhaps it was also due to the fact that he was haunted by the pale, sad face at Rahandabed.

All that Mr. Edgar saw of the young man but confirmed his first regard, and his praise of Carnew to Edna, when the two were alone, inflamed more ardently her desire to win him.

She was his constant attendant even in the tour of the house, when her father displayed to him the treasures of art which he had transferred from his English home, and she surprised him by her scholarly remarks. He did not know that, in the anticipation of talking to him about those very objects of art, she had made them a subject of special study and of particular inquiry from her father.

On the second morning of his stay, as he was about to enter the breakfast room, he met her bearing a number of letters.

"I was too impatient for the servants' distribution of them," she said, "so I went myself to the mail bag. I have been expecting a letter from Ned."

He started a little; having forgotten that the Misses Edgar were possible correspondents, it came to him now with a strange thrill of anxiety that Edna would, of course, write to Ned about her father's visitor. No inquiry for the young girl had been made by Mr. Edgar, and only a brief one by Edna when her father was not present, to which inquiry Carnew had replied that he had seen but little of Miss Edgar since Edna's own departure from Rahandabed, and to his relief she did not ask, as he had half expected her to do, if Ned knew of his coming to Weewald Place.

His start, however, was not perceived, and having entered the breakfast room, whither Mr. Edgar had not yet descended, she proceeded to look at the superscriptions on the letters. There were none for her, but the very last that she looked at was directed to Alan. He knew at once the stiff, crooked penmanship of his aunt, and he wondered what ill wind had borne to her his present whereabouts.

"If you will permit me," he said, "I shall read it now."

She bowed assent, and proceeded to arrange her father's letters by his plate, while Alan retired to a curtained embrasure.

He read with mingled feelings of astonishment and anger:

"NEPHEW ALAN——"

Mrs. Doloran had been too angry to insert the customary " My Dear."

" There was no necessity for such secrecy about your visit to Weewald Place ; everybody in the house knows it is after Edna you have gone, and we are all expecting you to return with her as your bride. But it is surprising that you should make such an early visit to this boor, Edgar, without acquainting me, your aunt. However, you are like the rest of your sex, unstable and unappreciative." (With woman's inconsistency, she had forgotten that it had been her wont to direct all such tirades entirely against her own sex, attributing to the sterner sex the very virtues for the lack of which she now censured her nephew.) " You will wonder, of course, how I got my information of your whereabouts. My own sharp wits gave it to me, for that fool Macgilivray, who brought me your note, couldn't or wouldn't tell me a thing beyond that you might have taken a train up, and then again, you might have taken a train down. I have spoken my mind pretty freely to Ned, and she quite agrees with the view I take of your conduct in this matter." (Ned had not opened her lips to express an opinion either way, for, had she even felt it her duty to speak, Mrs. Doloran's ceaseless garrulity gave her no opportunity to do so.) And then came the signature :
" Your indignant aunt,
" E. F. Doloran."

Carnew thrust the letter into his pocket, and turned as if to survey the winter scene without. But the angry flush mounting to his forehead, and the sparkle in his eyes, told that his thoughts were hardly upon the prospect before him. He well divined why she had inserted that about Ned ; it was that he might know how another than herself concurred in the judgment she had pronounced upon his conduct. It was well that she did not know how that paragraph in her letter had stabbed him in another way. It was that Ned would think he had gone after Edna. He forgot that he had never given Ned the slightest sign to make her suppose that he cared for her. And then his thoughts took another and an unkindly turn toward his aunt's "companion." Why was she so ready to concur in that adverse opinion of him? Why could she not in her woman's heart have found some excuse for his conduct, even though it did seem a little inexplicable? He was sure that he would have done it in *her* case. And yet in her case, where *her* conduct seemed inexplicable, he had condemned her many times. But we are so partial to ourselves, and so loth to extend to others the sweet, sweet charity with which we mantle our own feelings.

His first impulse, while all those thoughts coursed burningly through his mind, was to return to Rahandabed immediately and disprove his aunt's assertion of having gone for a wife; his next impulse, and the one which he obeyed, was to write a brief, cool note to Mrs. Doloran, in which he set before her very sharply how mistaken were all her conclusions, and how disagreeably officious she made herself by expecting him to accord to her the submission of a child in frock and pinafore. He ended by sarcastically thanking her and Ned for the kind judgment they had passed upon him.

Mrs. Doloran was as furious when she read that note as when she had been foiled in her endeavor to elicit information from Macgilivray, and she threw it to Ned to read, saying as she did so:

"He is a wretch! and I wish I had never seen him. How dare he insult me like that? The interest I took in him, the kindness I showed him was that of a mother, and this is his return. Have you read it?" pausing suddenly in her excited walk through the apartment, and almost glaring at Ned.

The latter rose.

"Yes, Mrs. Doloran, I have read it, and from it I infer that you must have made some strange statement of me. Mr. Carnow thanks me in his sarcastic manner for my kind judgment upon his conduct. As I at no time have given any opinion of his action, it is your duty to explain what he means. I have borne many things as your 'companion,' but it certainly does not belong to my position to bear misrepresentation by you."

She stood so firmly, and with such an unusually indignant look upon her face, that Mrs. Doloran shrank a little; but she covered her fear by answering immediately:

"Larks and daisies! what airs we give ourselves. You are only my 'companion' anyway, and as such it was your duty to concur in *my* views of things."

"Never my duty to concur in unjust views," broke in Ned, her voice tremulous with indignation, "nor, to my knowledge, have I done so."

"Well, when I censured Alan, you never brought forward anything in his defence," said Mrs. Doloran, glad of any statement under which she could shield herself.

"It was not my place as your 'companion,'" for the first time in her life Ned used a scornful emphasis, "to interrupt your tirades, and they were so unceasing that they gave me no opportunity to do so; but neither was it *your* place, Mrs. Doloran, to construe the silence incident to my position into an untrue statement of my opinion of your nephew's conduct."

"Larks and daisies," said Mrs. Doloran again, with a toss of her ludicrously bedecked head, "one would suppose you were in love with Alan yourself, you make such a fuss about these harmless remarks of mine; but you have no chance, Ned; Alan would never stoop to marry his aunt's 'companion,'" and then she laughed a shrill, forced laugh that showed the more plainly the crow's feet about her eyes, and even gathered one side of her nose into somewhat unsightly curves.

"I shall endure your remarks no longer," said Ned, quivering from head to foot. "It is not my duty to bear insult. I shall leave your house within an hour."

And she left the room before Mrs. Doloran had quite realized the sudden action. She was not prepared for that result, and she was a little dismayed by it; still she was too proud to seek an immediate reconciliation, and she determined to wait the hour before making any decision. Ned went immediately to her room and began a hasty packing of her trunk without well knowing where she was going. Albany suggested itself, but she shrank from going there without first acquainting the good people of her intended visit; then, the village of C—— came to her mind. Only the day before she had supplied Macgilivray with money that he might procure a temporary home with some of the villagers, with whom the Scotchman professed to be acquainted, for a maid of Mrs. Doloran who had been actually driven from Rahandabed by that lady herself. The maid was a prepossessing French girl, but a few months in the employment of Mrs. Doloran, and by her skill in hair-dressing and other feminine matters giving much satisfaction until it was evident her volatile, forward manners, and attractive appearance had brought her into serious trouble. Indeed, the guests were talking about it before even Mrs. Doloran's observation was awakened, and more than one gossip-loving tongue had not hesitated to say that one of the gentlemanly guests was the cause of it. The unfortunate girl herself maintained an unabashed face until charged with her conduct by Mrs. Doloran; then she burst into tears and acknowledged the truth, but refused to tell the name of him who had been the cause of her unhappiness.

The mistress of Rahandabed was righteously shocked. No sentiment of pity for the erring young creature entered her heart, nor was she touched when the girl, sinking on her knees, implored to be kept that she might earn that month's wages, as she had sent the last of her former earnings for the support of her little sister who was at school. Parentless, friendless, homeless, where could she go, what should she do? And her sobs were pitiful enough to rend the hardest heart. But Mrs. Doloran only answered sternly:

“ Ask him with whom you have sinned to help you.”

The French girl raised her streaming eyes.

“ Ah, madame ! I cannot,” and then she pleaded again, “ Do, madame, let me stay this month.”

But madame was inexorable, and Josephine was allowed just three hours in which to take her departure. Madame even told the story to Ned, who, owing to her somewhat isolated position among the guests, had heard no whisper of the tale before, and Ned’s sympathetic heart, for Mrs. Doloran had even told Ned of the French girl’s pleading to be kept, was touched to the core. She managed to see Josephine before her departure, and she was touched anew by the tale from her own lips.

The girl was very young, very pretty, and she had been brought up without a mother’s care ; surely a charitable heart could make many allowances for her ; thus thought Ned, while the dutiful provision which she made for her little sister, and the devotion that she showed in refusing to name her betrayer, though she might claim from him present and future help, evinced qualities of character admirable enough to enlist any one’s pity. So Ned’s heart went out to her, and Ned’s mind was quick and fertile in devising an expedient to help her.

Somehow, she had grown to like better and to have more confidence in Macgilivray than any of the other servants, due, perhaps, to the fact that the Scotchman was as respectful to her as to the most important of Rahanda-bed’s guests.

To the other domestics, being only the hired “ companion ” of their mistress, she was little better than an upper servant, and they treated her accordingly.

To the Scotchman, then, she applied for assistance in finding a temporary home for the French girl, and he, having friends, and even kin, living in the village of C——, promised to obtain a place for her immediately.

“ And there is nae need yet of the siller, Miss Edgar,”

responding to her offer of her purse ; "I ken there won't be muckle charge."

But she insisted, and he reluctantly accepted, and shortly after the three hours which Mrs. Doloran had allowed for the departure of Josephine, the girl found herself in the comfortable, though exceedingly plain little home of an elderly widow, whose only a child, a daughter, was at service with a wealthy family in the village. Whether Macgilivray knew the story which for a fortnight or more had been the theme of servant gossip, as well as of secret parlor talk, or whether he believed what Ned had simply told him, that the French girl had been summarily dismissed, and having no means and no home to which to go, was in distress for immediate shelter, she did not know, nor was she concerned to know ; but she was anxious to see the widow with whom Josephine would sojourn, feeling that, should the woman, when she knew the circumstances, object to furnish more than the most temporary home to the girl, at least she might advise something to be done in the case. So she called upon the widow that very evening, and found, to her unexpected satisfaction, a simple, homely, but good-hearted old Scotchwoman, who said, when Ned had told her all the circumstances :

"I kent well what was the matter, though Donald said never a word when he brought her here, only that the auld hornie had gotten as usual into his leddy, and made her drive this puir child out frae hame all in a minit. Its an ill wife that 'd noo do a gude turn to a puir lassie like her. Nae, Miss, she is welcome to a home here if she leeks it well eneuch to bide wi' an auld Scotch body leek me, an' I haud sense enough to hauld me tongue about her to the neebors. They'll be wanderin' an' talkin', but I'll jist say it's a freend o' me ain come to bide wi' me."

Thus was Josephine provided for through Ned's instrumentality, who little dreamed that in so short a time she would be herself in need of home, and as in the village of C—— the French girl had found so providential a shelter, why should not she find one also? And though the home of the widow was scarcely large enough to give her accommodation, still Macgilivray had other friends who might be induced to accept her as a boarder until she should give her friends in Albany timely warning.

And Macgilivray, though unable to control his surprise at her departure, was as prompt in promising to obtain an abode for her as he had been for Josephine, though he coupled his promise with an apology for the plainness of the home offered, at which Ned smiled, wondering what he would think of the plainness of the mountain home of her childhood.

"And are you sure I can go there immediately? I want to leave Rahandabed within an hour," she asked.

"There's nae doubt of it," he answered, "for they're glad enough to take a boarder or twa in the summer, and they haena noo objection to ain in the winter. But I'm sair troubled aboot the takin' o' you there mysel. You see, me leddy gart me drive some of the guests doon to the village as syne as lunch 'd be finished, and that puts a stoppit to me endeevor for you. But dinna greit," as he saw a shade come over Ned's face, "I'll tell Jim Slade (an under coachman of Rahandabed) where to bring you, and to tell the folk anent you. When they ken that I sent you they'll be civil eneuch, for they're me ain cousins."

Ned, with a relieved mind, returned to her room to complete her preparations, and when she was cloaked and bonnetted for departure, she sought Mrs. Doloran. That lady assumed a dignified pride and composure.

"I have come to say good-by," said the girl, her voice trembling a little.

"Oh, have you? Then you are determined upon going," was the coldly spoken reply; "and I suppose you have come also to ask for a recommendation. I assure you beforehand that I shall only recommend you for an unbearable temper and whimsical fits that make you turn the most harmless things into crimes." Her rage and chagrin at Ned's determination to go were now beyond all control, and she spurted out the first insulting words that came to her mind.

"I did not intend to ask you for a recommendation," the girl replied, her voice and face showing, in spite of her efforts to control herself, how she was stung and angered.

"I only came in a spirit of common Christian charity to see you before I left you forever."

"And I, in a spirit of common Christian charity," mimicking Ned's tones, "will order your wages paid before you go, though it is not customary with a *hired person*," the emphasis stingingly long and marked on the last two words, "to pay anything when the departure is as abrupt and impertinent as yours is."

"I have not asked for your wages," broke from Ned, now trembling from head to foot with suppressed indignation, "nor do I wish for any; and lest I should forget entirely the spirit in which I entered your presence, I shall say at once to you good-by."

And turning about, she went hastily from the room, leaving Mrs. Doloran a prey to the most violent rage. She had not intended nor expected that Ned would keep her word and really go away from Rahandabed, nor did she mean that it should be so even now; but her pride was too great to permit her to take any steps to the contrary just yet.

She would let Ned depart, but she would take pains to ascertain where she was going, and in a day or two she would send for her.

And with that resolution she hastened to find Ordotte.

"What!" he said, his tawny face showing greater dismay than it had ever expressed before in Mrs. Doloran's presence.

"You have actually let Miss Edgar go?"

"What could I do?" deprecatingly. "She would insist upon misunderstanding something I had said, and nothing would keep her after that."

Ordotte looked at her in a disagreeably searching

way that she peevishly avowed made her shiver, but he did not reply immediately. Probably he guessed better than the lady intended he should do, the cause of Ned's reported misunderstanding. When he did answer it was only to say quietly:

"Miss Edgar *must* return."

XXXIV.

Edna Edgar was happy. Her father each day declared himself better pleased with young Carnew, who seemed to enjoy Weewald Place with a heartiness that he rarely showed in Rahandabed.

His eyes glistened with pleasure over the rare objects of art that Mr. Edgar displayed with the pride of a connoisseur, and his dark cheeks sometimes glowed with color as he took his own animated part in interesting discussions with the well-read gentleman.

To Edna, as became the esteemed guest of her father, he paid the most delicate attention, but nothing that could be construed into any warmer feeling. Yet, she so interpreted every action on his part. She loved him as even in her brief, youthful infatuation she had never loved Mackay, and for a tithe of love in return she would have put her passionate, wayward heart under his feet.

In the solitude of her own chamber at night, when the ardor of her emotions banished sleep, she reflected upon his conduct to herself during the day, she took comfort and assurance from the fact that it was not his nature to be demonstrative, perhaps, not even to show up to the very moment of proposing for a lady's hand, any strong desire to possess the same. His attentions to her certainly were marked, and she was confident that before the end of his stay he would speak to her father.

For Alan—he was utterly innocent and unsuspicious of the feelings with which the daughter of his host regarded him ; did he dream of them, he would that moment, with becoming thanks for the courtesy that had been shown him, have shaken from his feet the dust of Wee-wald Place. One face alone had taken possession of his heart, and do what he would in the way of calling frequently to his mind all the adverse things he had heard of her, Ned's image retained its place. Often when he seemed to be most attentive to Edna, it was be-cause of her physical resemblance to Ned. One day that Mr. Edgar had taken him to inspect some very old pictures, and to ask his advise about having them retouched, he paused on their return before the door of a room next to his own apartment.

"Edna has not shown you this, I presume," he said. "I requested her not to do so."

"No, she has not," answered Carnew.

Edgar threw open the door. It was a small apart-ment, fitted up like a lady's *boudoir*, and having in the centre an easel, the front of which was covered with silken drapery. He threw aside the drapery, and re-vealed an exquisitely painted head and face of a lady. Carnew started, for it was such an exact likeness of Ned. As he looked longer, the resemblance to Edna came out, but neither so strong nor so startling as the resemblance to Ned.

"Whom do you think it is like?" asked Edgar in a tremulous whisper.

"Like Miss Edgar, who is Mrs. Doloran's companion," replied Carnew.

"You are mistaken, sir; it is an exact likeness of my daughter."

And the voice of the gentleman, before low and trem-ulous, was now loud and decidedly angry. Carnew turned to him in astonishment, at which Mr. Edgar seemed to recover himself, for he resumed in his natural tones:

"That, Mr. Carnew, is the portrait of my wife, painted when she was the age which my daughter is now. I have detected, or fancied that I have detected "—his voice sank a little— "a marked resemblance between it and my daughter. I requested Edna to leave it to me to

bring you here that I might hear you exclaim on your
first sight of it, how like it was to her. But I am disappointed, Mr. Carnew."

"Not entirely, Mr. Edgar," Alan hastened to say,
"for I can assure you that it does bear a marked resemblance to your daughter; the features are certainly an
exact reproduction of Miss Edgar's. It is the expression which is so striking a reminder of the young lady
with my aunt."

"We will go, Mr. Carnew."

He dropped the silken hanging, and taking Alan's arm,
turned from the room. But some strange mood had
seized him; instead of leaving the young man as it was
his wont to do when they had been, as they were this
morning, a couple of hours together, he still clung to him,
even when they reached the library, and after a moment's
hesitation, as if he were arguing with himself, he requested
him to enter.

"You will think me a strange man, Mr. Carnew," he
began, talking rapidly, as if to hide some emotion, "but
even at this distance of time, with twenty-two years
stretching their gap between us, I cannot look at the picture of my wife without feeling the old pain of loss,
the old keen yearning to behold her once more. That is
why I wish so wildly my daughter to resemble her, and
I only visit that portrait at intervals of months, that I
may trace the resemblance more assuringly, and that I
may save myself the pangs which come at every sight of
her pictured face. I love my daughter with greater
strength of affection perhaps, than many fathers love
their children. She is my only one, and as such I cannot bear to contemplate a day arriving when she may be
taken from me, when her love and her virtues may have
to grace a distant home, and her father be left to a childless solitude. But, even in such a contemplation, could
I be sure that he who may gain her hand would be worthy
of her heart, I might not look forward with such dread.
All this is strange to you, Mr. Carnew, but young and

unmarried though you are, still you can sympathize with the feelings of a father, and that father the father of an only child."

Alan bowed, wondering at Mr. Alan's unusual communicativeness, but having no suspicion of what further he was destined to hear.

" To know that Edna had given her heart to one whom I approved, and to one whom, judging from his natural kindness, would be content to make his home with father and daughter rather than separate them, such a prospect would make my old age indeed happy."

He paused, and looked with piercing earnestness into the face of his companion; but the latter still suspected not an inkling of the truth.

Both had been standing all the while; Mr. Edgar, too much engrossed by his own emotions to think of seating himself or of inviting his guest to do so, and Carnew, too much astonished and interested to think of another position than the one he had first assumed—standing by the library table.

And when that piercing look elicited nothing from the young man beyond the curious and interested face he already wore, Edgar went close to him; he put his hand on Alan's arm—a hand that trembled visibly—and said with a tremor which he tried desperately, but without success, to keep out of his voice:

" Mr. Carnew, I was once a lover myself. I can read the signs. You are in love with Edna, and you are the one I would choose for her—her heart she herself will give you, but her hand I can promise you."

Had Carnew been stabbed suddenly in some vital part he could hardly have been more shocked, or pained. Edgar's words were so unexpected and so undesired; then, how to tell this father that his only child was not beloved as the father's heart desired her to be. Oh ! it was hard. The color surged into his cheeks, and his own voice trembled a little :

" Mr. Edgar, I am sensible of, and I deeply appreciate

the honor you would do me; but it has surprised me, and all the more, that I have not been conscious of giving any encouragement for such an offer upon your part. My affections are pre-engaged."

"Pre-engaged!" It was the only word he could utter, so choked was he by disappointment and something even like resentment. But in a moment he recovered himself, and resuming that courtesy which he rarely long forgot, and with which he could mask every emotion, he seized Alan's hand and said:

"Forget, Mr. Carnew, that I have so far violated my duties of host as to speak to you upon such a subject; with that kindness with which I have already credited you, attribute it to a father's weakness. As Edna knew nothing of my intention, and indeed it was sudden and unpremeditated upon my own part, your friendly relations with her need not be affected."

And wringing Alan's hand, he turned to leave the room; but the young man called him, impelled by what sudden feeling to do so he himself could hardly tell, and looking strangely embarrassed when the gentleman turned at the summons.

"Mr. Edgar, as you have honored me by an unexpected confidence, so am I impelled to confide in you. When I announced to you that my affections were pre-engaged, I felt that I should also have told you to whom; the more particularly, that you have had at some time an interest in the young lady—Miss Edgar, who is the companion of my aunt."

Edgar became so rigid that he seemed to be rooted to the spot on which he stood, while his face paled, until it looked positively ghastly. It was on his lips to say:

"I cannot congratulate you on your choice;" but even in that moment of, to him, bitter agony, he restrained himself, actuated by a dictate of charity. Why should he blight by a word the prospect of his niece, unworthy and ungrateful though he deemed her to be? Besides, it would be the keener revenge to let Carnew, who had slighted an offer and affections every way worthy of him, fall into the trap he had himself prepared—let him marry Ned if he would. She had goaded Mackay to his death; she would probably break Carnew's heart when he came to know her true character.

"You do not speak," said Alan, unable longer to control his suspense, "and yet you have had some opportunity of learning Miss Edgar's character. To me she seems to possess virtues the most estimable."

"And it is not for me to disabuse you of your opinion," was the reply; "any interest which I may have felt in Miss Edgar, the 'companion' of your aunt, has completely ceased." He bowed and left the room.

Alan flushed, and unhappy paced the apartment. His stay now in Weewald Place must come to an immediate close; he even shrank from seeing Edna again—given to understand, as he was by her father, that she was not unwilling to yield to him her heart, he bitterly reproached himself for having accepted the invitation to Weewald Place. He had done it, he had to acknowledge to his secret soul, that he might be distracted from his persistent thoughts of Ned; and the result was, that her very absence threw a charm about her which was more potent than ever. Oh, that he could forget her! Now, when even Mr. Edgar, who was once her protector and her best friend, refused to say a word in her favor, that he could believe her to be unworthy of his regard; but up came the sad, gentle, lovely face, and he covered his own face with his hands and groaned.

Mr. Edgar deemed it best that his daughter should know at once what had passed between himself and his guest; he was all the more anxious to tell her in order to learn how deeply her affections had been won. And he sought her on leaving Carnew.

She bore the communication with an unexpected heroism; her pride was so great that not even to her father would she admit her suffering, and though she paled a little, and bit her lip until the blood wellnigh came, immediately after that, she laughed, and flinging her arms about him, more to prevent him from discovering her real feelings than through affection, she said :

"As good fish in the sea, papa, as ever were caught. If Mr. Carnew won't take me, Mr. Brekbellew will—you remember how devoted *he* was."

An expression of disgust crossed Mr. Edgar's features.

"Mr. Brekbellew is so contemptuously beneath your notice, my love, that I do not like to hear you mention his name even in jest."

"Very well, papa, I won't," caressing his hair, and letting her cool white fingers rest upon his hot forehead.

But in solitude Edna's heroism completely disappeared. She laid her head on her dressing-table and shed the most bitter and angry tears she had ever shed in her life. By what covert charms had her cousin succeeded where her own more exquisite beauty and accomplishments had failed? How she hated her. If one little word of hers could have averted from Ned the direst evil, she would not have spoken it. Rather would she have crushed her if she could, and then she sought to think what means were in her power of preventing Carnew's marriage with her. But she dared say no more evil of Ned than the insinuations she had already artfully made, lest all might recoil upon her own head. Could she have looked but a little way into the future, she would have beheld her revenge—a revenge awful enough to win even from her pitiless heart a cry of horror.

XXXV.

Carnew took his leave of Weewald Place with the best grace he could assume; and he found himself back in O—— just four weeks after his departure thence. He had not sent any word to his aunt, preferring to come upon her as suddenly as he had left her, and thus he was surprised to find Macgilivray with one of the Rahandabed carriages at the station when he stepped from the train.

"Not waiting for me, Donald, surely," he said, when he had returned the Scotchman's glad and respectful greeting.

"Nae, Mr. Carnew; me leddy sent me for visitors that's expected frae this train; but they're noo comin', as I ken," Carnew and another gentleman being the only passengers to alight from the car.

"I'll take the place of the visitors," said Alan, stepping into the carriage.

"Aye, an' mair welcome," responded the Scotchman half to himself.

"How are they all at the house?" resumed the young man.

"They're a' weel but me leddy hersel'; she's a maist daft since Miss Ned's awa'."

"Since Miss Ned's away! What do you mean?" And the young man paused in the act of comfortably adjusting his cushions, and almost glowered at the coachman.

Macgilivray's honest face wore a shade of sorrow.

"I thoucht it vera likely that you'd noo ken hoo it happened," and out of the fulness of his sympathizing heart he told Ned's story, Carnew taking his seat on the box beside him the better to hear. Donald had heard the account of her summary dismissal from Mrs. Doloran's maid, who had been an unintentional listener to the stormy interview between that lady and her "companion," when the latter announced her intention of leaving Rahandabed. He knew from servant gossip long before the unhappy tale of Josephine, and he had been told by the old Scotch wife, with whom Josephine abode, of Ned's constant charity to the unfortunate girl, so that he was sufficiently informed to give Carnew all particulars; and he did so in his homely fashion. Carnew listened with that tell-tale color that never came only when excited by strong emotions, and even with labored breath.

"And Miss Ned is now boarding here in C——, you say?" he asked, when Macgilivray had finished.

"Yes, she's wi' kinspeople o' me ain, and vera weel treated, she says hersel'."

"Drive me back to the village, Donald, to the hotel; I shall stay there for a few days; and tell me where Miss Ned is stopping. On your return to Rahandabed, say nothing of having met me."

"Dinna fear, sir; I kent hoo to keep me ain counsel this mony a day."

In his room in the hotel, Carnew was almost exultant. To have that about Ned which had so pained him in his aunt's letter quite disproved, as it was disproved by Macgilivray's story that gave the substance, if not the precise language, of Ned's denial of Mrs. Doloran's charge, and to hear of her tender charity to an erring one of her own sex, were like vindications of her character from Heaven itself. How could he longer do violence to his own heart by stifling his affection for one who evinced such admirable qualities? Her very spirit in leaving his aunt endeared her to him. What though there were some secret passages in her life in which she coquetted with affections, and perhaps even broke a heart—what woman was entirely free from the weakness of her sex? And to one who had such estimable virtues as Ned showed, surely much might be pardoned. Besides, she was more of a woman now, and increasing years in such a character as hers must develop unusual strength and steadiness. Thus did he reason with himself, and not until he was in the very flush of joy from his arguments did the ugly thought of Dykard Dutton come, the young man whom he had once met, and to whom he had seen Ned's letters addressed. Somehow, of late, in thinking of Ned, there had not intruded any thought of Dutton, her possible lover; it was only Ned herself, pure, simple, free, as Carnew's heart longed for her. Now, however, when he had worked himself into an enthusiasm about her virtues, Dutton's image rose up as if to forbid it; rose up with that honest, manly, *brave* look that had won such involuntary respect from Carnew on the night of their brief meeting. The remembrance of the joy she showed in his company that night, the money she had once sent him, but which had been so promptly returned, her letters to him—all came before him now in a most tantalizing manner. His joy was dampened, but even in the midst of his depression his kindly nature asserted itself. For the noble traits she had shown she deserved to be made happy, though her happiness should be bestowed only through his pangs. He would learn what prevented or delayed her marriage to Dutton; and if it were poverty, he would sweep away the obstacle. Thus resolved, he took his way to the address which Macgilivray had given him.

Ned had found such a comfortable home with Macgilivray's simple kinspeople, that she deemed it as well not to think of Albany for the present. Here she could, at least, without doing violence to anybody's feelings, pay her way; and why might she not remain thus until spring, when Dyke seemed so certain of being able to procure another situation for her? She need not even tell him, nor Meg, of her change, for it would cause them so much anxiety, and probably even bring Dyke from his business to see her.

Jim Slade, who had driven her from Rahandabed, was compelled to disclose her whereabouts the very same evening to Ordotte, for that gentleman had been indefatigable in his inquiries among the servants, until he ascertained who had driven the young lady to the village; and before Ned retired to rest that night, she was the recipient of a half-sharp, half-penitent note from Mrs. Doloran, asking her to return. The note was written in accordance with Ordotte's request. The reply was kind and respectful, but in it Ned firmly declined ever to go back to Rahandabed. Ordotte was dismayed, while Mrs. Doloran was furious, and the man who brought her that message owed it to his skill in evading a blow that his head was not broken with a small, but costly alabaster vase. The ornament shivered into fragments almost at his feet.

She sent again the next day, and the third day; by Ordotte's advice, she deigned to go herself in her most pompous state with her liveried lacqueys, which fashion she had copied, but grotesquely, as she copied everything else from abroad, and she almost overpowered the good people into whose simple little home she entered. But she was well known by reputation, her eccentricities being a frequent theme of conversation in nearly every house in C——.

Ned met her kindly, but as firmly as when she parted from her.

"And so you absolutely refuse all my overtures?" said Mrs. Doloran, the half-entreating air with which she had first spoken entirely disappearing, and a very angry one coming rapidly in its place.

"I think it is best for both of us," was the gentle reply, "that I should not return to Rahandabed."

"And what am I to tell Alan?" in her anger raising her voice as if she were at home.

"Since you accused me before of misrepresenting you, I refrained from writing to him of your unkind and ungrateful departure."

"I trust that it has been neither unkind nor ungrateful," was the response, "and if your own heart, Mrs. Doloran, does not prompt you to tell exactly why I left your service, then certainly nothing that I can say will avail."

Exasperated by the gentle firmness which neither entreaty, nor insult, nor threat could move, Mrs. Doloran screamed rather than said:

"Your audacity is only equalled by your impertinence, and I shall tell Alan how fortunate I am to be rid of you. You are a viper biting the hand that fed you."

"Mrs. Doloran," in a voice so full of indignant agony that it sounded hoarse and strange; but Mrs. Doloran flounced out of the room, her heavy-trailing silk dress making an alarming rustle, and out to her carriage without even a word to the amazed folk of the house. They had all heard the loud and angry tones, and knowing something of Ned's story from Macgilivray, and much of Mrs. Doloran's temper from the same source, all their sympathies went out to the young girl whom already, from her gentle, kindly ways they had learned to like.

Ordotte was more disappointed at Ned's refusal to return than he thought it prudent to express to the widow, and with similar prudence he refrained from telling her that he intended to have a watch kept upon Ned, lest she should leave without his knowledge.

Mrs. Doloran did not write to her nephew of Ned's departure; she knew, no matter what her version might be, that he would attribute the fault to her, and she preferred to wait his return, and answer his questions about Ned in her own sarcastic way.

XXXVI.

Ned, never dreaming of another visitor in her little quiet home, felt her breath almost taken away by the announcement one afternoon that a gentleman wished to see her. Could it be Dyke, was her first thought, and how did he get her present address? But a moment's reflection solved the latter query, as he could have ascertained it easily in Rahandabed. It must be he, she thought, with violently palpitating heart and some trouble perhaps, had brought him.

She hurried to the little parlor to meet, not Dyke, but handsome, flushed, gentlemanly Carnew. She was speechless from surprise.

"Miss Edgar," he said, almost tenderly, as he approached her with extended hand, "I have only to-day returned to C——, and learning, while on my way to Rahandabed, that you had left my aunt, I could not go on without seeing you."

She blushed brightly and answered:

"How kind of you, Mr. Carnew."

He shook his head disclaimingly.

"Hardly so kind as I might have been. I might have forborne my visit and remained at home to have protected you from my whimsical aunt. I have learned all about it, you see, though not from the lady I have just mentioned. Sit down," leading her to a chair, and seating himself near her, "and permit me to speak to you in a very frank, brotherly manner."

She could not conceal her surprise. Mr. Carnew's manner was so different from what it used to be. He was almost like Dyke in the kindly, protecting air he had assumed—he who had been so reserved—and she lifted her wide, clear eyes in a manner that showed her wonder, and also her pleasure. He smiled and continued:

"Will you give me the right of a friend, Miss Edgar, to question you upon your circumstances, what means you have of living now, out of position as you are, what you intend to do in the future?"

"I am not in any want," she answered, smiling back at him. "Mrs. Doloran's compensation for my poor services has been so ample as to place me beyond reach of need for some time to come. Regarding the future, I think I shall be able to secure another position in the spring."

"Another position! Do you mean that you will hire yourself out again as a lady's companion?"

"Yes," with a smile that was almost a laugh.

"Miss Edgar, may I be *very* frank, even to the verge of impertinence?"

"As frank as you please, Mr. Carnew," wondering what he wanted to know.

"I have sometimes thought that you were engaged to be married"— she started, and he regarded her emotion as one of astonishment that he had guessed her secret so well— "but that want of means prevented an immediate fulfilment of the contract; if such be the case, it will be my delight to remove the obstacle, to give to Mr. Dutton and yourself——" he could get no further, for she had risen to her feet, and exclaimed in an amazed, perplexed way :

"Mr. Dutton! Who said I was engaged to be married to him?" It was Mr. Carnew's turn to be confused. He also rose.

"Pardon me, Miss Edgar; no one has ever said a word to me about it; I surmised such to be the case from the devotion you seemed to show him."

"Poor Dyke!" said Ned, her voice very tremulous, "he is my brother, the dearest, truest, best friend I have, but not my lover;" and then with her eyes swimming, and her cheeks flushing until the color mounted to her forehead, she told the tale of her childhood; all Dyke's fatherly care of her, Meg's motherly tenderness, and all about the little mountain home which she loved so well. Her own deeply stirrred feelings made her eloquent, and never, Alan thought, had she looked so beautiful. Her love of and gratitude to these simple people was another virtue in her most estimable character, and when she had finished, unable to restrain longer the confession of his heart, he said, almost as tremulously as she herself had spoken :

"Since you are not engaged, may *I* sue for your hand? My heart is already yours."

Had she heard aright? Had he whom she loved so well, actually proposed to her? Was it true, then, that he had not gone to offer himself to Edna, but that he really loved *her?* Heaven was too kind, and with a gasp that was almost a sob, she put her hands into his so appealingly outstretched, and with a great, glad thrill of delight, he knew that he was answered.

"But your aunt," she said, when the violence of her emotion having passed, she was able to look up and to speak calmly.

Carnew felt like uttering some very profane exclamation in connection with his relative, but he repressed it and said instead :

"As I am quite of age and have ample means in my

own right, I do not know that my aunt will have any authority in this matter. I shall announce my engagement to her to-day, and I shall have preparations made for receiving you at Rahandabed."

"Oh, no!" she shudderingly responded, "after all that has passed between Mrs. Doloran and myself I cannot meet her."

" As my affianced, Ned, you will have nothing to fear. You will find Mrs. Doloran, the lady to whom you were companion, and Mrs. Doloran, the aunt of the party to whom you are engaged to be married, two very different persons. Also, my pride will not be satisfied unless the guests of Rahandabed receive you as an equal, which they will only be too well pleased to do now. They have had the pleasure of slighting you; I want them to have the agony of receiving you."

Thus he argued down every objection she interposed, and he was so lovingly firm about it that she was obliged to yield. When he left her she promised to be ready to accompany him to Rahandabed the next morning.

And when he left her she went up to her room and cried from very joy. Her happiness was so unexpected, so great. Then she wrote to Dyke a full account of everything that had happened, and a whole page filled with her own blissful feelings. Her pen seemed to dance over the paper, and she could have filled another sheet, but that she had some mercy on Dyke's eyes and time. She closed it with:

" I know, dear Dyke, all this will make you as happy as it has made me, and that you will give your choicest blessing to your   " Own Ned."

Dyke received that letter in the midst of one of his busy days; still he could have snatched a few moments for its perusal, but he only pressed it secretly to his lips and put it into his bosom. He preferred to read it in the solitude of his own room that evening when he could drink in all by himself the pleasure, the bliss which her letters gave him.   And that day something most unexpected came to him.

The head of the firm sought him, and offered him a partnership in the business.

"We have watched you closely, Mr. Dutton," he said, "and we have observed in you business faculties most valuable, but most rare. They will stand to us in the place of money you would otherwise have to give, and they will be of equal assistance to the firm."

Dutton went home with an elastic step.   Now would he be able to provide well for Ned without even waiting for the spring.   He could bring both her and Meg to New York for the remainder of the winter, and in the summer he could have the little mountain home improved into a pretty country residence.   He would have means for all that now.   Thus delightedly planning, he was in too high spirits to delay long at his supper, and he hurried to his room to read his precious letter.

After one perusal it fell from his hand, and his head dropped forward on the little table beside which he sat. What an agony shook him !   It seemed as if his heart would burst in that wave of sorrow.   And for the first fierce moments his soul cried out against fate, which ever seemed determined to snatch joy from him just as it was within his grasp.   Then his manhood returned ; that true manhood which is brave in adversity and disappointment. He called up all his own hopes and wishes for Ned, that she might be a lady, mingling in the society which she was so well fitted to adorn ; here was the fulfilment of all his wishes ; surely he ought to rejoice.   And he tried to do so, but his heart ached in the effort, and his temples throbbed with agony. Ned had been so dear, so *constantly* cherished.   He took out from a secret recess the packet of her letters ; every letter she had ever written to him, from the first childish epistle that she sent from school. He opened them one by one, and read them all. Then he folded them again, and tied them in their old position, adding the one he had that day received, and put them back.

How could he write to her with his heart so blistered? How could he congratulate her on a happiness that was his own death-blow? And for a little his head fell forward again on the table, and he yielded to his agony. But in it there was no reproach of Ned. He knew now that she had not understood any of his letters, and that she had never dreamed of his lover-like affection.

He looked up at last, the fiercest of his feelings conquered; and with a trembling hand he sought his writing materials. She never dreamed when she received that true, tender answer to her own letter, in what agony it had been penned; she did not even dream that the blister upon her own name was caused by Dyke's tear. She pressed the letter to her lips and to her heart, for it was so tender and so good; but even *she* did not know how self-sacrificing, how noble was the writer.

XXXVII.

Mrs. Doloran went into hysterics when told by her nephew of his intention to make, not Edna, but determined, impertinent Ned, his bride; her own peculiar hysterics, that threw the whole house into a confusion, and demanded fast and furious attention from those about her. She kicked with her feet, and worked with her hands, and jerked with her head, to the imminent danger of all in her vicinity, and then she paused long enough to stigmatize Alan for his ingratitude, and to predict for him dire unhappiness in his choice of a wife, after which she laughed and cried in a breath, and then resumed her violent contortions.

Everybody in the house, from the latest guest to the newest servant, heard in a very short time the cause of the commotion made by Mrs. Doloran, for gossiping tongues were plenty to repeat all that the mistress of Rahandabed said in her foolish temper; and consternation, disappointment, and envy, and even something like dismay actuated the hearts of most of the feminine guests, especially those who had treated Ned only as a hired companion.

Carnew knew his aunt so well that he was not unprepared for such a scene, and he retired to his own apartment until she should be in a more rational condition.

"Mascar, where are you, and where am I?" when her temper brought no result save the disappearance of Alan, and an array of attendants, and she raised her head from the couch to which, with main strength, she had been borne, and she affected to speak with so much feebleness that it was extremely ludicrous.

"Here, Mrs. Doloran," and Ordotte showed himself from a corner of the room, whither he had taken refuge until her pugilistic efforts should cease.

"Won't you give me my salts and find my fan, and arrange this cushion—I am so exhausted," and back went the head with feigned helplessness, while her maid stood aside to let the gentleman obey the many behests. But she opened her eyes and said, as if she were delivering her last will and testament :

"Does not your heart bleed for me, Mascar? Well has the poet said, ' Better is a serpent's tooth, than a thankful child.' " In her various emotions she was not conscious how she had twisted the quotation. "And what have I not done for him? Brought him up, and loved him as if he was my own son. Oh, my sorrows are greater than I can bear."

And again the eyes were closed, and the whole attitude that of one about to faint. With perfect gravity, Ordotte motioned the maid to attend her mistress while he surveyed the scene from a little distance. As soon as she pretended to recover he was at her side.

She sat up, trying to appear very weak, and very much of a martyr; her voice was most languishing as she bade her maid retire to the adjoining room, and as she again addressed Ordotte :

"You have not delivered *your* opinion of Alan's shameful conduct."

Ordotte stroked his mustache once or twice, and then answered quietly :

"*My* opinion is, that Mr. Carnew has shown excellent judgment in his choice of a wife. Miss Ned is a young lady quite worthy of becoming your niece."

"Mascar !"

She fairly shrieked his name, every trace of her pretended weakness gone. She was even sitting bolt upright, her hand clutching his arm.

"Think," she said in her high shrill voice, "Ned had to *earn her living;* I paid her for being my companion ! "

"And highly favored you were to get her to be your companion ; and working for one's living is rather to be commended. Come, Mrs. Doloran, be yourself again, and accept what can neither be controlled nor avoided. Alan will certainly marry this love of his, and if you continue to show your displeasure, you will drive him entirely from Rahandabed. I have heard you say that you loved him too well to give him up entirely ; besides, how the country will talk if you permit this rupture to be. Call your accustomed good sense to you, and receive Miss Ned. Accompany Alan when he goes for her, and my word for it, you will be much happier than by seeking to gain your ends in this manner."

But his arguments, weighty with her as they had been always heretofore, had to be repeated, and made still more forcible before she could bring herself this time to yield, and it was only when he had impressed upon her that Alan would have his way regardless of her, that she consented to send for her nephew. When she had thus consented, with her usual talent for quick transitions of feeling she became astonishingly changed, and Alan found her as ready to accede to his wishes as she was before opposed to them ; nay, even eager to hurry their fulfilment. She could scarcely wait until morning to go for Ned.

In the morning she insisted upon going in the same stylish equipage in which she had made her former call, and Alan, assured that she had the friendliest spirit, did not oppose her. He took his seat beside her without a word of remonstrance, and once more the good people with whom Ned sojourned were surprised by a visit from the wealthy and eccentric mistress of Rahandabed. · But this time, there were no loud and angry words from the lady to shock and amaze them, for she absolutely rushed at Ned and folded her in her ample arms in a way that took the girl's breath for a moment.

"You dear, charming, sly creature," she said, "never to let me know that you had won Alan's heart; but then Alan tells me you didn't know it yourself. And how mistaken I have been to think he loved that bewitching Edna. And Mascar speaks so beautifully of you. What have you done to win them all? And me! Can you ever forgive those dreadful things I said to you? But I didn't mean them, Ned; it was only my temper that spoke. See how good I shall be to you, now." And Ned was subjected to another uncomfortable hug, while Carnew looked on with an expression of such amusement that it came near evoking from Ned a burst of laughter.

Mrs. Doloran had actually worked herself into feeling all that she said. Hers was one of those shallow, emotional, though sometimes obstinate natures which may be easily turned, and she would continue to imagine that she had quite forgiven, and really liked Ned, while nothing occurred to lessen the esteem in which the young lady was held by Carnew or Ordotte.

So Ned was triumphantly re-established in Rahandabed; the guests fawned upon her, those who most slighted her being most forward in their attentions; the servants paid as much court to her as to Mrs. Doloran, and that lady fairly lavished attentions upon her. Indeed, Ned might be said to queen it in Rahandabed, and often she was so happy, she questioned the reality of it all. Carnew was most devoted, he rode with her, walked with her, and was by her side constantly in the evenings.

She bore her honors with a sweet, modest dignity; no one could detect an iota of pride or triumph in her manner; she was as gentle and simple and kind as in the old days, even insisting upon giving something of her old attendance to Mrs. Doloran, until Alan interposed.

"You are not a 'companion' in that sense of the word any longer," he said.

Sometimes Carnew yearned to ask about Mackay, for every word of what Edna had once said to him seemed to have been burned upon his brain; but as often he refrained from doing so. If she had been guilty of coquetry with him, a coquetry which had even sent him to his death, he did not, after all, want to know it, and if she were not, he would not for worlds pain her by letting her know that he had ever entertained such a suspicion. So he was silent on the subject, and she spoke only of the past as it referred to Dyke and Meg and her mountain home; she never spoke of Mr. Edgar, nor of her life in Weewald Place. It was such an unpleasant memory she could not bear to revert to it, and Carnew, divining her dislike to speak of it, would not intrude upon her silence by a single question.

She had not received any letter from Edna since Carnew's return from his visit to her father, so she felt that she might with impunity refrain from writing to her cousin. She was most reluctant to write, as her letter would have to contain an account of her engagement, and that might cause a pang to Edna.

The winter passed as never a winter since she was a child had passed to Ned before, for her life was so happy. Often, as the thought of Carnew's strong, true love thrilled her with delight, she exclaimed to herself:

"I am so happy; what have I done to deserve it?"

It was only the calm before the storm. A cup so bitter was to be ere long at her lips, that her worst enemies might look on aghast while she drank it.

XXXVIII.

In the second month of the spring Ned was to be married; a quiet ceremony performed in Rahandabed, followed by a wedding breakfast, after which the young couple were to take a brief trip to New York, Washington, and a few other prominent cities. In deference to his aunt, to whom Carnew was especially grateful for her kind treatment of his betrothed, he had agreed to make the trip thus short, but he intended to take his bride to Europe the ensuing winter.

And Dyke and Meg must be at the wedding; Ned sent the most loving letters to them, letters with affectionate postscripts appended by Carnew, entreating them to gratify her. But Meg was confined to bed from an attack of rheumatism that the doctor said would render her unable to travel for three months to come, and Dyke wrote in his tender, loving way that he could give no decided answer yet. She did not dream that his indecision came from the cowardice begotten of his love for her. He doubted if his heart could bear to see her given to another; whether his very manhood would not forsake him at the sight. He kissed her letter and put it away, but not with the packet of her former letters; those in some sense were more precious, more his own.

It became incumbent upon Ned to write at last to Edna, from whom she had not received a single line in all those months, in order to apprise her of her approaching wedding, and to write also to Mr. Edgar, which she did in her kindly way, thanking him for all that he had done for her, and asking him to forgive any annoyance or displeasure she had ever caused him.

What was her amazement to receive from Edna the following reply:

"MY DEAREST NED:—Can you imagine anything more singular? At the very instant I received your letter, I was about to write to you, to apprise you of *my* approaching wedding. Only, I shall be married at an earlier date, three weeks from to-morrow; yours will be three weeks later. My engagement has been very brief, and the ceremony will be quiet and hurried. We are going to Europe immediately after it, my husband and I; papa does not feel well enough to accompany us. But all this time, I declare, I have not told you who is to be the bridegroom. No less than our old friend, Mr. Brekbellew——"

Ned could read no further, for a moment, from astonishment. Brekbellew, who had been the butt of Rahandabed, he had only departed a month before; whose insipid conversation she had heard Edna frequently ridicule; who had nothing to recommend him save his wealth, and Edna surely had no need of that; could it be possible that she was about to give her heart and hand to that man? And how had her father's consent been won to such a union? She resumed the letter, but it explained nothing that so puzzled, and in some sense shocked her. It only said:

"You know how devoted the poor fellow used to be to me; I felt I must reward him. As our wedding is to be so quiet and hurried, I cannot invite you to be present at it; and as we shall leave in such haste, there will be no time to see you; but I know, my dear Ned, that you will give me your very best wishes, as I give you mine.

"Yours lovingly,　　　　　　　　　　EDNA."

A postscript stated that Mrs. Stafford had gone to England to make her permanent home there.

She also received an answer from Mr. Edgar, an answer that chilled her to the very soul—it was so coldly courteous. Miss Edgar having chosen to remove herself so completely from his authority or advice, he knew not why she should deem it necessary to ask his forgiveness for anything, or even to apprise him of her intended change in life. There was not the most remote allusion to his daughter's marriage, nor the slightest wish for Ned's happiness.

She crushed the letter in her hand, and thrust it into her pocket, with an uncontrollable feeling of anger and disappointment. This cold, aggravating man might surely, at such a time, have given her one kind word.

Edna's letter she showed to Carnew. He read it through without a word, and then he looked at her—a peculiarly amused and lingering look. For once, masculine wisdom had been greater than feminine astuteness; he divined, or imagined that he divined, the motives which prompted Edna's hurried and ill-matched marriage—*pique* at her disappointment in securing a more eligible offer, and ambition to be married before Ned should be. But seeing that his guileless companion had no such thoughts, he did not tell her what his own were, but returned the letter to her with a broader smile still, and a hope that Edna would be happy. She was on the point of showing him Mr. Edgar's letter also, but she refrained, thinking that, if she did, it would make Carnew dislike him; and since she owed her education and her home, for a part of her life, to the gentleman, she could not bear, in common gratitude, to diminish any friendship he might have won.

That same afternoon, Macgilivray brought a message to her from Josephine.

She's scarcely a' there," said the honest, sympathizing fellow, his expressive Scotch way of putting that her mind was not right, "an' the doctor says she'll dinna last till morning. She's sair tribbled, Miss Ned, an' she's ca'd mony times for you. Perhaps you wad nae min' gang to the puir creature."

Of course, Ned did not mind; she even gave up her afternoon ride with Alan, leaving a little note of excuse for him lest, did she tell him, he might object to her visiting Josephine just then. He had already demurred at the frequency of her visits to the girl, signifying his readiness to provide for the unfortunate creature in every other way than in allowing her any of the society of his intended. He could not bear the thought of his pure, lovely betrothed sitting at the bedside of that erring woman. But the erring woman was soothed and benefited by Ned's visit to such a degree that the old Scotch wife, with whom she stayed, regarded the young lady as little less than an angel; and Ned's own tender charity disposed her to minister, in whatever way she could, to the comfort of Josephine, even to the verge of offending Carnew. But, generally her plea for the poor girl won him, and he so far yielded as not to forbid her visits.

The secret that the poor French girl so well kept, not even telling it to Ned, preyed upon her with bitter effect. It made her ill, and sent her to her bed before even the birth of her child. For days she lay there, silent and uncomplaining, until the strain went to her brain, and she was "not a' there," as Macgilivray had expressed it. Then she called for "Mademoiselle" Ned; it was the one name upon her lips all that night and all the next morning, and the Scotch wife watched for Macgilivray when he drove to the village, which he did every day, either with or for guests, in order to ask him to tell the young lady.

When Ned arrived at the little cottage, she found all in commotion. Josephine's baby had been born two hours before, but still-born, and the young mother would hardly live through the night, the doctor said. But she was quite herself, with a consciousness of and a resignation to her circumstances almost touching. She asked for "Mademoiselle," begging that she might be sent for; and when informed that Macgilivray had promised to tell the young lady, tears of gladness and relief came into her eyes. When Ned came, she extended both of her thin hands to greet her:

"The doctor has told me that I will not live," she said, "and I would be so glad, only for my poor little sister— she has no one"——tears prevented her speaking, and she covered her face with her hands and let her tears have their way through her wan white fingers.

"I shall see to her," said Ned, "always see to her;

only yesterday Mr. Carnew paid her school bill a year in advance, and he has told the managers of the institute to draw upon him for all her expenses."

"O mademoiselle, how can I thank you? What have you not done for me; you are an angel. If the blessing of a poor, sinful creature like me can be of any use, you have it; but God will bless you."

She covered Ned's hands with kisses, and shed her happy tears upon them.

"They told you about my baby," she resumed, "didn't they? And how glad I am that it is dead; for, poor little one, what would it do? Draw your chair closer, mademoiselle, for I want to say something very secret. I want to tell you, you who have been so good to me, and now that I am dying, who the father of my child is; but you must promise me not to tell any one, for I love him, and I want to show my love of him by going down to my grave without giving his name to any but you. It is—" with a sort of gasp in uttering the words, "Harry Brekbellow."

Ned gave a violent start, and for a moment she became as pale as the poor sick creature beneath her.

"You are surprised, mademoiselle; you did not dream of him, for he never looked at me before anybody; but we met many times when there was no one to see, and he told me how he loved me from the first time I came to the house; and I grew to love him, until now, mademoiselle, even now, I love him so much I cannot say one word against him."

"But he has wronged you so," burst from Ned; "he has deserted you when it was his duty to marry you."

"I shall be soon gone, mademoiselle, and as my child is dead it makes no difference."

"But it will be *my* duty to speak of this," said Ned, her face very pale still.

"Oh, no, mademoiselle!" and she tried to raise herself in the bed in order to make her entreaty more effectual, "I could not die if his name were told."

There was but one course for Ned to pursue; to tell the dying girl that Breakbellew was about to be married, and that it would be criminal not to reveal his character to the lady he would marry. Her very soul shrank from the task, for she feared the shock it would give to her who "loved too well," but it was the only way to win her consent to the revelation of his name. And in the interest of justice, for the sake of Edna, whom she imagined as having full trust, at least in Brekbellew's upright character, it seemed to be her duty to do so. She stooped down and told it as gently as she could.

But all her gentleness did not temper the shock. Josephine could bear his heartless desertion in her hour of trouble, his cruel forgetfulness, for she was still buoyed with the hope that her devotion to him in the matter of not revealing his name would touch him, and that her very death would cause him to have a tender memory of her; but to hear that he was about to marry, proved so conclusively that he no longer cared in the least for her; indeed, that he had flung away all recollection of her, that every vestige of the slender hope that had animated her, fled.

" O mademoiselle!" she said, taking in her hot grasp both of Ned's hands, " that is the last pain. You can tell the lady his name, for my heart has broken now."

It seemed so, for relinquishing Ned's hands she turned her face to the wall with a great sigh, and she did not speak again. The young lady waited a long time, and the old Scotch wife came in and leaned over her.

" She's amaist awa'," she said, nodding her head at Ned. " She'll noo bide till night."

Her words came true, for, even as she spoke, there was a motion of the head on the pillow, a swift, upward opening of the eyes for a second, a gasp, and all was over.

XXXIX.

Ned was so pained and distressed, and even shocked by all the circumstances attending the death of Josephine, that she could scarcely hide her feelings from Carnew. He saw that she was pale and troubled, and at times most unwontedly pre-occupied, upon all of which he rallied her, and said that he was glad the French girl was out of the way, since, having such an effect upon Ned, what would it be if she had continued to live; and he hoped his betrothed would not happen upon any more cases of the kind. He liked sisters of charity, but not exactly in his own family; and then he laughed and made wry faces at Ned and his aunt, who had heard nothing of the young lady's good offices in behalf of Josephine until the death of the girl, when she exclaimed:

"Gracious, Ned! how could you? Don't you know you might injure your own reputation by going near such a creature? I wouldn't have her a minute in Rahandabed after what had occurred."

And Mrs. Doloran's nose went up to a much higher angle than its usual elevation.

Ned wrote to Edna, never doubting that she would break off her engagement immediately, when she learned the baseness of Brekbellew. But what was her astonishment to receive in reply:

"My Dearest Ned:—The circumstance you mention is by no means so dreadful as your imagination pictures it to be. Were you more acquainted with the world, you would know that it certainly was not sufficient to break off an engagement of marriage. In us of the frailer sex, virtue of the strictest kind is expected and demanded, but in our lords and masters these dreadful things are merely youthful indiscretions. So Mr. Brekbellew being only guilty of a 'youthful indiscretion,' it would be most unjust for me to punish him as severely as you seem to infer that I ought to do, and it would be most unwise for me even to hint that I had heard of his folly.

"Wishing you, my dearest Ned, a deeper wisdom in the future, I remain,   Yours,

"EDNA."

Ned was disgusted, and for once she fairly contemned her cousin. Was the latter utterly devoid of heart that she could write thus, when Ned had depicted in strongest language the love, devotion, and suffering of the unfortunate French girl and the heartlessness of Brekbellew? But it must be so, else how could she so easily and so soon forget poor Mackay?

In little less than three weeks all Rahandabed received the wedding cards of Mr. and Mrs. Brekbellew, and also the announcement that they had gone immediately to New York, thence to take passage for Europe.

"That beautiful girl," said Mrs. Doloran, "to marry such a monkey; but that just proves my theory about women; they're fools from the first to the last of them," evidently forgetting that she was including in the same category herself and Ned, for whom she now professed such an ardent affection.

"And that stiff, unmannerly old father of hers," she resumed; "it's a wonder how *his* pride could ever be reconciled to such a match—why, he snubbed that fool Brekbellew when he was here."

And Alan and Ned wondered also, but they were too much absorbed in the preparations making for their own wedding to give the subject over-much thought.

Dyke wrote at the very last that he was not coming; and it was true that his business (he being the newest partner in the firm) claimed very close attention, but he did not say that he was glad it was so, for he felt now that he could not witness unmoved the marriage of Ned. She had written that he must give her away, that Alan said so, and that that fact contributed so much to her happiness, all of which Dyke answered in the inimitably tender way so peculiarly his own—a way that told so much, and yet that told nothing he would conceal.

Ned cried from disappointment when she received the letter. Neither Meg nor Dyke to be at her wedding! All Rahandabed could not make up for their absence, and Carnew coming upon her, still in tears, also read the letter.

"It is too bad," he said, sympathizingly; "but we shall punish him, Ned. We shall stop long enough in New York to have him call upon us, and if this driving business of his won't even let him do that, we shall call upon him, if necessary, at his business place."

"O Alan, how good you are! I never thought of that," looking at him with smiles and tears.

"Well, prove your gratitude by drying your eyes at once, and permitting me to tell Ordotte that you will let *him* give you away. He is most anxious to have that privileged position."

"Is he, really?" half interested and half amused.

"Why, yes; he has been talking most mysteriously about his *right* to do so, and if I were not familiar with his strange innuendoes and strange insinuations, put forth to excite my aunt's laughable curiosity, I would say he knew some secret about you, Ned."

"No secret about me," she rejoined, laughing. "Everything plain as the day. I have had it from Meg a hundred times—a poor little English waif in whom Mr. Edgar became interested because I happened to bear the same name as his daughter, and he knew my parents; only for those fortunate facts, I might have grown up a poor, neglected orphan."

Alan did not answer; he loved her so well that he questioned nothing about her. She was the queen of his heart, and he wanted no more.

The wedding morning arrived, and even the weather seemed to have some nuptial design, for never had the sun shone more brightly, nor the foliage about the grounds of Rahandabed looked greener. The very birds were carolling in such a way that they woke up Ned even before it was time for her to arise. She could not sleep again, however, and she rose, as it were, to "nurse her joy." All night she had been in the little mountain home, a child again, talking to the trees in her quaint, childish language, with fond old Meg, and true, tender Dyke about her; and as she realized that all that was entirely gone, that on to-day she was to pass a Rubicon which would separate her forever from her maidenhood, that never in all the years to come could she ever experience any of her childhood's delights, burning tears started from her eyes, and rolled down her cheeks. Yet she did not for a moment doubt her happiness. She was only obeying the strange impulse of regret for something lost which to strong natures comes most forcibly in moments of greatest happiness, or perchance it was an unconscious sympathy with Dyke, something only to be explained on the principles of second-sight and presentiments, for at that same hour, early though it was—but he had scarcely slept all night—Dyke was reading her letters, reading them for the last time while she was a maiden, he said to himself.

When Ned found the tears on her cheeks, she brushed them away hurriedly, and then laughed as she did so, because of her silly superstition, for she had read somewhere that:

> "The tears of a bride on her wedding morn,
> Bring grief and neglect, and the finger of scorn."

Owing to Ordotte's frequent interposition, Mrs. Doloran's desire for vulgar display in the preparations for the wedding had been kept decently subdued, though in the matter of her own toilet she was provocative of mirth on every side.

Never was a sweeter bride than Ned. Her own exquisite, modest taste had prevailed in the choice of a dress, and as she entered the great state parlor where the ceremony was to be performed, and where the guests, and, in the background, the servants were assembled, everybody grew enthusiastic in admiration. She was leaning on the arm of Ordotte, and even his tawny face was somewhat flushed as if with pride and delight. Carnew, to many an envious heart in the assembly, never appeared so handsome. Happiness had given to his cheeks a rich flush, and to his earnest, dark eyes an exquisite sparkle.

The brief ceremony was over, and Ned was an Edgar no longer, but Mrs. Carnew, wife of the richest and handsomest man in C———. But of those advantages she never thought; he was her love, tender and true, and in that she rested, and had her treasure and her joy. The pleasant wedding breakfast also was over quickly, and then nothing remained but for the bride to put on her travelling dress, and speed away with her husband from Rahandabed. Mrs. Doloran hugged her very tight, and kissed her again and again, and then she hugged Alan, and kissed him, and after that she turned to Ordotte, and in her excitement seemed about to subject him to the same ordeal, only he, divining her intention, slipped out of her reach.

Macgilivray, honest, delighted Macgilivray, drove them to the station, and as he afterward expressed to his fellow-help :

'A bonnier bride ne'er steppit."

Never having travelled, beyond her journey when a child to the Pennsylvania School, thence to Barrytown, and afterward to Albany, the journey was a constant source of delight to Ned, and to Carnew, who had travelled so much both in the old world and in the new, her simple, unaffected enthusiasm was most refreshing. He loved to watch her silently, as, with the glimpses that she caught of the pretty places along the river, the color rose in her cheeks, and the sparkle came to her eyes. She was hardly wearied when they reached New York, and the thought of seeing Dyke seemed to imbue her with fresh spirits.

"I think, Ned," said Carnew the next morning, after an elegantly appointed breakfast in their own apartment in the Astor House—at that time one of the leading hotels in the city—"that we shall call on Mr. Dutton. I am afraid your impatience would never brook the delay of sending to him to call upon us. So if you like, we shall go immediately."

"Shall we?" her wide eyes alight with pleasure. "How very thoughtful and good you are, Alan!"

"Am I?" He was standing near her, and he could not resist the impulse to draw her to him and fold her in his arms.

"My own," he murmured. Was it the spirit of prophesy which occasionally, all unconscious to ourselves, comes upon us, that impelled her to say almost as if another and not she were speaking:

"Will the day ever come, Alan, that you will not find it in your heart to call me that?"

And he answered firmly; clasping her closely:

"Never!"

Neither dreamed of the black, cruel, horrid phantom which was so soon to separate them.

Dyke, in the private office of his business house, in consultation with the senior partner, was told some one wished to see him.

"Let the party come in here," said the senior partner, and he retired to a desk in a remote corner of the room.

Mr. and Mrs. Carnew appeared. It was Ned's plan to send in no cards, in order to surprise Dyke, and never was a surprise more effectual. Though knowing that their wedding trip was to include New York, he never dreamed of their visiting him, and now as he looked at the lovely, blushing, smiling bride, it seemed to be all a dream. But she did not leave him in dreamland long. Forgetful of everything but that the honest fellow whom she loved with all a tender sister's warm affection stood before her, she rushed to him, put her arms about his neck, and kissed him heartily. Even the senior partner could not help looking up, and wondering, and almost envying Dyke, for Ned was so lovely.

Dyke was crimson up to the roots of his hair and down to his shirt collar with surprise, delight, and a host of emotions. Something even like moisture came into his eyes, but he managed to conceal that and to avert a recurrence of it.

Ned drew him to Carnew, introducing:

"My husband!"

with a *naïveté* and pride that was charming, and Dyke wrung Alan's hand and congratulated him in a voice that to himself was unexpectedly steady. It was no use for him to beg to be excused from giving the day to the couple, for the senior partner, from his corner, overhearing some of Mrs. Carnew's entreaties, came forward, apologizing for his intrusion, but saying that, having heard the young lady's solicitations, he could no longer refrain from adding his request to hers that Mr. Dutton would take the day. Then followed introductions to the gentleman, and Dyke finally was induced to go out with his friends.

What a happy day it was! In the brotherly attention which Carnew paid him and the sisterly affection of which each moment he was the recipient from Ned, Dyke felt the pain in his heart lulled, and when he saw how truly happy was Ned, he rejoiced for her sake. With himself, all his agony should not weigh a feather against her joy.

Then he had some news for her. The relatives with whom Meg lived in Albany were all going to Australia—promises of most lucrative employment being tendered to them by friends already in that distant country. They were going in June, and by that time Meg would be able to travel, the doctor said, and Dyke intended to bring her to the little mountain home, at least for the summer. Meg was longing for it, and he himself was anxious to spend a few weeks there. The senior partner had told him that he could be spared at that season of the year for two months if necessary.

"Delightful!" said Ned; "and Alan and I shall visit you there. I want him to see the mountain home of my childhood."

Dyke blushed a little.

"I don't know about the propriety of your making a visit there now. Meg has dissuaded me from my desire to make some improvements in the little place. She says it would lose its charm for her if it were altered, and that, as she is so old and scarcely expects to live a great while longer, it will not be much for me to defer my plan."

"And she is right, dear old Meg," responded Ned, tears showing for a moment in her eyes. "I am glad she requested that. For me, too, it would lose its charm if you had it altered.

"But don't you see," said Dyke, "how little and how poor the accommodation is for you if you should visit it. The married lady, Mrs. Carnew, will hardly, I think, be content with what amply suited the little girl, Ned Edgar."

And Dyke smiled.

"Mrs. Carnew will be just as amply suited," mimicked Ned, "and as for Mr. Carnew, he has become so plebeian since he married poor little Ned Edgar, that I believe he could accommodate himself to a mud hut."

At which they all laughed, but immediately afterward it was settled that some time in the ensuing summer the young couple would visit Ned's mountain home.

That day ended, as all happy days do, far too quickly, and Alan and Ned continued their bridal trip.

XL.

The happy couple were back in Rahandabed, Ned flitting about in her handsome suite of apartments with the delight of a bird, and Alan settling down to the life he loved, of his wife, his books, and his long romantic rides about the country. Mrs. Doloran was most unusually amiable; some of the guests said that it was because she had proposed to Ordotte, and that he had accepted her. Whether such was the case, Ordotte was, if possible, more attentive to her, and she had become so much like ordinary women that she was now without a "companion," having dismissed two who had succeeded Ned, and further declared she intended to continue without one ; more than that, for a whole month she had not once broken into a violent temper, so that Macgilvray said :

"The auld hornie must have heavy work elsewhere, when he forgets me leddy so long."

The month of July came, and Dyke wrote that Meg and he were in the little mountain home. He had gone to Albany for her, made a stay of a few days while his relatives were preparing for departure to Australia, and now he was trying to live over again the old-happy times when Ned was like a little sprite of the mountains. It was his usual letter, bright, tender, cheerful, even in some sense amusing, for he had the faculty of telling commonplace incidents in a humorous way. Ned was so glad to receive it, and so sorry that it came just as Alan had set off on one of his long solitary rides, from which he would not return until evening. She was eager to show it to him, for he had only waited some such news, to prepare to accompany her on a visit to the home of her childhood. But she curbed her impatience, and flitted about the numberless little pretty things a woman of leisure finds to do, until it was time to go to her music. Alan wished her to cultivate that, and his slightest desire was her law. She had scarcely seated herself at the instrument, when a servant summoned her to Mrs. Doloran's private parlor.

Wondering a little, for such a summons was most unusual since she had ceased to be a "hired companion," she left the piano, continuing to hum the air she had just begun to play. She was so happy, that there was a strange feeling of wanting almost to hug the sunshine as it straggled through the half-closed blinds of the veranda which she passed on her way to Mrs. Doloran's apartments. There was no shade, no presentiment of how she would leave that lady's presence.

When Ned entered the parlor, there were more persons

in it than the mistress of Rahandabed. There was a middle-aged woman, evidently of the lower class, with a little, plainly dressed, sleeping girl about a year old in her arms, and beside her was a young, and well-dressed man. Though not good-looking, he would attract attention from his set, determined features. They were all seated in the centre of the room, and Mrs. Doloran was beside them, sitting bolt upright, a position she assumed only when she was excited, or angry.

Utterly unsuspicious of what awaited her, Ned came smilingly forward, but the smile froze upon her lips, when Mrs. Doloran, without moving a muscle of her rigid face, or inclining in the least, her stiff, erect form, pointed to the babe in the woman's arms, and said loudly and sternly: "Mrs. Carnew, this child is said to be yours; your child by a private marriage with Richard Mackay, who committed suicide some months ago upon these grounds."

Ned was bewildered; the accusation was so sudden and so outrageous, that the very emotions it called up as she recovered her voice, made her appear almost guilty.

"Such a charge, Mrs. Doloran, is too absurd even to be answered; if such be the purpose for which I have been summoned, I must retire immediately."

And she turned to leave the room.

"Not so fast," said Mrs. Doloran rising, and hastening to interpose her form between Ned and the door, "this is something more than an absurd charge, as you will learn before long. These people are armed with the most conclusive proofs of your guilt, and, to leave no link wanting, the minister who married you to Mr. Mackay, is to arrive here to day. I used to suspect that you were a sort of actress, Ned, but I never dreamed that you could have gone to the length of discarding your own child."

"Yes, ma'am," spoke up the woman with an unpleasant boldness of voice, "this *is* the lady's child. She was confined in my house a year ago this month, and I'd have always kept the little thing, for I'd grown to love it, but

Mr. Dickson, here, who was the bosom friend, it seems, of Mr. Mackay, come to me, and he says, says he:

" ' It would be an injustice to the child, not to reveal its parentage, especially. as its mother was a lady, and had made such a wealthy match, and——' "

" How dare you?" burst from Ned, no longer able to control herself, "how dare you tell such an atrocious lie? I never saw you before in my life."

"These heroics are very fine," said Mrs. Doloran, who, having heard the story of the strangers, had made up her mind to believe it. Anything that promised a sensation, even though it cruelly sacrificed some one, was hailed by her, and friendships for her own sex were too weak and fleeting to be permitted to stand in the way of an event that promised excitement, or novelty.

"I repeat it," she continued with an aggravating sarcasm, as she saw Ned trembling from indignation, "these heroics are very fine, but they carry no proof of your innocence. Why, this young man has in his possession letters of that unfortunate Mackay to him, in which you, Ned Edgar, are constantly mentioned, as the object of his love, and afterwards as his wife!"

"It is true, Mrs. Carnew," said the young man rising, but preserving a most respectful bearing, "I first met Dick Mackay abroad. and we formed so great a friendship for each other that he made me his confidant, when he became acquainted with you. He wrote to me frequently about you, and even sent to me a letter just before his death, telling me that he contemplated suicide, because though his wife, you did not return his love, but preferred to him a Mr. Carnew, and asking me to see to his child, for you, its mother, had discarded it. I could not get away from London where I then resided, but as soon as opportunity offered, I did so, and I hastened to this woman, who informed me that for ten months she had received no compensation for her care of the child, nor had any one called to see it.

" I confess, Mrs. Carnew, that I was indignant, not at

the father, who, because of his long silence, I feared had carried out his threat of death, but at the mother. I made it my business to come here and make secret inquiries. I found that poor Mackay had indeed committed suicide, and on these very grounds, and that his wife had unfeelingly married not a year after the event. That nerved me anew. I returned to this woman's house, and brought her and the babe back with me in order that the dead might be in some measure avenged, and that justice might be done to the innocent offspring.

"I have also written to the Reverend Mr. Hayman of Rhinebeck, who Mackay told me performed the ceremony, and he promised to meet me here to-day."

He had spoken very calmly but very firmly, and Ned had listened with a sort of strange curiosity mingled with her indignation. Before he had finished she understood it all. It was Edna's story he was telling, Edna who had confided in Ned to the extent of revealing her secret marriage, but who had forborne to tell of the existence of her child, and she answered with what calmness she could assume:

"You are entirely mistaken in supposing me to be the wife of Mackay, or the mother of that babe. I am neither, and I *shall* not longer remain to be insulted by such an accusation. If you, Mrs. Doloran, will not protect me from it, my husband will, when he returns." And without even a second glance at the parties, she went from the room.

But, in her own apartment, when she sat down to think calmly of what had occurred, there came to her for the first time since she had been so dreadfully accused, the remembrance of her oath to Edna. A sudden pain shot through her temples, and she could almost feel the blood receding from her face. Then, also, came before her the note delivered to her on the lawn, and addressed to Ned Edgar; through her own forgetfulness to demand it, she had never received any explanation of why her diminutive had been used.

Had Edna, fearing some such exposure as this, deliberately planned to have her swear? Was that a part also, of Edna's malicious deception, in order to save herself? The room swam about her with the thought, and for a moment it seemed as if she were going round with it. Though seated, she clutched the sides of her chair to save herself from falling. If only Alan would come! But if he were there, she could not tell him what she knew—she could only deny the accusation; but he, knowing and loving her as he did, would not for a moment credit the charge. There was comfort in that thought. But how should she prove her innocence to Mrs. Doloran, who evidently had given entire ear to the wretched story? And then she remembered what had been said about the Rev. Mr. Hayman coming that very day to Rahandabed. He would disprove the charge instantly, for she had never seen the gentleman.

Oh! for the day to pass, that Alan might come! And she spent the hours, never leaving her own apartments, in a restless, wretched manner. The fact that she so secluded herself was construed by Mrs. Doloran into a fresh proof of her guilt, and she appealed to Ordotte to second her opinion; but he shrugged his shoulders and said Mrs. Carnew should be granted at least the justice of being supposed innocent until fully proved to be guilty, upon which the lady looked angry, and said that Ordotte was entirely too partial to Mrs. Carnew.

Mr. Dickson and his companions were made especial *protégés* of Mrs. Doloran. One would think they had brought her news of some treasure, so grateful, so kind, and so considerate of their comfort was she. She insisted that Rahandabed must be their home until the dreadful thing was settled; and she lent a greedy ear to all the conversation of Mrs. Bumner, the woman who accompanied Mr. Dickson. He was evidently sincere and earnest in his undertaking, actuated by the motives that he had mentioned: love for his dead friend, and a desire to see justice done to the neglected offspring; but the woman evinced a disgusting garrulity—a readiness to tell, even to the very servants with whom she came in contact, all about Mrs. Carnew's neglect of her own child. So the dreadful story was known in all Rahandabed before Carnew returned, and it was believed (by some of those who had envied Ned, gladly believed) by all except two persons, Ordotte and Macgilivray. The latter, in his dry, honest Scotch way, scouted it at once, and had a war of words with more than one of his fellow-help about it.

Alan returned, but a watch had been kept for him, and before he could get to his wife, he was summoned to meet Dickson. Mrs. Doloran had a vein of shrewdness in her nature. With the tact of her sex, she divined that it was better to let Carnew and Dickson have an uninterrupted private interview before she introduced the woman, Bunmer. Dickson's quiet, gentlemanly, earnest manner would carry surer and quicker conviction to her nephew than to meet him first with the story of the garrulous, unprepossessing female. And she was right. After Carnew had recovered from the first sort of dazed shock that Dickson's story gave him, he actually found himself with a forced calmness, reading carefully every one of the letters which the gentleman produced.

There were nearly a dozen of them, none of them very long, but all well written, both as to composition and penmanship, and filled with accounts of the writer's affection for Ned Edgar. She was never spoken of as Edna, and was even referred to as, not the daughter of Mr. Edgar, but as one whom his bounty supported, and whom he loved as an adopted child. He came to the last letter, the letter which announced his contemplation of suicide ; that ran :

" Do not censure me, friend of my soul, for doing that which wiser and better men in harrowing circumstances have done before me. I can endure my life no longer. Ned will never acknowledge our secret marriage ; she will never consent to be known as the wife of a gardener's son. She is here in a place called Rahandabed ; hired companion to a wealthy lady, who has a handsome and wealthy nephew. She says she was there all the time I supposed her to be in Weewald Place, and during which time I was endeavoring to earn a living in New York, and, in accordance with her request, had refrained from writing to her. That she obtained permission to go to New York, where our child was born, and then that she returned here. I followed her in secret, and by hiding myself upon the grounds, I managed to see her.

"You wonder why I so deferred-to her; why I did not assert my rights and remove her from temptation. O my friend, if you have ever loved as I have done, you will understand, and pity, and forgive me. I loved Ned so madly that I could not lift my finger against the lightest wish of hers; and further, what means have I to support her—what kind of a home could I provide for her compared to the one she has now? I saw her, as I told you, and I suppose in my desperation I spoke wildly. I accused her of being willing to violate every law, of being ready to accept the attentions of this handsome, wealthy Carnew. She looked grave at that, and answered that Mr. Carnew too rarely noticed her for me to have any jealousy. O Walter, how I loved her; I felt, as I looked at her, as we both stood in the shadow of an old deserted mill, with the darkness of the evening closing about us, that I could make any sacrifice, after all, for her happiness.

"We were startled by the sound of approaching steps, and she fled to Rahandabed, while I hurried in an opposite direction.

"That night my resolution was made. She had said to me that no love was great which would not make every sacrifice. I would never be in circumstances to rescue her from the life of a dependent, and my existence would be a bar to her marriage to a better man. So I would make for her the greatest sacrifice it was in my power to make. I would end my life. I know not if she will see to our child; I sometimes think that she has as little love for it as she has for me; but, in any case, Walter, you will see to it. You have means, and you, I feel, will do your poor dead friend this service.

"P. S. They are having some sort of a *fête* in the grounds of Rahandabed, and I have dispatched a laborer, whom I have found on the road, with a note to 'Miss Ned Edgar.' He is to inquire for her among the gay company which, from my hiding-place, I can see assembled upon the grounds, but he is not to wait for an answer. I wonder, when she reads: 'Within an hour the last and greatest sacrifice I can make shall be completed. Can any love demand more?' if she will guess what it is; if she will shudder, if she will pity, if she will *love me*. And to-morrow, when they find my body cold and stark, will any thrill of compassion run through her frame, will any of her old regard for me come back? But what is the odds? I shall only have died for a woman's sake!

"Good-by, Walter, old friend. Would that my heart held only its love for you.

"Yours, in death,
"RICHARD MACKAY."

Carnew looked up, and across at his companion with eyes that fairly blazed, and a face so pale and rigid, that Dickson shrank from it. As the whole life of a person drowning is said to pass in instantaneous, but most distinct view, before the eyes that are closing forever, so every iota concerning Ned seemed to come instantaneously before Carnew. The note that so strangely had been given to her on the afternoon of Mr. Edgar's arrival at Rahandabed, and which evidently was the note referred to in Mackay's letter. Her two months' absence a year ago, during which she said she had been ill, and her sick appearance on her return fully corroborating her statement, but, O God! how all these facts substantiated the wretched charge against her. All that Edna had told him regarding Ned and Mackay rushed to him; Ned's appearance and evident illness just after the identity of the suicide had been proclaimed, all his old doubts and thoughts about her, even her very remark in the hotel in New York, ' would the day ever come, in which he would find it in his heart not to call her his own,' all came to him with a tantalizing minuteness that seemed fairly devilish. He rose, saying with a voice that had undergone as great a change as his face had done:

"I shall take these letters for the present."

Dickson did not object, and Carnew went out of the room, without expressing any wish to see Mrs. Bunmer. But he was met by his aunt.

"How has Mr. Dickson's account affected you?" she asked coldly, her eyes fairly glittering.

He did not answer her, but only pushed by her as if he had not heard her question. But she opposed his further progress.

"Are you not going to see this woman, Bunmer? And Mr. Hayman has arrived; he is waiting in the parlor for you."

Mrs. Doloran was in her most enjoyable element; not that, really from a spirit of viciousness, she wished to see Ned unhappy and disgraced, but because with childish credulousness, and that fickle disposition that formed such prominent traits in her shallow nature, she believed Ned to be fully guilty, and she disliked and despised her accordingly. She would show her as little mercy as she had shown the French girl. And, with characteristic selfishness, no thought of her nephew moved her to pity. Did *he* suffer, it would only be a little variety in his life, and something which he merited for having, against her wishes, married only a "companion." So there was no sympathy in her face and certainly none in her voice.

Alan put her aside again, and said in the same changed tones which he had used to Dickson:

"I am going to Ned."

Impatient, restless, fevered Ned! She had heard that Alan had returned. Her own maid had informed her, having heard it, when she went to tea, from the gossip-loving, watchful servants who knew that Mr. Carnew's return was looked for with great eagerness by Mrs. Doloran. And Ned wondered why he did not, according to his wont, come immediately to her. She never dreamed that he would see any of the strangers first; and, as for the tenth time she opened the door of her parlor to listen for his step along the corridor, her maid, who seemed to divine the cause of the anxiety, said respectfully:

"I heard one of the help say at the tea-table, that Mr. Carnew was talking to Mr. Dickson; that they were talking together a long time."

"You may go to your own room, Jane," said Mrs. Carnew coldly. "I shall ring when I want you."

So the wretched story had become servants' talk, since they knew the name of the strange gentleman, and that he was closeted with Carnew, and instead of coming to her, her husband had chosen to listen to the stranger's accusation. Pale before, she became deathly then, and her head throbbed as if it would burst; but at that moment Alan's step sounded in the corridor, and in another instant he was standing before her. She saw his face, and it struck a sort of terror to her heart; but she extended her arms to him, and she cried with an agonized entreaty:

"O Alan! my husband!"

He did not move; he did not even lift a finger to respond to her motion. He only looked as if he were frozen into that erect position, and as if his eyes were two burning orbs, looking over a blank of ice beneath them. Still she kept her arms extended, and she moved towards him, for it could not be that he, her husband, doubted her; but when she was so close that she might have thrown her grasp about him, as if she, too, had become suddenly frozen by the icy spell which seemed to bind him, her hands dropped to her sides, and she tottered back. He appeared to recover some volition then; for he approached her, and in that same altered voice, which seemed too much altered ever to give place to his own again, he said:

"Ned!"

At the sound of her name pronounced in that manner, a manner which was further horrible proof that her husband believed the wretched story, something of her old spirit came back; the old, sudden, flaring temper that had been wont to bring such trouble upon her childhood. She drew herself up, and while the color rushed into her cheeks, and even reddened her brow and neck, she answered:

"What would you say to *me*, if, during your absence, I listened to, and believed some miserable accusation against *you*? If I gave the traducers full ear, before even I asked one question of you? And this is what you have done to me, your wife!"

How beautiful and noble she looked as she stood gazing into his very eyes fearlessly and frankly, and how marked was her resemblance to Edna. To Carnew it had never seemed so great before. And how confirmatory of her innocence was her appearance. Guilt could never wear the expression that her face wore unless, indeed, she was a consummate actress.

He did not speak again, but led her by the arm to an inner room, then, placing a chair for her beside a little centre-table, he opened the bundle of Mackay's letters; one by one, beginning in order with them according to their dates, he opened them and placed them before her, and bade her read. She obeyed, growing like one in a ghastly nightmare as she proceeded, and he, sitting opposite, watched the varying expressions of her face.

Had Edna deliberately palmed herself upon Mackay as Ned, and as the latter remembered the life at Weewald Place, she felt that it would not have been a difficult matter. None of the Mackay family had sufficient intercourse with any one in Mr. Edgar's house to ascertain the truth. Edna could easily, for purposes of her own, have pretended to her lover that she was not the Edna Edgar who was Mr. Edgar's daughter, and the heiress of Wee-wald Place. With equal ease she could have gone further, as she evidently had done, and deceived her lover to the extent of making him believe that it was she who had gone to Rahandabed to earn her living; but for what purpose had Miss Edgar told so many malicious lies? If to conceal her own imprudent love, surely there were other ways and means than laying her guilt upon Ned's shoulders. When she came to the last letter, the letter that spoke of the note that had been delivered to Miss Ned Edgar on the grounds of Rahandabed, and of which she had first forgotten, and then neglected to demand any explanation, Ned gave a cry—a cry forced from her by the remembrance of that note which had been intended for Edna but given to her. She pushed the letters from her and rose to her feet. In that moment as she looked down at the mass of cruel lies, and then, as she looked across at the white, rigid face with its eyes burning into her own, for the first time in her whole life that she ever hated anybody, she hated Edna ; and yet her oath bound her from saying a word of the truth, and Edna was be-yond reach of any entreaty to undo the terrible wrong. With these feelings struggling in her bosom, she crossed to her husband; she took his cold hands in hers, she knelt at his feet, and looking up into his eyes, said in tones that, from their earnestness and their agony, seemed to be irresistibly convincing:

"Alan, as God is in heaven, I am innocent of this hor-rible charge. Richard Mackay was never my lover, never my husband. Oh! that I should even have to deny such as this to *you*. I thought your love was such that no doubt could ever cross it."

He raised her up, almost with his wonted tenderness, to his knee, and supported her there; but still he did not speak. His heart was yet too much torn with doubt and agony to allow him any voice. But his action had opened the flood gates of her heart, and she clasped him closely, and cried upon his bosom with the abandon of a child.

Some one knocked for entrance at the door of the outer room. Carnew put his wife down, and answered it. It was a message from Mrs. Doloran to the effect that Mr. Hayman was waiting, and as he was obliged to return up the river some miles that night, it would oblige him if Mr. Carnew would see him at once.

Ned also heard the message, the latter not being delivered in a very subdued key, and when Alan returned to her, her tears were wiped away, and she confronted him with something like a smile.

"I heard the message, Alan, and it has restored me. Let us go to this Mr. Hayman immediately, and he will disprove this horrible story; he will know at once that it was not *I* he married to Mackay."

She was so eager that it was she who rather led him along to Mrs. Doloran's private parlor; and she was so confident, and even so happy, feeling that convincing proof of her innocence was so near, that she was strong and brave, and smiling, and almost entirely her own old self.

Mr. Dickson was in the private parlor, and Mr. Hayman. The woman Bunner and the baby were in an ante-chamber, ready for instant production on being required. Mr. Hayman was a delicate-looking little gentleman, with very fair whiskers and a very weak, strangle l sort of voice, as if something within him was perpetually struggling with his vocal organs.

He rose, and Mr. Dickson rose, as Mr. and Mrs. Carnew entered, but Mrs. Doloran remained seated in her most severe attitude. On came Ned clasping her husband's arm very tight, but smiling and looking with all the candor and innocence of a child.

Dickson had been instructed by Mrs. Doloran to introduce the minister; probably because she wanted to devote her whole attention to watching the effect of the introduction upon Ned. The young man performed his part respectfully, and even gracefully, and then the Reverend Mr. Hayman said in his strangled voice, as he bowed to Mrs. Carnew:

"I remember distinctly the pleasure of meeting you before; it was on the occasion of your private marriage to a Richard Mackay, on the evening of the twenty-ninth of August, now almost two years ago. I remember it so distinctly, because both you and the young gentleman seemed very much flurried, and you were even married with your veil down. When you went into the vestry to sign your names, and I remarked upon the strangeness of such a name as Ned for a lady, you threw aside your veil for an instant, as if in forgetfulness, and I recognize now, only possibly somewhat more mature looking, the face that I saw then. Further, I ventured to inquire if the lady was any relative of the wealthy Mr. Edgar of Barry-town, and I was told that she was an inmate for the present, of his home, and supported by his bounty, for which reason it would be most imprudent to make her marriage known, and I was asked to keep my counsel about it. I promised to do so, and kept the promise until Mr. Dickson's letter reached me informing me what urgent reasons there were for breaking my pledge and begging me to come here."

All this he said, looking straight at Ned, whose smile vanished, but whose spirit rose at the very audacity of the charge.

"You are entirely mistaken," she said, her voice and her lips quivering, "I never saw you before in all my life."

A prolonged and derisive "oh" from Mrs. Doloran followed Ned's answer, while the minister for an instant seemed slightly nonplussed by the firmness and even hardly concealed indignation of Ned's reply. But he returned to the charge, even putting a little ministerial sternness into his accents:

"I regret exceedingly, Mrs. Carnew, to be obliged to repeat my statement: you *are* the lady whom I married to Richard Mackay on the evening of the twenty-ninth of August, now nearly two years ago."

"Can you swear to that?" asked Carnew leaning forward, and speaking still in his changed voice.

"I can," returned the minister.

"Then you would swear to a lie," burst from Ned, the indignant tears showing in her eyes.

"Heroics," said Mrs. Doloran sarcastically from her chair.

Alan turned to his wife; she had never relaxed her grasp upon his arm, and now her hold was so tight, it seemed as if her fingers were a vise. God help her! The anchor to which she clung, her husband's trust in her, was fast slipping away; she read it fully at last in his eyes, as he uttered but one word: "Come!" and then he turned with her to the door. Mrs. Doloran stirred herself:

"Alan, you have not seen Mrs. Bunner, nor the child."

He waived her back with a sternness that even she could not oppose, and he went on silently with Ned to their own apartments, to the inner room which they had left but a little while before. There, he withdrew himself from her grasp, and stood before her. For one moment his face was white, and stern, and rigid, as it had been in his aunt's parlor; but the next, all the agony of his soul broke into it, and, with a cry that pierced like a sword the heart of her who heard it, he threw himself into a chair, and covering his face with his hands, sat bowed and broken-looking, as if old age had suddenly overtaken him.

She flew to his side, she took his head in her arms, and she dropped her own burning tears upon it.

"O Ned!" he said at last, "why deceive me so? Why not have told me before our marriage that you were a widow? There was no crime in your having married two years ago, and I would have loved you the same, for I loved you so well, Ned, and I would have provided for your child."

"Alan! my husband! I am innocent of all this—oh!

if I could only tell you, but I am bound by an oath, by a solemn oath.”

“What oath?” looking at her with eyes that seemed to be burned back into his head.

“I cannot tell you. I am so bound, I cannot speak; but, if I could, O Alan! then you would know how I am wronged.”

“But what oath can disprove the minister’s readiness to swear that he performed the ceremony for you? What oath can give the lie to these convincing letters of the unfortunate Mackay? What oath can prevent the linking of your own actions into overwhelming proof against you? You obtained my aunt’s permission to visit your friends— you were absent at the very time that the child was born —you overstayed your time because, according to your statement on your return, you had been ill, and your feeble appearance when you *did* return, confirmed your story.

“O Ned! do not longer keep up the part you have assumed. Your duplicity now is breaking my heart more than all that has gone before.”

She clung to his knees again, and answered with a sort of piteous horror:

“I was in Albany, while I was away from your aunt; in Albany with Meg, and Meg’s relatives, and I was sick with a fever caught there. They can tell you ; they can all prove what I say,”—but even as she spoke, there flashed, in a sort of sickening way through her mind, that Meg’s relatives had gone to Australia,—“and Mr. Hayman may confound me with some one who resembles me.”

She seemed to speak with the energy of despair, and only that her sobs choked her, she would have continued.

But Alan, though his heart and his love pleaded for her, could not believe her. Mackay’s letters were such overwhelming proof ; then, she had not once written while on her reputed visit to Albany, another suspicious fact. He mentioned it.

“Because I was taken ill so soon after reaching there,”

she replied between her sobs, "and when I recovered I was deemed too weak to do so, and told that I could make all explanations when I returned."

"But some one could have written for you," he persisted.

"O Alan! can't you understand? They were all more or less illiterate people, and I did not have the heart to ask any of them to undertake the task of writing to a lady like Mrs. Doloran."

"But the minister, Ned; how could *he* mistake you for another?"

"I don't know; such things have happened—I have read of them. O Alan! if I could only tell you, but my oath, my oath."

Her face was buried on his knee, and she was sobbing passionately.

He looked down at her; down at the lovely head with its loosely coiled mass of soft, dark hair; down at the slight, willowy, quivering form, and he thought of her resemblance to Edna, of her own words, uttered a moment ago, "Mr. Hayman may confound me with some one who resembles me," but, in a moment he rejected as absurd the suspicion, the half hope which had come to him. The resemblance between the two girls, while it was certainly singularly marked, did not go to the extent of making their faces exactly alike; and the reverend gentleman had stated distinctly that he saw Ned's face. Also, it was impossible that Mackay could be so deceived: no; Carnew was certain, much as he tried to struggle against it, that his wife was guilty; there was even stealing upon him a horrible conviction that Ned's friends in Albany, if, indeed, she had any there, knew her secret, and would perjure themselves to save her; that this mysterious oath of which she spoke was only a subterfuge to explain her position; in short, that she had been playing a part ever since she came to Rahandabed, that she was acting now, and that her present grief was only a part of her clever *rôle*.

He stood up, and partly shook her from him; in a

helpless, suppliant way, she still endeavored to cling, but he stooped, unwound her hands, and went from her; went to his own room, and locked himself in.

XLI.

Ned dragged herself up also, and almost fell into the chair her husband had vacated. What should she do? Her brain seemed too much on fire to think, and her temples throbbed so violently, it was a relief to hold them. To whom should she go? How should she act? Again and again she asked these questions of herself in a senseless sort of way, much as a demented person might incoherently repeat a certain form of words: but at length, when more than an hour had passed, and another burst of tears had come to her relief, making her eyes feel as if they were only burned balls moving in a painful way in their sockets, her thoughts became a little clearer. Something she must do, and do immediately; she would go mad if she remained in that inaction. She would go to Mr. Edgar and demand to be informed where a letter could find his daughter, then she would write to Edna, adjuring her to release her from her oath, or to be Christian enough to undo herself the horrible wrong she had done. She would go to Meg, and bring her to corroborate her story of her Albany visit. She would summon Dyke, and at that stage of her resolutions her feelings gave way again, and she was sobbing once more.

Dyke, and Meg, and the little mountain home, and her happy childhood—oh! how in this hour of bitter anguish she longed for them all! but more than all for true, tender Dyke, who always loved her, and who, somehow, in this dreadful time, she felt would not have doubted her, in the face of a thousand such accusations.

Her bruised heart turned to him; he would understand her, and pity her as no one else could do; he would advise her, he would help her. Instantly her resolution was taken: she would go to Dyke—she would go that very evening.　Fortunately, there was a late train.　The necessity for immediate exertion lent her strength.

She summoned her maid and sent for Macgilivray, meeting the man in the corridor when he came.

Imperturable as his Scotch face always seemed to be to any emotion, it now showed an involuntary concern for the pallor and sadness of Ned's appearance.　But, without noticing his expression, she said rapidly, and in a whisper:

"Be ready to drive me to the station in a quarter of an hour.　I shall meet you a little beyond the entrance to the grounds."

As Carnew, esteeming the Scotchman for his honesty and prudence, had taken him into his own special service, Macgilivray, though wondering and having his own fears at such a strange request, was obliged to obey; so he bowed, and answered:

"All right, me leddy;" since Ned's marriage he would so distinguish her.

She knew it was unnecessary to caution him to silence about her journey; the Scotchman was proverbial for his reticence on the most trivial affairs.　But Ned forgot her maid, whom she had sent for the coachman, and who was not so proverbial for *her* reticence.

Mrs. Carnew went to her room.　With feverish haste, she threw off her handsome dress, and put on one that she had worn when she was only the "companion."　Of every jewel on her person which had been Carnew's gift she divested herself; her portemonnaie, filled with his hands, she placed on her dressing-table beside the jewels, and, going to her trunk, she took from it what little had remained from her earnings with Mrs. Doloran, after she had sent a handsome present to Meg.　There was sufficient to defray her expenses until she should reach Dyke.　Then, when she was apparelled for the road, she went and listened at her husband's door.　There was a hope that he would hear her; that he might even suspect her purpose and come forth, when she could once more re-iterate her

innocence before she left him. But everything was silent ;
not even a faint moan came to her ear; and in that grave-
like stillness she went back to her room, and wrote a note
to him—a note that she sealed and left on her dressing-
table beside his gifts—her jewels and portemonnaie. She
stole out then, passing by his door again, and stopping to
kiss one of the panels, as if to delude herself into the belief
that it was a kiss wafted to him, and then she went on.
But Jane saw her—Jane, who was supposed to be in her
own apartment until summoned to assist her mistress to
retire—and Jane had the hardihood to follow.

On through the darkened grounds, for the moon would
not rise until nearly midnight, the young wife fled. Flee-
ing from husband and home ; that was the thought in
her mind as she hurried to where Macgilivray waited ;
but it was from a husband who believed her unworthy of
his love, and a home that had ceased to be such when
Alan ceased to love her.

The darkness on the outskirts of the grounds was so
great that it struck a sort of chill to her, and it brought
up, somehow, the dark night when she accompanied
Edna to look at the dead Mackay. Again she saw the
suicide, and Edna kneeling beside him, and all the horrible events of that night. Little she dreamed then that it
would cast its influence so far ahead upon her own life ;
that it would blight and blacken her hopes, her love, her
existence. She drew her cloak closer about her, and hurried on.

" By your ain sel', me leddy ? " said the astonished, and
now very much concerned Scotchman, as he flashed the
carriage lamp on Mrs. Carnew's pale and somewhat frightened face.

" Yes, Donald; I am going to take the train up the
river. I have left word for Mr. Carnew. Now drive
quick, please. There is no time to lose."

She stepped into the carriage as she spoke, and Macgilivray felt impelled to obey her order. But, at the

station, when there were still some minutes to spare, the honest fellow could not refrain from saying:

"I'm sair tribbled, me leddy, at your gang like this; it's noo me place to speak, but the leck o' you takin' sich a journey at this time o' the night, and with none but your ain sel', it's—— "

The train was shrieking its near approach, and Ned stopped him by saying:

"Thank you, my good fellow, for your concern about me; but it is quite right for me to take this journey unattended, and I have travelled before, you know."

She smiled and waved her hand to him from the platform of the car which she had ascended, but it was too dark for him to discern either very plainly.

"Right for her to tae the journey," he muttered to himself; "aye, an' right for the folks that came to-day to break her heart. She's gang awa' her ain sel', because she's noo her husband's love any more, an' it's plain eneuch that she's gang frae his hame an' his heart."

But the honest Scotchman kept his own counsel, little dreaming that before Carnew himself should be apprised from Ned's note, of her departure, the whole servants' hall, through Jane's account of all that she accidentally (?) saw, would be discussing his wife's flight.

Carnew, absorbed in his agony, hardly noted the flight of the night. When the garish dawn of the morning looked in through his windows, it found him in the same position, flung across his bed, on which he had thrown himself after entering his room and locking his door. Everything passed in review before him, from the moment that he saw her first, to the day of his marriage; every suspicion, every doubt that he had entertained of her, returned to him with a sort of new and horrible significance; even the forgotten fact of Mr. Edgar's coldness to her—Mr. Edgar who had been her educator, her benefactor—there certainly must be grave reason for the withdrawal of *his* interest, and perhaps even graver cause for the departure of Ned from Weewald Place to earn her own living. And yet, through it all, through his doubt and suspicion, through his grief and indignation, through every outraged feeling that seemed to be mastering him like so many demons, the pale, tearful, reproachful, beautiful face of his wife appeared, and he found himself clasping it in imagination to his heart, and letting fall upon it the unmanly tears wrung from him by his fierce sorrow.

Like a drowning man clutching at straws, he cast about him for some help, some hope; his great love was desperately pleading for her, and desperately struggling with the stern passions which rent him, and it won a sort of victory at last. He would hold in abeyance his entire conviction of her guilt until he saw Mr. Edgar. That gentleman would be able to throw some light on all which was now so dark; he could at least tell what Ned's conduct had been while she lived in his house, and whether he thought it probable that she could be guilty of so much duplicity. Having come to this conclusion, and being wearied in body and soul by his long hours of fevered thought, he dropped at last into a heavy slumber. But still his thoughts were busy with Ned. It seemed as if she came to him, softly, for fear of awaking him, and dropped a light kiss upon his forehead, that he opened his eyes and smiled at her, that he extended his arms to invite her to his embrace, but she glided from him, wearing the sad, reproachful look he had seen last upon her face, and then, as she disappeared entirely, not going through any door, but vanishing in that impalpable way in which people do in dreams, he saw that she was dressed for a journey; that she even carried a little travelling reticule. He tried to call her back, but his tongue refused to move, and his agonizing effort to produce some sound awoke him.

It was full day; the sun was shining brightly through his open windows, and there came faintly to him the sound of voices from the garden below. He started up, still under the influence of his dream, and unlocking his door, staggered forth into the adjoining apartment. There he was met by Jane.

"O Mr. Carnew! I was just going to ask your valet to waken you. I thought I heard Mrs. Carnew ring for me, and I went to her room, but she is not there. As I am always summoned to go to her before this hour of the morning, I couldn't help being a little uneasy, some-how."

She told the truth in some measure; she was uneasy, but from curiosity, for all night she had kept herself awake to learn if Mrs. Carnew returned; she had even the hardihood to prowl about in the vicinity of her master's room to discover whether he were really in his own room and ignorant of his wife's proceeding. With the first light of the morning, she had stolen to Ned's private dressing chamber. She saw the jewels, and the porte-monnaie, and the note beside them addressed to Alan, and she drew her own inference—an inference that made her company quite agreeable at the servants' breakfast table.

Carnew did not answer her; he hardly looked at her, but went to find Ned.

He was yearning for her presence, as it seemed to him he had never yearned for it before. He entered her room, and he saw her portemonnaie, and her jewels, and the note. With a hand that trembled so he could scarcely steady it to break the seal, he opened it.

"My Darling Husband:—I am going to Dyke; he will help and advise me. He is the only friend to whom I can turn now, for were a thousand vile accusations brought against me, his love for, and trust in me would cast them all aside. And he may be able to devise some means of proving to you my innocence. Until that time, until you can hold me to your heart again, feeling that I am as worthy of your love as you thought me on our wedding morn, I think it is better that I should remain away from you. But you will be with me always, Alan; my heart holds only you, and it never, *never* held any one else in the relation you bear and have borne to me.

I kiss you, my own, a thousand times, and may God bless
you and keep you.

"Your loving and innocent wife,

"NED CARNEW."

The letter fell from his grasp, and he sank with a groan
into a chair. Instead of softening and winning him, the
little, pathetic note only closed the tender springs of his
heart that had been opened despite himself during his
vigil of the night, and that had been made to flow even
more plentifully by his dream of the morning. She had
chosen to flee from his home, his protection, and to Dyke,
of whom she spoke even in her note in terms of endear-
ment only befitting a lover, or a husband. With strange
inconsistency he became violently jealous of Dyke. He
called to mind all Ned's fondness for Dutton, the very
kiss she had so openly given him in the office in New
York, her solicitude for him on all occasions, and at
the same time he quite forgot the right, the duty
which was hers to love him.

He quite forgot that he himself had thought that very
affection a noble trait in his wife's character, and that *he*
had even loved Dyke, because the latter was so fond of
Ned.

As men violently disturbed by passions of their own
rousing are seldom capable of seeing, even in an indistinct way, an unbiassed side of the case, so Carnew drove
on to another rock that threatened the destruction of his
happiness.

Ned had deserted him! He would not lift a finger to
bring her back, but he would go that very day to Edgar
and satisfy himself upon the point he had raised the previous night. Ah, down in his secret heart were the hope,
the wish, the passionate yearning, that, in spite of what
Edna had once told him regarding her father's little
regard for Ned, in spite of what his own eyes had witnessed
of Mr. Edgar's coldness to Ned, in spite of the fact that
Ned had always been strangely silent upon the subject,

Mr. Edgar would say something that would imply his own doubt of Ned's guilt. If Edgar doubted, could not he, her husband, doubt also? And if he doubted, could he not take her to his heart, to his love again?

O Ned, how hard your sweet face fought for the victory!

XLII.

Mrs. Carnew slept no more upon her night journey than did her husband in his bitter vigil. So impulsive had been her action, and so absorbed was she in the emotion by which her very soul was torn, that she never thought of the difficulties to be encountered in a journey to her mountain home at that unseasonable time.

The train deposited her in a village opposite Saugerties, at a late hour, and then there was the river to be crossed, and a twelve-mile drive that led up the mountains.

For the first time she realized her awkward situation, an unprotected young woman out at that hour of the night, and her heart beat violently. Still, she assured herself somewhat by remembering that she was very plainly and darkly dressed, and that her veil concealed as much of her face as was possible without obscuring her vision. And, as she looked about her in the little waiting-room, she had some thought of seating herself quietly in a corner until morning. The impracticability of that idea, however, showed itself in a moment, for a couple of loungers seated themselves at no great distance from her, and though the light in the place was too feeble to discern their faces plainly, she felt they were looking at her. Not even daring to hazard a question of them, she left her seat and went forth. She knew that hotel facilities were much greater than when she was a child, and she hoped that that there might be something of the sort convenient. She had not walked long before the appearance of a certain building seemed to promise a fulfilment of her hope, and to her satisfaction she found it was so. But the accommodations were most rude, only intended for railroad employees the people told her civilly enough, and then they as civilly added that, as she had been belated, and knew not where to go until morning, they would try to accommodate her, which accommodation not only furnished her lodging, but included her breakfast for what seemed to be a very moderate sum. She had some delay in crossing the river, the rude boat used for the transportation of passengers being slow in crossing the stream, and not over-prompt in starting; but that being at length accomplished, she had only to hire a conveyance for the mountain drive. At the place where she decided to apply, the man looked hard at her, when she said she wanted to go to Mr. Dutton's; but he made no remark further than to tell her the price of the drive, and how long it would take to reach her destination.

How the lumbering ride and the scenes about her, the familiar aspect of which came back with a suddenness that seemed to bridge over at once the gap of years intervening since she passed through them last, brought to rhe mind the old, happy days!

Changes in those times were not quite so rapid as in these days of scientific speed, and Ned recognized, or at least thought she recognized, the same unpainted houses, at such long distances apart, and even the very same roomy, open, shaky-looking barns belonging to the unpainted houses, but situated from them the length of a field. Even the mountain road, which the horse so slowly and laboriously ascended that the sleepy driver seemed to awake a little to the difficulty, and to sympathize with the beast to the extent of panting somewhat on his own account, was apparently the same she had driven along in her childhood. There were the stately trees that once to her had such human significance, and now they were passing the ravine which she used to people with the elves that Dyke told her about. Again, they came in sight of the gorge, with its unknown and dreaded depths, and then some grand old peak of a majestic mountain came in sight, with the sunlight gilding it, and the light blue sky kissing it, and all nature about it shrouding it in solitude and sublimity. Not a sound disturbed the stillness save the creaking of the wagon and the occasional puffing of driver and beast, but to Ned it seemed as if the solitude was peopled with voices—voices that cried "lost," to signify that all she was leaving was lost to her forever. She tried not to look about her, so that the voices might cease, and she tried, by thinking alone of what Dyke would say when he saw her, to shut out the memories of her childhood. But they only came the more, making her heart and her head ache; and for the last hour of the ride, she held her clasped hands on her forehead, to endeavor to lessen the violent throbbing of her temples.

At length they came in sight of the dear old dwelling. It had the same mottled appearance she remembered so well. True to his promise to Meg, Dyke had not altered an iota of its old, simple fashion. She stopped the sleepy driver and told him he need come no farther. She would alight and walk the rest of the distance. She wanted no stranger's eye on her meeting with Dyke, and she waited until the vehicle had turned about and was proceeding down the road before she went on. Then, though she had been so impatient to reach her journey's end, she walked very slowly. Her heart was beating as if it would burst from her trembling frame, and the color was going and coming in her face with fitful rapidity.

Some one came out of the little dwelling—some one who walked slowly also, as if grief or care might have weighted his steps. In a moment, she saw it was Dyke, and he was coming toward her; but he did not see her, for his head was down. She threw her veil far back and quickened her steps. He raised his eyes on the sound. On she came, opening her arms to him, and with a cry of strangely mingled joy, and sorrow, and relief, she threw herself upon his breast.

He put out his hands and held her there, too much astounded to utter a single word, and yet somehow divining that her singular visit was not made in pleasure.

Tears came to her relief, and she sobbed upon his bosom, as she had sobbed the night before on her husband's knee. He knew now that she had come to him in trouble, and he did not ask a single question while her burst of grief continued. He only held her to his heart as if, despite what terrors, what troubles might menace her, he would shield her from them all. But his face had grown very pale, and his heart was beating almost as violently as her own was doing.

When her tears had ceased, and she had lifted her head from his breast, he said:

"Now, Ned; what is the matter? And how have you come all this distance alone?"

"Come off the road somewhere, where we can talk," she answered, continuing as she took his arm, "not into the house, I don't want to go there yet; I don't want to see Meg until I have told all to you. I am so glad that I met you."

" Yes, Ned; I also am glad that I met you before you saw Meg."

There was a strange and sorrowful significance in his tones, but she did not notice it.

"Come to the wood," she said, "I can tell you all there."

And to the wood they went; the old beloved wood of her childhood, with its serried ranks of trees, now somewhat thinner, for the age of progress had penetrated there in the shape of a greater frequency of the woodman's axe. They seated themselves beneath one of the stately trees, she, with her hands clasped upon his knee, and her anxious, tear-stained face lifted to his own; he, stooped forward in his eagerness to hear, and his mouth compressed and rigid as it always became when his heart was stirred.

She told her pitiful story; from the first to the last of all that had happened, save that she did not break her oath to Edna, but she said as she had said to her husband, that she was bound by an oath, which, if she could only divulge, would immediately prove her innocence.

"But don't ask me where, nor to whom I gave the oath," she added, "for I cannot tell you."

Dyke did not answer that plea, but he said, while the rigidity about his mouth became more marked;

"And your husband did not believe *you?* He believed instead what these strange people said."

"But Dyke, how could he do otherwise in the face of so much against me. These letters of Mackay, the minister's assertion, all that I have told you? How can we blame him for thinking me guilty?"

"His love for you, Ned, should have been stronger than all that."

He arose then, as if to shake from him some painful feeling, and he walked away a few steps. Then he returned and seated himself again:

"I want a little time, Ned, to think what is best to be done for you; and you, after your long journey, and all that you have endured, sadly need rest; so, when you have had some refreshment, and have gone to bed, I shall try to form some plan for us."

She rose at once, but he gently pulled her back:

"I have something else to say. There is a change in Meg; she is not quite herself. I do not mean that she is insane, nor yet idiotic, but there is a sort of strange dotage upon her which might shock and pain you if you came upon her suddenly. She has lost her memory to a great extent, and while she will know you and greet you with affection, she will have forgotten those things that it might be your delight to have her remember. When I went to Albany for her, I noticed the change, but it was very slight then. I remained with her in Albany after our relatives had gone to Australia, in order to consult a physician. He said it was a gradual softening of the brain; that she would probably live a long time, but that she would never recover. I found a good honest woman who was willing to accompany us here, and I did not tell you about this change when I wrote, because I could not bear to sadden your anticipations of your visit to your old home. But I was glad to meet you to-day in order to prepare you before I brought you into the house. Now, Ned, we shall go."

He gave her his hand to assist her, and she with the other hand brushed away the tears his recital had caused. How everything that she loved was changing! Would Dyke change too? In appearance he had changed, and sadly so. He was slightly stooped, he who had been so erect; and his face was lined, and his hair was slightly gray, and his whole manner was touchingly indicative of silent suffering. Even in her own sorrows Ned sadly noted all that, but she also knew that while his heart continued to beat, and his intellect remained unclouded, he would never change to her.

Meg knew Ned, and evinced as many extravagant signs of delight at seeing her as she might have done in the days of her soundest mind, but her malady was soon apparent; she remembered nothing of Ned's marriage, nor of her visit to Albany where she had seen her last, nor did she make a single inquiry about the cause of Ned's present and unannounced appearance. Some indistinct remembrances of the young girl's childhood she had, and of her school-days, and that she had gone to live with Mr. Edgar, but further than that everything seemed a blank. She would nod and smile when reminded of certain incidents, but it was evident she did not remember them. She comprehended perfectly when Dyke spoke of refreshment and rest for their visitor, and she even busied herself in helping the hired woman to set the repast; afterward, she accompanied Ned to the latter's own old room, and waited until she was comfortably in bed. Then she stooped and kissed her, and Ned held for a long time to her own, the precious old face.

Her fatigue caused her to sink at once into a deep slumber, and when she awoke the long bright day was nearly done. For a moment as she looked about her on

the old, familiar surroundings of her childhood, it seemed
as if all the years which had intervened were only a dream,
and that she was really a happy child again.   In that one
brief, whirling moment, Rahandabed, Mackay, even her
husband, were no longer realities, and under that impression she started up ; and then the delusion fled.   The
cruel weight came back to her heart, the wild, burning
thoughts to her brain. She thought, while she bathed her
face, of Dyke's promise to think out some plan ; in all
those hours he surely must have done so, and she hurried
her toilet in order to join him.   But, when she came out
of her room, Anne McCabe, the strong, stout, good-
natured looking hired woman, said that Dyke had left a
note for her, and then she got the note, and Ned read :

"Dear Ned :—I have been thinking a good deal while
you slept, and I have come at last to a course of action ;
but I would rather not tell you what it is, until I have
tried it.   You have sufficient trust in me to bear with my
secrecy.   This plan of mine will take me away, for perhaps some days, but you, Ned, remain quietly as you are.
Anne McCabe is quiet and good-hearted, and little given
to curiosity. She will do all she can for your comfort.
It is a pleasure to Meg to have you, and the quiet and rest
will be beneficial to yourself.   Be as cheerful and hope-
ful as you can be, dear Ned, and He who guides us all
will steer you also safely into light and happiness again.
You shall hear from me soon.

"Dyke."

As she read it over and over, wondering what could be
the plan that took him from her side at such a time, no
inkling of the truth came to her.

Dyke, with a singular, far-seeing prudence, would not
spend one night under the roof that gave shelter to Ned.
If her husband's love had already succumbed to accusations against her, might it not further yield to suspicion
from any trifling source?   Might not her very secret
flight to Dyke, who after all was no relation, be construed

into something more against her character? At least such
were the fears that came to him, and that made him de-
termine, before he reached any other resolution, to leave
the house while Ned slept, for he could not explain his
motive to her who was so guileless, so unsuspicious. And,
when that was settled, he seemed to see his way clearer.

As he remembered Edna's character, when she was a
child, and as from what little he had managed to glean
about her in her more mature years, that character did not
seem to have lost any of its unlovely traits, he did not
think it improbable that she was in some way the source
of all the mischief. The oath of which Ned spoke, begging him not to ask where, nor to whom she had made it,
somehow confirmed his suspicion. To him, from the first
time the children saw each other, Edna had been a sort of
evil genius to Ned, and though the letters of the latter,
when she was a child at school, never complained of Edna,
still he felt that every one of her childish troubles there,
were due to her cousin. And the evil genius possibly
had not become less as the children grew; it had flamed
probably on many occasions, until it had cast this last
blight. Such were Dyke's thoughts, and he could not
curb them. He knew that Edna had married and gone
abroad. Ned had given him that news in one of her
letters just after the event, and even those facts somehow
convinced him the more. He was almost prepared to
swear that Edna was Mackay's wife and the mother of the
child. And since he was so convinced, he determined to
repair at once to Mr. Edgar and confer with that gentleman. Afterward, he would see Carnew. So, leaving
the note for Ned, and instructing Anne McCabe to be
very attentive to the young lady, he packed what he
needed for his journey, kissed Meg, who, while she returned his kiss fondly, expressed no surprise at his departure, and taking the hired man with him in order that
the vehicle might be returned, he drove rapidly to
Saugerties.

XLIII.

All Rahandabed was in commotion on the morning
after Ned's flight. Every servant in the place knew it.
Mrs. Doloran knew it, and the guests knew it almost as
soon as Carnew himself knew it. Were he not in such a
state of grief and perplexity, he must have wondered a
little how her flight became known so speedily; but, as it
was, he thought of nothing only that she *had* gone, and
gone to Dyke, that she had not taken with her one of his
gifts, that the evidence of her guilt was most conclusive,
but that in spite of it all he passionately loved her. For
some time it did not occur to him how she had gone, and
whether to New York, or to the little home in the mountains, for he had not heard Dyke's letter which told of his
return from New York. At length, however, he found
himself wondering about it, and becoming anxious for her
safety on such a journey at such an hour. He sent for
Macgilivray, as being the most likely to have driven Ned
to the station, and Macgilivray told him all that he knew.
He had driven Mrs. Carnew to take the late train up the
river, and he had purchased her ticket for Tivoli. Carnew asked no other question, but dismissed him. The
honest Scotchman was convinced then of the truth of the
impression he had received the night before; the young
wife had indeed "taken hersel' awa' frae her husband's
heart and her husband's hame," but, as before, he prudently kept his own counsel, though he was vexed and
indignant and puzzled, to find that his fellow-help knew
so much. They even asserted to his face that he had been
in waiting with the carriage for Mrs. Carnew the night
before, and that he was like the rest of his long-headed,
canny race, in keeping the affair to himself, but it didn't
do him much good, for they had found out anyway. To
all of which he replied in his dry manner:

"Then it's frae the auld hornie you got your information, and mebbe the same auld deil wouldn't mind tellin'
you where Mrs. Carnew's gang." Knowing their ignor-

ance upon that point, he gave that shot with supreme satisfaction to himself.

But one of the help retorted:

"Wait till Mrs. Doloran sends for you, as she'll be sure to do, when she finds out *you* drove Mrs. Carnew away last night. You'll not carry such a bold face with her, even though you are not in her special employ just now."

But the Scotchman answered with the same dry gravity he had used before:

"Dinna greit! me lady has tackled me before, and Donald has noo been wantin' in his ain way o' answerin' her."

The servant's prediction was verified. The moment that Mrs. Doloran heard from her own maid, who was of the kind to retail all sorts of gossip to her mistress, that Macgilivray was implicated in the flight, he was summoned to her presence; it was her way to get all the information she could from menials, before taking any other step.

The coachman was as wary, innocent, and non-committal as he had been on a former occasion, when she had endeavored to extract information about Alan; and in a perfect burst of fury, she threatened to have him summarily discharged.

"Vera weel, me leddy; when Mr. Carnew bids me I'll gang, and have noo to say but to thank him; but till then I'll noo greit."

She fairly drove him from the room, in her vulgar fury actually hurling after him a silken-covered foot-stool. It missed him, owing to his own dexterity, but it shattered two of the stained-glass panes in a window that lighted the passage leading to her apartment.

Then she sent for her nephew; an imperative summons, to which he returned a respectful reply, but one declining to see her. Such an answer did not diminish her anger, and with her face blazing, and even so swollen that her very temples seemed to project, she descended to find Ordotte. He was just entering the breakfast-room with his hands full of roses; it was his self-appointed morning task, while the roses were in bloom, to put bouquets of them beside each lady's plate; but everybody saw that Mrs. Carnew always received the largest and the handsomest flowers.

With a pleasant good morning to Mrs. Doloran, he was going to Ned's plate, selecting the roses as he went.

The lady's anger gave way to scorn.

"You can save yourself the trouble, Mascar; I suppose you have not heard, but Mrs. Carnew, overwhelmed by the disgrace of having her guilt found out, has fled from Rahandabed. She went away, secretly, last night."

Ordotte had *not* heard of the flight, and he was, perhaps, the only person in the whole place who had not, owing no doubt to his little intercourse with the servants; there was a something about his tawny face and strange manner that both awed and repelled them. Now, as he listened to Mrs. Doloran, he dropped the flowers in his surprise, and ejaculated:

"What?" in such an astonished manner, that one would think he had received an internal shock.

"Yes, she's gone, the brazen jade," resumed Mrs. Doloran. "She knew she couldn't face it out, and so she thought she had better go."

"But where has she gone?" asked Ordotte; "and what does Alan say?"

The lady shrugged her shoulders.

"That fool, Macgilivray, drove her in the carriage from here last night, but he is as close as an oyster about it; and as for Alan, like the fool that *he* is, he's shut up in his own room, and won't see anybody. I am sure we're well rid of her; Rahandabed would have been disgraced while she continued here. Faugh! how I detest her."

"Poor creature! Is there no loop-hole for her?" said Ordotte almost involuntarily.

"Poor creature!" repeated Mrs. Doloran, anger and

contempt struggling in her tones. "Do you wish to insult me, Mascar?"

"Not for all the rajahs in the Punjaub, madam," replied the gentleman with assumed penitence, and bowing profoundly, "but I was only thinking, had the proofs of her guilt been so very clear, so entirely conclusive——"

"Mascar Ordotte!" shrieked the lady, "have you taken leave of your senses? Do you want any more conclusive proofs than those letters from Mackay that you read, than what I told you of how Mr. Hayman acted, and what he said; than all the woman Bunmer tells?"

"My dear Mrs. Doloran, men have been hung on the very strongest circumstantial evidence, and after their death their innocence has been proven."

"Well, *you* had better undertake to prove *her* innocence," her voice fairly hissing from anger and scorn.

"My dear Mrs. Doloran," he had assumed what to anybody else would have been a most comical attitude, and mock expression of penitence and humility, "we shall allow the dear young lady to be quite guilty; we shall not raise the ghost of an event to prove her innocence."

He was actually on one knee, with Mrs. Doloran's hand to his lips, a scene stealthily witnessed by the butler, who had retreated to his pantry when the two entered the room, and afterward detailed by him to his fellow-help with an actual impersonation of Ordotte's attitude, that sent the whole servants' hall into convulsions of laughter.

But Mrs. Doloran was appeased, and she forgave the suppliant, and arm in arm they continued the tour of the table, placing the roses, and leaving Ned's place significantly vacant.

Early in the day, Alan was ready for his journey to Weewald Place, and Macgilivray drove him to the station, feeling certain that his master was going after the runaway wife.

Mr. Edgar was at home, and he responded in person to Mr. Carnew's card. But what a change had taken place in him! Alan started when he saw him, and extended

his hand almost as if he were in some uncertainty about
the gentleman's identity.   His hair had become entirely
gray; not a black streak was to be seen in it, and his beard
and moustache were equally bleached.   Heavy furrows
indented his face, and his eyes had the deep, hollow look
of one accustomed to long and painful vigils.

For a moment, it seemed as if he were struggling with
himself in order to be cordial, and he evidently succeeded,
for after that moment's indecision he shook Carnew's
hand warmly, and wanted to conduct him at once to one
of the guest-chambers.   But Alan kindly declined.

"My errand," he said, "is too important and too unhappy to allow of my taking any rest until I have stated
it.   I have come"—a sudden flush rushing to his face—
"to ask you some questions about my wife; to ask you
to tell me frankly what *you* know of her character.   What
was her conduct while under your roof, if the charges
here brought against her" —he drew out of his pocket
Mackay's letters, "seem likely to *you* to be true?"

And he put the packet into Edgar's hand.

"Come to the library," said Edgar, "we shall be more
comfortable there," and he led the way.

Carnew, in a fever of doubt, fear, and expectation,
watched Edgar's face while that gentleman slowly read
every one of the letters.   He did not speak when he had
finished, only put the packet aside, and looked across at
the haggard, anxious face of his visitor.

"Speak," implored Carnew, "what weight do these
letters carry to you?"

Edgar answered deliberately, as if he were testing his
words:

"Let me tell you first what I know of her pertaining
to this unfortunate Mackay."   And then he recounted in
in the same deliberate manner how he had received his
first intimation of Ned's secret acquaintance with the
gardener's son, by one day, during her stay in Weewald
Place, meeting a servant carrying to her a rare exotic, the
gift of this same Mackay.   How he had interrogated his

daughter Edna upon she subject, and what that young lady had told him; and lastly—most damaging statement of all—what Edna had told him of their secret visit to the body of the suicide when it lay on the grounds of Rahandabed; how Ned had gone to Edna and requested her to accompany her.

Carnew's heart seemed turned to ice, though his head and his eyes were burning. The very blood in his veins seemed to have frozen; he found himself wondering in a vague, incoherent way if all power of motion had gone from him; but the summit of his agony was reached; with a low, bitter cry, he threw his head forward until it rested upon the table, and then he was motionless.

Edgar rose and went to him. He put his hand softly, tenderly upon his shoulder, and he said with tones that trembled from emotion:

"Mr. Carnew, you are not alone in suffering."

Alan raised his head and perhaps seldom did two more agonized faces gaze at each other.

Edgar resumed:

"In me you behold a man who has carried a hidden agony for years. A horrid doubt was engendered for me by a near relative—a doubt that cankered all my pleasures; a doubt that, if it slumbered for a little, only awoke to gnaw and torment me with new vigor. And so it continued until a very few years ago. Then I *did* conquer it, and I was happy. In the love of my beautiful child alone I lived, and I fancied she reciprocated my affection. I imagined her devotion to be such that she could make no choice of a husband unless first assured that he would meet my approval—I who would have sacrificed my life to give *her* happiness; and yet, Carnew, how am I rewarded? How does she repay *my* love, *my* devotion? By giving her hand to one who should have been almost beneath her contempt—to one with whose imbecility I was disgusted."

He stopped, as if overcome by his emotions.

"And yet she was married with your consent?" broke

from Carnew, interested, despite his own emotions, in this strange recital from a man like Edgar.

"Because she *would* marry him, Carnew; because she dared to say that she would defy my opposition. Brekbellew could support her as luxuriously as I could do, and she did not seem to care for anything more. To save her, and to save myself from the unpleasant gossip that would ensue did I refuse my consent and close my doors to her, I yielded; but she married without my blessing, and she went abroad without my good wishes. You cannot be blind, Carnew, to the change in my appearance. The chords of my heart seem snapped. I am sick of life."

He sank into a chair and covered his face with his hands.

Both were silent for a long time; then it was Edgar who broke it by rising and saying, as again he crossed to Carnew and placed his hand on the young man's shoulder:

"We can sympathize with each other; our griefs are akin; you have an unworthy wife, I an unworthy child. In both cases, the proofs are too plain to be disputed, to be doubted, and it only remains for us to bear our sorrows with what fortitude you may."

As a fellow-feeling is said to make us wondrous kind, so the fact that both were suffering made Edgar singularly tender; he was drawn to the young man, as if he were bound by some tie of blood, and he forgot all the feelings which had been engendered by Carnew's former refusal of Edna's hand. He was almost impelled to repose full confidence in him; to tell *what* the horrid doubt had been of which he spoke; and to lay bare the thoughts that Edna's rebellious marriage had awakened in his mind; how the very obstinacy and even temper she had shown upon that occasion had recalled to her father, with a pang of horror and dismay, the disposition of his hated brother; never had the character of the latter been so reproduced, possibly because never had his beautiful daughter so boldly exerted her own headstrong will.

And when she had gone from Weewald Place, with her brainless husband, he had shut himself up to give full vent to his dreadful reflections. Could he, after all, have been mistaken? Was Edna not his own, but poor, despised Ned, who, because of her very position in his house, might perhaps be pardoned for her secret notice of the gardener's son? All this he was strangely impelled to tell, and to tell further, that again his feelings toward Ned had been changed by the perusal of Mackay's letters. His daughter could not be guilty of such duplicity; she came of too noble a race; so Ned, since the proofs of her guilt were so great, *must* be his brother's child.

But he did not tell this to Carnew. Some unaccountable repugnance to open his sores further than he had already done kept him silent.

There was nothing to restrain Carnew from disclosing all the feelings of *his* heart; he felt that nowhere could he meet with so sympathetic, so pitying a listener, and he told everything: his doubts, his fears, his suspicions, before his marriage; his amazement, his agony, his horror since; and through it like a refrain ran the confession that under all circumstances he passionately loved Ned.

" But everything is over now," he said with a bitter sadness; " I shall settle an ample amount upon her, but I shall never live with her again."

He rose then, and by a sort of tacit consent, though he remained over night, and though both gentlemen sat together until long past midnight, neither Ned nor Edna were again mentioned.

He left early on the following morning, being in feverish haste to confer with his lawyer on the subject of the settlement for his wife; he thought of going abroad after that, but he was not quite decided.

XLIV.

On the afternoon of the day of Carnew's departure from Weewald Place, Dyke arrived there, and he sent up *his* card to Mr. Edgar. That gentleman looked very much displeased upon receiving it, having yet fresh in his mind the story of Carnew, in which the latter had even confessed his jealousy of Mr. Dutton, and remembering how boldly, on more than one occasion, the same Mr. Dutton had spoken to himself, it was hardly strange that he felt disinclined to accord much favor to him. However, he descended to the reception room where Dyke waited, and bowed with his wonted courtesy, as he requested to know the object of the visit.

Dyke paused a moment to steady his tones; he even spoke with more than his usual slowness, that his feelings might be well restrained.

"I have come in the interest of Mrs. Carnew, to ask you, as her near relative, to assist in proving that she is innocent of charges that have been made against her; to —— "

"Stop!" interrupted Edgar; it will probably save time to tell you that Mr. Carnew has been here. He came, like you, with some hope that I might be able to refute these charges. He told me the whole story, and he submitted to me the proofs of her guilt which had been given to him. The interests of truth and justice demanded that I should be frank in telling what *I* happened to know of Mrs. Carnew; what I accidentally learned while she was in this house, what I heard after she had left it."

"May I ask what these things were?"

Dyke's tones were very slow still.

Edgar warmed a little while he answered him, while he told what had given the knell to Carnew's hopes.

The young man's feelings were gaining the mastery, and they were slipping from so tight a rein, that they threatened to be all the more violent. His deliberate manner of speech gave sudden way to a rapid, impassioned tone:

"Has it never occured to you, Mr. Edgar, that Mrs. Carnew is the victim of a very web of calumny; a web deliberately woven to shield another, and a guilty party?

No doubt, Mr. Carnew has told you how his wife spoke of an oath she was forced to take. That, to a clear judgment, must tell its own story, and ought to bring home to you at least a desire to investigate the case."

"I do not understand you, sir," broke from Edgar, flushed and perspiring from anger.

"Then I shall make my meaning clear. Has it never occured to *you*, as it has occurred to *me*, and as it ought to have occurred to Mr. Carnew, that Edna Edgar, now Mrs. Brekbellew, and your reputed daughter, may be the guilty party, the wife, married in secret to Mackay, and the mother of his child?"

Edgar fairly reeled for an instant; then he caught a chair, and steadying himself by it, responded fiercely:

"Never!"

He seemed unable to say more, and Dyke resumed:

"Then it is time that you entertain this suspicion; it is time that you reflect——"

"Cease!" thundered Edgar; and his manner and tones recalled to Dyke how he had once before, when Dyke was a mere lad, spoken to him in just such a manner. "How dare you make such an insinuation to me, her father! Leave this house, and never again presume to enter it. Go!" He pointed to the door.

Dyke did not move.

"I shall go, Mr. Edgar, when I have said something more, to which you *must* listen. You have no absolute facts upon which to base your belief that Mrs. Brekbellew is actually your daughter, and what, if in the future, in the strange dispensations of a retributive Providence, proofs should be forthcoming that she is *not* your daughter, but that she, who to-day is so vilely calumniated, whose love is outraged, whose heart is broken, is your child, what in such a time will be your feelings? Look to it, that retribution in that shape does not overtake you. Good-by."

He was gone before Edgar could answer a word, but

he had **put** a barbed arrow into that proud, quivering heart, that no effort could draw out.

On to Rahandabed was Dyke's next proceeding; on, to force Carnew into the belief that he himself held of Ned's innocence; on, to wring from those who accused her the justice they would not give. His impatience could scarcely brook any delay, and allowing himself time for neither rest nor refreshment, he reached C—— late that same night. There he had to stop, for he could scarcely present himself in Rahandabed at such an hour; so he supped and lodged in the hotel, and early the next morning continued his journey.

Carnew had not breakfasted when Dyke was announced, and the servant who brought up his name told it to another servant, who managed to convey it to Mrs. Doloran's maid, who gave the information to Mrs. Doloran, and that lady, driven by her curiosity into unwonted hardihood, actually went to her nephew's suite of apartments, and ensconced herself in his parlor, in order that she might see the stranger as he came out of Carnew's study; her information being to the effect that Mr. Carnew would receive Mr. Dutton in his private library.

As Carnew had been surprised at the change in Mr. Edgar, so was Dutton surprised and even shocked at the change in Carnew. Scarcely more than two months before he had seen the young man in the full bright flush of a handsome, vigorous manhood; now he beheld him, worn and haggard, as if weeks of illness had passed over him. The change softened Dyke's heart. He felt that it was grief for Ned which had caused it, and he broached his errand kindly and even tenderly. But Carnew was not disposed to be softened; he had suffered so much; he was so sore from the accumulated proofs of his wife's guilt, and, more than all, he was so weak from the struggle that he had waged with himself all the preceding night to cast her entirely out of his heart, and in which he fancied he had succeeded, that he was not inclined to receive Dyke in any friendly spirit. Further, his unreasonable jealousy made him regard his visitor as one who would even perjure himself in the interest of Ned. With such feelings *he* was not stirred to pity, as he saw the premature age and suffering in Dyke's appearance, and with coldest courtesy he motioned him to a seat, and seating himself opposite, listened politely, but that was all.

Dyke told his story with simple brevity : what he knew of the character of the two Ednas when they were children, and his suspicions.

Not a muscle of Carnew's face moved, and he answered a little wearily :

" This is absurd on your part, Mr. Dutton, and preposterous as well, that you should, in the face of the clearest evidence against Mrs. Carnew, attempt to fasten the charges upon Mrs. Brekbellew. In the first place, if the latter had the cleverness for such a course of deceit, there would not be wanting times and circumstances, during such a protracted period, of betraying herself in some manner. Your supposition is most illogical."

He warmed a little as he continued :

" There is hardly a link wanting in the evidence against Mrs. Carnew ; her very visit, ostensibly to Albany, made at the very time this child was born, is a most significant circumstance."

It was Dyke's turn to fire up, and he answered indignantly :

" Mrs. Carnew's visit *was* made to Albany at the time of which you speak."

" Was it ? " spoken coldly, for here was an opportunity for Dyke to assert what was untrue, in order to serve Ned ; and the same cold voice continued :

" Can you prove it ? Were *you* there at the time ? "

" No ; I was not there at the time ; but I can prove that *she* was there and——" he stopped suddenly, remembering his little means of proof ; Meg remembered nothing of the visit ; her relatives were on their way to Australia, and he could not even write to them until he should receive their letter.

Carnew smiled grimly at the sudden break in the hotly spoken speech, and he said with an unmistakable decision as he rose :

"It is no use, Mr. Dutton; we cannot banish nor dispute the facts which stamp Mrs. Carnew as being, when I married her, the widow of Mackay, and the mother of his child. As such, she ceases to be my wife. I shall go to New York to-day in order to have settled upon her a sufficient annual sum, and then, I shall forget her."

Dyke could not control himself; he also rose.

"Since she ceases to be your wife, she shall also cease to be dependent upon your support. Discarded wife though she may be, she is not without friends, Mr. Carnew."

The indignant, defiant speech roused Alan's hot, jealous blood, and he answered with a bitter sarcasm :

"No doubt, since she has your home and your *heart*." with a taunting emphasis on the last word, "to rush to, when she flees from her husband's protection."

"Say but another word like that, Mr. Carnew, and I shall forget that you are her husband." Dyke advanced threateningly, the blood firing his cheeks; but Alan did not move, nor did the expression of his face change.

"Your wife is as pure as the snow when it falls," Dyke continued passionately; "and that even you, whose trust in her should have been great enough to shield her in the face of every accusation, could have no taunt to throw at her, I left my home within two hours after she had entered it. I have not seen her since, nor shall I return to her while she claims its shelter. But, as I hold a brother's right to her, I can work for her support. I did it before, and now that she is wronged, calumniated, discarded; that you, her husband, refuse to believe her, it will be my duty, more than ever, to provide for her."

It was impossible not to admire the young man; he seemed so noble, so brave, so true, and even Carnew felt a brief involuntary admiration and respect; but after that, his old feelings returned, and he answered with his former coldness :

"Mrs. Carnew can do as she chooses about using her allowance. It shall be made regardless of her feeling in the matter." He rang for a servant to escort Dyke out, and he waited until the servant came, and Dutton with a brief, "good morning," had departed.

Mrs. Doloran had an excellent view of him as he passed out, and she was still surveying the door through which he had gone, when Alan came from the study into her presence. He started when he saw her, and then he colored with resentment at her intrusion.

"What is the meaning of this unannounced visit ?" he asked sternly.

"Now, Alan, none of your tragics," by which she meant that her nephew was not to show any indignation. "I am going to know the meaning of the way you're acting. You haven't let me know a word about Ned——"

"Why should I ?" he interrupted ; " you settled her fate by declaring that she should never enter Rahandabed again."

"And you have really sent her off—you dear, good, sensible boy."

"No, I did not send her off. She went herself," becoming petulant.

"I know she went herself ; but you have sent her word that she is never to come back ; that you will never receive her again as your wife ?"

He bent his most stern and piercing look upon her.

"How much of my conversation in that room," pointing to his library, " have you heard ? "

She pretended to be indignant.

"Not a word. Do you suppose I came here to listen to your private conference ? I came here to know what you mean by shutting yourself away from everybody since Ned's flight, and where you went the day before yesterday, when you took that journey, and who that man is, calling upon you so early this morning ? You are just involving the whole house in mystery, and treating me, your aunt, shamefully.”

“Then I must continue to treat you, my aunt, shamefully, for I shall satisfy your curiosity no further than to say, that I did not send word to my wife that I would not receive her again. As I have not yet breakfasted, you will please excuse me.”

He left the room. His aunt was furious with disappointment. She had not gained an iota of the information for which she had come, but she consoled herself by reporting to the guests that word had been sent to Ned never to return to Rahandabed; her husband would under no circumstances ever receive her again.

A couple of hours later, she was thrown into further dismay by the announcement from Ordotte that he was going abroad; he would leave Rahandabed that very evening, in order to secure an early passage to England. Her surprise and her regret were so genuine, that she forgot to indulge in the hysterics with which she usually received unpleasant announcements. Instead, she held up her hands, and continued to gaze at the speaker in a sort of speechless horror. Ordotte laughed a little at the spectacle she presented; then he composed his face, took her uplifted hands within his own, and led her gently to a seat, where he bent over her and said very softly :

“My going away has to do with a secret; with a mystery, in which even you, my dear Mrs. Doloran, may find yourself somewhat involved. But you must not reveal this to a soul; you must not even tell that I have gone anywhere but to England for a few weeks; whereas, I am really going to India after I leave England. But I shall not be absent more than a few months. Next winter will see me here again, and with such a sensation as shall make Rahandabed famous for generations.”

The lady’s dismay had vanished; delighted interest had taken its place.

“Can it be possible, Mascar ? ” she said. “ How novel, how beautiful! But why may not Alan and myself accompany you? In the present state of his feelings, this journey would be the very thing for him."

The tawny face affected to be distorted with horror.

"My dear Mrs. Doloran, were *any one* to accompany me, it would prevent forever the unravelling of the mystery. Do you not remember what I told you of those strange people in India who can leave their bodies in one place. and stalk forth in a visible spirit to a great distance? Well, I mean to visit one of those; having lived as long in the country as I did, I made the acquaintance of some of these people, and to good purpose, for the acquaintanceship will serve me vastly now. But, were I to go accompanied, they would refuse to cast any spell for me, and my journey would be in vain."

"But we need not accompany you just there," persisted the lady; "we could even remain in England until your return."

Ordotte shook his head.

"I have a task to do in England which necessitates my going alone. I regret that it should be so, as much as you do, my dear Mrs. Doloran, and nothing but the fact that I am about to unravel a tremendous mystery sustains me in my effort to tear myself from Rahandabed."

"Tell me the mystery," demanded the lady

"Do you wish me to kill myself?" he answered, assuming a passion that somewhat frightened his companion. "I should have to do so if I breathed a word of this *awful* mystery;" with an awful emphasis on the next to the last word, "and I have only told it to you, that you would sympathize with my anxiety," changing his manner to one of sorrowful tenderness, "that you would wish me good speed on my journey, that—" his voice became very tender— "you would cherish my memory during my absence; not that you would harrow my soul by wishing to accompany me when it is impossible for me to consent."

He drew back a little, and looked the picture of dejection.

The lady was touched, as she always was when Ordotte seemed to be affected.

"O Mascar! why accuse me? I never meant to harrow you—you know I love—I think too much of you—I——" the rest of the sentence was lost in a hysterical sob.

Ordotte came back to her, and dropped on his knees at her feet.

"Cease to weep, my dear Mrs. Doloran ; I believe you, and I know the depth, the sincerity of your friendship for me "--he always studiously avoided the word affection—" and I know that though my stay abroad should extend to six months, your friendly feelings will not diminish ; the hospitable doors of Rahandabed will not be closed to me.".

"Never, Mascar, never; *I* am mistress here, and you shall always be received with open arms."

And, as if she would exemplify her words, she opened her own arms and seemed about to fold them round the kneeling gentleman, but he evaded her endeavor in some sly, skilful way of his own; and then being certain that he had pacified her, and quite reconciled her to his solitary departure, he seated himself beside her, and began to discuss the probable length of his journey.

When the hour of his departure came, Mrs. Doloran *would* accompany him to the station, and what was her surprise to see her nephew there; he had just stepped from his carriage, and was giving some order to Macgilivray. Regardless of all propriety, she leaned from her own conveyance, and called to him.

He was obliged to go to her, but he bit his lip with vexation ; he had the strongest objection to being questioned on his intended journey—an objection that was not lessened as he caught sight of Ordotte's face.

But Mrs. Doloran for once was not so anxious to seek information as to give it. She began with impressive volubility :

"How strange and how delightful ; both of you going

to New York; and when I tell you, Alan, that Mascar is going away for the purpose of unravelling a mystery, an awful——" she stopped short and suddenly, for the gentleman she had mentioned, finding no other way to remind her of her promise of secrecy, brought his foot heavily down upon her own; but even that did not improve her memory; it only extorted from her an—

"O-o-o-oh! Mascar, you were very awkward just then. You have hurt my foot dreadfully," and then she went on with all that she knew of the motives for Mascar's journey, while he, with a most expressively amused look, muttered something about attending himself to his ticket, instead of allowing the footman to do it, and left the carriage.

Mrs. Doloran, in the full tide of her account, did not oppose him, as she would have done at another time.

"Isn't it all very wonderful, Alan?" she still continued, when she had repeated every word that had passed between Ordotte and herself; "and if he could only have taken you and me, as I wanted him to do."

"I should certainly have declined the privilege of accompanying him, if he had consented," returned Alan ironically.

"Then may I ask where you are going now?" she retorted angrily.

"As you have already guessed, to New York."

"And what are you going to do there?" she questioned in the same angry tone.

"Nothing that concerns *you*."

And after that there was no further time for conversation, for the train was in sight, and all of Mrs. Doloran's feelings were absorbed in her parting with Ordotte. She cried upon his shoulder in spite of all his efforts to prevent her, and she even managed to get her arms around his neck, from which embrace he was obliged to use violence to release himself, or he would have missed the train. And all the way home she cried to herself; being alone in the carriage, there was no one to help her if she went into hysterics.   But she soliloquized upon her aggravated trials, how unprotected she was left, Mascar and her nephew both gone ; and then she called her nephew a brute, and otherwise stigmatized his treatment of her.   She did not dream that his treatment of her was due to her own harsh judgment of Ned.   Had she expressed one pitying word for Mrs. Carnew, had she uttered one doubt of her guilt, Alan would have gone on his knees to serve her ; but the more severe she grew to the discarded wife, the more the young husband felt like being cold and insolent to her.

Promises with Mrs. Doloran were most unstable things. She kept one only so long as it suited her; and thus it was with the promise of secrecy which Ordotte had exacted from her.   No sooner had she returned to Rahandabed, than all the guests were regaled with the mysterious object of Ordotte's journey.   And by that time, her imagination having had time to work, her account was so mysterious it would have puzzled Ordotte to recognize even the bare elements of that which he had said to her.

XLV.

On the train, Carnew selected the most retired seat he could find, even drawing his hat over his eyes in order to signify more unmistakably his desire for his own companionship.   But as he neared New York, he felt some one drop into the vacant seat beside him; even then he did not remove his hat, nor make any motion, not until a familiar voice pronounced his name.   He looked up to meet the tawny, smiling face of Ordotte.

" Pardon my intrusion," he said in his cool, easy manner, " I have not done so, you see, until the last moment ; and I would not do so, only to clear some undefined notions about my journey which your aunt may have left in your mind."

Carnew roused himself a little.

"I really have not given myself a thought about your journey. I scarcely heard what my aunt said."

"Then so much the easier to explain myself," with a manner that was proof against any rebuff. "You see, my dear fellow, when I bound Mrs. Doloran to secrecy, I did it knowing perfectly well she would repeat everything I said to her, just as she did to you, despite my painful reminder of stepping on her foot. And when you return to Rahandabed, you will find upon all sides of you such a version of the mysterious causes which led to my journey that you will ha·dly recognize me, or your worthy aunt. In order, then, to clear up beforehand these mysteries that await you——"

Carnew interrupted him.

"I assure you, Mr. Ordotte, I have not the slightest interest in anything you mention. I must beg to be excused from listening any longer."

Once more he drew his hat over his eyes and leaned back in his seat.

Ordotte leaned over him and whispered, if that could be called a whisper which had to be spoken loud enough to drown the noise of the cars :

"Will you make me the same reply when I say that you are most deeply concerned in this mystery I am going to have explained ? "

Carnew sat bolt upright.

"I do not understand you, sir."

"Nor can I explain myself further; but that perhaps is sufficient to win me your attention for a few minutes."

Carnew looked cold and haughty still, but he did not make any attempt to relapse into his former position, and Ordotte continued, with an expression of face not at all in accord with the serious words he was saying ; but that was his *ruse* to make the people about him think he was only holding a light and bantering conversation.

" You have never given me much friendship, Carnew, and you have done your best to make my stay short in Rahandabed. You have been most dissatisfied and worried about your aunt's · preference for me, fearing that she might do the desperate thing of marrying me; not that you would lose anything by her marriage, but because you did not want the family disgraced by her union with such an Indian mountebank as you regarded me. Nay, don't disclaim my assertion yet; I have not finished," as he saw Carnew about to speak; but the latter would interrupt with :

"Instead of being about to disclaim your assertion, I was going to say that you certainly had read correctly my feelings toward you."

Ordotte laughed so that his exquisitely white teeth were quite visible for a moment, and resumed :

"Well, I am leaving Rahandabed now, without having married your worthy aunt, and if it be decreed that I should never return, then will be dashed for you one of those singular joys which only come once in several generations. I have watched you, young man, as I watch everybody with whom it is my lot to be thrown, and despite your unfriendly feelings toward me, I have liked you. Not knowing that I should meet you on the train, I had some intention of seeing you privately before I left Rahandabed, in order that I might say a little of what I have just now stated; but your good and worthy aunt really left me no opportunity. Come now; are we friends ? "

He laughed again, as if he had been telling a good story, and had with an effort restrained his mirth until it was finished. And he did not give Carnew time to reply, for he resumed immediately that his laugh had gone back to a smile :

"Do not take the trouble to protest your suddenly acquired friendship for me, nor to display your penitence for your treatment of me in the past. I should be overcome if you did; but think of me as one who has gone abroad in your interest; and should success reward me and enable me to restore to you something that you now deem lost forever, why then overwhelm me with your contrition and your friendship. Until the arrival of that time, farewell!'"

He glided away before Carnew could stop him by word or motion, and as the train was just then rushing into its destination, he was not able, in the bustle that ensued, to catch even a glimpse of him.

The young man regarded it all as the senseless vagaries of a man who, now that he was leaving Rahandabed, wished to create in his favor a diversion on the part of one whose dislike he had so clearly read. What could *he*, a foreign stranger, do toward restoring that suddenly vanished happiness? Oh, no; the mysterious innuendo was of a piece with the singular conversations in which Ordotte always indulged, and that so easily won foolish, credulous Mrs. Doloran. For him they had neither truth nor charm, and his lip curled with scorn as he reflected upon the recent attempt to enlist *his* interest and curiosity. Even the suspicion that he once had of Ordotte's secret knowledge of something pertaining to Ned, and that now recurred to him, no longer affected him.

His mind was irrevocably made up. Ned was guilty beyond the merest shadow of a doubt, and doubly so since she had chosen to desert him and flee to the protection of Dyke; and with an inflexible will he executed his plan of the settlement for her. But when it was all concluded; when he had signed his name to the last of the documents required in the case; when he knew that the cold, hard legal announcement, unaccompanied by any softening word from himself, would go to Ned—a strange film came over his eyes, that made him hasten his adieu to the lawyer, and almost stagger forth into the sunshine. After that, he tried to mature his plan of going abroad, but it was useless. Every impulse of his heart pleaded for a return to Rahandabed, and he tried to excuse his indecision by thinking that his presence was necessary to protect his aunt from being victimized by her own follies; but that was only a species of self-deception too flimsy for even his wilfully obscured vision; for he knew that the secret and all powerful motive was the fact that Rahandabed was redolent of Ned's presence, and not after all at such a great distance from her; to go abroad would place thousands of miles between them. So back to Rahandabed he went, leading a more secluded life than ever, with his books and his solitary rides that always took the direction of Ned's mountain home, and daily increasing in petulance and irony to Mrs. Doloran.

Ned had received at last the anxiously looked-for letter from Dyke; every day, since his departure the hired man had gone down to the post-office in Saugerties, but only to return empty-handed until Dyke had been gone five days.

Then he bore a packet with the well-known superscription. She tore it open, and read:

"DEAR NED:—My news is so unsatisfactory that I have scarcely the heart to write. Still, into the blackest darkness may come, when we least expect it, a streak of light, and I feel that it will be so in your case. My little plan in your behalf has quite failed. I thought perhaps to learn from somebody something that would cast a doubt on these cruel charges; but I have learned only that your husband intends to settle upon you a large amount yearly. Use your own judgment about accepting it, but remember, dear Ned, that if your heart should shrink from taking any support from one whose trust has turned to doubt, my home is yours as it used to be in your childhood, and my means are ample for your support. Nor need you hesitate to accept what I offer, through a proud fear of being dependent, for, my business demanding my constant presence in New York, with whom could I trust poor, dear old Meg? Anne McCabe is good, it is true, but in dear Meg's present state, it would make me very anxious to know that there was only Anne McCabe with her. So you see, dear Ned, what a charity will be your acceptance, at least for the present, of the proposition I submit; that is, in case you think it better to refuse your husband's offer.   But even should you accept the latter, your present home can continue to be such, can it not?

"I shall be unable to return to you, as I resume business to-morrow, but you shall hear from me often, and now, dear Ned, no matter what occurs, do not lose heart nor hope. Remember that the clouds cannot always lower, and that your innocence, and trust in Heaven, will win at last the reward that Heaven alone can give.

"Yours,

"DYKE."

He had been very careful not to say of whom he had tried to learn something that might cast a doubt on the cruel charges; not to hint that he had called upon Mr. Edgar and upon her husband, and not to intimate that his sudden and premature return to business was due to his resolution to keep away from his home while it sheltered Mrs. Carnew.

And none of these things dawned upon her mind as she read the letter; nothing but the desolate fact that her husband had indeed repudiated her, when he intended to make a settlement upon her; in her misery she never questioned what Dyke's plan had been, and though she recognized his noble soul in the gentle, generous, and delicate wording of his letter, still it took nothing from her wretchedness.   She went to her room and sobbed over the letter, until its neatly written page was a mass of blisters.

That same evening, when she had begun her answer to Dyke, thanking him for his offer and accepting it, since she could be useful to dear old Meg, one of the neighbors, who lived a little further down the mountain, and who had been to Saugerties that afternoon, brought up another letter addressed to Mrs. Carnew, in the care of Mr. Dykard Dutton.   It was the letter from the lawyer, announcing the settlement that her husband had made upon her.   Not a word from Carnew.   Just a few brief, legal lines, and nothing more.   Her old temper rose, and, for the time, indignation supplanted every other feeling.   He might at least have sent one kindly word. She was convinced that, if an hundred such charges had been brought against him, *she* would not have doubted, and with that fiery spirit still sustaining her, she pushed aside her half-written letter to Dyke, and wrote to her husband:

"Mr. Carnew :—Since you evidently consider our married relations sundered, I cannot accept the settlement you have made. I do not need, nor shall I touch one cent of the amount.

"Ned."

She was determined to be as brief and cold as possible, and she swallowed the gulp in her throat, and brushed the film from her eyes, resolved to give way no more to her unhappy feelings. But that was so easy to resolve, and so hard to do; when her letters were finished, and addressed and sealed, and she retired to the darkness and solitude of her own little room, where Carnew's image came tender and trusting as he once was, and the dreary future spread before her, in which, perhaps, she was to know him no more forever, her fortitude again gave way, and the pillow upon which she rested her head was saturated with her tears.

Was there no way out of this horrible blank, nothing which *she* could do to help herself? Yes, there was something; something of which she had thought before, but had not done. She could write to Mrs. Brekbellew, making her appeal so strong that a heart of stone must be touched by it. But then came the thought, would Mrs. Brekbellew be willing to take any steps in Ned's behalf, when so doing must expose herself? "But why should *I* suffer so bitterly when she is the guilty one?" moaned Ned.

"And *her* husband may not think it so dreadful if the story comes to him from her own lips. At all events, it is her duty to clear me; to release me from my oath. To-morrow I shall write to her father for her address."

And on the morrow she did so, a brief, polite note, containing no more than the request for Mrs. Brekbellew's foreign address.

The three letters went forth together, the hired man starting early with them in order to be in time for the first mail from Saugerties.

Mr. Edgar received his first, and he smiled a little scornfully, wondering if the note was of Dyke's prompting, remembering the latter's insinuations against Mrs. Brekbellew, and what he or Ned could expect to gain by writing to his daughter. However, he answered it, but saying respectfully and briefly that, as Mrs. Brekbellew was travelling upon the continent, preparatory to an extended stay in London, he could not give her exact address; but any letter addressed for her, to "Brekbellew & Hepburn, Strand, London," would be forwarded to her.

A little later in the day, Carnew received Ned's communication. He was indignant at her rejection of his settlement, and divining that her independence was due to Dyke, he was more violently inflamed than ever against that individual. He tore the little note into pieces, and flung them into a large empty vase that rested against one side of the fire place. He would not answer it, and the settlement should remain.

The day after, Dyke received *his* reply, and when he had read it, he put it away with a sort of sad satisfaction; he was glad that Ned had refused the settlement, and it was a joy for him to work for her; but he wished that he could entertain a little less bitter feeling for Carnew. As it was, he almost hated him for his distrust and doubt of Ned.

XLVI.

"Ordotte, old fellow! where *did* you come from, and how do you do, and where have you been, and what have you been doing, and when did you arrive, and where are you stopping, and——" the numerous questions were cut short by the speaker's positive inability to continue them.

He was a short, thick-set man, with a very red face and puffy cheeks, and a mouth that seemed always on the point of blowing something away. He had little light-blue eyes, however, which had a certain trusty winning sparkle, and a way of clasping a friend's hand that went right to the friend's heart. He was still shaking Mr. Ordotte's hand with a vigor and significance that quite atoned for his loss of speech, when that gentleman good-humoredly broke in:

"You swoop down upon me with so many questions at once that it will be an hour's task to answer you. I came yesterday from Liverpool, where I landed from New York, the day before; I am in excellent health; I have been, as you have been aware from my letters, sojourning with a Mrs. Doloran, of Rahandabed; I have been doing nothing in particular, and I am stopping for the present at the Grosvenor Arms."

"Capital, old fellow," accompanied by a vigorous slap on Ordotte's shoulder; "you have answered all my questions in a very neat manner. And now come along; we'll have a chop together down here at the Picadilly, and this evening I'll introduce you to our club. By Jove! how your letters used to amuse them. Why, we had extras the nights your letters came. I used to read them to the whole assembled club—I mean the parts that described that place Rahan—— something (but no matter for names), and that odd Mrs. Doloran. Everybody used to go into fits, and call them devilish fine."

"Read my letters aloud to the whole assembled club!" repeated Ordotte, stopping short in the walk both had begun, and looking at his companion with a sort of horrified stare.

"Why, yes, old fellow. I didn't tell you so when I replied to you, lest the fact that they *were* going to be read aloud might impede your style. Now don't be cut up about it. Of course, I did not read anything pertaining to private affairs, only your amusing descriptions and your capital hits at the different characters you met. For instance, that imbecile fellow Brekbellew, whose uncle I wrote to you was in business on the Strand with the father of one of our fellows, Hepburn. The fellows in our club laughed about him till the tears ran down some of their cheeks."

By this time Ordotte had either been quite appeased, or he deemed it best to appear so, and both had resumed their way to the Picadilly, Ordotte's friend continuing:

" Didn't he make a lucky marriage, though—a beautiful girl and an heiress. When they came here on their wedding trip, they stopped at old Brekbellew's for a day or so, and Hepburn, of our club—he's the youngest and the richest man in it—saw her. He raved about her for a fortnight afterwards. Whatever induced her to marry such a man ? Why, his uncle says he hasn't the brains of a calf, and what with his idiocy, and his capacity for being gulled and victimized, and his insane desire to create a princely impression about himself, even *his* large fortune will dwindle in a little while ; but then his wife is said to be immensely rich."

By this time they had reached The Picadilly, and Mr. Munson's volubility was inspired afresh when an appetizing lunch was placed before him and his friend.

" Nothing like our London porter," he said with a blow of satisfaction as he put down his empty glass, and refilled it. " You have gotten into American ideas," as he saw that Ordotte's had scarcely touched his.

" You people over there don't know how to breed bone and muscle as we do," touching with a gesture of pride his own short, stout arm.

" You forget," answered Ordotte, laughing, " the effect of my Indian life. Remember I have been ten years in that ghastly country with not much opportunity for making bone and muscle."

" That's a fact, old fellow," speaking with his mouth half-full. " I remember when you came from India to get all that money that was left to you; you were even more of a scrawny, tawny-looking being than you are now. And then you went to Italy, didn't you, and met that queer Mrs. Doloran there ? "

Ordotte nodded.

" And how long are you going to stay here ? and how did you come to leave Rahan—— devil take the name ? You didn't say anything in your last letter about coming to London."

" I didn't know it myself at the time ; something happened shortly afterward to make me decide on the journey, and I am not going to stay in London longer than to made arrangements to go to India."

" To India again ! " Mr. Munson's glass, on its way to his mouth, was stopped at about a foot from that capacious receptacle, and his little sparkling eyes were transfixed with astonishment.

" What the devil are you going to do there ? "

" A little business bordering perhaps on the occult. You know there are jugglers there, and persons having the gift of second sight, and people who approach you visib'y in spirit, and converse with you, and tell you mysterious things, but whose fleshly bodies may be at that precise time fifty miles distant."

" Don't, Ordotte, don't tell me any more ; you are withering the marrow in my backbone," and in order to restore the vigor of the said marrow, he emptied his glass and called for another, making the third measure of porter.

But Ordotte, without noticing the interruption, continued :

" I am going to see one of these persons, an old man who dwells in the Terai, and with whom I have had, when I lived in India, more than one mysterious conversation. If I can find him, I shall ask his help, and I do not think he will refuse. If I cannot find him, I shall search for another of his kind."

" Upon my soul, Ordotte, you talk as if you had been studying the black art."

" Perhaps I have—the black art of reading other

people's hearts"—and then he finished at a draught his first glass of porter.

Manson ate on in silence, looking as if he were strangely divided between his desire to satisfy his voracious appetite and his wish to ask more questions. At length the latter prevailed, and as the grease from his well-buttered chop trickled smoothly down his ample chin, he inquired how long would Ordotte's stay be in India, and whether he would return to England, or to New York.

"I cannot tell the length of my stay in India, as my errand may require more time than I think, and I shall not return to New York from there unless I can learn that Mrs. Brekbellew has also returned to that city. I have quite a desire to see her for the sake of old times; you remember what interesting accounts I gave of her, and if she should remain abroad, I shall certainly make the effort to meet her somewhere."

"Well, old fellow, I think *I* can keep you posted as to her whereabouts. You know her husband writes to his uncle regularly. I guess he does it as a stroke of policy. He may be his uncle's heir, and, anyhow, every letter directed to them comes to Brekbellew & Hepburn first, and the firm forward it to the young couple. The're in Paris now, spending lots of money, and Mrs. Brekbellew's beauty and accomplishments are the theme of every *salon*. I shouldn't wonder if her poor idiot of a husband hadn't by this time become like most French husbands of a certain class, a sort of figure-head."

And having finished his chop and his porter simultaneously, and his companion also having finished his slighter gastronomical operations, both sallied forth, after a little, taking leave of each other, and Ordotte walked slowly back to his hotel, ruminating on all that he had heard about Mrs. Brekbellew.

That evening he sent a note of excuse to Mr. Munson, pleading fatigue as the cause of his inability to be present at the club meeting, and expressing deep regret that he

should be obliged to forego the pleasure. And while
Munson, having read the note to the assembled members,
was discanting upon his own unexpected meeting with
the writer of the same, and the mysterious object of his
journey to India, Ordotte was penning a letter to Mrs.
Doloran. It was the first he had written her since he left
Rahandabed, and he filled it with the items which he
knew would most please her. In an incidental way he
mentioned what he had heard of Mrs. Brckbellew's
triumphs, and he promised to write again as soon as he
reached India.

XLVII.

Life in Rahandabed moved at its old gait; indeed, it
was faster and more vivacious than ever, owing to Mrs.
Doloran's desire, now that Ordotte was away on such a
mysterious journey, to fill up the time with excitement so
that it would pass the quicker.

The house was so constantly crowded with guests that
it presented more the appearance of a hotel than a family
country mansion, and excursions by day and parties by
night continued without intermission.

Carnew was disgusted with it all, but as no one, not
even his aunt, dared to invade his solitude, he was not
disturbed further than by seeing occasionally a little of
the lamentable folly. He knew it would be useless to
attempt to check it, or even to remonstrate, as Mrs. Doloran's self-will was now roused to such a pitch that even
the restraint Alan used to exercise upon her seemed to
have lost its power. In one thing he *did* interfere, and
by so doing called down upon himself the real or seeming
animadversions of pretty much the whole house, for the
entire society of Rahandabed was formed of fashionable
satellites, who revolved around the mistress, and possessed
their souls only through hers. It was, when she announced her charitable intention of keeping the woman
Bunmer and her baby charge, in Rahandabed. For Mr.

Dickson she had actually obtained, through the influence of her friends, a very lucrative position in New York, and to Mr. Hayman she had sent a handsome donation, with the promise of renewing the same annually; but for Bunmer and the child, since Mrs. Carnew had so shamefully discarded her own offspring, it became "her duty," spoken in accents of the most stern virtue, to provide for them in a tender manner. So, in the servants' hall was Mrs. Bunmer installed, with a very comfortable apartment entirely to herself, and no labor required of her but the careful nursing of the baby.

Alan swore when he discovered all that, but his aunt assumed a greater appearance of virtuous indignation than ever, and went into such hysterics that the whole house came about her, and her nephew was glad to retreat to his own solitary and secluded apartments.

When the letter came from Ordotte, she read it to everybody, and insisted upon reading it to Carnew, for that purpose sending for him. He returned a short but respectful reply, declining the proposed pleasure, as he had no interest in Mr. Ordotte.

"But he shall hear it, for all that," persisted Mrs. Doloran, and straightway she went to his apartments. He was in his own room, and that was locked against her. Down she went on her knees, so that her mouth could be on a line with the keyhole.

"My dear Mrs. Doloran——"

"Good God!" said Alan to himself, as the words, fairly shouted through the aperture, made him start in his chair, and sent into convulsions of subdued laughter some of the servants who were surreptitiously listening in the next apartment, "how shall I rid myself of her?"

"I have had a most pleasant voyage," pursued the stentorian tones, "and one that I should have enjoyed exceedingly were it not for my regret at leaving Rahandabed and you——"

"Thank Providence, some one appreciates me," thrown in from herself by way of a reproachful parenthesis.

" When I arrived in London, I met a dear old friend, Mr. Munson by name ; " " but what's the use of reading the whole of such a nice letter to you ; you wouldn't appreciate it.   I'll just go on to what it says of that lovely Mrs. Brekbellew ; she's in Paris, with the Emperor himself at her feet. If you had married *her*, now, as I wanted and begged you to do "—she had never asked him to do anything of the kind, but that didn't make any difference in the present instance—" instead of that shameless, brazen, good-for-nothing Ned——"

She was cut short by the sudden opening of the door, so sudden that, as the door opened outwards, it sent her flat on her back in a most ungraceful sprawl.

The hot words on her nephew's lips could come no further as he saw his aunt's position, and if they could, they would not be heard, for she set up a succession of screams that brought the whole corps of listening servants into the room.   Alan, seizing his hat, fled from the apart-ment, and ordering his horse, dashed away on a frantic ride.

But he had taken his wonted direction, and as he rode through the fresh, blooming country, somehow there stole into his troubled thoughts the reminiscences which Ned had told him of her child-life, when she talked to the trees ; and then there came conjectures about her present life, what she was doing, how she employed her days, whether Dyke *did* refrain, as he had said he would do, from visiting her, and whether her heart had become really as cold to him as her last brief note would indicate ; and lastly, he felt such a wild, uncontrollable yearning to ascertain something about her, that he actually turned about and rode straight to C—— again, where he put up at the hotel, and dispatched a messenger to Macgilivray to request the latter to take home his horse.

Then he took the train up the river, crossed to Sauger-ties, found a better place of refreshment than Ned had discovered, and the next morning sallied forth, hardly knowing what the object of his journey had been, nor what he now intended to do.

The village, though quite worthy of the name then, was not so populous nor so well-built as in these progressive days, nor did the people have such a smart, half-city look. And everybody stared at him; so elegant a looking gentleman had not greeted the eyes of many of them before, and all unconscious of any rudeness upon their part, they continued to look from the well-brushed nap of his hat to his brightly-polished, snug-fitting boots. Finding that staring seemed to be in perfect propriety, he did a little of it on his own account, and at length, felt his eyes to rest with unusual curiosity upon a very old man, apparently blind, who was sitting on a bench in front of a cobbler's shop. His face had that winning serenity which is not infrequently seen in the faces of the blind, and that seems to speak of a peace in their souls unknown to those who are in possession of their eyesight. His attire was poor but scrupulously clean, and his small hands and attenuated fingers showed that they had never been employed in much rude labor.

He was quite alone on the bench, and Carnew, impelled he scarcely knew how or why, seated himself beside him; at the same time three pair of round eyes looked at him from the cobbler's window, and three little, round, strawberry mouths were opened wide in childish astonishment at the stranger.

"Excuse my speaking to you," said Carnew kindly, "but I am a stranger here, and would like to ask a few questions."

The old man turned his sightless eyes on the speaker, with that singularly intelligent way that the blind occasionally have, and answered in a voice that evinced education and natural refinement:

"There is no apology needed for speaking to me, sir; and ask as many questions as you choose, I shall be happy to answer them."

"Have you lived long here? Do you know most of the people about?"

"I have lived here forty years, and I know everybody within a reach of ten miles, and everybody knows me. I came here from Edinburgh, where I was educated in the university; I came here because I had failed to get along at home. I fancied that I had a turn for farm labor, and that in a new country I'd make a good hand. I was mistaken; my taste for books was too strong, and I threatened to be as great a ne'er-do-weel here as at home. But Providence was good to me. From one and the other of the neighbors, though there weren't near as many then, I got something to do in the way of teaching the children. As my own wants were small, and as I never married to increase them, I managed to eke out enough for my support."

"Since you know the people within such a range, do you know any one by the name of Dutton?"

"Dutton!" the sightless face kindled with delighted animation. "Do you mean Dyke Dutton, that lives out here on the mountains?"

"Yes, I think that must be the same."

"Do I know *him?*" returned the old man. "It was I who educated him, and a pleasure it was to me to do so, he was so quick to learn, and so grateful, and so noble; yes, sir;" placing, in his enthusiasm, his hand on Carnew's arm, "noble is the word to apply to him. Why, he never forgot me. Others that I have done more for grew up, and got rich, and wouldn't know me if they saw me; but he, even in his adversity, didn't forget me. My Christmas and Easter present of money came to me just the the same. He thought to conceal from me the poverty he was in, when that scoundrel Patten, to whom he trusted the getting of his patent, deceived and robbed him, but there's not much like that can be concealed in these parts, sir. The whole village somehow got hold of it, and if that scoundrel Patten was to show his face here, he wouldn't have life enough left in him to get back to where he came from. But, speaking of Dyke's goodness, sir, one day, about six weeks ago, when he was in a great hurry, going down, he said, to Barrytown, he stopped for a minute to see how I was getting along, because he said it might be a good while before he would be up here again. I knew by the tone of his voice that he was troubled; but as he said nothing about it, I didn't like to ask him. Afterwards, however, when they got it here in the village that letters had come in his care for Mrs. Carnew, and when farmer Dean, who lives just a couple of miles from Dyke, brought the news that Mrs. Carnew was staying there with old Meg, I couldn't get it out of my mind that he was troubled about *her*. You see, sir, she was raised with him, and only went away to go to school; but afterwards she made a grand marriage, and perhaps she isn't happy. But, excuse me, sir, for talking so much; I am so fond of Dyke that I can't stop myself when his name is mentioned; and then maybe you knew all that I have told you. You see, if it wasn't for his kind presents," going again into the subject of Dyke's goodness, "I'd have to be more beholden to these good people," motioning back to the cobbler's shop, "than I am. And now, sir, what did you wish to know about Mr. Dutton?" forgetting in his childish simplicity that he had imparted pretty much his whole stock of information.

Carnew was a little puzzled what to answer, in order to pretend that he knew very little of Mr. Dutton, and seizing on the first idea that presented itself, he answered:

"I have heard that his home is situated in a very picturesque spot, and I thought as I was in this part of the country I should like to see it."

"Well, about its situation," responded the old man, in a tone that indicated a little of his disappointment at not being asked something directly relative to Dyke's self, "that depends on individual taste; before I lost my sight, ten years ago this very month, I thought it was a pretty, romantic spot, but I have heard since that some people think the scenery is too wild. As to seeing it for yourself, sir, there will be no difficulty about that; at the very next corner you will find people glad to let you have a conveyance and a driver to guide you."

"Do you think I should find Mr. Dutton at home?"

"Oh! no, sir; whenever *he* is at home, somebody down here knows it; for every time the hired man comes down for letters, or anything else, he is always asked about Dyke. Last time he was down, he said Dyke was back to his business in New York."

"Well, then, whom do you think I shall find at home."

"You'll find old Meg; she's a sort of daft now, they say; has what the doctors call softening of the brain, and so doesn't remember what happened last week. And you'll find Mrs. Carnew there, and a hired woman."

"Have you ever seen Mrs. Carnew?"

"When she was a little girl, but not since; she was as handsome as a picture then; and how Dyke loved her! They say she has grown up beautiful."

By this time, the owners of the three pair of round eyes and the three strawberry-mouths had become so venturesome that they dared to get into exceedingly close proximity to Mr. Carnew, and were even about to lay rather familiar hands upon his clothes. Within doors, the honest cobbler and his good-natured helpmate had been holding a whispered conversation about the stranger.

Alan smiled, as he noticed the encroaches of the little ones, and while he felt in his purse for a coin apiece for them, he asked the old man for his name.

"Peter Patterson," was the reply.

"Well, Peter," said Carnew, shaking the old man's hand, and leaving in it a golden douceur, "I have quite enjoyed listening to you, and now I shall go to the corner and hire a conveyance to take me out to Mr. Dutton's home."

The conveyance was soon procured, and the driver, being a voluble fellow and well acquainted with the topography, not alone of his own village, but seemingly of all Ulster County, entertained his passenger with the history of the occupants of every farm-house they passed, an account of the last new road that had been projected and partly made through the mountains, with a view to building a sort of hotel on one of the most accessible peaks for summer tourists. That capitalists from New York were already on the ground, and that both road and hotel would be completed in another season.

"The place is just four miles beyond Mr. Dutton's, sir; if you'd like to see it, I'll drive on, and you can stop at Mr. Dutton's coming back."

"I do not want to stop at all at Mr. Dutton's; I only wish to drive by his place to see its situation."

"Well then, shall I drive you the four miles beyond?"

Carnew assented, and the driver continued his communicative strain, until they came in sight of Ned's home.

"That's Mr. Dutton's house," said the driver, pointing with his whip to the little mottled dwelling, and Carnew leaned forward, his heart beating violently, and his cheeks flushing. The smoke was curling in a lively, home-like way up from the chimney; a fat, speckled cow was grazing in a field near-by; and a man was working at something just outside the barn. The door of the little house itself was open, and some one, at the sound of the wheels passing, came to the doorway to look out. Carnew shrank behind his companion and pulled his hat over his eyes; but it was not Ned, it was only a stout, middle-aged working-woman. He wondered if she were Meg, about whom he had heard so much; but he thought not, for Meg had been described as quite old. So, reassured that Ned was not in sight, he pushed his hat back again, resumed his first position, and once more looked about him. There were the woods, *her* woods, about which she had told him such quaint tales of her childish fancies; and beyond were the grand, old mountain peaks, looking in the sunlight of the summer-day like gilded monuments of a primeval age. What peace there was about it all! A peace that seemed to make Carnew more tired than ever of his own unsatisfactory life, and of the hollow, heartless people who made up the society of Rahandabed.

The additional four miles lay through scenes as picturesque, but wilder than those they had passed, and late in the afternoon they came upon a perfect hive of laborers. A temporary structure had already been erected in the doorway of which stood what were a couple of evidently city gentlemen, though dressed in the easy costume that bespeaks men who have renounced all the restraints of fashion. They looked with a good deal of curiosity at Carnew, who, tired of his somewhat cramped position in the wagon, had alighted to stretch his limbs.

He bowed to the gentlemen, and then advancing, told how he had heard of their undertaking, and had come to gratify his curiosity by seeing it; after which he presented his card.

"What? Carnew is it?" exclaimed the younger of the two gentlemen, with delighted surprise. "Are you, my dear fellow, the Alan Carnew of some place along the Hudson—some place with an odd name?"

"The very same," replied Alan laughing.

"Well, I am Charles Brekbellew, cousin of that poor idiot, Harry Brekbellew, who made a long visit at your place with the odd name, and who ended by marrying a great beauty and an heiress. Now, if you have formed any personal and private opinion of that same weak devil, Harry Brekbellew, who, like other devils of the same ilk, get the best plums from fortune, don't let that opinion extend to your humble servant. I am his first cousin, son of his father's brother, and shipped from England here, six years ago, because I wouldn't truckle to a rich old uncle, a banker in London, and another Brekbellew. Harry used to write to me once in a while about his times in —well, in that place with the odd name; and that's how I came to hear about you. He said you were a good sort of chap, but not much for mingling with the rest of them, which course on your part, if the rest of them were like my cousin, did you much honor. He didn't have the grace to ask me to his wedding—but here I am rattling on and forgetting all the courtesies. Mr. Carnew, allow me to present to you my friend and partner, Mr. McArthur."

As Mr. McArthur was an Irishman of the type whose hearts entirely rule their heads, it is needless to say that he responded to the introduction by giving Alan's hand a most cordial shake, and then he followed up his cordiality by wanting to know if Mr. Carnew wouldn't step within and join them in a bit of lunch, to which Mr. Brekbellew responded by taking Carnew's arm, and insisting that he should do so, saying as he led Alan within:

"Now that you are with us on the mountains, why not make a stay of a week? We have everything you need in the way of dress, and I am sure our manner of living will be a pleasant novelty to you. Come, say you will, and let me dismiss this man of yours. One of us will drive you down to Saugerties at the end of the week."

Carnew's heart leaped at the offer; to be for a whole week in the very vicinity of Ned; to have, perhaps, opportunities of making, in the gloaming of the day, surreptitious visits to the immediate neighborhood of her home, and to catch secret glimpses of her, perchance, were enough of themselves to make him inclined to accept the invitation, even if his companions had been less sincere and genial than they were. And then both pressed him so earnestly, tempting him with all the wild, novel pleasures of the place, that he found it difficult to resist. So the driver was dismissed, and Carnew remained with Mr. McArthur and Mr. Brekbellew.

XLVIII.

Carnew found his new abode to be one of pleasant novelty; life there seemed to be something like what he used to read when a boy of the life of the people in the backwoods; everything was done simply, in a manner almost primitive, and there was such a genial glow shed over it all by his two pleasant companions. he very second day he found himself entering into all their ways with a zest that was refreshing to himself, and most agreeable to his friends. They took him quite into their confidence.

"You see, Mr. Carnew," said Brekbellew, who in neither countenance, voice, nor manner resembled his cousin, and who, while he could not lay the slightest claim to physical beauty, bore that evidence of manhood which wins involuntary favor. "You see," he repeated. we haven't undertaken this enterprise so much to make money out of it as to give ourselves a new object of interest. If it just pays the expense, we shall be satisfied; if it does not, McArthur there will lose pretty heavily, but he won't mind, for he is pretty rich, and hasn't any wife to call him to account. As for me, I'm a poor devil anyhow, and the little I sunk in the enterprise won't beggar me. There is no one to call *me* to account except that old uncle on the other side, and as I told you, he washed his hands of me six years ago because I dared to hold some opinions of my own. My cousin Harry will come in for all that fortune."

"You are better without it, Charlie," said McArthur, in his rich Irish voice; "carve your own way in the world as I did."

Carnew looked at the last speaker, thinking he was rather young to have carved his own way to the wealth he was said to possess; but he also thought, as he continued to look, it was hardly to be wondered at when one noticed the physiognomy of the man. Perception, judgment, observation, memory were all most strikingly developed, while benevolence shadowed all, and mirth, the true, Irish, witty mirth, stood out as strongly as the other qualities. It was a face, like Brekbellew's, not possessing the beauty that goes to silly women's hearts, but a face to delight the physiognomist, and the form which it surmounted was somewhat slender, but well-knit and compact.

"We came up here," pursued Brekbellew, "last summer, Dan and I, and we stayed a fortnight tenting it. Don't you think we are pioneers? Well, that was the way the idea came first, the idea of building a sort of summer-house up among these mountains, and running it for tourists like ourselves. It came to McArthur who was rusting for something to do, and he broached it to me, allowing me, just to say that I had *some* money in it, to put in the magnificent sum of one hundred dollars. Yes, sir; that is the extent of *my* share in this great enterprise."

And the speaker affected to swell with most laughable importance.

"Of course," he continued, "the hardest job would be making the road, and getting the materials up here for our building. We looked about us for awhile, and finally hit on that place of Dutton's"—Carnew started slightly, but he was not observed—"four miles below here; it was such a pretty spot, and not quite so high as this, and instead of having any new road made, we could have improved the old one. But Dutton wouldn't sell; it was an old homestead, and he couldn't part with it. I saw him down in New York, at his place of business, and I never was so much taken with a stranger in my life. There was such an air of simple honesty about the man. I was so impressed by him, I had to take McArthur to see him on the pretense of business, of course, and he came away with the same feeling; didn't you, Dan?"

Dan nodded his head.

Carnew bit his lip with secret vexation; this was the second time within two days that Dyke's praises had been pressed upon him.

"It would have been a desirable site," he answered, in order to get the conversation out of the channel of encomiums. "I noticed it as I was driven here. And would you object to *my* becoming a partner in this undertaking? I also, like Mr. McArthur, have some spare funds——"

"Couldn't think of it, my dear fellow," interrupted

McArthur; "I cannot share the honors of this enterprise any further than I have done ; the success or the failure must be ours alone, must it not, Charlie ? "

To which Charlie responded an emphatic

" Certainly."

That was the honest-hearted Irishman's way of refusing to entrap even a rich friend into what *might* prove a failure.

That evening Carnew took a walk, a solitary walk that led him down the mountain in the direction of Mr. Dutton's house. It was a brilliant sunset when he started, but it was moonlight when he had traversed the four miles which intervened. The little mottled, well-remembered house was in sight, with the light from a lamp shining through one of the windows. Like a culprit trying to escape from justice, he stole nearer and nearer to the little dwelling. If he could only get one sight of her, he would be satisfied, he would be happy.

Every wooden shutter was thrown back, so that if the lamplight would not expose him he might steal in turn to each of the windows that were situated at accessible heights from the ground, and perhaps a kind Providence would reward him. He did so, and through one of the open windows near which he stood, he beheld with a great throb of his heart the object of his search. She was seated by a little table in the centre of the room, on which stood the lamp that sent its rays so far, and she seemed to be reading a letter to an aged woman by her side.

As only her profile was toward him, he could not see what ravages separation from her husband had made in her countenance ; he could only see the clear, chiseled profile, the low, coiling mass of soft, abundant hair, and the slender, graceful figure. Then the tones of her clear, sweet voice floated out to him, and he caught that she was reading a letter from Dyke. He strained his ears, but that was scarcely necessary, for her words came to him distinctly :

" You will not mind, dear Ned, that I still remain

away. And, perhaps, even you will be comforted a little by knowing that I am relieved of so much anxiety in feeling that your gentle care is about dear old Meg. Surely He who forgets nothing that is done for His name's sake will reward you for your unselfish affection, will reward you by proving your innocence, and restoring to you your husband's love and trust. Have courage and hope a little longer, and this night of trouble will be followed by a clear and perfect day."

At this juncture, whether by that magnetic pressure, which makes us feel that eyes we do not directly see are looking at us, or whether Alan, in his eagerness, forgot himself so far as to incautiously shift his position, Mrs. Carnew stopped her reading abruptly, and turning so that she faced the window, she saw her husband's countenance.

The suddenness of the sight, the seeming impracticability and impossibility of his being in such a place at such an hour, and in such a manner, all combined to make her think it was an apparition, an apparition that boded some evil to him, according to the old superstitious legends of her childhood, and with an agonized scream she attempted to stand, but reeled, and fell back fainting to her chair.

Alan fled ; though a moment before he was softened, and touched even in Dyke's favor, by the hearing of that letter, which had not one harsh word of himself, now his old pride had returned. He would not be caught thus surreptitiously looking at his wife, for the world, and he fairly dashed along the mountain road by which he had come, not relaxing his speed until he had run a mile or more.

When Mrs. Carnew recovered, knowing that old Meg would not understand her, and Anne McCabe would be unable to help her to any solution of the mystery, she decided not to say a word of what had caused her swoon, and she satisfied the sympathizing inquiries of the woman by answers which, while they were truthful, still did not betray what she wished to conceal. Poor old Meg asked nothing; only put her arms around Ned, and pillowed her head on her breast as she used to do when she was a strong and comparatively young woman, and Ned was a little, helpless child.

But Mrs. Carnew thought about the strange cause of her fainting fit all the more because of her silence upon it, and when she replied to Dyke's letter, which she did that very night, she begged him to find out something about her husband's health. She did not tell him why she made such a request, further than to say it was owing to a sudden and strange anxiety, because she felt that Dyke would think what she saw was only an hallucination of her own disturbed brain, and that he would deem her weak and unwomanly for yielding to it.

And Dyke *did* smile a little when he read her request, but he loved the writer none the less for it, and as he slipped the letter into the fastening which bound her other letters—he kept them all together now—he resolved to go to Rahandabed, that he might ascertain in person the information desired by Ned.

Alan had regained *his* mountain quarters in such a state of breathlessness that his companions wanted to know if he had met a bear, and if the killing of it had thrown him into such a panting condition.

"No; but I've had a long quick walk up your mountain, equal in exertion to an encounter with a bear," answered Carnew laughing, and then he fell to the late supper which had been delayed for him, and took his own animated part in the bright, genial conversation of his companions, as if his heart and his head were not on fire with thoughts of his wife.

At midnight, when his friends had retired, he stole out to walk and think.

If but one message would come from her; one little word of wifely love, or remembrance, he felt he would be willing to condone everything, and implore her to return to him. But this wilful obstinacy and pride upon her part, made him equally determined and proud, and as he looked up to the clear, moonlit sky, he shut his teeth hard together, resolving no love on his part should betray him into yielding one iota, until she had made the first advance. But, when he turned in at last to sleep, his fitful slumber was beset by visions of Ned as he saw her that evening, reading Dyke's letter.

He remained with his mountain friends a week as he had promised to do, and every evening he rambled in the direction of Ned's home; but only far enough to be in sight of the house; he was afraid to risk again a nearer view, for, though on the first occasion he had fled so quickly that he was certain he had not been recognized, he might not be so fortunate again. Sometimes one or both of his friends accompanied him, and though they remarked the lingering look with which he turned from Dutton's place, they little dreamed, not knowing that Carnew was married, of the dear, dear object under Dutton's roof.

On the day of his departure, Brekbellew drove him to Saugerties, and obtained from him a promise to revisit the mountain quarters before the setting in of cold weather.

" And next season, Mr. Carnew," he said, as he shook Alan's hand, " we'll be able to give you the welcome of a prince," to which Alan responded, by reminding him of the promise he and McArthur had given to visit Rahandabed during the winter.

As Carnew neared C——, his last interview with his aunt—when she had attempted to read Ordotte's letter through the keyhole, and had failed so disastrously—came to his mind for the first time since he had dashed away so frantically, and filled as his thoughts were with disturbing and weighty matters, the ludicrousness of the scene struck him as it did not do at the time of its occurrence. He laughed to himself, laughed even after he had reached C——, and had taken his seat in the conveyance he hired to take him to Rahandabed.

It was evening when the vehicle turned into the broad,

admirably kept road which led to the house, and the wonted festivity was under way.

Scarcely looking at the flashing lights, and the gaily dressed ladies flitting past the open windows, he directed the man to drive to the side of the house, and having paid and dismissed him, he went quietly to his own apartments. He had hardly entered when a servant knocked for admission.

"Mrs. Doloran desired to know the moment you returned home, sir, and having been told that you are here, she wants to know if you will go to her, or if she will come to you."

Carnew frowned, thinking, that perhaps she meant to renew her attempt at reading Ordotte's letter, and he concluded, that he had better consent to the interview in order to prevent a repetition of the keyhole scene.

" Tell Mrs. Doloran that I will see her here."

He had no desire to traverse the gay house as he would have to do to reach any place of interview appointed by her.

In an incredibly short space of time, as if she might have been waiting in the next passage for the servant's answer, Mrs. Doloran presented herself. Her very dress, devoid as it was of taste, or becoming color, was an eyesore to her nephew, and the way in which she rustled and rattled her ample silken skirts, caused an aching in his ears ; but he saluted her respectfully, and waited for the announcement of her errand.

" Alan Carnew," she had evidently worked herself up to the pitch of anger at which hysterics usually supervened, but for some purpose of her own she seemed determined to waive the hysterics for the present, if not indefinitely. " I demand this instant from you an explanation of your conduct ; what do you mean by shutting yourself up with a strange man for a whole hour early in the morning, going off after that for a week, nobody knows where, and having during your absence that same strange man coming here asking for you, and when *you're* not to be had, asking for me, just to know how your health is, and when I told him that you had the health of all fools, without a pain or an ache that disturb people of brains, he just bowed and thanked me, with the air of one of the rajahs that Ordotte talks about? Now, sir, I demand a full and instant explanation of all this."

Carnew pursed up his eyebrows to indicate a surprise, which he certainly felt, that Mr. Dutton—of course it was he, since he was the gentleman who had been closeted with him, though not for an hour, on the morning of his departure—should have come again to Rahandabed, and only for such a purpose as his aunt stated. Could it be that he had brought a message from Ned? But no, in that case he would not have asked for Mrs. Doloran; so, with his eyebrows still pursed, and his whole manner indicative of grave wonder, he replied :

" I am as much astonished as you are, madam, that information of *my* health should be the single object of any person's visit to Rahandabed."

" Now, Alan, don't provoke me to something desperate. You know I have not Ordotte to soothe and protect me. I want to know immediately who that man is? "

" What man? " questioned Carnew, with perfectly simulated innocence.

Mrs. Doloran stamped her foot, and fairly roared :

" The man who called here yesterday, and who was with you in your study there," pointing to the library-door, " the morning that you went away in such a huff."

Alan stroked his mustache.

" If you really saw this mysterious man yesterday, and answered his question about my health, it is a wonder to me that you did not then avail yourself of the opportunity to learn his name. Certainly, when he sent his request to see you he sent his card with it."

" No, he didn't ; he just sent a request to see me without any card, and told me to my face that it was only because he could not see you that he asked for me."

" And you did not inquire his name ? " in a tone full of doubt and sarcasm.

" Do you think I was so stupid as not to ask that ? I asked it the first thing and the last thing, but he wouldn't give it. He smiled, and said it made no difference. What do you think of that ? "

" That he is to be admired for his prudence ; that he is to be commended for not pandering to a foolish woman's insensate curiosity."

Mrs. Doloran could scarcely speak for temper, but there must have been some still more powerful motive at work, for she managed to prevent a violent outbreak, and said as firmly as her raging passion would allow her to do :

" Since *he* would not give the information I wanted, I demand it from you."

" What information ? "

Knowing of how little avail anger and firmness had been in the past with his aunt, when she was as decided as she seemed to be now, he determined to try an entirely new plan, regardless how soon it brought on her hysterics, for in that case she would be removed, at least from his presence.

" His name, booby—the name of this man ? "

" What man ? "

And thus Alan provokingly kept it up, affecting complete ignorance of what he was to answer, until Mrs. Doloran, fairly beaten on her own ground, and beaten in such an ignominious fashion, broke down at last, not into her usual hysterics, but into a very storm of crying.

" When you know how it would relieve me," she said, " just to tell me his name, you ungrateful boy that I've loved, and loved, and loved——" but Alan had shut and locked himself into his study.

XLIX.

Ordotte had made his mysterious journey to India and had returned, not, however, to New York, nor yet to London, but, directed by the contents of Munson's last letter, to Paris. To Paris, where Mrs. Brekbellew was still the lovely butterfly of fashion, fluttering around the flame of destruction, and where her husband was fast sinking into the vortex made by his own follies.

While he had that kind of cunning and bravado in small and mean things which is often to be found in very weak characters, he utterly lacked the cunning to save himself from being thoroughly victimized, and the courage to command his wife to desist from her extravagant course. He smarted under her open contempt of him, and he winced beneath the extravagance into which she forced him, but he had not the manhood to resist either.

By nature he was economical without being parsimonious, but she taunted this quality in him to such a degree that he rushed to the gaming-table, with the hope that his winnings would make him indifferent to her folly.

That course made him an open mark, and while Mrs. Brekbellew, by reason of her beauty and extravagance, was the boast and the toast in fashionable *salons*, Mr. Brekbellew was to be found nightly staking large sums, and accepting his losses—he rarely won—with a sort of imbecile indifference, which was stimulated, perhaps, by his deep, and often secret potations.

Ned's appealing letter had been carefully forwarded to Mrs. Brekbellew, and she had received it before she was a month in Paris; but the only effect it produced was to make her laugh quite heartily; so heartily that her husband heard her from the next room, and he ventured to thrust his head in and inquire the cause of the mirth.

"Nothing that concerns you, this time," was her light and contemptuously spoken reply, "though your idiocy is a constant source of mirth. I don't know what I should do, if you were to get brains like other people. I would have nothing to laugh at."

He withdrew before she had quite finished; her sarcasm and ridicule pricked him like pins driven deep into tender places, but he had not the courage to resent it.

"I knew that would send him back, the fool," she soliloquized. "And now, Mrs. Carnew, you have come to the wrong one for justice, or mercy. I, to expose *myself* for the sake of clearing *you*, give an opportunity to *that* idiot—" pointing to the room into which her husband had retreated—"to taunt and perhaps denounce me in revenge for all my reviling of him, and cause myself to be thoroughly hated by my own father? Oh, no! I should be as great an imbecile as Harry Brekbellew is, if I did. You swore an oath, Mrs. Carnew, and you shall have to abide by it, even if it *does* separate your husband from you forever. It is only fair that you should have some unhappiness in your married life. I have misery, utter misery in mine. I *hate my* husband."

For an instant she bowed her head to let the bitter tears that welled into her eyes have way. Then she roused herself, tore the pitiful little letter into scraps, flung the latter into the great open fire-place, touched them into a flame with a match, and watched until the last shred had gone into ashes.

That was how Ned's appeal was answered. .

When the couple had been four months in Paris—he continuing to gamble with the recklessness of a madman, and she to reign a very queen of beauty and fashion—he was brought up in short order by a very angry and threatening letter from his uncle Brekbellew, of the firm of Brekbellew & Hepburn.

"What are these reports that I hear?" the old gentleman wrote in firm, large, black characters, "that your gambling losses have eaten into the very capital of your fortune, and that just how soon the gaming houses themselves will be enriched by the balance of the capital has been openly discussed by every *roué* in Paris, and that your fine wife has taken to herself, instead of *your* escort, the attendance of fashionable counts and dukes, and out-does even her French friends, the mesdames, in setting the example of wifely estrangement. Are these reports true, sir, and what do you suppose shall be *my* course if they are? I'll throw you to the devil, sir, you and your fine wife, and leave every pound of my money to that other scapegrace, Charles Brekbellew. *He* is doing well, sir; *he* has gone jointly into some railroad enterprise in America, and if he *did* contradict me to my face, and not agree with *my* opinions on public matters, at least he has proved himself a thrifty, sensible man.

"I expected to have my bachelor home made bright and cheerful, and my declining age rendered pleasant, by the residence of you and your wife with me; but as it is, sir, I suppose you would both scorn such a proposition. Either write immediately that you are coming to live with me, or prepare to be totally disin-herited.

"Your indignant uncle,
" HENRY BREKBELLEW."

That letter caused young Brekbellew to reflect—that is, to do as much of that admirable and oft-commended action as his little, addled brain was capable of doing. He *was* going to the devil; he saw that in a sort of misty, help-less way, and his wife did not care how soon he reached his infernal destination; he saw that also, with an impotent rage. A couple of months more of her present extrava-gance and his own gambling expenses, unless luck should turn in his favor, would quite impoverish him. To be sure, there was her fortune to expect. On her father's death it would be very large; but then, after all, he could not be certain of enjoying that. Mr. Edgar's openly expressed dislike of him, his coldness on the very morning of the wedding, and the meagre dower he had given to his daughter, all told unmistakably, even to his weak in-tellect, that his chances of enjoying Mr. Edgar's wealth were rather poor. If the gentleman should conveniently die, he might bequeath his wealth in such a manner that only Edna could touch it, or he might, as even affectionate fathers were known to do sometimes, entirely disinherit her because of her marriage without his approval. The outlook was unpromising in every direction save that proposed by his uncle, and, regarding himself, he was willing enough to pursue that course. A quiet life in England would repair in his health and purse the ravages made by his Paris excesses, and he exerted all his feeble determination to insist that his wife should agree with him. But he dreaded the effort, knowing how she lived in the adulation and excitement about her; he felt that she would scorn his uncle's invitation, and he groaned as he thought of the contempt with which she would treat *him*. Still, when he should tell her how near he was to financial ruin, and should suggest his fears regarding her own fortune, he thought and hoped she might be affected in the right direction.

To fortify himself still more for the interview, he drank a whole bottle of wine, and then sent a request to his wife to be permitted to see her.

Mrs. Brekbellew was just then in the hands of her maid, and any request from her husband was so unprecedented and so audacious—she having completely humiliated and snubbed him since they had come to Paris—that she replied to the messenger with a ludicrous surprise:

"Mr. Brekbellew wishes to see me?"

"Yes," answered the girl in French, which language Mrs. Brekbellew had also used, "he is most anxious to see madame immediately."

"When Nanette finishes, he may come in; tell him I shall ring when I am ready."

So poor Brekbellew waited, like the obedient cur that he was, until a silvery little tinkle told him that he might enter his wife's dressing apartment.

She was seated before her mirror like some lovely vision, and the infatuation of the days in Rahandabed

when the spell of her beauty ravished him, seemed to come
to him again. He saw so little of her recently, that his
present sight of her was almost like the renewal of an old
acquaintance. And it rendered the announcement of his
errand still harder. Indeed, he only stood before her increasing her contempt for him, by his awkward, embarrassed manner.

"Well, Breky," that was one of her derisive terms for
him, "what do you want? Please be quick, for the
Count de Chamont is to be here this evening. I expect
him every moment." A slight flush rose to Brekbellow's
cheeks. Weak as he was, he winced more beneath the
taunt implied in her haste to forsake him, her husband,
for the company of another of his sex, than at her open
contempt of himself. But he choked down his resentment, as he was accustomed to do, and took from his
pocket his uncle's letter.

"Read that," he said meekly, extending it to her.

She did so, and, having finished its perusal, looked up,
asking lightly:

"Well, what has all that to do with me?"

"To do with *you*?"

Her coolness astonished him into something that seemed
like spirit.

"Why, madam, it has to do with your means of living.
In a couple of months more at the rate of our living here,
I shall be a beggar. Has not *that* something to do with
you?"

"Why, Breky, you poor fool! that is the very thing I
want you to become; then I can write to my father with
a good grace that you have ruined me by your gambling
excesses, that I cannot live with you any longer; and he
will either come and take me home, or come and allow
me to continue to live here. *His* fortune is ample enough
for all *my* wants."

Brekbellow's little spirit still sustained him.

"Perhaps you ought not to be so sure of his fortune.
He didn't behave very handsomely when you were mar-

ried, and he may carry his dislike to the husband you chose, so far as to leave you to the beggary caused as much by your own extravagance, as by your husband's gambling."

She laughed—a long, low, musical ripple—before she replied, shaking her head at the same time in a saucy, coquettish way, that to even the poor wight before her, was most aggravating:

"You are mistaken, Breky; as you always are when you attempt to use your poor little brains in the way of forethought, or reflection; I am my father's only child, and it is *you* he dislikes, not me. He will be so rejoiced when he learns that I do not care for you; that I have discovered he was right in his estimate of you, a poor, little, contemptuous imbecile, that no woman with ordinary brains could possibly esteem, that he will instantly take me to his heart, and his home, and his fortune again."

For once, the poor little creature's temper was fairly aroused. His wife's lash had cut so deep, that, like the trodden worm, he had turned at last; the fumes of the wine were also rising to his brain, and he actually almost threateningly advanced to her, at which she rose, and confronted him with exceeding dignity, while he retorted:

"Who was it that wrote to the poor, little, contemptuous imbecile, that no woman with ordinary brains could esteem, to come to Weewald Place and propose to her, that she was ready and eager to marry him. Who did *that* unwomanly thing, answer me that, madam?"

But Mrs. Brekbellew replied with great stateliness:

"Have you the letter which contains that *unwomanly* proposition?"

The next to the last word was pronounced with sarcastic emphasis.

"No; fool that I was to give it up to you, after we were married."

"Then don't taunt people with statements that you can't substantiate."

"Why did you marry me?" resumed Brekbellew, the wine, and his unwonted temper, giving him extraordinary courage: "You were rich and did not not need my money; you never cared for me. Why in thunder, madam, did you marry me?"

"Why?" she repeated with provoking deliberation and calmness, "because I loved Alan Carnew, and hearing that he was about to marry Ned Edgar, I would not give her the satisfaction of having a husband before *I* had one. You were the most convenient suitor at the time, and you evinced the dog-like qualities of faithfulness and obedience which always mark the model husband; hence, I proposed to you." With another long, low, silvery ripple of laughter.

"And you actually married me without loving me in the least, without even meaning that show of affection with which you greeted me in Weewald Place?"

"Actually, Breky, actually."

"Then you are a devil, madam, and the sooner I go to my uncle, and tell him how *I* was duped, and forced by your very treatment of me to the gambler's life I am leading, the better for me. He will recommend a separation instantly, and I shall adopt his recommendation."

She retorted, but in the calm, passionless voice she had used throughout:

"And you, sir, are a deceiver, and the sooner I go to my father, and tell him how *I* was duped into marrying a man who had deceived and deserted a poor French girl, leaving her and her child to die in the village of C——, the better."

Brekbellew retreated as if he was shot. *That* secret he deemed so safe, not having heard a word from any quarter which connected *his* name with his unfortunate victim. *How* did his wife, of all others, obtain possession of it? And he continued to stare at her, speechless and aghast.

She resumed, having for a moment silently enjoyed his discomfiture.

"That was *your* secret, and I respected it. It was re-vealed to me before I married you, and the writer implored me not to risk my own happiness by wedding a man so lost to every sense of honor, so heartless as you were——"

"Josephine herself told you," burst from Brekbellew.

"You are mistaken; I did not hear a syllable from Josephine; but, as I was going to say when you interrupted me, I never intended to reproach you with it; I never intended to let you know it was in my possession, but this evening you have driven yourself upon it. Now take your course: return to your uncle if you choose, but do not include me in any of your plans."

She rang the bell for Nanette, and poor, little, crestfallen, dismayed Brekbellew retired from the apartment, like the miserable whipped cur that he was, and she descended to the elegant *salon*.

An hour later, and she was surrounded by her admirers. She seemed to be in excellent spirits, giving out witty French repartee with a clever archness surprising in one to whom the language was not a mother tongue, and eclipsing by her beauty every French woman present.

A servant brought her a card. She glanced at it, looking not quite pleased when she read the name, and seeming for the moment to hold some mental debate. Then she gave an assent, and in a few moments, Ordotte, smiling, gracious, and with as distinguished an air as marked any of the Frenchmen of title in the *salon*, presented himself.

L.

Mrs. Brekbellew, notwithstanding her secret dissatisfaction at meeting any one from Rahandabed, and particularly Ordotte, of whom she had always a strange, undefinable dread, gave to him a most cordial welcome, and presented him with charming grace to every one in the company. Her secret displeasure arose from her fear that Ned might not have continued to keep her oath, though in that case she was prepared herself to swear a hundred oaths, if necessary, to her own innocence, and she doubted not, now that Mackay was dead, and her own previous plans being so well laid, that she would be able to prove it, at least to her father, should the story ever reach him.

Ordotte exerted himself to charm, and being quite conversant with the language, having been educated in Paris, he succeeded, as he usually did when he chose to do so.

Mrs. Brekbellew forgot, in the affability and charm of his manner, all her fears, and she threw herself into the pleasure of his society with the same zest that others were doing.

In the middle of one of those accounts of mysterious incidents which take their rise from the lightest trifle, and yet sometimes lead to consequences that shake a throne, he had paused, ostensibly to wipe his brow with his handkerchief, but really to watch Mrs. Brekbellew, for he had invented the very story he was telling, and was leading it up to a certain point in order that he might have an opportunity to say something else.

She was listening to him, her eyes glistening, and her pretty lips apart in intense and delighted curiosity.

"As I was saying," he resumed, withdrawing his gaze from her and looking about him carelessly for a moment, "the strangest things happen in the most trifling way. Just from the fact of my having made an acquaintance, at first a mere prosy acquaintance, in India, consequences have ensued that have changed, not only the whole tenor of my life, but actually caused me to leave America on a a second and most mysterious journey to that land of rajahs and tigers. And while there this time, I had the singular fortune to meet one of those old wizards who seem occasionally to do such startling things. He appeared to favor me, possibly because I had been in the country before, and knew somewhat how to humor him; and one of the souvenirs which he gave me was a sort of essence, looking merely like colored water, but exceedingly fragrant."

While he spoke, he took out of a leather case, in his breast pocket, a vial not more than a half-inch in length. It sparkled as he held it up, and when he took out its tiny stopper, the odor was almost overpowering for an instant. Everybody bent forward, aglow from surprise and interest, but Mrs. Brekbellew seemed to be fairly breathless.

"This essence," Ordotte continued, "is for the purpose of making marks on human flesh." A sort of shudder went through the little circle, which he perceiving, smiled, and hastened to add, "not any mark to torture, but a mark for some reason to be made without being afterwards detected until this essence is again used, when the mark, whatever it may have been, stands out once more distinctly for a few moments and then disappears. Suppose we try it on the wrist of some lady present? Who knows," laughingly, "but we may get at some lost fortune in this way, or some romantic history. Mrs. Brekbellew, will you give me the privilege of putting it upon one of your wrists?"

Laughing and disclaiming against the fact of any secret mark being found upon her, she extended her pretty wrist, the Count de Chamont gallantly unclasping her bracelet.

"We will take the left wrist, if you please," said Ordotte; "being nearer to the heart, it would be more certain to figure in any romance." And the gallant count immediately unclasped the heavy bracelet of that wrist.

Ordotte poured a single drop upon the beautifully-moulded and snow-white wrist extended to him, and it was singular how far the one drop seemed to diffuse itself, spreading a full inch in every direction, so that if there had been a secret mark anywhere in the vicinity of the wrist, and the essence possessed the power claimed for it, it must have shown distinctly. But nothing appeared save a slight discoloration of the skin, for an instant, and Mrs. Brekbellew withdrew her hand, saying smilingly:

"I told you, you would find nothing there."

"Shall we try the left wrist of some other lady?"

asked Ordotte with ludicrous earnestness. "I insist that it must be the left wrist, for never was romance spoiled yet by anything so far removed from the heart as the right wrist."

Another pretty hand was extended to him, and he again applied his mysterious test, but with no other effect than it had upon Mrs. Brekbellew.

"Now," he said, "will some gentleman permit me to mark letters upon his hand, or wrist, in order to test *all* the powers that are claimed for this wonderful substance."

The Count de Chamont obligingly extended his hand, and Ordotte took from his leather-case a tiny brush having an ivory handle. Dipping this into the essence, he proceeded to make on the back of the Count's hand a large capital letter C. It stood out distinctly, showing a dull-red color, and, after the lapse of a few minutes, began to fade, until not a trace of it could be discerned. Then Ordotte poured a single drop of the essence upon the spot, as he had done on the wrists of the ladies, and again the dull-red C came plainly forth, for a few minutes, then died away.

After that, Ordotte affected to be anxious about any further waste of his precious essence, and he put it back into his leather-case ; and to the remark that secret marks were rarely placed upon the wrist, he answered that the fact of their being rendered so secret by the essence might make the wrist a very convenient and probable place to mark.

Then he turned the conversation into the channel into which, for a purpose of his own, he had caused it to drift before he had spoken of the essence.

"We were speaking about the part that trifles play in the most important affairs. Nature has strange plans of her own in every one of them, often making the consequences that ensue only the retributive justice for some law transgressed ; just as in her similitudes she has a purpose for an end, though, before the end be attained, an innocent person may have to suffer for guilt of which he or she knows nothing."

He turned his eyes quite carelessly to Mrs. Brekbellew's face.

"Which fact brings to my mind," he pursued, keeping his eyes upon her face, the singular likeness you bear, Mrs. Brekbellew, to Mrs. Carnew, and the unpleasant circumstances in which you might have found yourself had you been in Rahandabed three months ago."

The color fled from her countenance so suddenly and so completely that it looked ghastly, and it occasioned more than one comment of surprise and curiosity among those about her. But she recovered herself in an instant, and forced a smile to her lips, as she said:

"What do you mean? How could my resemblance to Mrs. Carnew cause *me* any unpleasantness?"

Had not her betrayal of herself, a moment before, by her startling loss of color, convinced Ordotte that the tenor of his own shrewd thoughts about her was correct, he might have been imposed upon by her present appearance; she seemed so full of a pleasant, innocent surprise, and nothing more; even as it was, he hesitated a moment before saying what was upon his lips, lest he *might* be mistaken, and his bold stroke be a venture even too deep for him; but his instant's reflection convinced him, and he answered very slowly, very significantly, and looking straight into her eyes all the while:

"With your living likeness before all her accusers, Mrs. Carnew might have been able to show them that suspicion could, with equal propriety, have attached itself to you."

Mrs. Brekbellew fairly held her breath in her desperate effort to show no outward sign this time, but it seemed for an instant as if her very heart would burst in the agony of the endeavor, and despite all that she could do, her voice trembled, as she said:

"I know now to what you refer—poor Ned's unfortunate story. She wrote to me about it."

"She wrote to you," repeated Ordotte in those same slow, significant tones which made Mrs. Brekbellew feel like strangling him, "and you, no doubt, replied, comforting her and sympathizing with her."

She could endure no more; she felt that if one word further was to reach her from his detested lips, she should scream, or faint, or do some other startling thing; so she rose, making some remark about the intense heat of the room, and taking the arm of the Count de Chamont, who had also risen to assist her, she went into one of the adjoining apartments.

Ordotte was secretly delighted. He had settled in his own mind, beyond the reach of any further doubt, the fact that Mrs. Brekbellew was the wife of Mackay, and not Mrs. Carnew; and he felt assured that when he should send the next morning a request for a private interview with Mrs. Brekbellew, he would not be refused, as he might have been, had he not touched so keenly her sense of safety that evening; so, with the happy air of a man who has won an unexpected triumph, he addressed himself to the rest of his little audience, and interested them so much that they forgot to comment upon Mrs. Brekbellew.

That lady had requested to be left alone, and retiring to a part of the house where no sound of her gay company could reach hear, she strove to calm and reassure herself.

That Ordotte believed *she* should have been the one accused, instead of Ned, she had read unmistakably in his eyes, but how did he *know*, she asked herself over and over. Had Ned then broken her oath, and told him, and had he come to Paris to beard her with her guilt? But why take this roundabout course, if such were his object? Why not openly and briefly accuse her? Did her father know? Had Ned told him also? And then she remembered how particularly cold and short was Mr. Edgar's last letter.

She beat her foot into the carpet in her rage, and

clasped her hands together, until the nails cut into the flesh; but all brought her no help. On every side she seemed to see a confirmation of her fears that Ned had broken her oath and told everything, and that nothing she could do would avert now the guilt from her own shoulders.

Then she reverted to Ned's letter, which had been so explicit and so touching; Mrs. Carnew had detailed every link in the circumstantial evidence against her, so Mrs. Brekbellew was in full possession of every particular, from the arrival of the woman Bunmer with the child, and the statement of the minister, to Ned's own departure from Rahandabed. And as she thought of it all, still beating her foot and clinching her hands, she strove to reassure herself by saying:

"Why am I such a coward? Since every one of them, from Bunmer to that dolt Hayman, took Ned for *me*, why cannot I face all this out? *My* word, *my oath*, if necessary, will have as much weight with my father as Ned's will. Why do I let *his* random remarks cow me in this manner? And I *shall* not. I shall send word to these people below that I am indisposed, and then I shall have *him* up here, and extract the worst from him, and show him my scorn and indignation for what he has had the effrontery to say to me."

Thus Ordotte found himself privately requested to go above stairs, and a prudent servant conducted him to Mrs. Brekbellew.

She was seated, and in the subdued light of the room he could hardly tell the difference between the color of her face and the white hue of her dress.

With a motion, she desired him to take a chair near her own, and then she said in a tone of cold, and offended dignity:

"I have sent for you, Mr. Ordotte, to give you the opportunity of explaining what you said to me this evening: why the mere fact of my resembling Mrs. Carnew should make it possible for me to be accused of what she may have done?"

Ordotte answered with the easy manner of one replying to the most ordinary question :

" The only explanation of what I have said is to accuse you boldly, madam, of what has been visited on poor, slandered Mrs. Carnew ; you were the wife of Mackay, and you are the mother of his child."

She rose then, in her haste and anger upsetting her chair, and he also stood up, but in the same calm, easy way in which he had spoken.

" You forget yourself, sir ; you transcend every privilege that admission to my presence has given you, and I can only regard your statement as proceeding from a brain disordered by wine or by a madman's frenzy."

She strove hard to speak with the same cool dignity with which she had first addressed him, that she might the better impose upon him, and force him at least to a partial retraction of what he had said ; but in spite of all her efforts, her voice and her form trembled

Ordotte, looking at her sharply, deemed it as well to come to *his* point at once.

" Mrs. Brekbellew "—his voice had changed to such a deep, firm tone, it seemed to be like another person speaking :

" All your dissimulation with me is wasted. I *know* what you have done, and had you not sent for me to-night, I should have sent to you to-morrow morning for the purpose of saying what I shall say now. I desire from you, over your own signature, a statement to the effect that you *were* the wife of Mackay, that you *are* the mother of his child, and the successive steps by which you contrived to have Mrs. Carnew accused of all that *you* have done. I desire this statement in order to show it to Alan Carnew. As you have been the cause of his separation from his wife, so you must effect their reconciliation. I also desire this statement to show to Mr. Edgar."

"Pray," she said with tremulous sarcasm, "is there any one else you desire to show this statement to?"

"No," he answered, in the same deep, firm voice; "I shall spare you any further disgrace. As my object alone is to prove Mrs. Carnew's innocence to those who are nearest to her, I shall be satisfied in attaining that. Your husband and your husband's relatives shall be left in ignorance of your prior marriage."

"Mr. Ordotte," she fairly hissed his name; "I regret that you have come upon such a foolish errand. If I *had* forgotten myself so far as to marry in secret a gardener's worthless son, and if I *had* given birth, also in secret, to his child, I say, if I *had* done these degrading things, do you think I would be so unjust to my own interests as to grant what you so coolly request? You certainly have reckoned most insanely, and since that alone, to use your own words, was the object of your intended call upon me, we shall consider this interview ended."

She crossed to put her hand upon the bell, but he intercepted her.

"Although," he said, with an air and tone which she could not oppose, "the sole object of my desire to see you was, and is, to obtain the proof of Mrs. Carnew's innocence, still, I have something more to say, and as that something more will be rather lengthy, I advise you to be seated."

He drew a chair forward for her. She motioned it disdainfully away. He bowed, and resumed:

"A gentleman was once placed, through the ill-feeling and spite of his brother, in such circumstances as not to know his own infant daughter from the infant daughter of his brother, whose wife was a low woman of ill-repute. The brother asserted that *he* knew, having privately marked the child with a certain subtle essence that had been obtained from India in some way by one of his riotous companions. The peculiarity of this marking essence was that only for the few moments which it lay upon the flesh could be detected whatever might have been imprinted there, and as the brother refused to say where he had marked the child, but that somewhere upon her person were the letters E. E., and that he alone had the secret of reproducing these letters, the father was unable to tell which was his own child. The brother, having lost his wife shortly after the birth of the children, departed to some foreign country, and the unhappy father, fearing to do injustice to his own child, took both the infants."

He paused abruptly because of the labored breathing of Mrs. Brekbellew. With a vague dread of she knew not what, she was linking his story with the senseless marking scene of an hour before, and the very gleam of his eyes—those eyes that even in Rahandabed seemed to be constantly reading her through—now acting upon her like a painful probe, made her almost unconsciously breathe hard and heavily.

"You had better be seated," he said, again attempting to place a chair for her, but she waved it away as she had done before, and he resumed:

"The brother went abroad, and at length to India, where he met some one who became in time his most confidential friend. To this friend the brother in his softened moments, which only came when his health was broken, and his mind was filled with regret for the happiness that in his earlier years he had thrown so ruthlessly aside, opened his heart. He told the story of what his own malice had accomplished with regard to his brother's child, and at the same time confessed that he could not conquer himself sufficiently to take any steps of reparation; but he said that after his death his friend might tell all he knew, and he told this friend in what part of India this marking essence had been procured.

"Strange, very strange circumstances, sent this friend to the very house which sheltered two young girls marvellously alike in appearance, bearing the same name, and in every particular corroborating the story told by this brother. The friend marked it all, and waited. He knew that his lips were sealed until he should hear of the death of this brother. From the time that he had left India he had heard nothing directly of the brother, and only very indirectly, that the latter had disappeared no one seemed to know where.

"At length, when a time came in which one of those young girls was vilely accused, and, the friend thought from his careful observation of her character, unjustly so, he conceived the idea of going to India and searching for some trace of this brother. He did, but found nothing more than that he had left the country in an exceedingly feeble condition of health, shortly after the friend himself had gone, and it was supposed he must have died in some foreign hospital. That information the friend deemed sufficient to free him from his oath, and having secured the marking essence, he came to Paris to test it first on one of the young ladies to whom he has referred. He did so to-night, and by it he has made the discovery that she who passes for Mr. Edgar's daughter is not sustained by any proof. Do you now recognize the characters in my story, Mrs. Brekbellow? The gentleman of whom I spoke is Mr. Edgar; his brother is your father, and the friend is your humble servant:" bowing profoundly as he said the last words.

"I refused to use any more of the essence to-night, lest there might not be sufficient to make the test upon the wrist of Mrs. Carnew."

He stopped, but his listener did not answer him. She seemed frozen in her horrified amazement, and he fancied that her eyes, beautiful as they were, resembled the wild eyes of frantic animals he had seen in the jungles.

But, at last her voice came to her; a broken, husky, and utterly changed voice.

"I do not believe you. This tale is an invented Indian story, like those you told in Rahandabed."

He bowed, as he replied:

"Thank you for the compliment to my veracity, but you shall have the proof of the truth of my story in a few weeks, when not only Rahandabed, but Paris and London shall gossip of the downfall of Mrs. Brekbellew, who had been a usurper all her life."

She turned from him and wrung her hands. O God! how her cruel wrongs to another were about to be visited upon her own head. Then she turned back and extended her clasped hands to him in entreaty :

"Have you no pity for me? I never did you a wrong. What will *you* gain by exposing me?"

"Had *you* any pity for her whose happiness you have blighted? And you ask what I shall gain by exposing you? I shall gain the approval of my own conscience for having unmasked evil. No, Mrs. Brekbellew, I have no pity for *you* further than to refrain from proceeding to the extreme measure of acquainting your husband with what you did prior to your marriage to him, and that you are not the daughter of Mr. Edgar. And further, I shall guarantee that Mr. Edgar and Mr. and Mrs. Carnew will preserve the same silence. I know, that in consideration of all that I shall tell them, they will be easily won to the pledge I shall exact from them. The only source you will have to fear will be the gossip of Rahandabed, for, in justice to Mrs. Carnew, the whole truth must be told, not alone to the mistress of that place, but also to each of the guests. However, gossip so distant may not be wafted here, and if it should be, perhaps your fertile brain may find some means of depriving it of its effect. This is the utmost I can do for you, Mrs. Brekbellew, and this I pledge myself to do, if you will give me the clear, written statement for which I have asked."

He retreated a little, as if he considered all argument at an end, and she turned away as if to reflect upon his proposition ; but she was unable to think. Her head seemed to be on fire, even while her limbs were trembling as if from a chill, and she had a sort of wild desire to clutch at something, like a person falling from a height. At length she compelled her thoughts to fall into something like order. What if she still braved it all by a firm denial? Since Ned had been mistaken for her by the very persons who alone could have told the difference, what proof of her guilt *could* be obtained apart from her own admission?

There was indeed one, Annie Mackay, who she feared could be got to testify against her, if she had not become the crazy, though harmless creature her brother's suicide had made her. And that she still remained demented Mrs. Brekbellew was well aware, for in every letter she wrote to Mr. Edgar, she requested to be informed of Annie's condition, and he as often answered that she was still with her aunt in Rochester, and was still harmlessly, but entirely and incurably insane. So, with that one, fierce, defiant impulse uppermost, and forgetting for the instant the other sword suspended above her, in the fact that Ordotte would prove she was not Edgar's daughter, she turned, and said quickly:

"You have no *proof* of what you assert of me in regard to this Mackay, and I deny it all; and I shall continue to deny it."

She had forced to her aid a courage the reaction of which she knew would be sickening, but its present help was worth that, for it enabled her to stand very firmly, and very erect, and to speak with something of her own old voice.

But Ordotte answered, almost as if he had expected such a speech, and was quite prepared for it:

"Then, Mrs. Brekbellew, I have only one course to pursue; to-night, I shall see your husband—I am well aware of his nightly resort—and acquaint him with *all* that I have told you; in the present state of his reduced fortune, it will concern him a little to learn that you are *not* the heiress he supposes you to be. Immediately after that, I shall write to a friend in England who will make it *his* business to acquaint your husband's uncle, the wealthy old bachelor, Mr. Henry Brekbellew, with the fact that the wife of his nephew is but the portionless niece of Mr. Edgar. And my third proceeding shall be, to cause it all to become common gossip in every club-room in Paris and London ; not alone the fact of your be-ing no heiress, but the fact also of your secret marriage to Mackay, and your unmotherly treatment of your own child. I have ways and means to circulate such news rapidly, and scandal-loving people will believe all, despite a thousand denials from you. Good-night, Mrs. Brek-bellew."

He turned away, and had reached the door. She glared after him like a madwoman, but she seemed to have no power to speak. His hand was upon the knob of the door. With a gasp she rushed to him.

"Stay," she cried, " give me a moment to think."

He turned back, but still kept near the door.

She sank to her knees.

" O Mr. Ordotte! have *some* pity upon me. To do what you say will deprive me of everything. My hus-band is his uncle's heir, and if his uncle should hear these things about me he may insist upon a separation between us. If my husband should hear them he may become in-dignant enough to sue for a divorce. Then, what means of support should *I* have? O Mr. Ordotte! listen to me. Let your heart be touched ! "

Tears were streaming down her cheeks, and were he not fortified by the thought of Mrs. Carnew, away from her husband, and suffering for the wrong-doing of this very suppliant, he might have been touched, and have actually yielded to the frantic plea, but as it was, he answered only :

" By agreeing to the plan I propose, Mrs. Brekbellew, you may preserve your husband's affections and those of his uncle. I can do nothing else for you."

" Nothing else," she moaned, and then, seeing how cold and determined was the tawny face above her, she rose, gasping:

" Come to-morrow, then ; I shall have the statement for you."

" Pardon me, Mrs. Brekbellew; to-morrow will not do. I must have it to-night."

" To-night!" she repeated, and again feeling that there was no appeal from that hard, determined man, she said, through her tears:

" Come into the library."

He followed her, and as they went, stray sounds of the music and mirth below floated up to them, causing the wretched woman to shiver and groan inwardly. Would she ever take part in the same again?

Ordotte dictated the statement, and she attempted to write, but her hand trembled so she could not form a legible letter. She took a second sheet of paper, but the result was the same; then a third, and so she continued, until the first page of five successive sheets was blurred and spoiled.

" I cannot write it to-night," she said; " you see I cannot. Come in the morning."

" Oh, no!" he answered coolly, throwing himself back in his chair. " I can wait until you become calmer, wait until morning if necessary."

Finding that there was no escape, she forced herself to the task at last; wrote from his dictation a clear, confirmatory statement of all of which he had accused her, at the end signing her name and dating it.

She was rising from her chair then.

" Wait a moment, Mrs. Brekbellew," he said quietly; " you have not done all yet. I require a letter from you to Mr. Edgar, stating what you have done to-night, and explaining how you were able to escape from his espionage long enough to contract this secret marriage, and long enough afterward to give secret birth to a child. This statement," taking the latter from the table, " would scarcely be sufficient without something of the kind to convince Mr. Edgar, and if necessary, to convince Alan Carnew."

" Such a letter is outside of your proposition, sir," she said, aghast at this new requirement.

“ I require it now,” he answered quietly.

If only she could have strangled him as he sat there ; and for an instant she glanced down at her small white hands and then at him, as if she might be measuring her strength for an attack.

He arranged himself more comfortably in his chair, as if he expected to have to wait some time for her compliance with this additional demand, but his face preserved its cold, hard, determined expression.

She resumed her seat, and tried to think that a letter such as he required would make her fate no harder than would the written statement she had already given. And what difference could it make, since she was after all not Mr. Edgar’s daughter ! She felt, somehow, that having angered him so much by marrying Brekbellew, he would have little difficulty, perhaps even he would be rather glad of the excuse to cast her altogether out of his paternal affections. Then, she thought, what if Ordotte’s story were not true : but there was so much within even her own experience to convince her of its truth ; the strange resemblance between herself and Ned, the similarity of their names, and Mr. Edgar’s interest until recent years in Ned, all these circumstances were certainly strongly corroborative of his tale. But, what if the essence should fail to produce any more mark upon Ned’s wrist than it had done upon her own ? Even, not doubting that the letters *had* been ingrafted, might not—despite what Ordotte had said of length of time making no difference—the twenty-three years that had elapsed since the time of the marking, have obliterated them beyond even the power of the mysterious essence to recall ? And, in that case, Mr. Edgar would be in as much doubt as ever, and she could still claim to be his daughter. But, somehow, she could not get herself to adopt that doubt, and looking back again at the tawny face reclining against the crimson cushion of the chair, she seemed to read in every line of it a sort of undeniable assurance that everything he said was true—it was almost as if some one had told her that he had already tried the essence in secret upon Ned, and that it had worked as he expected it to do.

She turned back to the table and resumed her pen. But what or how should she write to him whom she was accustomed to address as "my dear father"? She could not say that now, neither could she bring herself to write Mr. Edgar, or even Sir; and at length, in desperation, she determined to begin without addressing him at all, and to write it in a brief, business-like way. So, she drew the paper to her, and wrote with nervous haste a mere repetition of what she had written at Ordotte's dictation. When she announced that she had finished, he rose and stood beside her while he read it.

" This will not do, Mrs. Brekbellew," he said with stern determination, as he returned her letter to the table, " it makes nothing clear; you do not give a single explanation of how in any instance you contrived to escape from Mr. Edgar's espionage sufficiently long to further your plans. I shall have to dictate this letter, as I have already dictated your statement."

He drew his chair close to hers, placed another sheet of paper before her, and said as he resumed his seat :

" Please state there how you first became acquainted with young Mackay, how, when, and where you were married to him, and by what means you deceived him into believing that you were Miss Ned Edgar, and not Miss Edna Edgar. When you have done that I shall dictate the rest to you."

Even if the circumstances about her were not the desperate ones they were, she could hardly have resisted the stern determination of the will opposed to her own; something in the keen, glittering eyes, which never turned for an instant from her face, frightened and subdued her, and left her helpless as an infant in the toils of her own making. She wrote as he had commanded her to do, and thus it was with the rest of the letter. Ordotte compelled her to disclose every link in her hidden chain of guilty facts; it seemed at times, from his sharp dictation

as to what she should write, as if he must have known of
those secret events from some marvellous intuition, and
often she stopped to look at him with a sort of ghastly
surprise, but his face, with its keen, glittering eyes, presented no other aspect than that of an indomitable resolution.

It was finished at length, and as she looked at the
closely written pages, and thought how fully exposed in
them was every circumstance of those acts which, even
were she Edgar's child, must fill his heart with anger and
loathing for her, she bowed her head involuntarily on
the table and sobbed aloud.

Ordotte merely pushed back his chair a little and
waited.

While she sobbed she had some wild desire to append
a few words of penitence ; to beg her father, or uncle,
whichever he was, not to cast her memory entirely out of
his heart; but, when she lifted her head and dried her
eyes, she thought half scornfully that such an appendix
would only be an additional humiliation, and productive
of no benefit. No ; her letter might go as it was, and she
would put out of *her* heart every remembrance of the
past. Not even a throb of motherhood for her abandoned
offspring came to her. It was Mackay's child, and the
hatred which she had for him as the cause of her present
trouble and disgrace extended itself to the neglected little
one. Its future was nothing to her, so long as it was kept
out of her way ; and that, Ordotte had promised her should
be done.

" Do you wish to write anything more ? " he asked, when
her emotion had quite ceased, and he had assured himself
that her letter was completed, so far as regarded the facts
which he had requested.

" No," she answered sullenly.

" Then direct it, if you please."

He folded it for her; and when she had written Mr.
Edgar's name, he sealed it with the wax at hand, and put
it, together with her statement, into the leather case, a

compartment of which contained the vial of essence.
Then he said a respectful good night, to which, if she
heard it, she was quite indifferent, and he left the room,
guiding himself to the porte-cochère, where he met some
of the other guests also taking their departure.

LI.

For a long time Mrs. Brekbellew sat staring at, without seeing, the handsome lamp in front of her, and with
her hands lying listlessly in her lap.　Her thoughts were
drifting in a wild, helpless way to Rahandabed, to Weewald Place, where, as soon as her letter and her statement were read, she felt that execration would be heaped
upon he —execration from every one; from him whom
she had o long called father; from Alan Carnew, whom
no excitement into which she plunged could make her
forget; and from Ned, whom, as she pictured the happiness fast approaching the latter, in the restoration to
her husband, and the finding of a father, she fiercely
hated.　Not even the fact that Ned had so faithfully
and nobly kept her oath had power to touch her, and
if in her present blight she in some way could utterly
crush Mrs. Carnew, she would not deem her own fortune
so hard.　But it was maddening to think of Ned in the
full enjoyment of all of *her* lost pleasures.　She shuddered at the contemplation; and then she thought of her
poor, weak husband, for whom she felt the same sort of
contempt she would have given to a drivelling idiot.　But
all that must be changed now; she could not afford to
scorn him any longer; instead, she must propitiate him,
and propitiate his wealthy uncle.

She dragged herself up wearily, and looked at her tiny
watch.　It was an hour past midnight; how the time had
flown during that horrible interview and since, while she
had been yielding to her own equally horrible thoughts.
But her husband must be in his room by this time, though
she could scarcely be said to know anything about it, never

having troubled herself before about the hour of his return from his nightly play. However, he was in his room, having been put to bed in a state of wild intoxication by his valet, who had to assist in carrying him from the carriage that had brought him home.

When his wife entered, he was tossing about on the pillows, ejaculating between his hiccoughs:

"Fifty thousand, by Jove! Won't the old coon think I went it—hic. Such a steady hand, too; no flinching. I lose with as much *sang froid* as other fellows win—hic— Mrs. Brekbellew—whew! she'll be glad to know I took her advice so soon. Gone to the devil at last, as she told me to do—hic—let her father support her—hic—no woman of ordinary brains—hic——"

But Mrs. Brekbellew waited to hear no more. He was in no condition to listen to her communication; and, impatient as she was to make it, she felt that it must be deferred until the morning. But his random words, maudlin as they were, caused an added weight upon her heart. Had he really lost that night at play another fifty thousand? If so, from what his uncle's letter had stated, his fortune must be almost entirely gone, and in that case ruin for him must be also ruin for her.

She dismissed her maid, who had been sleepily waiting for her, and threw herself dressed as she was upon the bed, to obtain if she could a little slumber before the morning came. But her slumber was fitful and feverish, and the first streak of dawn, as it shone garishly through the window, awoke her with a start, and utterly unrefreshed. She could rest no longer, and waiting only to bathe her heavy eyes, she hastened to her husband's room.

He was sleeping heavily, and as she stood by his side, looking down upon his face that, with its utter want of intellect, and its marks of constant and deep dissipation, was a most unsightly object, she felt as if her very soul rose against him in utter disgust. To obtain some control of her abhorrence, she turned away and walked to the window; but even there his breathing reached her.

She turned back after a moment, and seating herself in a chair by his bedside, called him. He stirred uneasily, but he did not open his eyes. Forcing herself to the task, she grasped his shoulder, as she called him again.

He awoke, and in his bewilderment, caused both by her unusual presence and his own disordered brain, he sat up and looked wildly about him.

"Try to recall your senses, Harry," she said in a voice which she partly succeeded in making gentle; "I have something to say to you."

Was that really his wife who spoke? *His* wife using a tone that was not contemptuous, and actually calling him Harry, instead of the scornful diminutive of Breky! He rubbed his eyes and looked about him again as if to assure himself that he was not dreaming. And as he looked, the events of the preceding night returned to him. His uncle's letter, the interview with his wife, his loss at the gaming-table—a loss which would impoverish his fortune to even the desperate extent for which Mrs. Brekbellew had wished. And then he wondered if she already had heard of it, and had come to announce her immediate departure from him. He felt convinced that such must be the object of her most unusual visit, and that perhaps in a sort of pity for him she had determined not to inflict her wonted contempt.

So, in resignation to that which could not now be averted, and in a sort of thankfulness that it was to be in some measure tempered, he turned his eyes upon her again, noting for the first time that she was still dressed in her reception toilet of the evening before, and that her face was frightfully pale and weary-looking.

If the morning light was not by this time streaming brightly into the room, he might have thought it was yet night, and have wondered how he came to be in bed at such an hour. But every moment his mind was becoming clearer as to recent events, though he could not remember how or when he retired, having, immediately after his loss of the night before, gone to drown it in a deep potation.

"Do you think you are quite able to comprehend what I am going to say?" Mrs. Brekbellew resumed, when she thought she had given sufficient time for him to collect his disordered wits, and being careful to preserve the same tone that she had used before.

He nodded, being almost afraid to speak, lest somehow the sound of his voice might bring upon him the old and dreaded contempt.

She leaned toward him a little.

"I have been thinking about your uncle's letter and about your circumstances, and about what is my duty in the matter."

"Here it comes," he thought with a sinking heart, "she's going to say that it's her duty to go back to her father." But Mrs. Brekbellew, quite unsuspicious of his thought, continued :

"I have been thinking about these matters all night, and I have decided"—he looked at her piteously—"to agree to what your uncle proposes. You may write to him, as soon as you choose, that we accept his proposition. We will make our home with him."

Poor little Brekbellew hardly dared to believe that he had heard right; and it never occurred to him to think that anything had happened to make this change in his wife. If he could be quite sure that his hearing had not deceived him, that he was not dreaming, that his wife really had spoken those wonderful words, he could be happy, for he felt that, by telling everything to his uncle, the latter, in consideration that the couple would make their home with him, would not at least disinherit him ; and, by quiet, economical living for the future, the remnant of his fortune might be saved. Revolving these things in his mind, he sat so still that he hardly breathed.

His wife said again :

"Did you hear, Harry? And when will you write to your uncle?"

Her questions were surely proof that he had heard aright in the first instance ; he could not doubt his hearing any longer, but he answered very softly, as if he were under some spell :

" I shall write to-day."

" And tell him," she said, " that I shall be devoted to you both ; that I shall make his home as pleasant as I can."

She rose to go. He put out his hand as if to detain her, though for what purpose he would have been unable to explain, feeling still as if he were under some magical spell. She looked back at him, compelled herself to smile and vanished.

LII.

Ordotte was in such glee over what he had extorted from Mrs. Brekbellew that his gay spirits might be taken for the effervescence of a true Frenchman ; and as sleep, because of grief and mortification, did not visit Mrs. Brek- bellew until nearly morning, so the same quiet restorer, owing to satisfaction and delight, kept away from Or- dotte's couch ; and as the unhappy woman he had left had her mind filled with harrowing thoughts, so was his imagination fed, but with most pleasant pictures. He perplexed himself trying to decide which he should do first—go to Mr. Edgar, or to Alan Carnew ; but at length he decided upon the latter course, as it was more important that Mrs. Carnew should be restored to her husband with- out delay than be made acquainted with the father, whom she had never known as such. And then he became im- patient for the arrival of the morning, when he should take passage on the first vessel going to New York.

.   .   .   .

Mrs. Carnew was still an inmate of the little mountain home, devoted to Meg and trying to interest herself in the lighter household duties. But the constant struggle to bear her trial was telling upon her ; and as day after day and week after week wore on without bringing that for which her very soul was crying—one word from her husband, her health began visibly to fail. Even Anne McCabe, the hired woman, noticed that; and though she knew nothing of the sad part of Ned's history, she often thought within herself that there was some secret trouble weighing upon the young lady, and her warm, honest heart often grieved about it.

She wished that Mr. Dutton would come home to see it; he might be able to help it in some way. But Mr. Dutton considered it his sacred duty to remain away, for the reason already stated; and as Ned, in her replies to his frequent letters, never said anything about her health, he could not be expected to know that she was rapidly losing health and strength.

She never said anything about her husband, after the letter in which she had asked Dyke to get information to his health, and to which she had received in reply that Dyke had obtained undoubted assurance of his perfect health.

Perhaps that which seemed like the surest knell of all her hopes was the cruel neglect of Mrs. Brekbellew to answer her appealing letter. Sometimes Ned was inclined to hope that it had miscarried, but that was only a brief, vain hope, for she felt in her inmost heart that Mrs. Brekbellew had received her letter, but *would* not answer it.

In Rahandabed there was little difference in the gay life that still reigned there, save that Mrs. Doloran was, if possible, more eccentric and more fractious than ever. She received letters regularly from Ordotte, which she read to the whole house—her nephew excepted—interjecting comments of her own that made it hard to know whether the writer was not absolutely deficient in common sense. Alan shut himself away from her more determinedly than ever, feeling that she was now entirely beyond his influence, and in his anger that she should judge Ned to be so guilty—though with strange inconsistency by his own course toward Ned, he seemed not to think her less so—he hardly cared what victim she might become through her own absurd folly.

If Ned would but send one word to him; but, as the days and weeks wore on, and not a syllable came, he tried to resent her neglect, by compelling himself to forget her. He shut away everything that could remind him of her; and he even wrote to his mountain friends, McArthur and Brekbellew, to excuse him from paying his promised autumn visit; and he tried to think the reason alleged in his note—reading in which he was engaged, preparatory to a trip abroad—was really true; but under that he knew was another and more powerful motive: he would not trust himself again in such proximity to Ned; did he do so, he must break through every barrier imposed by his own pride, and go to her. He reminded his friends, however, of *their* promise, and won from them a renewal of their pledge to visit Rahandabed before the winter passed. Carnew was resolved to go abroad early in the spring.

The winter holidays were approaching, and even in their snowy dress the grounds of Rahandabed had an interesting, and to one sufficiently well wrapped to defy the cold, inviting look. Within the house, every apartment, heated as it was with ample, blazing, and most cheerful-looking fires, and furnished with the most comfortable and luxurious furniture, had the air of pleasant ease especially adapted to Mrs. Doloran's idle, pleasure-loving guests.

On this morning, three days before Christmas, Mrs. Doloran was in high spirits; in such spirits that her exhilaration seemed to have communicated itself to the very help, and to have bred among them a state of glee that anywhere else might have been considered quite demoralizing.

Even Bunmer, as she was called by the domestics, who, in imitation of Mrs. Doloran, dropped the appellative of "Mrs.," shared in the general joyful bustle, though she was not quite sure what it was all about, and she ventured at the breakfast table to ask again for information on the subject.

" Didn't we tell you once," replied one of the waitresses, who had good-naturedly taken upon herself the serving of the coffee, "that Mrs. Doloran had a letter from Mr. Ordotte, saying he was coming home, and such news as that will just make her like an angel for a week ? The house will be topsy-turvy until he comes, preparing for him."

" And what is he to her, that she should be so glad to see him ? " ventured Bunmer again.

" He's her right-hand man in everything; and a good sort of fellow, too. Isn't he, Dan ?" and the waitress turned to the butler seated at her right hand. " Didn't you hear him sticking up for that Mrs. Carnew, when Mrs. Doloran and the rest of them were down on her ? "

" That I did," replied Dan, but his mouth was too full and his breakfast too tempting for him to say more.

Macgilivray, however, who was seated at the opposite end of the table, and who never could resist an opportunity of speaking in favor of Mrs. Carnew, especially when there was present the woman Bunmer, whom he disliked and distrusted, said in his dry way:

" And you wad noo be an honest mon if you did nae rejoice in your heart at the same; for if ever there was a puir wronged chiel, Mrs. Carnew is ane."

His fellow-help were so well accustomed by this time to his frequent assumption of the cudgels in Mrs. Carnew's behalf that they manifested little surprise, but Bunmer, at whom the Scotchman invariably looked whenever he spoke of the lady in question, could not be quite so easy. As a "guilty conscience makes a coward," so her own secret consciousness made her somewhat fear the Scotchman's steady glance, and on this particular morning impelled her to the suspicious course of defending herself before even she was charged with anything.

She said, bridling up:

" I don't know why, Mr. Macgilivray, you should look

at me every time you speak of Mrs. Carnew. I haven't done any wrong to her."

"When the cap fits a body, it's right encuch for that body to wear it," answered the Scotchman, growing more determined and bolder in his defence as he saw the woman irritated by it. "And it wad noo be onleekly if you had wronged the puir chiel; such things ha' happened before, for there's a power in siller to makit mony an evil."

His random words made a hit of which he little dreamed, and the woman, coloring, rose from her chair, saying she would not remain to be longer insulted. Every one looked up surprised, but no one opposed her retreat to her own room, and Macgilivray merely remarked, as he resumed his breakfast:

"It's noo insult to speak as a body thinks."

Three hours after, it was discovered that Bunmer had gone. Her disappearance was found out by the prolonged crying of the child, whom she had left, and who had awakened from the slumber in which it was at her departure. When a thorough search had been made for her, her disappearance was announced to Mrs. Doloran, but that lady was too much absorbed in her preparations for the arrival of Ordotte to give herself much concern about the flight of Bunmer. And when asked what should be done with the baby, she answered impatiently:

"Don't bother me about such a trifle now. Do anything you chose with it."

A license which did not help the servants out of their dilemma, for no one of the female domestics could be spared from her duties to give the attention, or care which was needed by the poor, little, abandoned child.

It was Macgilivray who assisted them out of their difficulty.

"I'll take it to C——," he said, "and find some o' me ain folk to tak care o' it. Puir little bairn, we can't leave it to dee!"

And that same afternoon he took it, carefully wrapped

up, and lying close to his honest heart, to the village,
where he found at least a temporary home for it. As he
returned to Rahandabed, he muttered to himself :

"Bunmer knowed vera weel what she went for, an
syne may be the auld Hornie 'll find things not all his
ain way; the puir wronged chiel that had to gang frae
her ain hame may be back again. You can nae mair
keep innocence doon than you can break an egg in an empty
poch."

LIII.

Alan was aware of the preparation going on about him ;
he could scarcely have been otherwise from the noise and
bustle almost at his very door, but, absorbed as he endeavored to be in his books, it concerned him very little.
In the midst of it all, however, a letter came to him,
which changed the whole tenor of his thoughts. Indeed,
he read it twice to be sure that he had not mistaken its
contents. It was from Ordotte, and ran :

"I have arrived in New York from Europe, and I
shall delay my return to Rahandabed in order to meet
you here. I have news to communicate, which you will
enjoy better hearing it out of proximity to your aunt.
Indeed, I cannot see her until I have seen you. Come
to me immediately. I am sojourning in the Astor House,
and I can scarcely contain my impatience to meet you.
"MASCAR ORDOTTE."

For the moment Carnew was inclined to regard this
letter as a part of Ordotte's other eccentricities ; that, if
he obeyed the summons it contained, he should find himself in New York on a very objectless errand ; but, again,
its tone seemed so earnest that he could not disregard it,
and at length, after he had read it five times, he decided
to go. So, that evening, he found himself in New York,
and waiting in Ordotte's apartment in the Astor House
for that gentleman to appear.

He came in almost immediately, his anxiety to meet

Carnew the moment he should arrive, not permitting him to be absent long.

Without speaking, he rushed forward and grasped Alan's hand, shaking it with such joyful cordiality, that, in spite of Carnew's dislike for the man, he felt compelled to return it at least in part.

Then Ordotte drew a chair forward so that he might seat himself very close to Carnew, and opening the breast of his coat, he took out the leather case that contained the articles which were to prove so much.

Carnew was deeply mystified; all the more that not a single word had been spoken so far, and that still without a syllable, Ordotte opened and placed before him a closely-written paper.

Carnew read it; it was the statement Mrs. Brekbellew had written, and when he had finished, he raised his eyes like one in a strange, troubled dream.

Then, for the first time Ordotte spoke.

"What do you think of it?" he said, manifesting such a youthfully eager delight, that it gave to his wonted sober appearance something of a grotesque look. "But, before you say a word," he continued, "let me give *my* story." And in a rapid, but clear and distinct manner he told everything. How his interest was first awakened in Mrs. Carnew, by hearing her name from her own lips when she came to Rahandabed; his judgment of her character derived from his own close observation, his unfavorable opinion of Mrs. Brekbellew when she visited Rahandabed, and his confidence in Mrs. Carnew's innocence, even when circumstances seemed most desperately against her. Then he explained the true object of his journey abroad, and all that had resulted from it, even to a minute account of his interview with Mrs. Brekbellew, and he added that should further proof of the truth of what he had stated be required, he could furnish it in the letter that he held for Mr. Edgar from Mrs. Brekbellew, having no doubt that Mr. Edgar would consent to show the letter as soon as had he read it himself.

Carnew did not interrupt by a word; it seemed to him as if he could not speak if he would, and when Ordotte had ceased, he still continued to look like one in an awful night-mare. Nor would his companion say any more. Intuitively he divined the feelings that must be at work in Alan's breast, and he sympathized with them too keenly to break upon them by any comment of his own.

The fact that Ned would shortly be proved to be Edgar's daughter, instead of Mrs. Brekbellew, was nothing to him beside the fact which he had read in the statement of her innocence, and which Ordotte had confirmed. Fool that *he* was to have been so blind, so deficient in suspicions of anybody else than his wife. Why could he not have remembered the resemblance between Ned and Edna, and have given the former the benefit of at least a doubt; and as before, every trifling circumstance rose up to confirm his conviction of her deceit, so now, with equal impulsiveness and haste, many trifling circumstances arose to confirm the story of her innocence. He forgot what had been an overwhelming proof of her guilt in the fact of the minister's recognition; and his love for her, roused with new violence as he thought of her bitter wrongs. Unable to endure his thoughts he staggered to his feet, and as if he forgot the presence of Ordotte, covered his face with his hands and groaned. Then, uncovering his face he began to pace the room. His companion did not disturb him, feeling that it was better to let the young man's feelings have their vent.

"What should he do?" How could he ever repair what he had done? What atonement could he make to poor, calumniated, outraged Ned? How could he convince her that he had never once ceased to love her? If he had only gone to her when he was near her; if he had only entered her little home the night on which his presence was so nearly detected! And then he cursed himself for the pride which had kept him from her. And what if now he should be punished by finding her ill, dead perhaps, unable to listen to his penitence, to say at least that she forgave him!　He was maddened at the thought, and he stopped a moment in his walk, seized by a wild desire to flee to her immediately.　But, somehow, in the same instant there came to him the thought of Dyke; his last interview with Dyke, when the young man had pleaded for her who was so wronged; when he had shown in his declaration not to return to his home while it held Mrs. Carnew, *his* noble regard for the honor of the wife whom her husband neglected, and in that moment Carnew hated himself almost as much for his treatment of Dyke, as for his neglect of Ned.　And then the thought came to him to seek Dyke first.　He would probably find him at his place of business in the morning, and he, perhaps, being the noble fellow he was, would find an easy way of reconciliation to Ned.

That decided, he seemed to remember the presence of Ordotte, and going up to that gentleman, who had remained very quietly seated, he grasped both of his hands and said in a voice husky from emotion:

"What shall I say to you, my friend, for what you have done?　How shall I thank you?　And what amends can I make for my coldness in the past?

Ordotte jumped up nimbly, and partially turned his head, perhaps to conceal a sudden moisture in his eyes, as he answered:

"You do not need to say anything; and as for thanks, I am so happy in being the means of re-uniting Mrs. Carnew and yourself, that I am amply rewarded.　Regarding amends, why, in the future, when you see me endeavoring to entertain that amusing aunt of yours, do not judge me too harshly.　That is all."

The protracted and hearty grasp of his hands by Carnew assured him that much more than he asked was granted.

LIV.

Dyke seemed to himself to have become an old man, though he had hardly reached his prime.　Suffering often ages much more quickly than years, and life had given him such bitter disappointments. But his sorrows had not soured him; he still retained his simple, healthy trust, accepting good wherever he found it, and never suffering the dross of human nature to blind him to the fact that there was often beneath it the gold of some noble quality.

Knowing so well what it was to suffer, his heart went out in boundless sympathy to all forms of the same, and the gentle, kindly gravity of his manner won general respect and liking. He had schooled himself to a resignation that did not complain, even in secret, and he had from his earliest years that Christian philosophy that sees in everything the wisdom of a higher power. Thus the happiness which was so wanting now would be complete in another sphere, and he could, like many more brave spirits, labor and wait.

Was Ned's innocence proven, and was she restored to her husband, there would not be quite such a weight upon his heart, nor would he add to the precious packet of her letters each one as it came from her now, with such a trembling hand, and such a great, quivering sigh. Occasionally, he permitted himself to read them all over, from the first little cramped epistle of her school-days to the very last, that so carefully concealed all *she* was suffering. He fancied that the reading of them made him braver for his own duties, and more resigned to everything that had befallen him. She seemed so noble, from the first simple expression of her warm affection for himself and Meg down to her brave, uncomplaining acceptance of the bitter cup prepared for her, and he always kissed the letters and put them away, breathing a heartfelt prayer that her innocence would soon be cleared.

The same evening that Ordlotte told his story to Carnew had been one of the times when Dyke permitted himself to read Ned's letters, so that the next morning he went to his business more absorbed in her than usual, and feeling with an unwonted irritation his impotence to help her in the matter of her wrongs.

How was he astonished to be summoned a little after his arrival to meet a gentleman, and to find that gentleman Alan Carnew!

They were alone in the private office, so that Carnew was spared the necessity of putting any great restraint upon his feelings.

" When last we met, Mr. Dutton," he said, " you came in a measure to sue to me; now, I have come to sue to you; to beg your interference in my behalf with Ned. I have discovered that she is innocent of everything with which she has been charged, and that I—I have been a brute."

He stopped, for emotion had unmanned him; and together with the sleepless night he had passed, and his absolute refusal to touch nourishment—protesting to Ordotte's entreaties that it would choke him, until he had seen Dutton—had made him a little dizzy.

Dyke strove to calm his own feelings, excited by this sudden and unexpected statement, and he drew a chair forward for his visitor, and said as quietly as he could :

"Sit down, Mr. Carnew; you appear so feverish and unwell that you had better rest a little."

He dropped into the chair, but, having recovered his voice, immediately resumed :

"I must tell you at once all that I have heard."   And he did so, pouring forth in an eager, impassioned way everything that Ordotte had told him, adding when he had finished :

" Do you think she will ever forgive *my* blindness and stupidity? Do you think I shall ever have her heart again as I once had it?   You know her so well, you who have known her from her childhood. Forget the taunt I once flung upon *your* honor regarding her, and speak, Dutton, as I feel you alone can speak. O God! that I should have thrown her from me as I did ! "

He broke down utterly then, strong man though he

was, and covering his face with his hands, something like a great sob escaped him for an instant.

Dyke was white to the very lips; white even while he exulted at this strange fulfilment of all his wishes for Ned, for the sight of Carnew's suffering, arising as it did from his love for her who had dwelt so long and fondly in his own heart, aroused again in some measure his own past anguish.

But he bent forward, and answered in his grave, kindly way :

"You have always had her love. It needs but one syllable from you to tell her that *your* heart is still hers, to bring her to your arms again."

"Then we shall go to her this minute, Dutton."

He rose wildly.

Dyke gently forced him back into his seat.

"Wait a moment," he said, "I have a little advice to give."

"Anything, Dutton; I shall do anything you say, as long as you tell me that I may win my wife again."

And he looked up with the submission of a child.

Dyke smiled.

"I think it would be better to wait a couple of days. In the mean time, with your permission, I shall write to her of these wonderful tidings, and tell her you will be with her almost immediately. That will be better, perhaps, as it will prepare her for your visit, and for her new-found happiness."

"But a couple of days, Dutton! How can I wait a *couple of days ?*"

Dyke's white lips parted again into a smile. The color had not yet returned to his face, but no suspicion of *his* suffering entered into the mind of the impatient man beside him.

He resumed :

"Since you think it the better course, Dutton, I consent to it. But you will come with me. We will go to Ned together."

Dyke shook his head.

"Your meeting will be better with as few witnesses as possible. And Ned will understand when you tell her how much I rejoice in her happiness."

Something in the tone of the speaker, and an instant after, something in the expression of his grave, pallid face caused for the first time a suspicion of Dyke's real regard for Ned to enter Carnew's mind; but with it came also, as it had never quite come before, the realization of Dyke's true nobility. It forced him to compare him with himself, and the comparison shamed him. He rose, a little unsteadily still, and, grasping Dyke's hand, said tremulously:

"Dutton, you are a noble fellow. May God forgive me for my treatment of you; but if the future can make amends, it shall do so. And now——" he hesitated, as if with sudden diffidence.

"What is it?" asked Dyke, reassuringly, and returning the warm pressure of Carnew's hand.

"When you write, I would rather that you refrain from telling Ned what we have learned of her relationship to Mr. Edgar. I want nothing to come between her thoughts of me."

And he looked with a sort of pitiful wistfulness into Dyke's face.

"It shall be as you wish," answered the latter, the smile still about his lips. That proposition accorded with his own thoughts just then. It was better that for the present Ned should have nothing to think of but her husband.

They parted, Carnew to return to Ordotte, who decided to go to Weewald Place, where Carnew would also repair after he had rejoined his wife, and Dyke to write to Ned.

He wrote immediately, so that the letter would be certain to reach her in time—a long, full, clear letter that stated nothing obscurely, and omitted nothing save what he had been requested to omit. At the end he said simply of his own feelings:

"I thank God in my heart for you, dear Ned, that the day of your happiness has dawned at last.

"Your brother,
"DYKE."

He took pains to place in addition to the direction "in haste," knowing that would facilitate its carriage to Ned should there be no one in Saugerties from the immediate vicinity of the mountain home at the time of the arrival of the letter; the mail master, to whom Dyke was well and favorably known, seeing those words upon it, would find means of forwarding it immediately. And so it happened. The letter was brought up by one of the residents of Saugerties, and reached Ned shortly after mid-day. Catching sight of the words "in haste," her heart leaped to her mouth. Could the letter be a summons to her husband, that he was ill, or dying? She could scarcely steady her trembling hand to open it; but when she did so, and read it, and realized fully its glad contents, a scream of joy burst from her, and, rushing to Meg, she put her arms around her and cried like a very child from joy.

Meg laughed, and petted her darling without comprehending or questioning the cause of her tears, and Anne McCabe ventured to ask when Mrs. Carnew's burst of emotion had spent itself a little:

"Was there any trouble in the letter?"

"Trouble, Anne? Oh, no! but such joy. How shall I contain myself, how shall I wait? My husband is coming; he will be here this very day."

Then Anne guessed a little to herself of what might have been the secret trouble which seemed to press so upon young Mrs. Carnew—that it had reference to the husband who was coming so speedily—but she forbore to ask any further question, feeling that perhaps in time she would be made acquainted with everything, and she began to busy herself in preparation for the visitor. Ned took up her station at the window—it was too cold to remain at the door—but as the window commanded a full view of the wide, bare, snow-covered road, her view was quite as good.

There was no one to pass by their isolated place, Dutton's being the highest abode on the mountain, so that when it was almost evening, and she could just discern some vehicle coming along the road, she felt that it contained her husband. She rushed to the door, opened it, and unmindful of the piercing cold, darted down the path leading to the road.

On came the sleigh, but before it reached its destination, Carnew saw the slender, graceful, girlish figure.

"You need come no further," he said to the man who had driven him from Saugerties, and springing out before even the vehicle had quite stopped, he rushed to the figure on the path.

In another moment, she was folded in his arms with her face pressed to his own.

LV.

Edgar had become so much of a recluse that he was never seen beyond his own grounds, and the only person to whom he seemed to care to speak was Mackay, the gardener. Whenever he took his walks about the place, he always stopped for a brief conversation with the old man. It might be that the rich, cultured gentleman felt a sort of secret sympathy with this poor, old father whose offspring, like his own, had given a cruel stab to the paternal heart. But he would not acknowledge such a reason even to his own inmost soul, and while he himself was careful not to reveal any of the facts that he had heard of young Mackay's secret marriage, it never occurred to him that the story might be carried to the old man's ears from another source, and so it finally happened.

The gossip of the help of Rahandabed extended itself to the help of other country seats, and a few days before the winter holidays it actually got into the kitchen of

Weewald Place. Some of the shocked servants were for keeping it carefully from old Mackay, while others deemed it their bounden duty to tell him. And the latter had their way.

That same night the old man was told why his son had committed suicide, and that his abandoned child was in Mrs. Doloran's care.

The poor old creature was dazed, and even the gossip who broke the story to him felt that it would have been a truer kindness not to have disturbed his ignorance.

"You say he was married," he said at last; "married to Miss Ned Edgar, and that she's married again, and that his child is living. I must do something about it. I must see Mr. Edgar."

And straightway he went to the grand house, in his bewilderment ascending to the great, grand entrance, and asking to see Mr. Edgar.

That gentleman, being near the entrance hall at the time, heard his voice, and, much surprised, came to him immediately.

"Come in here, Mackay," he said, seeing that the gardener was laboring under some strong agitation, and he opened the door of one of the reception chambers.

"You seem to be in trouble," he said as kindly as the exceedingly stern gravity which his manner had recently assumed would allow him to speak; "what is it?"

"It's about me boy, Mr. Edgar, me boy that killed himself," his lips quivered, and for an instant he paused to pass his sleeve over his sunken eyes. "I was told to-night by one of the help in your kitchen that he married the lady who used to live here—Miss Ned Edgar they called her—and that his child is in one of the village down the river. I have heered that Miss Edgar was no flesh of yourn, that it was only your kindness as kept her here, and I didn't come to say anything to you about that. I've only come to ask if there wouldn't be some way of my getting the child. I was told that the mother left it, that she's married again, and doesn't want to own it. But it's *my* flesh and blood, it's the child of me poor, misguided boy, and I'm an old man, Mr. Edgar, and I might say a childless old man, for Annie, the doctors say, will never be better. Will you tell me some way of getting the little one?"

His eagerness, and the emotion he tried to suppress were pitiful; even the cold, stern man who had imagined himself rapidly dying to every sympathy was touched. He was obliged to turn away for an instant before he could trust himself to speak with his ordinary voice. Then he said:

"Perhaps I have been to blame, Mackay, in not letting you hear from *my* lips what you have heard to-night; but I refrained from doing so in kindness to yourself, and"—he lowered his voice a little as if he were speaking only for his own ears—"perhaps, to spare a little my own feelings, that any one who had ever been of *my* household should have brought such sorrow upon you. But," raising his voice again, "I can still make amends. Leave the matter to me for a day or two, and I shall devise some means of getting your grandchild to you."

"Thank you, sir; may God bless you," and the old man turned from the room, remembering as he re-entered the hall that it was his place to descend to the lower entrance, but Edgar called him back, and dismissed him through the grand door by which he had entered.

Then he sent for the butler.

"Summon immediately all the servants to their dining hall. I wish to speak to them there."

The order was obeyed with astonishment and consternation. Such a thing had never happened before; and while Edgar, because of his grave, stern manner and extreme reticence, was excessively feared by his help, his generous treatment of them prevented their fear being accompanied by its usual attendant—dislike.

He had adopted the English custom of a full set of servants, even though such a number seemed to be quite unnecessary, so that the large dining-hall contained quite

an assembly of men and women when he entered it to
speak to them.   And, unconscious as they were of his object in thus gathering them, most of them quailed befor
the keen, stern look of his eyes, as he turned them upo
every face before he spoke.

" I desire to see the man or woman among you wh
recently told to old Mackay the cause of his son's suicide."

His voice was so loud and distinct it fairly rang through
the room, causing those who had quailed before to quail
still more; but the female servant who was the culprit
was not deficient in something of the courage that dis-
tinguishes the virago, added to which she thought it better to face the matter bravely of her own account than to
be discovered by some informer among her fellow-help.
So she rose from her place, and said quite loudly and distinctly:

" I am the person, Mr. Edgar, who told Mr. Mackay
about it."

Edgar turned his eyes upon her with a look that the
rest of the help afterwards averred was enough to riddle
her through, and he said in the same tones he had used
before :

" You will present yourself this evening for payment
of whatever may be due to you, and you will leave this
house before nine o'clock to-morrow morning.   Barnes,"
to the butler, " that is all."

He turned and strode away, leaving the help too dumb-
founded to speak until they ceased to hear the last sound
of his steps.

The next day brought Ordotte to Weewald Place, and
Edgar, when he received his card, was in little mood to
see him.   He remembered him with dislike as the man
who in Rahandabed had spoken with such irritating
mysteriousness, and he felt somehow as if this interview
would be an unpleasant repetition of the same.   Still he
could not decide on a refusal to accord him an interview,

and so he descended to the reception chamber where Ordotte waited.

Bowing coldly and haughtily, he desired his visitor to
be seated, which invitation the latter accepted immediately, saying as he did so:

" I have so long a story to tell you, Mr. Edgar, that I
must request you also to take a chair, and to give me your
closest attention."

" If your story should be as pointless as the one to
which I listened when I met you in Rahandabed, I doubt
the propriety of giving it very close attention," answered
Edgar, making no attempt to seat himself.

" I have come to explain that very pointless story," responded Ordotte, " and to supplement it by a still more
extraordinary tale ; but I must beg, Mr. Edgar, that you
be seated. My tale is too long, and, as you will find before I have proceeded very far, too interesting, for you to
hear it standing."

Edgar took a chair at some distance from his visitor,
but without any relaxation of his cold, haughty manner.

Ordotte was not abashed ; he felt too certain of his
power to produce a speedy change in that rigid countenance, and he began at once:

" When your young wife died many years ago, she left
to you an infant daughter whom you dearly loved. When
the child was two weeks old the house was broken into, it
was supposed by gypsies, and the babe was stolen. A
fortnight after, your brother sent to you that your child
was in his house. You found such to be the case, but
found also that his own babe, of the same age, so exactly
resembled your own that you could not tell them apart.
Your brother swore that *he* could do so, having put a
secret mark upon your child which would only reappear
under the action of the Indian essence that had been used
to make it. That secret mark comprised the capital letters E. E. on the child's left wrist."

A change *had* come into Mr. Edgar's countenance ; it

was losing its pallor, and becoming flushed and heated. But Ordotte did not seem to notice it. He continued :

“ In your dilemma, you proposed at last to take both children, giving a large sum of money so as to have legal claim to your brother’s child. Your brother then left England, taking his wife with him, and seven years afterward I met him in India.”

The flush had increased in Edgar’s face, and the perspiration stood in great drops upon his forehead, but he made no motion to wipe it away, and Ordotte still seemed not to notice any change in his companion.

“ When I met Henry Edgar in Calcutta,” he continued, “ he was poor, having dissipated everything he had ever possessed ; he was a widower also, and childless, having lost his wife and son a couple of years before, and he was in somewhat failing health ; but at times he was a genial companion, and having it in my power to better his position, he became attached to me. After we had been some time associated he gave me his confidence ; all that I have told you.

“ Hating you for being your father’s favorite, and for being the cause, as he imagined, of his own disinheritance, he thought that nothing would stab your heart so keenly as to steal from you your motherless infant. It was a bold undertaking, but he knew the house so well that he felt he could venture it. He did so, and succeeded in stealing the sleeping babe from the nurse’s arms. He brought it home, intending to start with it almost immediately for the gypsy camp, which he knew was within a few miles of the neighborhood. He felt that he could dispose of it there. But when his wife saw the child, so like her own, the springs of pity in her maternal heart welled up ; she begged her husband to forego his plan, to do anything he would, but not to give it to the terrible fate that might await it among the gypsies. He, too, noted and was surprised at the exact resemblance of the babes, and it caused another thought to enter his mind. Only a week before, one of his riotous companions had been affording amusement to his friends by experimenting with a little vial of essence that had been brought from India by a sailor uncle. This essence produced on human flesh, marks which only remained while they were subjected to its action. Henry Edgar, much interested in it, begged from his friend what remained in the vial. He remembered that now, brought it forth, marked his brother's child as I have told you, disclosed to his wife how he intended to harrow his brother's soul, and, as she was very much in awe of him, frightened her into the most abject submission.

"Suspicion settling in some manner upon the gypsies, Henry Edgar was enabled to secrete the little stranger in his own home for a fortnight, during which time his wife nursed it with her own child. He did that in order to make assurance doubly sure; that the very fact of nursing at the same breast, might help to cement, in some way, the singular resemblance.

"When he sent for you, Mr. Edgar, he was defiant of every consequence; he had gained his revenge in depriving you of the certain knowledge of which was your child, and he was equally satisfied, when you proposed as the last way out of the dilemma, to take both children. Knowing with what detestation you regarded the low woman he had married, he felt that in thus confounding her child with your own, he had given you a lasting wound.

"His wife, apart from the submission which she was compelled to yield to her husband, was satisfied to resign her child when she knew it was going to your care. It would be better provided for than with her.

"All this Mr. Henry Edgar told me, and after that, I studied him with more interest, feeling that I understood the cause of his odd impulses.

"The story I told you in Rahandabed, giving my hero the name of Klip Kargarton, was a true one; only the hero was Henry Edgar. We hunted in the jungles as I then described, and brought the cubs of a tiger away. I explained to myself his strange anxiety to get the cubs

to the tiger who had lost her own, and his disappointment
when the beast did not seem to know the difference, by
thinking that it was a sort of experiment to assuage, perhaps, his own remorse. He wanted, if even by such far-
fetched and absurd means, to assure himself that you
had been able by a sort of instinct to know your own
child at last. But when I ventured to speak to him about
it, to suggest the propriety of his return to you, and to
venture to predict your forgiveness in consideration of the
atonement he would make, by proving to you which was
your child, he would not listen to me.

"His hatred of you at such times seemed to come up
with as much vigor as it could ever have done. Once,
when he thought he was dying, he said to me that if he
should die, I might, if I ever met you, disclose the confidence he had given me. He could not help me in the
matter of the essence, for there had been none of it left
after he had marked your child, but he and I both knew
that if it had been once obtained from India, it could
surely be obtained again.

"He did not die then, however, and when I was about
to leave India for England in order to take possession of
a wealthy bequest, he said to me the last night we passed
together:

"'Should anything ever occur in your future life, should
you ever make any acquaintance that might cause you to
wish to reveal my story, you may do so, if you will ascertain first the fact of my death; or, if you cannot get an
absolute certainty of that, but still can discover nothing
to tell that I am alive, you may consider yourself released
from your promise.'

"We parted then, and though we corresponded infrequently for a time, before a year had passed, I ceased to
hear anything from him.

"In Rahandabed I met Miss Ned Edgar, and as I heard
her name from her own lips, I thought of Henry Edgar.
There was a family likeness between them, and I was
satisfied in my own mind that she was one of the children

of whom he had spoken. Later, I met the other Miss Edgar, and shortly afterwards, you. *Your* likeness to your brother was startling, and knowing so much of your secret history from his lips, I could not resist the temptation of probing you a little.

" I did so, as you have admitted remembering, with the story of Klip Kargarton, and the result convinced me that the wound given by your brother rankled still. Much as you fancied you loved the beautiful being whom you called your daughter, there *were* moments when you feared that you *might* be mistaken.

" I was not at liberty to settle your doubts, because I had made no effort to inform myself of your brother's death ; nor did I have with me the essence without which I could not *prove* which was your child. In order to get that, I should have to journey to India, and I was enjoying myself so well in Rahandabed, that I could not bring myself to leave the place. Also, there seemed to be no very good reason why I should disturb the existing order of things.

" Miss Ned Edgar, from my close observation, bade fair to become in time Mrs. Carnew, though she was too modest and too humble to dream of such a thing for herself then, and in that case she would be quite as well off as if she were acknowledged to be *your* daughter.

" As I told you during the conversation we had in Rahandabed, I have been enabled from early boyhood to divine character, sometimes with a sharpness surprising to myself. .And having this power I exerted it fully in reading the characters of the Misses Edgar, discovering that while one, she who has since become Mrs. Carnew, had a rigid principle of rectitude, and a most unusual capacity for self-sacrifice, the other had a marvellous power for sacrificing her friends whenever they opposed her own interests, and an utter disregard for all the little ways of honor. This discovery, however, I kept quite to myself, not even acting upon it in any way, until Mrs.

Carnew was accused of that of which I felt her cousin, Mrs. Brekbellew, had been guilty."

He was obliged to pause, for Edgar had risen to his feet, as if he were about to utter some angry interruption But he only sat down again, and for the first time wiped the perspiration from his face.

"Shall I proceed?" asked Ordotte.

Edgar nodded.

"Then," resumed Ordotte, "it seemed to be my duty to exert myself to go abroad for three reasons; the first, to obtain what proofs I could of Henry Edgar's death, if indeed he had died, as, remembering the feeble state in which I left him, I felt convinced he must have done; the second, to get the Indian essence of which he had spoken, and the third, to extort from Mrs. Brekbellew a confession that would clear her calumniated cousin.

" Regarding the first object of my journey, I succeeded in tracing Henry Edgar only to the time that he too left India, eight months after my own departure thence, intending to enter some European hospital, but, with that, my clew ended; I could ascertain nothing further about him. I considered myself released from my promise to him, and having, after much travel through India, obtained the essence, or what, from Edgar's description of it, seemed to be such, I went to Paris, and called upon Mrs. Brekbellew.

" Without letting her know my object, I, in the presence of her company, tried the essence upon her wrist. It failed to bring forth any letters. Shortly after, in a private interview with her, I told her much of the story I have now told you, revealing the real object of my experiment upon her wrist, and convincing her that it had proved she was *not* your daughter. But I did not say to her what I shall now say to you; that it may be the essence will not work upon Mrs. Carnew's wrist. Not knowing the name of the drug, I have nothing to assure me that I have really obtained the right article, save as it tallies with the description that Henry Edgar gave of it.

But its possession helped me to obtain that which was even of more importance than what it was expected to prove—the innocence of a cruelly wronged woman.''

He stopped for a moment to take from his breast Mrs. Brekbellew's statement. Placing it in Edgar's hand, he resumed:

"Read, in the words of her whom you have regarded as your daughter, a confession that fully exonerates Mrs. Carnew.''

Edgar mechanically opened the paper, but again he had to wipe his perspiring face before he could read it. When he had read it, he arose.

"I must retire for a little, Mr. Ordotte.'' he said with a sort of strange, sad entreaty in his voice, that was in pitiful contrast to the manner with which he had first addressed his visitor. "Will you excuse me?''

"Certainly,'' replied Ordotte, rising also and bowing; "but permit me to give you this letter from Mrs. Brekbellew,'' and he drew from his breast the letter that he had also extorted from her.

Edgar took it, and retaining the statement, he turned with both from the room.

LVI.

The bowed, broken, blighted man ascended, not to his own apartment, nor yet to his private study, but to the room that contained the painting of his wife. Flinging aside the silken curtain that hung before it, and placing loosely in his breast the papers given him by Ordotte, he dropped on his knees, and covering his face with his hands, leaned the latter on the base of the frame of the easel on which the picture rested.

All the anguish that he had ever suffered since he had looked last on the fair, dead face of the original of that portrait, now swept across his soul anew; he experienced again every harrowing doubt, every fear which he had so often felt during those long twenty-four years. His pride in, and his love for Edna, so frequently—despite the assurance that he endeavored to give himself—disturbed by the thought that after all he *might* be deceived; his studied coldness to Ned, his satisfaction at hearing anything of her which might justify that coldness, and put down the gentle, reproachful face that occasionally visited him in his fevered dreams; the ungrateful return which Edna had made for his love and lavish indulgence; the positive heartlessness she had shown regarding his feelings; the lack of womanliness in her choice of a husband, and now, the discovery of her dreadful deceit, all came before him with a sickening vividness and horror. But that which harrowed him more than all the others was the thought that he had been giving his love and tender, fatherly care to her who had proved herself so miserably undeserving, and who after all was *not* his child; while to the one who had actually made the very marriage he had sought for Edna, and in other things, according to the recent account, had comported herself in a way worthy of his affection, he had given coldness and contempt. He buried his face deeper in his hands and groaned aloud.

Still, the next instant he felt that he could not be sure of what Ordotte had stated; for had not Ordotte himself said that the test might fail when it should be applied to Mrs. Carnew? And in that case he would be in the same horrid doubt as ever.

An involuntary motion that he at that instant made, disturbed the letter he had placed in his bosom; it fell in a rustling manner to the floor. He was attracted by the sound, and uncovering his face he looked down at it.

The superscription was uppermost, and he recognized Edna's penmanship with a sort of shrinking horror. Still, he lifted the letter, and rising, seated himself directly in front of the picture. Then he broke the seal and read:

"This is to certify that the statement I have written to-night, and given to Mr. Ordotte, is correct. I became Richard Mackay's wife after I had deceived him into believing that I was Ned Edgar. I met him for the first time when Ned and I were out riding on horseback. He gave me a drink of water from a cup, which he formed of a leaf, and I was struck with his beauty, as I knew he was with mine.

"I contrived to see him afterward many times, allowing him at first to think that I was Miss Edgar the heiress, but afterward duping him into believing that I was Ned. I did that, when I found my affections involved, to save myself, and to test his attachment.

"He, glad to find that I was only a friend, dependent upon Mr. Edgar's bounty, urged me to marry him, saying if I would do so he would go to New York, and endeavor to make a living by which in the future he could support me; that the very fact of being my husband would give him ambition and courage.

"I consented, stipulating for the strictest secrecy; and one evening, during the week before Ned's departure for Rahandabed, I retired early to my room on the pretense of a headache. There, telling my maid not to come to me until late next morning, I arranged my dress so as to make my resemblance to Ned even more perfect than I knew it was already, and I stole from the house.

"A distance down the road I met Mackay, who was waiting with a conveyance. We drove to Rhinebeck, where we were married by Mr. Hayman, and I registered as Ned Edgar. Then we went to a hotel, remained until the early morning, and drove back to Barrytown.

"I knew that Ned was accustomed to early walks about the grounds, and so closely resembling her, I hoped to escape any unpleasant recognition, and I succeeded. I reached my room without being discovered, and it was not suspected that I had been away from home all night.

"Mackay had promised me to go to New York immediately. He did so, and I wrote to him that I had accepted a position as companion to Mrs. Doloran in C——. In a few months, I accompanied you to New York for the purpose of being introduced into society. While there I found means of frequent secret communication with Mackay, to whom I explained my presence in New York by saying that I had been requested to accompany Miss Edgar, and for that reason had left Rahandabed; that Mr. Edgar's kindness allowing me to have a maid, I had given the situation to his sister.

"I brought Annie Mackay with me from Barrytown as my maid, because I knew that she was her brother's sole confidant, and because I felt that I also, during the fast-approaching month of June, must have a confidant. She, never having seen me in company with her brother, and knowing that I was Mr. Edgar's daughter, did not dream that it was I who was her brother's wife; for, as he had told her all when he supposed that I was the heiress, so did he undeceive her when, as he imagined, he was himself undeceived. So, she also supposed it was Ned he had married; and when, being obliged to tell her the truth, I did so, she was startled and horrified. But I told her that I had practised this deception on her brother because I loved him so passionately, and because I knew if he should discover how much I was above him it would break his heart. She was consoled, and she pledged herself to keep my secret as faithfully as I myself kept it. Not even to her brother would she give a hint of his mistake.

"I did love Dick Mackay when I married him. I loved him so wildly that I thought I was willing to make every sacrifice for him; but, afterward, when I reflected upon what I had done, I became desperate from remorse and fear. I no longer loved him. I wanted to get away from him forever. But I had to be cautious, and to pretend that I cared for him still, lest he might betray me in some way.

"I passed sleepless nights in endeavoring to contrive some means of getting away from you during the month of June following my marriage with Mackay, and during which you intended to have me accompany you to some seaside resort in the vicinity of New York. Fortune favored me. Just when I had begun to be in absolute despair, you were summoned to England——"

Edgar looked up from the letter to recall that English visit upon which he had been summoned.

He had gone on information sent to him by one of his English friends, a gentleman who was chaplain to an hospital, and who knew Edgar's early history. The information was that a man in exceedingly weak health, and giving the name of Henry Edgar, but who refused to tell anything else, had obtained admission to the hospital, and by his name, and other things about him detected by close observation, aroused the suspicion, and finally firm conviction of the chaplain, that the dying man was the long unheared-of Henry Edgar. On such information had Edward Edgar hurried to London, praying that it might be his brother, and that he might live long enough to clear the horrible mystery of which he had been the cause. But the man on Edgar's arrival had been in his grave a week! He thought of all that now, as he continued to look away from the letter, and he thought also how it tallied with the last clew of his brother which Ordotte had obtained.

At length he resumed reading, beginning again at the words : " you were summoned to England, and you pressed me to accompany you. I refused, alleging my fear of the voyage, my dislike to leave the society by which I was surrounded, everything that I could think of as an excuse. You reluctantly gave me my way, and I saw with relief your departure upon a journey that must certainly occupy a couple of months. There only remained Mrs. Stafford to be disposed of, and that I succeeded in doing by feigning to accept an invitation to Staten Island.

"Mackay managed everything else for me. He had found an humble but respectable widow in a part of New York City willing to offer me a refuge, and thither I went, accompanied by Annie Mackay, instead of to Staten Island.

"Mackay showed this widow, Mrs. Bunmer, our marriage certificate, and told her that we wanted everything so secret, lest Mr. Edgar, upon whose bounty I depended, should find it out, and in his anger at my making such a marriage, would cut me off entirely. But we did not tell her where Mr. Edgar lived.

" My child was born in her house, and I remained there until July; then I joined Mrs. Stafford, who was quite unsuspicious, even though I had told her not to write to me while I was away, as it was an unpleasant exertion for me to answer any letters save those from my father. Almost immediately, I was invited to visit Rahandabed by the very friends with whom Mrs. Stafford and I were spending a few weeks preparatory to our return to Barrytown. I accepted the invitation intending to take Annie with me. I felt as if I must never lose sight of her. But she became ill, pined to go home, promising me sacredly, however, to keep all my secrets ; and when Mrs. Stafford volunteered to accompany her, preferring to do so that she might return to her own home in Weewald Place, I did not object. Mrs. Stafford felt no uneasiness at leaving me, as I was with friends. I went to Rahandabed, writing to Mackay that I was going back there with Miss Edgar, and that on no account must he come into the neighborhood. I would always communicate with him in writing, but, as he loved me, he must not come within miles of Rahandabed. That as *I* could not attend to our child, he must be father and mother to it. I felt assured that he would do all I asked, for I knew how madly he loved me.

" Rahandabed was so gay, so delightful, I tried to throw away every care and be happy, too. I tried to forget Mackay ; only when through very fear I wrote to him. I expected to meet Ned, but she had gone to visit some one in Albany, and did not return until I had been a fortnight the guest of Mrs. Doloran.

I met Mr. Carnew, and deeply as I once had fancied I loved Dick Mackay, I now loved Carnew. I struggled against it, but I could not resist being delighted with his attentions, nor could I bring myself to reject them. But I did not intend to do any great wrong. I meant if he should propose to me to tell him then why I could not accept him.

"But Mackay disobeyed my wishes. He came into the neighborhood of Rahandabed. I caught sight of him one afternoon as I was riding on horseback with some of the guests. My blood boiled with anger and hatred, for I feared that he would accost me. But he did not; only stood there looking at us, and as I passed, making a motion that seemed careless to others, but which I interpreted to mean for me to come out to meet him upon that road. I did so that same evening, and found that I had interpreted his motion aright. I pacified him as well as I could, and won from him a renewal of his pledge of secrecy, by promising to meet him again in a more secluded spot.

"But that second secret interview was partially overheard by Ned, who recognized my voice. I fled when I found her searching for me, and afterward I contrived to make her think that she was mistaken.

"When Mackay decided to take his own life, he sent a note to Rahandabed, intended for me, but directed to Miss Ned Edgar, for I had not undeceived him. I saw her open the note and read it, and I knew at once, from the bewildered expression of her face, that she had received a communication which was intended for me. But there was no opportunity for me to recover it, much as I burned to do so, until Mackay's suicide was discovered. My heart misgave me that it was he. In my fear and horror, I confided part of my secrets to Ned, but I bound her by oath, never to reveal them. Together we went to the out-house where they had laid him, and I recognized my husband——"

Edgar threw the letter from him, in a sudden paroxysm of anger and disgust; he remembered so distinctly the very words of Edna, when she had told him that Ned had sought her for company in going to view Mackay's remains. And then he remembered Dyke's plea for Ned, her oath of which he had spoken as a very link of evidence in her favor. And yet he, Edgar, had been so cruel, so blind!

He arose and paced the little apartment for a few moments to endeavor to gain some control of his agitation.

Then he forced himself to finish the dreadful letter.

"As I have told so much," it continued, "I may, in justice to myself, say that I married Brekbellew because I could not win Carnew, and also that I might go abroad to get away from any consequences of my secret marriage.

"EDNA BREKBELLEW."

The letter was finished, and finished without a word expressive of penitence or remorse for the terrible wrongs of which she had been guilty. In her statements, there had not been the faintest trace of sorrow for the poor, old man whose son she had killed, nor for the wife whose happiness she had blighted; and, more than all, she had not shown for her abandoned offspring even the common regard of motherhood.

Surely, here were traits to warrant her being the child of low parentage; no daughter of her, to whose portrait he now lifted his eyes, could have had such a character. Once again he went and knelt, as he did before, in front of the picture to let his anguish have its way; then, when he had somewhat calmed himself, and felt that he could return to Ordotte with some degree of composure, he descended to that gentleman, who, finding that he was expected to pass so long a time in solitude, had wandered to the other rooms on the hall, and was interesting himself in every object that he saw.

"Pardon me," said Edgar, when at length he found him, "for forgetting so strangely all the rules of hospitality. But I shall try to atone for my negligence. I may claim your company for some days, may I not?"

He seemed so absolutely broken in appearance and voice that Ordotte, through sheer sympathy, had to make an effort to answer him.

"Mr. Carnew and his wife will be here to-morrow. I

intended, with your kind permission, to remain to meet them.”

“Certainly, Mr. Ordotte; and are they coming because ”—he hesitated strangely—“because Mrs. Carnew has been told that she may be *my* daughter?”

“No; Mr. Carnew was desirous that she should be told nothing about it, in order to have nothing to distract her from her reunion with him. So we arranged that she was to learn nothing about this mysterious proof of her parentage until she should learn it here, in your presence.”

A pleased look came into Edgar’s face.

“I am glad of that,” he said, “very glad; and will you satisfy me further by promising that Mrs. Carnew shall not be told until I give permission? Her reconciliation with her husband will be so much happiness that it can make little difference to defer for awhile the story of her parentage.”

Ordotte bowed, as he answered:

“I think I can promise that any revelation made to Mrs. Carnew shall be made only with your consent and approval.”

“Thank you, Mr. Ordotte.”

In his voice, as well as in his manner, there was painful evidence of the struggle going on within him; as if he wanted to depart from his wonted cold, stern bearing, but was still bound to it by the pride with which he so constantly masked his feelings.

The signal for the late lunch sounded, and Edgar summoned a servant to conduct his visitor to one of the guest chambers, in order that he might be refreshed by an ablution before he descended to the dining-room.

LVII.

Happy Ned! Her joy seemed so complete that she almost doubted it, and she feared to go to sleep, lest she should wake and find it all a dream. The visit that she had contemplated making with her husband to the home of her childhood could never have been so full of delight as was this one, when he was with her after so cruel a separation. And when she heard from his own lips how he had never ceased to love her, how his love had driven him to make that secret visit which had so frightened her, and how he had only waited for one word from her to make him flee to her, she threw her arms about him again and murmured:

"My own true husband!"

They were so absorbed in themselves that they forgot the presence of Meg, to whom Carnew had been introduced lovingly by Ned, and with whom he had warmly shaken hands. The old woman had smiled and nodded, and seemed as pleased as Ned could wish her to be, but evidently without comprehending what it was all about. They had not even closed the door of the room in which they sat, and Anne McCabe, in the apartment adjoining, where she was engaged in preparing as sumptuous a supper as the larder of the little home afforded, heard sufficient to fulfil her own prediction of some time knowing what had been the trouble in Mrs. Carnew's life.

"Can you tell me now, Ned," said Alan, as she lifted her head from his breast, "to whom you gave the oath of which you told me, before you left Rahandabed?"

"Yes, I can tell you now. Mrs. Brekbellow confided to me, at the time that Mackay's body was found, that she had married him in secret, first making me swear never to reveal it. As she has herself revealed it, I do not consider that I am any longer bound by my oath."

"And how could you keep that oath in spite of all that afterward happened?" asked Alan, holding her a little from him and looking down into her face, with new marvel at the character that could thus sacrifice its own dearest interest to a principle of honor.

"I wrote to her, telling her everything that had occurred, and begging her to release me from my pledge; but, if she received my letter, she has never answered it."

"Received your letter?" broke from him in a burst of

indignation. "I feel sure she received it, but to have answered it would have been to disclose her own perfidy," becoming so hotly indignant, as he remembered how artfully Edna had once insinuated to him that Ned had a secret acquaintance with young Mackay, that he could not restrain himself from coupling Mrs. Brekbellew's name with a curse.

Ned put her hand over his mouth.

"We are so happy now," she said, "you and I, we have so much to be grateful for, that we can afford to forget Mrs. Brekbellew. We shall neither mention, nor think of her any more."

And then she stopped by repeated kisses the further stigmatizing of Mrs. Brekbellew, to which his feelings with regard to that lady fain would have given vent.

Anne McCabe announced the supper, and Ned conducted her husband to the homely little dining-room ; but that evening it seemed the most charming place in all the world to the re-united couple. Ned headed the table, and served the tea to Alan and Meg with the joyous vivacity of a child. Indeed, she could hardly be still, she was *so* happy, and though she looked very sweet, and very lovely in her simple dark dress, unrelieved by anything save a plain white collar and bands to match at her wrists ; still, for the first time, as Alan sat opposite to her, he noticed how slight she had grown; how even her face had lost its fulness, though that fact was now somewhat concealed by the bright, happy flush on her cheeks; and he felt with a throb of pain that possibly the reconciliation had come none too soon. A few weeks more of what she had already endured, would have placed her beyond the reach of any earthly reparation.

It was hardly to be. expected that either could eat, though both made absurd pretenses of doing so, and then when each discovered the other's clumsy feint, there was so much ridiculous protestation, that it set them to laughing heartily. If Dyke had only been there to enjoy it all—but Ned was consoled when Carnew assured her that he intended to make Dutton often join them in the future.

Anne McCabe was in some concern about sleeping accommodations for the handsome gentleman; the rooms were all so small and plain—but Ned assured her with the brightest smile that her husband could accommodate himself to any circumstances, and Alan surveyed with actual pleasure Dyke's room—the apartment assigned to him—when he entered it.

"Its difference from what you have been accustomed to, will make it a delightful novelty, won't it, dear?" said Ned laughingly, as she insisted upon making him closely acquainted with every object in the room.

"If it were far less, to know that it was under the roof with you, would impart to it the sweetest of all charms," he said gallantly, and then he dropped into a chair, and insisted on drawing his wife down to his knee.

"I must talk to you Ned; I must hear you talk to me. My heart is so full, it seems as if nothing else will satisfy it."

And so it happened that everything came to be discussed once more, and even more fully. The conversation took such a turn, that Alan found himself again excusing his conduct, by laying before his wife every link of what had seemed to be such dreadful evidence against her. Her unaccountable absence from Rahandabed, her sick appearance when she returned, all of which had given such color to the charges against her. And Ned, as she listened to him, could hardly blame him for entertaining conviction in the face of so much proof; but then, she, in her turn, told all about that unfortunate visit to Albany, and how Meg had nursed her through the fever, and how afterward the people who had been so kind to her had gone to Australia. Carnew remembered then what Dyke had said to him relative to that visit, and he understood now Dyke's silence when he had asked for proof of Ned's Albany sojourn, for he saw Meg's mental condition.

The better part of the night passed before either thought

of slumber, but then everything had been explained, and Carnew realized that never before had he appreciated, or known, the guileless, truthful, noble heart of his wife.

After breakfast the next morning, she would take him out to show him everything about the farm, regretting that the severity of the season prevented her taking him to the old, loved wood of her childhood.

" But, next summer, Alan, you *must* see it."

" Yes; next summer, Ned; and now, can you get ready immediately to accompany me from here?"

" Immediately?" with surprise, and a little shade of dismay in her voice, " I was hoping you would stay here a week at least."

She was on the point of adding something about delaying as long as possible her meeting with any of the people at Rahandabed, but she checked herself, fearing that she might give him pain.

" I should be glad to stay a week, a year, if you wished it, Ned, but we both owe something to Ordotte for what he has done, and I have promised to meet him some time to-day."

" Ordotte!" she repeated; "indeed, we do owe a great deal to him since he has been the means of proving my innocence. Where are you to meet him?"

" In Barrytown; in Mr. Edgar's house."

" Mr. Edgar!"

A new, strange, and half melancholy light came into her eyes.

" I had forgotten about him," she continued, " is *he* to be told of what his daughter has done?"

They had returned from their survey of the farm, and were about entering the house, when Ned asked the last question, and Alan waited to answer it until both were in the little sitting-room. Then he turned to her:

" Ned; do you suppose Ordotte or myself could permit Mr. Edgar to remain in ignorance of his daughter's conduct, when Mr. Edgar himself, having heard the calumny against you, fully believed it? Simple justice to you de-

manded that he should be told.   By this time, no doubt,
he is in possession of the whole story.”

She colored a little, and the melancholy light in her
eyes increased.

“ How must Mr. Edgar feel,” she said softly, “ if he
has learned it all. He loved his daughter so well; he
was so proud of her ! ”

“ How did *you* feel, my darling, when your whole
happiness was dashed by the very acts of this daughter he
loved so well ? It is but a just retribution perhaps, for
the unmerited coldness with which he has always treated
you.”

She did not reply to his speech, only after a moment’s
silence she asked again :

“ Am *I* to meet Mr. Edgar ? ”

“ Yes ; in company with me. Do you shrink from the
meeting ? ”

“ A little ; I fancy that even the knowledge of my
innocence may scarcely change his wonted distant manner
to me, since my guiltlessness has only been proved at the
expense of his daughter’s character.”

“ Well, we shall see ; ” answered Alan, kissing her ; and
then he left her, to give an order to the hired man to be
ready to take them to Saugerties, in time for the next
down train.

LVIII.

It was Ordotte who met Mr. and Mrs. Carnew on their
arrival in Weewald Place, and after he had shaken hands
with the lady, and bowed in grateful pleasure to her murmured thanks for what he had done, he begged to be excused while he drew Alan aside ; there was a brief
conversation between them in a very low voice, and then
both rejoined Mrs. Carnew. Immediately after that Edgar entered the room. Neither Alan nor Ned were prepared for the change in him ; he seemed such an utterly
broken *old* man. His hair and beard were quite white,

while his eyes, that had been so keen and large, seemed
now to have shrunken in size, and to have lost their
lustre. He was strangely stooped, and even his gait had
a sort of totter; while his manner, that manner which
had been so stern and so repellant, was strangely, almost
touchingly gentle and submissive.

He came forward like one about to plead for some
favor, and as Ned watched him, both shocked and touched
as she was, the tears sprang to her eyes. It was to her he
came first, addressing her in a voice that was in full keeping with his appearance, cracked, and even husky.

"Mrs. Carnew," he said, "I am such an old, blighted
man now, that perhaps you will waive the apologies I
ought to make for my treatment of you in the past, for
what I ought to say since you have been so wronged by
one of mine."

Ned could control herself no longer. Over the hand
he had extended, and which she had warmly grasped, she
bent her head and let her tears fall as they would.

"You weep?" he said in some surprise.

"For you," she answered, looking up; "I am so sorry
for you."

He turned from her to the two silent and sympathizing gentlemen, asking in the same cracked, husky
voice:

"Has anybody told her? Does she know?"

Both gentlemen simultaneously shook their heads,
and he seemed to be satisfied. Withdrawing his hand
from Mrs. Carnew, he crossed to Alan.

"Once before I bade you welcome here, when I did
not dream of such a cloud as this, and thought perhaps
to cement my own happiness before your visit should
end; now you are also welcome. You will remain for a
few days, will you not? All of you?"

He turned to each successively, and Ordotte, with a
look at Alan, meant to convey to that gentleman that it
was better to consent, undertook to answer in the affirmative for the party.

Upon which Edgar rang for servants to conduct them to their rooms.

It required all Alan's comforting powers to make his wife cease to grieve about Mr. Edgar.

"I am so sorry for him," she said; "he seems so utterly blighted. If the change had been described to me I could not have believed it. If Edna were to see him now it would surely break her heart."

It was the first time she had mentioned Mrs. Brekbellew's name since the subject of that lady had been closed between herself and Alan, and he could not refrain from saying:

"I doubt if anything this side of the infernal regions could break her heart."

Poor old Edgar, as we also are impelled to call him, since he has all the marks of age, met his guests at the dinner-table; it was painful to watch his struggle to retain his old wonted dignity; and the very evidence that he gave of his own consciousness that his old power was gone, made the exhibition still more painful.

Carnew and Ordotte, for sake of the pale, troubled lady who sat opposite the host, endeavored to lighten the gloom of the meal by cheerful conversation; but the weight still remained, and all were glad when they could retire.

Almost immediately after, a message was brought to Alan, requesting him to meet Mr. Edgar in that gentleman's private study. He kissed his wife as he left her to obey the summons, and he entreated her to have out of her face on his return, the troubled look that made him so anxious. She smiled as she promised to endeavor to do so, and in order to keep her word, she threw herself on a couch that slumber might dissipate her thoughts of Mr. Edgar.

Edgar was seated when Carnew entered his presence, and he motioned the young man to a chair near him.

"Ordotte has told me that he made you acquainted with everything," he said, in the cracked voice that seemed to have taken permanently the place of his own.

Carnew bowed an affirmative.

"And you are quite convinced of the entire innocence of your wife?"

He spoke with a slow, trembling voice that, in addition to his cracked tones, made it somewhat painful to listen to him.

"I am quite convinced," was the reply. Edgar fumbled at something in his breast-pocket, and drew forth Mrs. Brekbellew's letter. He placed it open before his companion.

"That, Mr. Carnew, will insure still further your convictions. Read and know how your wife has been wronged."

Carnew pushed it from him.

"I do not need to have my conviction still further insured. I know my wife's innocence, and I only regret my stupid blindness to it before."

"But read this letter, Mr. Carnew, in obedience to my desire to have you do so;" and Edgar placed the closely-written letter under Alan's eyes.

Thus requested, Alan read it, his face flushing and his lips setting themselves more firmly together in the effort required to suppress his indignation, as he learned the long tissue of cruel deceit that had been practised by the writer. When he had finished he made no comment, at which Mr. Edgar seemed relieved; and he hastened to prevent any remark upon it, for he said, as he took the letter and hurriedly replaced it in his breast:

"We will not refer to that subject again, Mr. Carnew."

Alan bowed; he could not trust himself to speak just then, for if he did, he must have given vent to his indignation, and that he would repress for the sake of the unhappy man beside him, whose stabs were deeper than any that had been inflicted upon himself.

Edgar spoke again:

“It was my wish that Mrs. Carnew should not be told
for a little of her relationship to me.”

Alan having mastered his indignant feelings, replied :

“Yes; so I was apprised by Ordotte immediately on
my arrival here.”

“And would you mind, would you object,” speaking
like one about to prefer some pitiful petition, “if I
asked you to let her ignorance continue ?” In his touching earnestness, he leaned forward and placed his trembling hand on Carnew’s arm

“If this test of which Ordotte speaks were to be applied to her, it might fail as it did——” he hesitated because he would not mention Mrs. Brekbellew’s name—
“on its former application, and then I should be in the
same dreadful doubt, for Ordotte is not sure that the essence is the same that my brother used. But—” he
leaned forward a little more, and placed his other trembling
hand on his listener’s knee, “ make your home with me,
Alan, you and your wife, and give me an opportunity
of atoning to her for my conduct of the past.”

His whole blighted soul seemed to be in his eyes as he
raised them to Carnew’s face, and he waited for the answer with the appearance of one expecting a life and
death decision.

Alan was a little startled at the proposition, not that
so far as concerned a residence in quiet and elegant
Weewald Place, he would not have been better satisfied than in noisy and somewhat vulgar Rahandabed, but
he was astonished that Mr. Edgar should manifest such
a desire, and especially immediately after he had disclaimed against telling Ned of her relationship. Like
his wife, however, he could not help being touched by
the blight that had come to the poor gentleman, and also
like her, he wished to give him some comfort. He answered kindly :

“I must consult Mrs. Carnew before I reply to your
request, and if she should consent, it must not be as the

recipient of any of your bounty. As in Rahandabed, her husband's means *shall* and must provide for her."

"As you will," responded the cracked voice, "only consent to what I ask; and go now, and see Mrs. Carnew, so that my suspense may be ended."

He leaned back in his chair, and closed his eyes to wait while Alan should be absent.

Ned was awakened from the slumber she had courted, to hear the errand upon which her husband had returned to her. Her wide eyes were alight with pleasure in a moment.

"To live here! O Alan! I should be delighted; and now that poor Mr. Edgar is so changed, and so lonely, it will be one of our sweetest tasks to keep him company, and to cheer him as much as we might. Besides," throwing her arms in coaxing entreaty round her husband's neck, "life here will be so much more pleasant than in Rahandabed; it will be quiet, and gentle, and genial, and there it would be——" she stopped suddenly, remembering that her remark would possibly reflect painfully upon his aunt, but he playfully took up the sentence.

"And there it would be noisy, and vulgar, and uncongenial."

She blushed, and tried to hide her face by burying it on his shoulder, but he gently forced her head up, and compelled her to meet his eyes, all blushing as she was.

"I know it all, Ned," he said, an accent of deep earnestness underlying the outward playful seeming of his voice, "and my feelings have warred against it as much as your own; but I intended it this time to be of short duration for both of us. In a couple of months at most we should have embarked for Europe."

"I would rather remain here," she replied; "and if you will only consent to do so, Alan, I shall be very happy. You see, it will avert that which I have been most dreading, a return to Rahandabed. I cannot meet Mrs. Doloran—I cannot meet any of those people."

"But you must return with me for a short time, that

amends may be made for that horrible calumny; that these very people in Rahandabed may know how grossly you have been wronged," he urged with some impatience.

She pleaded all the more.

"Don't ask me to do so, Alan. Surely, whatever amends may be required can be made without my presence," and, at length, she won her way.

He left her to take her answer to Edgar, who received it with a sigh of relief, and such expressions of grateful satisfaction as made even Alan glad that he had granted the request.

When Ordotte was made acquainted with it he approved most heartily, indorsing everything that Mrs. Carnew had urged, and adding that there would be little difficulty in setting Mrs. Doloran's mind right on everything pertaining to Mrs. Carnew, when it was strengthened by the presence of Mr. Carnew and himself. "That is, my dear fellow, if you are willing to trust to my mode of execution, this delicate and interesting mission."

"Willing to trust you," said Carnew, grasping Ordotte's hand. "After all that you have done for us; owing, as I do, my present intense happiness to you——"

"Stop, stop; my dear fellow!" interrupted Ordotte, laughingly. "You forget the intense happiness I have given myself in all this, not the least of which has been your friendship for which I always longed, but could never succeed before in winning."

And he wrung heartily the hand in his grasp.

Thus it was arranged that the two gentlemen should repair to Rahandabed, where Alan would make only the briefest possible stay, after which he would return to make his home in Weewald Place.

Before they went, Edgar visited old Mackay; it was a rare thing for him to call upon the old man in his little, lonely home, and the latter, though surmising the business upon which the gentleman had come, felt honored by the condescension, and he tried in his simple way to express his appreciation of it. But Edgar stopped him.

The soreness of his own heart had strangely levelled all social distinctions.

"I have come about that of which you spoke to me the other evening," he said quietly; almost with the air of one talking of business foreign to his own thoughts, but that his melancholy appearance denied the seeming suggestion.

"I have commissioned some one who is going to C—— to have your grandchild sent to you; do you understand? It shall be sent to you; a nurse shall be found for it, and she will come with it, and she will live with you, and take care of it; and I shall defray the expense that may be incurred."

Old Mackay's lip began to tremble from emotion, and he was about to speak, to pour forth his thanks, but Edgar continued:

"I have more to say; there is an error to be rectified—an error under which you and I and many others have labored." He stopped short, and looked away from the eager old face before him for a moment, as if to recover from some sudden emotion, or, it might be, to reflect upon the words he would use; when he turned back, he resumed in the quiet way that had marked his communication from the beginning:

"The mother of your son's child is *not* the young lady who has been accused of being such, but another person."

"Another person," repeated the old gardener in a dazed way.

"Yes; another person," resumed Edgar, speaking as firmly and decisively as his cracked voice would allow him to do. "All the proofs of the innocence of her who was charged with being the mother of your son's child are in my possession, and she, with her husband, will henceforth make her home with me. So, from now, Mackay, you will remember not to link her with your grandchild, and you will correct, whenever you have an opportunity of doing so, the wrong impressions of others. That other person, she who *is* the mother of your son's child, will never trouble you in the possession of it, and I shall provide always for its care. In consideration of that, Mackay, you will not ask any question about the mother of the child."

And old Mackay, absorbed more in the thought of getting possession of his grandchild than in any speculation about its mother, gave a quivering assent.

LIX.

The Reverend Mr. Hayman was surprised, and even thrown into a little consternation on the reception of the cards of two gentlemen who waited to see him in his pretty, cozy parlor, " Alan Carnew" and "Mascar Ordotte." The owner of the former name he well remembered, since his own never-to-be-forgotten visit to Rahandabed, where he was confronted with such a strange scene ; but the latter name was quite unfamiliar. However, he repaired immediately to the presence of his visitors, and was introduced by Alan to Ordotte, who, at once, in his own peculiar, original way told the object of their visit.

" Strange circumstances, Mr. Hayman," he said, " have made us think that even you, careful and accurate as your ecclesiastical profession enjoins you to be, may have been mistaken in the identity of the lady whom, a few months ago, you were summoned to C—— to recognize as the person you had privately married to a Richard Mackay some time before. As you recall *all* the circumstances now, the mere glimpse of her face which you obtained, as she forgetfully lifted her veil, the possibly not over-bright light by which you saw her features, might you not have been mistaken in supposing her to be the lady whom you saw in C——, especially if she resembled closely in figure and height, and even somewhat in countenance, another lady of her own age ? Take time to reflect, dear, reverend sir, and then answer us as you would do if at the last moment of your life you were asked to give an account of this."

The reverend gentleman was exceedingly conscientious, and being thus gravely adjured, he *did* call to mind, as closely as he could remember, every circumstance of that private marriage, and he *did* come to the conclusion that he could, very possibly, and very probably, too, have been mistaken in his recognition of the lady in C——, especially if there were another lady who closely resembled her.

And he thus expressed himself at the close of his reflections.

"Then, dear, reverend sir," exclaimed Ordotte, jumping up, and seizing the reverend's hand, "we congratulate you on your discovery, and you may congratulate us upon ours. *We* have discovered that the lady whom you met in C——, Mrs. Carnew, is entirely innocent, having been the victim of some one who resembled her, and who artfully used her name. But, 'all's well that ends well,' and she and her husband here are having a second honeymoon," upon which Mr. Hayman bowed, and shook Alan's hand in congratulation.

When they had left the little parsonage, and were once more on their interrupted journey to Rahandabed, Carnew said, a little impatiently, to his companion:

"What was the need of that visit, Mascar? In Heaven's name did you suppose I wanted any more proof of my wife's innocence?"

"No, Alan, no; I would not wrong you by such a thought. I did it for our mutual satisfaction, and to disabuse the minister of his error. Every one who has believed that horrible calumny ought to be told the truth."

"You are right, Mascar; and how shall I thank you for your forethought about it all," answered Alan, his impatience quite gone.

"As I have told you before, my dear fellow, I am so well rewarded that I do not need your thanks. And now "—with a quiet humorous chuckle—" just bend your mind to the task of devising some means for me to escape the scolding of your aunt for not having written a line to her since the letter that announced my departure from Europe."

"You do not need my help," replied Carnew, laughing; "you are such a favorite in Rahandabed that my aunt will easily forgive you. Hint to her that you have acquired a new stock of Indian stories, and she will hasten to be reconciled."

"By George! I have it," burst out Ordotte with assumed rapture. "When we arrive in Rahandabed, you go immediately to your own apartments as if nothing had happened, and allow me to manage everything."

"Agreed," said Alan, laughing heartily, for he could imagine the extravagant proceedings of his aunt.

All Rahandabed had been in a state of flurry since the arrival of the letter of which Ordotte had spoken, and when more than sufficient time had elapsed for the traveller not only to have reached New York, but to have been safely housed in Mrs. Doloran's hospitable mansion, her anger and disappointment knew no bounds. She raved at everybody, and even sought her nephew to compel him to share her violent discontent. But he had taken his departure, no one knew where, and, as usual, Macgilivray, who could have told at least that he had driven him to the station to take a down train, amusingly evaded giving any information; he could do so with the greater impunity as he knew that Mrs. Doloran was powerless to disturb his place with his master. And when her violence reached such a pitch that no pastime was free from the disagreeable ebullition of her temper, both guests and servants ardently wished for the advent of some one who could restore peace to the house.

Every day, at the arrival of every train from New York, by her order a carriage was in waiting for Ordotte, and Jim Slade, who had been promoted to Macgilivray's place on the departure of the latter to Carnew's especial service, devoutly prayed each time that he would not be disappointed.

"For," as he expressed it to his fellow-servants, "sure she sends for me, and badgers me as if I had the divilish little foreigner in one of me pockets; and only that I learned to dodge when I was a boy, I wouldn't have a whole skull on me to-day."

Macgilivray met the trains also, not knowing when his master would return, but feeling that he ought to be on hand. Thus both gentlemen found conveyances for them when they did at length arrive in C——, and while, when they reached Rahandabed, Alan went quickly and quietly to his own apartments, Ordotte was ushered into the presence of Mrs. Doloran. But that lady considered herself intensely aggrieved, and for once she was going to show even Mascar Ordotte her offended dignity.

She received him in her most pompous state, her tall, erect figure held with a ramrod-like stiffness, and the expression of her face, surmounted by its grotesque head-dress, combining the utmost severity and anger. But Ordotte was not dismayed. He had rehearsed his part to himself, and he lacked neither the desire nor the skill to play it.

With an exact imitation of the lower classes of the East, he acknowledged her august presence; then he waved his hand in a mysterious and pathetic way to the company about her, after which he dropped on one knee before her, raising his hands and clasping them in supplication, and at last he stood up, folded his arms, shook his head in a very sad manner, and then let it drop forward upon his breast in an attitude of unutterable dejection. As he had shrewdly supposed, Mrs. Doloran's curiosity was so excited that her anger and dignity were forgotten; she fairly rushed to him, seized one of his folded arms with both of her heavily jeweled hands.

"What is it, Mascar? What has happened?"

In obedience to the rest of his *rôle*, he slowly unfolded his arms, and lifted the forefinger of his right hand to his lips, where he pressed it very firmly; then he pointed to an inner apartment, and motioned that she should accompany him there. She took his arm at once, saying in her loud, impetuous manner :

"You have something to tell me, my dear Mascar— some secret." And bowing distantly to her surprised and amused companions, she repaired with him to the room to which he had motioned.

"Now tell me," she said, hardly waiting to be well within the room. But Ordette provokingly delayed his communication. Not content with pretending to assure himself that the door was quite closed, he went about, knocking on the walls and peering into the corners, until his companion, even in the midst of her intense curiosity and impatience, began to wonder if he had not become a little insane. He desisted at length, and approaching her, said in a very solemn voice :

"I am now about to reveal to you the sequel of all my Indian stories. I have solved a great mystlery, and I shall tell you a wonderful tale."

She was so impressed by his manner, his voice, and his words, that she was powerless even to make a reply ; she could only stand and stare at him as if she had partly lost her own reason. He pulled her down into a chair, and seating himself beside her, lowered his voice to a most mysterious whisper. When he finished his long story, to which she had listened with the same dumb amazement that had characterized her at its beginning, her comprehension of it all was as mysterious as had been the manner of the reciter of the tale. Somehow, she had caught the story in this wise, that Ned Edgar, Mrs. Carnew, was a very wonderful being ; so wonderful, that the wise, fortune-telling people of India, had cast her horoscope, and discovered that she had been dreadfully wronged, and they had put Ordotte, who was one of their favorites in the way of finding out how she was wronged, and they had commanded him to see that full reparation was made to her, threatening, that upon whoever refused to make this reparation they would work their charms, so that the most dreadful punishment should ensue, that Ordotte, owing to their help, had discovered it was Mrs. Brekbellew who was guilty of everything of which Mrs. Carnew had been accused.

These were the facts that Mrs. Doloran had gained, and she was so imbued with fear of the awful people in India, that she became instantly amenable to Ordotte's directions. Indeed, she begged him to tell her what she should do, promising the most abject and implicit obedience.

His advice, so earnestly solicited, enjoined first, a gentle and kindly interview with her nephew, then an assembly of everybody in Rahandabed, even to the servants, when Ordotte would tell the story of Mrs. Carnew's innocence, and proclaim the guilty party, and thirdly a most contrite and affectionate letter to Mrs. Carnew, all of which directions Mrs. Doloran so faithfully observed that the same day saw the fulfilment of the three.

Thus Rahandabed was again the scene of exciting gossip in reference to Mrs. Carnew, and Macgilivray in his delight lost so much of his Scotch gravity, that he became an object of amusing wonder to his fellow-help. And he became also somewhat of an object of envy when Mrs. Doloran, in obedience to Ordotte, having discovered what disposition had been made of Mrs. Brekbellew's deserted offspring, sent for Macgilivray to receive both from Ordotte and Mrs. Doloran a substantial reward for his kindness, and to be further commissioned to find if possible, among his kin in the village a woman who would be willing to go with the child to Barrytown, and take permanent charge of it there. It is almost needless to say that Macgilivray succeeded in executing his commission, and word having been sent to that effect to Mr. Edgar, that gentleman sent his own carriage to meet the woman upon her arrival at the station, and she and her charge were driven to the small and plain, but comfortable home of poor old Mackay. We draw the veil upon the emotion with which he received his grandchild. He forgot everything, but that he saw the eyes of his unfortunate son in the eyes of his little one, and that it was Dick's own expression which played about the mouth of the laughing babe.

LX.

Mrs. Doloran had never been so amiable, surprising even those who knew to what to attribute its cause; whether it was that Ordotte during his absence had acquired new powers of interest, or that her friendship for him had been increased by their separation, even that gentleman with all his fully credited penetration of character was unable to tell. But, nevertheless, it delighted him to bask in it all himself, and to know at the same time that it was adding to the general happiness of the house. First, however, when the lady's manner to him assumed a greater sweetness than it had ever evinced before, and an intimacy strongly suggestive of affection, he said to Alan:

"Will you object, my dear fellow, if my attentions to your aunt should become very tender? If, in fact, should she reciprocate them, I should ask her to become Mrs. Ordotte?"

Alan could not forbear laughing at the expression of the tawny face; it was so unusually serious, and even perplexed, and he asked, as soon as he recovered his voice:

"Are you in earnest, Mascar?"

"Never more so; you see, Mrs. Doloran's friendship for me quite touches me, it is so disinterested, and she yields even her dearest whims to my wishes."

"Well, Mascar, if you really can esteem my poor, foolish aunt sufficiently to make her your wife, and she is willing to renounce her widowhood, I do not know of a greater service you could render to us all. Your very presence here, marvellously subdues her temper, and she willingly yields a deference to you which she would do to no one else."

"Then you are willing to accept me for an uncle, if I can win Mrs. Doloran to bestow her hand upon me."

"With all my heart, my dear fellow. I wish even that it could take place very speedily, for then I could renounce all anxiety about my aunt, and not feel as if I were neglecting something every time that I leave Rahandabed."

"I don't know," replied Ordotte dubiously shaking his head, "perhaps if I were to attempt to precipitate matters, I might spoil everything. But when shall you return to Weewald Place?"

"I would go immediately this very day, for everything that I wished to attend to here is settled now, but that I feel I must remain to receive young Brekbellew and Mr. McArthur, of whom I told you. I invited them here, and this morning I received a note, saying they would arrive before the end of the week. Ned writes that she is intensely happy, having just the life of quiet which she always enjoys, and that, though she does not see much of Mr. Edgar, she still contrives opportunities of ministering to him a little, which add to her own delight; also, while she is longing to have me with her again, still, as she hears from me frequently and knows that I am well, she is quite willing to resign my return to my own convenience. So, in that case, I suppose I ought to remain, but every day that I am away from her seems like a year."

His patience was not put to the test he anticipated, for the close of the week brought not his two friends, but a letter of apology and regret; young Brekbellew had been imperatively summoned to London by his uncle, and the tone of the summons convinced both himself and his friend, McArthur, that it would be most unwise to disregard it. He would sail for England the very day on which he wrote, and McArthur would accompany him; but, on their return both would fulfil their promise with pleasure.

Alan was delighted to be free to return to Ned, and when his aunt parted with him, it was with the strictest injunction upon her part to come back with his wife as as soon as possible, at least for a brief visit, to which command Alan promised obedience.

Jim Slade drove him to the station, and Macgilivray sat upon the box beside Jim ; for the Scotchman was not only going to the station with his master, but was going to accompany him to Weewald Place, where Alan had promised him he should still be Mrs. Carnew's coachman. And Donald had a light heart in his bosom, and a very cheerful glow all over his honest Scotch countenance, for he could have served Mrs. Carnew in the love of his heart, and without a penny of hire.

Mrs. Carnew *was* intensely happy ; the great, quiet house just suited her, and to know that it must occasionally be in her power to minister even in little ways to the poor, changed, lonely master of the house, was a comfort to her. He seemed determined, however, not to give her much opportunity, for, after the first day of her husband's absence, in which he requested her to avail herself of the music-room as long and as often as she choose to do so, he seemed to keep studiously out of her sight, save at meal times. Then, however, she was so quietly and tenderly attentive to him, that it touched him in spite of himself, and more than once she found his eyes fixed with a mysterious earnestness upon her face. She wondered a little at it, and could she have seen him immediately after such times repair to the chamber that contained his wife's portrait, and there, seating himself before it, view the pictured face with the same mysterious earnestness that, in his gaze at herself had so puzzled her, she would have wondered a great deal more.

He made those studies of the portrait because somehow, Ned's face, when occasionally at table it was raised with such a commiserating expression to his own, strangely resembled the portrait, and he studied the latter to assure himself that he was not mistaken.

Ned had written to Dyke more than once—long,

fond, faithful letters, descriptive of everything about herself, and he rejoiced in her happiness.

"They cannot have told her yet of the relationship she bears to Mr. Edgar," he soliloquized, as her letters spoke of him as Mr. Edgar, and nothing more, "and perhaps it is as well," he continued; "she is as happy without knowing it."

And his answers to her were all that her affectionate heart could wish them to be.

When Alan returned to Weewald Place, his efforts succeeded in winning Mr. Edgar somewhat from his seclusion, and Ned had further opportunities of paying him little, kindly attentions. Once, as she met him on her way to put a letter in the mail-bag, she dropped it accidentally, and he, stooping for it, saw the name "Dykard Dutton." He seemed painfully startled as he lifted it, and returned it to her hand.

"Dykard Dutton," he repeated; "do you write to him frequently?"

"Yes," she responded with a smile, "he was the first companion of my childhood, and ever since he has been my brother."

"Yes, yes," he answered somewhat quickly; "I know. I remember all that. And he had an aunt, an old woman, who was kind to you, too. Invite them both here. Say that I desire very earnestly that they should come."

"His aunt, poor old Meg," replied Ned, "is not herself any more; she has softening of the brain, the doctors say. But I shall give your kind invitation to Dyke."

"Softening of the brain," repeated Edgar, as if he were speaking to himself, and then he put his hand to his forehead, and passed it back and forth for a moment, as if he might be trying to realize that *his* brain, with its constant weight of harrowing images, might not also be softening. Then he turned away, saying as he did so:

"Invite them here very soon."

But to that invitation which Ned hastened to tender, Dyke replied very respectfully and very gratefully that it would be most inconvenient for him to accept it at present, this being the brisk season of his business, and that for Meg, a change from her own accustomed surroundings would hardly be well for her. He had written the truth strictly, but he did not add that he was glad at being enabled so to write. Ned was happy, and work and absence from her, were the best things for him.

So, the quiet, short winter days went on in Weewald Place, and whatever little gossip had ensued among the servants relative to Mrs. Carnew, who, from having been deemed so dreadful and guilty, was now, in a sense, the honored mistress of them all, had been most secret, for they all remembered the summary way in which Mr. Edgar had treated the last newsmonger. Old Mackay had made it his business to tell them that Mrs. Carnew had been wronged, and that she was not the mother of his grandchild.

In the midst of this quiet life came a letter from Mrs. Doloran, giving information of her intended marriage to Ordotte in a fortnight, and begging Alan and his wife to be present at the ceremony. It was accompanied by another letter from Ordotte, couched in amusing style, and also begging the pleasure of the company of Mr. and Mrs. Carnew. He had induced his affianced to have the ceremony quite an informal affair, and to let Rahandabed to some responsible parties while they should be abroad on their wedding tour. She had begged to be taken to India, to look with her own eyes upon the scenes of the wonderful stories she had heard, and Ordotte intended to gratify her. That news determined Alan upon leaving Weewald Place for a few days, and Ned could not refuse to accompany him.

But Edgar, when he heard that even Mrs. Carnew was going away for a little, seemed to be strangely affected. He took her hand with a touching childishness, and holding it fast, he looked into her face for some moments without speaking. Then he asked, using his voice with difficulty:

" How long shall you be gone? "

She turned to her husband, who replied for her:

" Two weeks."

He sighed then, but said no more.

LXI.

Love, or some equally powerful influence, had so mastered Mrs. Doloran, that Ned hardly recognized in the unusually quiet-mannered, and what was even more unusual, the low-spoken woman, who met her with a succession of embraces, the loud, imperious creature she had left. Even her dress had undergone a marked change; its color and its mode were not in their wonted grotesque contrast to those about her, and she looked decidedly better in consequence.

As Rahandabed was to pass so speedily into the temporary possession of strangers, all of the guests had gone except the few specially invited to be present at the wedding, and immediately on the conclusion of the ceremony, and the subsequent breakfast, everybody would take his or her departure.

The day before the wedding, Ordotte and Alan had a private conference, during which the former attempted to transfer to his companion the little vial of essence.

Alan declined to take it.

" Of what use is it to me? " he said. *My* happiness nor my love of Ned would not be increased by having it proved that she is Mr. Edgar's daughter. I would rather she should *not* know it, for then, perhaps, he will not burden her with property of which she has no need. *I* am as rich as he is, and I want my wife to be beholden only to me."

" Still, take it, my dear fellow. You do not know what circumstances may arise in which you may wish to have it."

And he continued to press it in such a manner that Carnew at length accepted it.

That same day a letter arrived to Alan from young Brekbellew.

" I am in wonderful luck," the epistle ran ; " my uncle thinks I have done so well in America, that I deserve a lift from him, and he has taken a fancy to McArthur. Together I think they will make a sort of Aladdin's fortune for me. He insists on McArthur dining with him three times a week, and he has a wonderful spread for us. My cousin, Harry Brekbellew, and his wife, live with him. He made them come over from Paris, when he heard that Harry had lost nearly all his fortune there, and he has actually compelled the poor fellow to work as a clerk in his counting-house. McArthur and myself sometimes drop in there to see poor Harry perspiring and secretly swearing over his toil. His beautiful wife, whose extravagance in Paris, they say, was the main cause of the ruin, has a most desolate life, that is, for one of her gay temperament, in my uncle's house. She has no society, my friend and I being the only ones ever invited, has only a meagre allowance, and expresses in her face her dreadful unhappiness. I think my uncle gloats over it all. Mrs. Brekbellew has not the tact to please the old man, and he retaliates by twitting her sarcastically on her present privations. I tried to talk about you several times, but the topic seems to displease Mrs. Brekbellow, for she always either turns it, or leaves the room. Harry is pleased enough to talk about you ; he told me that you were married to a lady bearing the same maiden name that his wife did, and who resembled her closely in appearance.

" When you were with us on the mountains we thought you were a bachelor like ourselves, but some day McArthur and I shall claim the privilege and pleasure of being introduced to Mrs. Carnew.

" Answer as speedily as you can.

" Your friend,

" HENRY BREKBELLEW."

Alan showed that letter to his wife. She was so happy that she could afford to pity sincerely the unhappy Mrs. Brekbellew, and a tear of commiseration fell upon the letter.

"She deserves it all," said Alan, savagely.

Mrs. Doloran became Mrs. Ordotte, and she seemed to become her new honor well; she was blushing and radiant as a much more youthful bride might have been, and she leaned upon her husband's arm with all the grace of one who, having gone through the ceremony a second time, might be supposed to know how to avoid every awkwardness of such an ordeal.

When the hour came for her departure, her farewells were characterized by a feeling unusually sincere, and that made her nephew experience for her a deeper throb of affection than he had felt perhaps ever before.

And so Rahandabed was left at length to the care alone of the servants whose task it was to prepare it for the reception of its future temporary owners, and while Mrs. Ordotte was whirled with her husband to New York, Mrs. Carnew, with her husband, returned to Weewald Place. There, Alan united with Ned in contributing to Mr. Edgar's happiness; but the poor, blighted gentleman seemed incapable of responding to their efforts, and he continued to sink until he could no longer leave his bed. Then Ned constituted herself his chief nurse, and the old man grew to feel that no voice was so soothing, no touch so tender as was hers. Sometimes he caught her hands, and held them while he looked into her face with such melancholy wistfulness that she was fain to turn her eyes away. Alan was sometimes present on these occasions, and he also was fain to turn away from the wistful look; to him it conveyed so plainly the struggle of the *father* to claim that which he still strangely hesitated to be convinced was his own.

One evening, when Ned had retired for a little, leaving her husband with the invalid, the latter said suddenly and with a much stronger voice than he had used for some time:

"If Ordotte were here I would have him apply the essence of which he spoke, to Mrs. Carnew."

"He gave the essence into my charge," replied Alan.

"Did he?" speaking with a sort of joyful animation, and raising himself slightly in the bed. "Then, Alan, you can apply it to-morrow; but do not let her know our object; pretend that it is only to test the power of this wonderful drug—that it forms letters which speedily erase themselves. Can you? Will you do so?"

He raised himself still more, and he looked with wild longing into the face beside him.

"Yes;" said Alan, feeling that it would be no difficult task to keep from Ned the true object of the application.

So, the next morning at the breakfast table, Carnew told his wife of Mr. Edgar's desire, and unsuspicious Ned saw in it only the vagary of a sick man; in his various travels he possibly had obtained the drug, and now in his illness it had occurred to him to test its reputed properties. Such was the impression which she retained when Alan finished speaking, though he had not said more than Mr. Edgar wished to test the power of an Indian essence by applying it to her. It did not occur to her to wonder why the application should be made more to her than to Alan, or to Mr. Edgar himself, for she gave the subject no further thought than to assent smilingly her readiness to submit to the test.

And when an hour later, in Mr. Edgar's room, Alan asked her to bare her left wrist for the application, she did so with the same unsuspicious readiness with which she had heard about the essence at the breakfast-table. Had her eyes been lifted from the hand she was extending, to the prematurely aged face watching her from the bed, she must surely have felt that there was some unusual significance in the proceeding, but they were not lifted, and it was with the very brightest of smiles she watched the tiny vial in her husband's hand. She did wonder a little that his hand should be so tremulous, but even that momentary wonder was absorbed in the interest with which she watched the dropping of the liquid. Over what a surface that single drop spread! And what a vivid color it produced! And would it do what she had been told it so wondrously did—form letters on human flesh? Yes; there they came, two capital E's in garnet color, distinctly visible upon her wrist as if they had been printed there. Alan looked at Edgar. He was sitting bolt upright in the bed, his face convulsively working, and his hands clutching the air.

"Take her away," he said hoarsely, "and tell her who she is; then bring her back to me."

As if exhausted from his effort to speak, he fell back heavily, his head sinking among the pillows like one who had lost consciousness. But to Alan, who hung above him in alarm, he motioned to have Ned taken away.

Roused at length to the fact that something extraordinary was being enacted, and suddenly and strangely oppressed, Ned looked at her husband, piteously begging:

"What is it, Alan? What does it mean?"

He did not answer her, but he put his arm about her to reassure her, and then ringing the handbell just within his reach for the nurse who occupied the adjoining room, he drew his wife gently out of the apartment, taking her to the library, where, still holding her to him, he told her the whole story of her birth, and what Ordotte had discovered.

"And *I* am Mr. Edgar's daughter," she said in a dazed way, when Alan had finished.

"Yes; you are Mr. Edgar's daughter, and ever since we have been in this house he has been struggling desperately with his conviction of that fact. But he is quite assured now, and he is waiting for you, Ned."

She rose from his knee where he had held her, and she went in an unsteady way to the door; then she looked back at where her husband still sat, and extending her arms to him she cried:

"O Alan! my husband! come with me; I cannot meet my father, knowing him to be such, without you."

He went to her, and caught her in his hands.

"My brave little Ned," he said, "Heaven at length has done you justice."

Then he accompanied her to the door of Mr. Edgar's room; further he refused to go, saying:

"Your meeting this time will be too sacred for witnesses."

And she was forced to enter alone.

Mr. Edgar seemed to be asleep; the nurse whispered that she thought he was asleep, and then, in obedience to Mrs. Carnew's wish, she retired, and Mrs. Carnew stood looking down at the white, still face. It was *so* white and still, that it made her tremble even more than she had done on her entrance to the room. What if it were death that made it look so, and that he should never wake to tell her with his own lips that he now fully believed her to be his daughter. She stooped to him until her breath fanned his face. He stirred, and woke, looking at her in a bewildered and half unconscious manner for a few moments; then his memory seemed to return, and his eyes regained their old earnest, wistful look. At length, it all came back; the scene of an hour before, his own wild emotions soothed by the opiate the nurse had administered, and his impatience—before he had fallen into that slumber—to have Ned made acquainted with the story of her birth. He lifted up his arms to her, and cried huskily:

"My daughter."

"My father."

She responded, as she wound her arms about him, and shed upon his breast her happy tears

LXII.

Now that his doubt was gone, that he possessed in Ned a daughter in whom he constantly discovered new resemblances to her idolized mother, Mr. Edgar seemed to rally.   He was able to leave his bed for a portion of each day, and he insisted upon inviting Dyke and Meg to make their home in Weewald Place.   Failing that, they must at least promise to spend some weeks with Mr. Edgar; and Ned, when she had written the letter, was obliged to read it to her father to assure him that she had made the invitation most urgent; but even then he was not satisfied until he had appended in his own trembling hand a repetition of the invitation, and Ned, in the privacy of her own room, wrote again beneath that:

"By all the love you have ever borne me, Dyke, do not refuse this favor; my happiness cannot be complete until you and dear old Meg are here to witness it;   so, if you will not make your home with us, at least come to us for a little while.   Come and see my father.

"Your own NED."

And Dyke, when he read the letter, could not refuse her.

"Since," he said to himself, "it will gratify her so much, why should we not go for a little while?"

And he put her letter away and strove to be happy in the thought of her great happiness; but, despite his efforts there remained the old pain in his heart; for Ned was so dear, and his nature was so strong and tender, it was still hard to let her be to him only the sister she supposed herself to be.   But his feelings were known alone to his own secret soul; not a word, not a sign should ever betray to any one his hopeless love.   Being a partner in the firm, he could easily arrange for a fortnight's absence, and he departed for the little mountain home in order to bring Meg to Barrytown.

When he arrived in Saugerties, he was surprised to find a crowd gathered almost in front of the post-office, and still more surprised to learn that the object of the gathering was to witness the castigation then being vigorously administered to some victim.   Dyke worked his

way to the front of the crowd, and beheld with new astonishment that the subject who writhed beneath the
lashing strokes of a stout whip, was his old enemy, Patten. The man who was giving the punishment was the
stout, powerfully-built smith of the village, and one of
Dutton's numerous friends. He was spurred on to his
work by the delighted cries of the spectators, but more
than all by the enthusiastic applause of old blind Patterson, to whom the strokes of the whip as they fell seemed
to convey as much as if he actually saw the proceeding.

"Don't spare him," urged Patterson, "let his scurvy
hide have it for his treatment of honest Dutton. Give
it to him well. Don't let his body have a sound spot in
it."

By this time, Dutton was recognized, and a cheer went
up for him, while the castigation went on with new vigor.
He tried to raise his voice in behalf of the miscreant, but
no one would listen to him, and it was only when the
smith's arms were tired of their work that Patten was
released. He was more dead than alive, and he skulked
away like a miserable cur, not knowing where to hide
himself, and followed by the hoots of the village boys.

"It was I spotted him, Mr. Dutton," said old Patterson
in a glow of delight, as he wrung Dyke's hand, "just
there above the post office; he was asking about some
parties here, and I knew his voice, and I collared him. I'd
have given it to him myself, but Jim, the smith, just then
came along, and he rushed and got a cowhide and gave
it to the villain. I suppose he thought we didn't know
of his doings or that you hadn't friends here to take
your part, but he's sensible of his mistake by this time,
and I don't think Saugerties will be cursed by his presence again."

And a second time Dyke's hand was shaken heartily,
while others pressed about him to assure him of their
satisfaction at the punishment of the villain.

Meg was like a child preparing for her journey to Barrytown; of course, Anne McCabe had to accompany her,

for the old creature was not capable of waiting upon herself; and one afternoon, when Weewald Place looked its brightest in summer attire, Dutton and his two humble companions arrived.

The servants wondered at the welcome which these humble people received. Princely guests could not have been the object of more attention, and Mrs. Carnew was seen on numerous occasions to embrace the old woman. But it was all made plain when they were informed, as Mr. Edgar insisted upon doing himself, that Mrs. Carnew was his daughter, and that Mr. Dutton and Meg Standish were the people with whom she lived when a child. No further explanation was vouchsafed, and remembering the lesson they had received regarding indiscriminate gossip, they were careful to pass but few remarks.

Dyke was hardly prepared for the warmth with which Mr. Edgar received him; and he was touched by the almost abject penitence he showed for his former treatment of him.

"I did you such a gross wrong, Mr. Dutton," he said, continuing to hold Dyke's hand, "you were the only one of us who believed in her always. Do you remember when I offered to dower her if you married her, how nobly you refused my offer?"

"Say no more about it, Mr. Edgar," answered Dyke, averting his head a little, and speaking with slight huskiness; upon that subject he could not and would not speak. But, though Edgar respected his wish, he read more than Dyke dreamed he did, and he knew now, as he felt he had known five years before, that Dutton loved Ned with a lover's love.

The fortnight passed, and Dyke would take his departure. No inducements from Edgar and Carnew, no affectionate entreaty from Ned could alter his determination. The little mountain home, he said, was the place for Meg, and the utmost they could win from him was the promise of an annual visit. Edgar felt that *he* knew the reason of Dyke's refusal to make Weewald Place his home, but he also kept Dyke's secret, and while he pitied him for his silent, hidden suffering, he admired him for that strength of character which made him so firmly reject the sweet temptation of being often in Ned's presence.

A year elapsed; a pleasant, peaceful year varied only by letters from Mr. and Mrs. Ordotte, in which was enthusiastically described the pleasure that lady took in her Indian travels; indeed, so much enjoyment did they afford her, that it was possible their stay would be prolonged another twelve months. Letters had come also from Brekbellew, giving glowing accounts of the regard in which his uncle still continued to hold him and McArthur, and doleful details of his cousin's married life. One letter contained:

" A rupture between him and his wife seems imminent, not a little hastened by the penuriousness and severity of his uncle. Young Mrs. Brekbellew has grown daring and defiant, and of late has formed acquaintances not at all to the old gentleman's taste, nor, for that matter, to the taste of her poor, little, brainless husband. But these acquaintances are enabling her to see something of the gay life she evidently longs for, and none of us will be surprised to hear some fine morning that she has actually left her husband."

The prediction seemed to have been verified very shortly, for his very next letter contained an account of Mrs. Brekbellew's flight from the house of her uncle, and her temporary shelter with one of her fashionable acquaintances.

" And she absolutely refuses to see her husband," the letter continued, " and report is already busy coupling her name with that of a dashing military officer."

That letter Carnew showed neither to his wife nor to Mr. Edgar.

The end came suddenly to Mr. Edgar; so suddenly that the physicians, in making an autopsy, said he had developed a new and sudden affection of the heart; and when his will was read, it was found that he had be-queathed his fortune to Dykard Dutton. "For," the paper ran, "knowing that my beloved daughter is amply secured in the love and fortune of her husband, I would do a late justice to the man who so nobly has proved him-self worthy of my regard."

The bequest of his wealth, while it was a delight to Mr. and Mrs. Carnew, was an intense surprise, and even a source of some regret to Dyke, for it placed him above the necessity of pursuing any business. But his active mind soon found outlets for his means in schemes of benevolence, and his leisure was employed in the scientific studies which he liked so well.

Not even then would he consent to make Weewald Place his home, nor even after Meg's death, which took place quietly and painlessly. He preferred his home among the mountains he said, which home he enlarged and beautified, so that Mr. and Mrs. Carnew could spend a part of each summer season with him.

McArthur and Brekbellew found so many inducements to remain in England, that they did not return for some years, and then Brekbellew showed Carnew a paragraph from a French paper.

"Died in one of the hospitals here, of cancer in the face, a Mrs. Brekbellew. Her maiden name was Edna Edgar, and she is said to have been once a great heiress, and a woman of extraordinary beauty."

One day, Carnew received a letter from a Catholic priest in New York. It contained news that made the last link in the chain of superabundant evidence of Ned's innocence.

The letter ran :

"I am desired, dear sir, by a woman named Anne Bun-mer, to state to you some facts the concealment of which has troubled her conscience. These facts refer to her as-sertions of the identity of Mrs. Carnew with a Mrs. Mackay.

"She desires me to tell you that, when confronted with

Mrs. Carnew, she was perfectly convinced that lady, though very closely resembling Mrs. Mackay, was not Mrs. Mackay, but that, fearing to lose the remuneration which she hoped to get for her care of Mrs. Mackay's child, she persisted in her false charge. Her fear of detection made her flee from C——, and her conscience afterward so tormented her, that she has at length requested me to inform you of the truth.

" Respectfully,
" REV. CHAS. A. HARRINGTON."

Alan hastened to show the letter to Ned, and both thought with thankful, swelling hearts, how ample and how complete was the justice that had been rendered for that foul wrong.

There is little more to be told. The Ordottes returned to open again an hospitable mansion in C——, but one conducted on less indiscriminate principles than in former days, and it is to be hoped that our heroes and our heroine lived for many years in the enjoyment of that happiness which must come at some time from a life of rectitude.